WINNING HAS A PRICE.
HOW MUCH WILL YOU PAY?

SUMAN DUBEY

RUPA

Published by
Rupa Publications India Pvt. Ltd 2020
7/16, Ansari Road, Daryaganj
New Delhi 110002

Sales Centres:
Allahabad Bengaluru Chennai
Hyderabad Jaipur Kathmandu
Kolkata Mumbai

Copyright © Suman Dubey 2020

This is a work of fiction. Names, characters, places and incidents are either the product of the author's imagination or are used fictitiously and any resemblance to any actual person, living or dead, events or locales is entirely coincidental.

All rights reserved.

No part of this publication may be reproduced, transmitted, or stored in a retrieval system, in any form or by any means, electronic, mechanical, photocopying, recording or otherwise, without the prior permission of the publisher.

ISBN: 978-93-89967-36-4

First impression 2020

10 9 8 7 6 5 4 3 2 1

Printed at Nutech Print Services India

The moral right of the author has been asserted.
This book is sold subject to the condition that it shall not, by way of trade or otherwise, be lent, resold, hired out, or otherwise circulated, without the publisher's prior consent, in any form of binding or cover other than that in which it is published.

*I dedicate this book to the four women in my life
I admire the most—*

My mother, Purnima, for her dignity and grace even during adversity

My mother-in-law, Sikha, for her passion for life and free spirit

My sister, Chaytali, for her ability to find purpose in life and reinvent it for herself

My wife, Binda, for her strength in compassion and calmness

'When the gods wish to punish us they answer our prayers.'
—Oscar Wilde

*'You are what your deep, driving desire is.
As your desire is, so is your will.
As your will is, so is your deed.
As your deed is, so is your destiny.'*
—Brihadaranyaka Upanishad

Contents

Prologue .... *xiii*

Part 1
AWAKENING

No Place in the Sun	3
The Smell of Leather	6
Whiskey Tales	10
Big Brother Is Watching	14
Bloodless War	17
A Billionaire in Thirty Minutes	21
A Long Dead Career	25
A Butcher's Fantasies	28
The Darkness of Diwali	31
Backchannel Negotiations	36
Low-Hanging Balls	40
Almost a Father	43
Buried Under Stardust	46
Brother from Another Mother	50
Vision Statement	54
Missed by a Mile	58
Gratefully Numb	61
Schadenfreude	64
Pull of the Umbilical Cord	65
Enforced Pride	68
Mr Assistant Coach	71

Part 2
DESPERATION

Rottweiler Turned Pug	75
The Guru's Disdain	78
Test Team for T20	81
Hell Hath No Fury	83
Halley's Comet	87
Thanks for Not Helping	91

Square Peg in Round Hole	94
Hara-Kiri on the Horizon	97
Room Service	100
The Lady in Purple	105
Newspapers Lie	109
The Prodigal Son	112
The Edge of Compromise	115
Coach or Ballboy?	118
Pebble in the Shoe	122
Booze and Brawl	126
Rebel with a Cause	130
A Goat Is the Leader of Sheep	133
Fire, Smoke and Then Water	135
Never Say Never	138
Blast from the Past	142
Till Death Do Us Part	145
One Step Forward, Two Backward	148
From Ass to Ash	151
A Question of Loyalty	153
Faint Light of Dawn	155
The Greasy Pole	159
Coronation	162
First Blood	166
The Writing on the Wall	168
A Cat and Mouse Game	170
Abrupt End to the Honeymoon	172
Face Behind the Mask	175
The Slippery Slope of Adulation	177
The End Justifies the Means	179

Part 3
REDEMPTION

Overdose of Emotions	185
Milk and Cookies	187
A Game of Glorious Uncertainties	189
Be Warned	190
Accident or Attack?	192
Family Comes Last	194

2 + 2 is not 4	197
5 for 26	200
Sniffer Dog	204
The Smell of Information	205
Between a Rock and a Hard Place	208
Polite Enquiries	210
Hormone-Struck Teenagers	211
Hiding in Plain Sight	214
The Tragedy of Passionate Fans	217
The Great Escape	221
Reboot	224
Prisoner's Dilemma	226
Nothing Succeeds like Success	229
Fait Accompli	231
The Visitor	232
Surrender	235
Et Tu, Dad?	239
Volte-Face	243
Blood Is Thicker Than Water	246
Epiphany	250
The End of Innocence	254
Cutting the Cord	257
The Last Supper	259
Femme Fatale	264
Gone for a Toss	267
Deception	270
Controlled Demolition	273
Trump Card	277
The Antihero	280
Ode to the Master	282
Flight of the Legends	284
Epilogue	287
Acknowledgements	289

Prologue

In a flash, The Visitor put a gun to Neil's head, choking him with the other arm. 'You bastard...' he hissed, 'never question me again.'

'What do you want?' Neil rasped, fighting to breathe.

The Visitor pushed him onto the couch, pinning him with his leg. 'Lose the final...'

Neil sucked in air, struggling to clear his hazy vision. He peered at the gun pointed at his face, wondering if he was hallucinating.

'I am only a coach,' he croaked. 'Can't force eleven cricketers to play badly. They are monitoring us...at every step. It is impossible to pull it off; we will get caught.'

The Visitor grunted as he clicked open the safety latch of his gun. 'Did I ask you for your opinion?' he asked in a low, calm voice. He stabilized the gun using both hands and fired. With a loud cracking sound, the bullet ripped through the backrest a few inches from Neil's head. The fabric and wood were burning, emitting foul black smoke.

Neil lay terrified as The Visitor sprayed water to douse the fire.

'Now listen carefully, so I don't have to fire again,' said The Visitor, hitting Neil with the empty water bottle. 'Don't use your head...just follow instructions.' He paused, touching his temple with his finger. 'Otherwise I will bore a hole into your head. Got it?'

One look at The Visitor's stoned lifeless eyes convinced Neil that the game was over; nothing would move that maniac to reconsider his demands. He wiped his face, nodding to show he agreed.

The Visitor fiddled with his beard. 'Good! But just in case you stray from the line...apart from killing your family, we will kidnap your girlfriend and sell her as a sex slave in the Middle East. She will be in high demand both before and after she dies. Some customers pay big dollars for the experience of doing a dead body.' He licked his lips. 'And her kind of body will get high premium. Enough incentive for you to comply?' The Visitor grinned, hauling Neil up by the collar. 'Do you understand?'

Neil managed a feeble yes.

'I can't hear it. Louder!'

'Yes!' shouted Neil.

The Visitor dropped him on the couch and left the apartment.

Neil lay cold and shattered, with his face dunked in a toxic sludge of bile, dust and burnt leather. The bullet hole on the couch emitted the odour of gutted self-respect and fractured morale.

Fuck! I just wanted to coach the team. That's my big crime—I tried to help the team win. Couldn't bear to see it become a victim of hustlers and looters. But I failed, just when I thought I would succeed. I failed. Eight months of getting my ass busted for this godforsaken team…the humiliation, struggling to hold up my head. Twenty years of international cricket has come to this. A goon almost shoots at me, threatening to kill and rape unless I sell out the team I built, betray the game I lived for, abandon my only chance at redemption.
I need help.
I surrender.
Akash!

Part 1

AWAKENING

'A single event can awaken within us a stranger totally unknown to us. To live is to be slowly born.'

—Antoine de Saint-Exupéry

No Place in the Sun

Eight Months Ago

Late October, 2007
Feroz Shah Kotla Stadium, New Delhi

'Excuse me, sir...please vacate your seat.'

A tall, thin man in a black suit stood uncomfortably close to Neil, struggling to control his tie fluttering in the strong wind.

Srikant Kale bowled out Mark Stewart, and the stadium erupted to celebrate Australia's fifth wicket.

'Sir! For your comfort, I will move you to another seat,' said Mr Black Suit.

'No, thanks! I am comfortable here,' Neil said.

What a googly; superb; we can win from here!

Animated chatter ensued in the VIP box. Should India continue with spin? Only 35 overs left; will India make it?

Saurabh Goyal favoured spin bowling. 'The wicket is dry and dusty; spinners will get an unpredictable turn,' he said.

Neil smirked at the stereotype of favouring spin bowling on Indian pitches.

I had taken 5 wickets for 26 runs on the last day of the test match, and I was no spin bowler. Pacers can use the strong wind from one end. But who can oppose the legendary Saurabh Goyal? Huh?

Mr Black Suit spoke again. 'Excuse me, sir...'

The late afternoon October sun had cast long shadows covering a part of the pitch. From a distance, the players in their white uniforms resembled pieces on a chessboard. Neil noticed a problem in the field placement. The wind was slowing down the ball; fielders in catching positions should stand a few steps closer to the batsman than they usually do. He remembered the test match from eight years ago when he had terrorized the same opponent on the same ground, winning the game for India. The crowd had bayed for blood that afternoon, terrifying the Australians.

I was a hero then. Who cares for my opinion now?

'Sir! This whole area is being vacated.'

Another stocky, senior-looking person in a grey suit joined Mr Black Suit.

'In the middle of the match?' snapped Neil.

Neil turned to look as Stuart McGill hit Srikant Kale for two consecutive sixes. The cheering in the stadium stopped.

Fuck! Use the fast bowlers, idiots!

'Sir, we need this space for the home minister. Please cooperate.'

'Listen! I won't move. Park the minister somewhere else,' Neil said.

He shook his head. 'You know I played for India?'

Mr Grey Suit nodded. 'Yes, sir! And that's why we will find another seat for you.'

Other guests vacated the VIP box, except Saurabh Goyal who sat undisturbed in the front row. Obviously they couldn't touch the grandmaster. Lesser cricketers were lesser humans as well.

Neil pointed to the front row. 'Who else are you moving?'

'Everyone, sir, except the senior players.'

'And I am not senior?' fumed Neil. 'Call the DCA secretary. I got an award today at lunch, for God's sake…'

'Okay, sir!'

'Neil, come sit next to me,' Saurabh called out.

'And do what?' Neil gripped the handle of his seat and tried to smile.

Yeah right! So, now you will rescue me? The Messiah will save the downtrodden!

'We never meet; let's catch up,' Saurabh rose from his chair. 'Are you okay?'

Mr Grey Suit returned, this time accompanied by two more people. 'Sir, the DCA secretary has gone to receive the minister.'

'Okay, fuck off then…'

'What's the problem?' Saurabh asked Mr Grey Suit. 'Don't create a ruckus here.'

'Saurabh, please don't interfere.' Neil fumed under the garb of politeness. 'Just because I have played fewer matches than you…'

'Fewer than Saurabh? You are comparing yourself with him?' somebody said, causing laughter, smirks and giggles in the VIP box.

Neil shivered, drowning under the deluge of public mockery.

His phone slipped from his palm and slid under the seat after hitting the ground.

'Sir! There is no time. Please!'

A roar went up in the stadium. Mr Grey Suit caught Neil's right arm and tried to yank him to his feet, but his hand slipped and tore his shirt instead.

Neil pushed Mr Grey Suit in reflex action, throwing him near the seat. Mr Grey Suit slid across the polished floor with hardly any friction and banged his head against the wall with a loud grunt.

The stadium cheered the loss of another Australian wicket, but the VIP box had better entertainment. After a brief struggle, the police evicted Neil just before the home minister entered with his entourage.

Neil immediately left the stadium.

The match ended in a draw.

The Smell of Leather

After Three Days, in Gurgaon

'Are you dead?'

Nandini's blazing eyes seemed to bore a hole through Neil's head. 'I have been calling you for the last two days like an idiot,' she screamed.

Neil smiled as she entered his apartment. 'Relax, relax.'

'What happened here?' Nandini gasped. 'It's a war zone.'

'Sorting stuff to throw away,' said Neil.

Several piles of old sports magazines occupied the couch. On the floor lay heaps of batting pads and cricket bats, some new, others with numerous cracks and stains bearing evidence of their checkered services to the game. A large open wooden box housed hundreds of used cricket balls, some having writings on them in black to record landmarks and achievements. Dozens of dirty sports shoes rested against the wall. Beside them sat a pile of blue and white tees and tracks—the Indian cricket colours.

He waddled across the living room trying to create space where there was none.

'Never mind...I will stand,' she said, and leaned against the wall. 'Why are you hiding?'

Neil grinned and checked his phone. 'Sorry, it conked off.'

'Since when?'

Nandini wrinkled her nose and he walked over to open the window.

'The smell bothering you?' Neil asked.

The dirty cricket gear stink like the memories they represent.

'What happened in the stadium?' Nandini hopped over the clutter to join Neil near the window. She peeked outside and breathed in the fresh air.

Neil sighed. 'Read the newspapers.'

The boom of firecrackers bursting outside disturbed his train of thought.

Diwali crackers? Already celebrating?

'You got an award?'
'Yes.'
'For?'
'Exceptional performance against the Australians...' He shook his head. 'It doesn't matter.'

Nandini held up a newspaper. 'It's not here.'
'Fight stories are more juicy.'
'Why didn't you move?'
'Saurabh didn't.'
'Who?'
'Saurabh Goyal.'
'Oh! The big guy?'

Neil pointed at the front cover of a magazine.

Saurabh Goyal...included in the ICC Hall of Fame

'Yeah!' he said. 'We debuted for India in the same match. In the first game, he got only 12 runs, but I got 5 wickets. Over time, he did much better...ninety international centuries.'

Nandini flipped through the magazine. 'Smart people avoid trouble.'

'Compromise?'
'Not exactly.'
'Like you?'

'You know my story,' snapped Nandini. Her lips quivered. 'Very unkind of you to...'

'We do what we think is right,' snapped Neil. 'So don't question me.'

'Why are you avoiding people?'
'The press is hounding me...and the police...'

He flinched at the deafening sound of the firecrackers.

Nandini covered her face with her palm. 'Is there an FIR against you?'

'There will be if I speak about the matter.'
'Dad called you?'

Neil shook his head.

'Grandma?' Nandini sighed. 'They won't care when it matters.'
'Don't blame them for my faults.'
'But not everything is your fault,' said Nandini. 'I read in *The*

Indian Age how Gagan and Akash's fight sabotaged your coaching business.'

'Who said this?'

'No idea; did not mention the source,' said Nandini.

'Is it true?' asked Neil.

'Well! Can you explain why your business stopped at just one academy in five years?' asked Nandini. 'Gagan is plain incompetent... but is that the only reason?'

Gagan convinced me to retire early...promised to make my cricket coaching academy a big business. Fuck! It was supposed to redeem my career. No wonder I was evicted from the stadium where I was a hero eight years ago.

'Does Ramesh uncle know?' asked Neil.

'Yes, but dad doesn't care,' fumed Nandini.

Neil fumbled around in the clutter. Several firecrackers burst outside in quick succession, shaking up the place.

'God! Can't bear this noise; I am leaving,' said Nandini.

'Going somewhere?'

'Will pick up Abhi from mom's and then prepare for a party my great husband is hosting tomorrow evening.'

Neil smirked. 'Celebrations?'

'Yeah! Celebrating Delhi's great pre-Diwali rituals,' scoffed Nandini. 'Men will drink all night while the bored wives will watch them gamble away their ill-gotten wealth.'

'Sounds very interesting,' Neil smirked.

'Hey...can you come?' said Nandini in a pleading voice. She joined her palms and begged. 'Please! Please! Please!'

Neil shook his head. 'Can't. Your husband hates me.'

'Please!'

'But why?'

'Show everyone you are fine,' Nandini patted his shoulder. 'You don't have to hide.'

'No, thanks.'

'Neil! I need your support on a tough evening,' said Nandini in a stern voice. 'Are you man enough?'

Her husband will nail me. It will be a disaster.

Neil hesitated but gave in. 'Okay, I'll be there.'

'Oh, I almost forgot...' Nandini smiled and produced a newspaper clipping from her wallet. 'A new cricket league is starting...the ICCL;

it's a great opportunity.'

Neil frowned and shook his head. 'Not real cricket. A circus for rich people to show off.'

'Stop acting like a crybaby,' Nandini stormed out of the door. 'Do something to help yourself.'

Neil hurried after her. 'Okay! Will think about it.'

Nandini entered her car and rolled down the window. 'Keep your phone on,' she said. 'Can't babysit you; I already have Abhi to worry about. Today it took me two hours to drive from Greater Kailash to Gurgaon.'

'Don't worry about me.'

Nandini's eyes twinkled as she grinned. 'It's weird. The disgusting smell in your apartment...evoked memories of childhood.'

'How?'

'Your room in the farmhouse has the same smell. It was dreadful, but later I got used to it. Funny, I always think of you whenever I get that smell.'

Neil laughed. 'The advantages of being dirty.'

Nandini peered with unfocused eyes. 'Do you remember how the farmhouse used to be lit up for Diwali? The diyas on the front porch? Crackers bursting in the lawn?' She sighed. 'Those were carefree times, when life was so full of possibilities.'

'True; but ancient history,' shrugged Neil. 'Why think about them now?'

Life has become a graveyard of aspirations. Things were going so well... ICC Emerging Cricketer of the Year, the only genuine fast bowler in India after Kapil Dev. I was destined for greatness, but couldn't hold on. It all slipped away in the blink of an eye.

Whiskey Tales

Next Day, Late Evening

Captain Jayshankar Pandit (fondly called Cap Jay) presided over an animated discussion about the difference between Scotch and Bourbon. He detailed the difference in ingredients and manufacturing processes—one used malted barley, while the other used corn; one was from Scotland while the other was from Kentucky. Bourbon must have at least 51 per cent corn in its mix of grains, as per the US Federal Standards of Identity. It is distilled at 160 proof or less, in a new charred oak barrel. He described his visit to the Jack Daniel's distillery in Kentucky and gloated about how the owner had appreciated his vast knowledge of spirits and beverages. He spoke about his incredible experience as a whiskey taster in Scotland, and answered the questions of his guests with the patience and grace of a guru.

'As if they are dying to learn!' Nandini rolled her eyes. 'Fucking freeloaders who wouldn't care if it's Scotch or local hooch, as long as it's free. What a purposeful life...spent in the holy pursuit of whiskeys,' she marvelled at her husband's penchant for nonsense. 'Thanks for coming; it will be a long night.'

'But I will leave soon...don't feel well,' said Neil, patting his stomach.

Nandini smiled. 'You need better excuses.'

Cap Jay's card party buzzed with people. Bearers clad in white served from an extensive bar stocked with many bottles of liquor. Gamblers thronged the poker tables in the middle of the enormous living room, throwing money, accompanied by curses, insults and prayers. A smooth jazz tune played in vain from a boombox in the corner, failing to cheer up a group of women huddled together nearby. They occasionally adjusted their makeup or hair, looking like a herd of sheep waiting for their turn at the executioner's table. Other women had joined the cheerleading squad near the table. Small groups of people chatted in various parts of the room with glasses in their hands, and others sat by themselves, too drunk or bored to interact.

'Remember that woman I told you about?' Nandini pointed

towards a tall, slightly plump woman, wearing a very short red dress standing with a boisterous group near the bar. She laughed with gay abandon as the adoring men swooned over her.

Neil nodded. 'What about her?'

'Her name is Deepika, and she works in Jayshankar's office.'

Neil vaguely remembered Nandini mentioning Cap Jay's extramarital affair with a woman in his office.

What should I do about it?

'She is harmless here, in a room full of people,' said Neil.

Nandini clenched her fists. 'He dared to bring her to this house. Bastard!'

Gagan arrived and headed straight for the bar. Neil dropped his feeble attempt to sympathize about Deepika's presence and hurried over to talk to him.

Gagan rejected Neil's query about the newspaper article regarding his coaching business. 'Don't believe this nonsense. Akash is not so powerful,' he said.

'When are we getting the land? And the finance?' asked Neil.

'I am busy with other stuff,' scowled Gagan.

'You promised thirty academies in five years.'

Gagan avoided eye contact and scanned the room, as if searching for somebody.

'You have time for parties?' Nandini asked Gagan, catching up with them.

'Urgent business with your husband. So...'

Nandini seemed perplexed. 'Business? Here in this debauched party?' She pointed towards Cap Jay. 'He is barely sane.'

'It can't wait...kind of an emergency,' Gagan looked uneasy. 'Need another drink...will talk later.'

Neil walked outside and dissolved in the pitch darkness of the lawn. Cap Jay would soon use the incident in the stadium to make fun of him. He dreaded the prospect of returning to a room filled with revellers hungry for entertainment from the misery of a fellow human being. Ditching Nandini would be wrong. But there was no place to hide there. The endless sequence of tragedies in his life had ensured humiliation at every step. Losing his parents in a car accident had made him dependent on his uncle and grandma at an early age. They ridiculed him for his father's decision to shun the family business.

Breaking his ankle in a practice game just before his India debut had set his career back by two years. Kanika's sudden disappearance from his life had set off a chain of events that ruined his career. He faced hostility from teammates, coaches and managers in the Delhi cricket team. Cricket bosses had hated his independent attitude and sidelined him to settle a score with his uncle. His coaching venture had flopped. Let alone finding love, even meaningful relationships had eluded him since Kanika.

People confuse my misfortune with lack of talent or intent, and blame me for bad luck and the malice of others.

Neil was tired of feeling sorry for himself. His challenges were bigger than just countering Cap Jay, and life was prodding him to act and elevate himself above humiliation, above self-pity, beyond the reach of society.

Can't join the family business; I am a cricketer, not a businessman. Grandma will taunt me—like father, like son, she will say. Nothing new, she has ridiculed me all my life.

Underutilized potential is a crime. I have to impact cricket; leave a legacy. The coaching business is the only way forward.

Gagan won't do anything; I have to take charge.

When Neil returned to the party, Cap Jay called out to Nandini, 'Ask Neil to drink—have fun.' He lifted his fat arms and they jiggled. 'He is hurting.'

'Alcohol reduces your pain,' someone around him said in a mocking voice.

Cap Jay put a few fingers in his mouth and whistled.

'Don't worry, he will handle it,' Nandini snapped.

'Ladies and gentlemen, we have a new gangster in town,' Cap Jay pointed towards Neil. 'The great cricketer, WWF champion, Neil Upadhyay.' He clenched his right fist, puffed up his face and moved his hand, as if striking an imaginary boxer. 'And he took on the home minister.'

A woman giggled from behind Cap Jay. 'So, it's true; they threw him out.'

Cap Jay stuck out his tongue. 'Yesssssssssss. To fight the high and the mighty,' he shook his butt and patted his right bicep with his left palm, 'you need muscles.' Cap Jay burst into laughter and held his stomach, struggling to control himself. 'A mouse is fighting a lion. It's too small to even become the lion's meal.' Suddenly Cap Jay cleared the table by sweeping the playing cards and currency notes to the ground. He emptied the contents of a black pouch on the table and rolled up a 100-rupee note. Then, with one end of the pipe in his nose, he snorted the powder off the table. 'Gagan, you want a hit?' he blurted out.

'He is not here.'

Cap Jay wore a wicked grin and winked at Nandini. 'Go find Gagan.'

Neil rued his inability to react. How come he had defended himself at the stadium but not there? He could finally see the reality of his situation. Would Cap Jay mock Saurabh Goyal? Cap Jay was right. A mouse cannot demand respect from a lion. To challenge the powerful, you need muscles.

And I have none.

Nandini shook Neil out of his trance. 'Do you see Deepika?'

'No. Why?'

'Nandini! Get me a drink,' Cap Jay snapped his fingers. His lips twitched, and with a violent shudder, he collapsed on the table.

She winced and looked away. 'My husband fixed my brother with his whore…and he is doing her in my house.'

'Really? How do you know?'

Nandini replied to his stupid comment with a steely stare devoid of emotions.

Cap Jay keeled over the table, looking unconscious. People started leaving before he suddenly sat up and yelled, 'Let's play.'

'I chose money over a middle-class life in the US. I deserve this,' Nandini said, misty-eyed.

Neil hugged her and felt despondency radiating from her body.

'Please leave, Neil. Sorry I made you go through this,' she said and rushed out of the room.

Big Brother Is Watching

After Two Days, Late Afternoon

After three hours of waiting in a cramped reception area, Neil's time had finally come. 'Mr Upadhyay, the minister sahib will see you now.'

Neil hobbled into the minister's room in the new leather shoes he had bought for this meeting. He buttoned his coat and collapsed on the nearest chair with a grunt.

Damn these shoes!

He checked his folder, searching for no document in particular. The minister looked up from his papers. 'What's the emergency?'

'Sir, please help my cricket academy.'

'What?'

'We need land, sir; we applied two years ago…'

'Impossible.'

'But I am helping cricket.'

The minister laughed. 'Cricket doesn't need help. The cricket board is already filthy rich. The Delhi government's policy is to promote other sports in the state.'

'Sir, I want to coach…'

The desk phone rang, and the minister indulged the caller with a lengthy pitch about how cow's milk could improve stamina.

What luck! Our sports minister is a nutrition specialist. And I am enlightened by his knowledge and vision.

The minister failed to convince the caller and banged down the phone with a curse. He returned to his file, seemingly oblivious to Neil's presence in the room.

Neil fidgeted in his seat to attract attention.

'Yes?' scowled the minister.

'I want to grow my coaching business.'

'Can't happen.'

'Why?'

The minister glared at him. 'Neil! My nephew forced me to meet you. Don't push me…'

Neil squeezed his eyes shut. 'Sorry, sir. I am desperate.'

'I have my limitations,' said the minister.

'I want to create a legacy; impact cricket.'

The minister went and sat beside Neil and patted his back. 'Don't worry about more impact, son! You have already done enough.'

Neil smiled. 'Give me something to work on...'

'Talk to your cousin.'

'Gagan?'

'Akash! Gagan is useless.'

Neil scratched his head. 'But Akash is not involved.'

The minister pulled out a large handkerchief and wiped his face. His small black eyes looked like buttons on his large red face. 'Akash doesn't want anyone to help you or Gagan.'

Neil gasped. 'Akash and I have no issues...'

'Can't say...ask him.' The minister joined his palms in a namaste and looked uneasy. 'Please! Don't mention me.'

'So, my powerful cousin is crushing me?'

'Powerful? Huh! You have no idea.'

'And you can't help?'

'No one can.'

'What if I buy land from a private party?'

'Buying land is easy; running the academy is tough,' the minister fiddled with a paperweight. 'Akash will shut it down in two seconds through the government.'

'Under what rule?'

'Rules get made as needed.'

'You are trying to scare me, right?'

'Fine! Try it then,' snapped the minister. 'You don't know what I know. Within the next hour, Akash will know you were here, without me telling him.'

The desk phone rang again, and the minister moved back to his chair to take the call.

Neil slumped in his chair and blamed himself for Akash's malice. His selection in the Indian team had delighted Akash. He had taken Neil under his wing, travelled to see him play, bought him the best cricket gear—Slazenger bats and shoes imported from England—best cricket balls and world-class apparel. He had hired a personal fitness specialist, manager and dietician for Neil, and convinced Raghav Bedi to mentor him. Akash had acted as the big brother and had done his best to support him.

But I did not value his affection. When we scorn our best supporters, they end up as our worst enemies.

Neil had ruined their great relationship by appointing Kanika as his manager when Akash had promised Divya that her cousin would get the position. He had then lost face in front of his wife and never forgotten the humiliation. Neil had supported Gagan during the union strike in the Omkar Group and criticized Akash in public without realizing that it was a conspiracy by Gagan to topple Akash. Neil's foolishness had made Akash an enemy forever.

I was then a cricket star. Never thought he would be able to harm me.
This isn't about family politics any more. Akash has a problem with me.

He felt dizzy and short of breath.

Can Ramesh uncle help? Grandma? Maybe Nandini? Akash has a soft corner for her.

After the minister finished his phone call, Neil rose to leave.

'Son, life is unfair, but we must move ahead,' said the minister. 'Just clear it up with Akash, and you will be fine.'

Neil detested sympathy. He nodded out of politeness and collected his folder.

'I always loved your bowling. But I am helpless.'

Neil ignored him and moved towards the door.

'Wait, Neil!'

The minister tossed a magazine towards Neil, which struck his chest and fell on the floor. A photo of Akash occupied the whole front cover along with the following words:

The Most Influential Tech Companies in Asia—AlphaX Tops List

'Read the article; it mentions his net worth,' said the minister. 'He is the fifth richest man in India. What kind of influence do you think he has? I would flee if this man was my enemy.'

Bloodless War

Next Day, Early Afternoon

Neil ached for Nandini's attention as she read the menu for the fifth time. The waiter approached for the order, and Nandini gave him her acid tongue instead. 'What's the hurry? Should we leave?' Nandini discarded the menu. 'Let's go somewhere else. This restaurant is pathetic.'

'I will be late for a meeting,' mumbled Neil.

'Meeting whom?'

'Former teammate from Kolkata.'

Nandini stared, narrow-eyed, a sure sign she had read through his lies.

I have hurt her. Now this conversation will be useless.

Neil held her hands. 'Sorry, I lied.'

Nandini smiled. 'You are a terrible liar; it's so attractive.'

'How did you know?'

'You stammer.'

She wants to spend time with me, but I am so selfish.

'Let's order salad,' Neil patted his stomach.

'What's your Plan B?'

'I can try my luck in South India, perhaps.'

Nandini fiddled with her sunglasses. 'Akash can screw you anywhere.'

'Should I apologize?'

'What is the guarantee he will actually forgive you even if he says so?'

'Should I ask Ramesh uncle to help?'

Nandini rolled her eyes. 'Yeah! As if dad will intervene.'

'I am sure he will,' said Neil. 'Should I list the things he has done for me? Adopting an orphan like me is more than enough.'

What's wrong with her? So ungrateful; uncle has supported the whole family.

Neil shook his head. 'He fought against grandma to let me play cricket. Got me transferred to Kolkata when I was struggling in Delhi; helped me get back into the Indian team by speaking to the cricket board president. Cricket training in England, rehabilitation in

Australia when I broke my ankle, mentors, coaches, cricket equipment, money...whatever I needed. No questions asked. So please don't say he won't do anything.'

Nandini grinned. 'Right! You are his top priority.'

'Yes, I am,' snapped Neil. 'I realized the importance of my family when they threw me out of the stadium. I thought people respect me, but in reality, they respect my family. Would they have dared to throw me out if uncle would have been with me?'

Nandini fiddled with her sunglasses again.

She always fiddles with things when she is not sure. Hopefully, she will now drop her absurd ideas and give useful suggestions.

'Why do you think he encouraged your cricket?' asked Nandini.

'Because he loves me.'

'No, you moron...to ensure his sons have a free run in the family business.'

Neil laughed. 'Are you reading a lot of fiction?' Wide-eyed, he put his hand to his face. 'Thrillers? Complex plots? Conspiracy theories?'

'Will you cut the crap?' screamed Nandini.

Neil flinched as their altercation attracted unwanted attention from the other tables. 'Why are you shouting?'

'Because you refuse to change.'

We can't agree about the family. There is no point escalating a useless issue.

Nandini kicked the table, and the glasses toppled, soaking the tablecloth with water and wine. 'If dad and grandma could blackmail me into marrying a stupid debauched half-man...can you be sure he had no selfish reasons for helping you?'

Nobody had forced her to marry! She could have lived in the US.

A waiter arrived and cleaned the table.

Neil knew the danger of opposing Nandini. She might fly off the handle again and lose focus from the main issue. He tried to give a neutral answer. 'But uncle helped me all my life. I owe everything to him.'

'So why not with your coaching business?'

'Gagan was in charge.'

'The only person he ever loved is Gagan,' Nandini spat and chucked a used napkin on the table. 'God knows why he tolerated Gagan's nonsense. It harmed Gagan more than it helped him. Do you remember your marriage proposal?' she fumed. 'Dad tried to sell you to that obnoxious Gupta family because they promised some contracts to our company.'

'I regret turning down uncle,' said Neil. 'Marriage might have given direction to my life.'

Nandini scowled. 'Yeah? That girl is a spoilt with a reputation worse than that of a whore.'

'Maybe I could have adapted to that lifestyle. Her father's strong connections would have helped me.'

'Neil! The Guptas were interested as you are tall, muscular and good-looking. They didn't care for you as a person or for your cricket dreams. Would you have been happy being a sex slave to satisfy their nymphomaniac daughter?' Nandini shouted at Neil. 'They would have made your life a living hell. And, dad wouldn't care as long as he made money.'

Neil grinned. 'Again your fictional stuff. Your dad is not a criminal.'

'Dad said you are selfish like your father, just because you protected yourself,' she said in a stern voice almost ready for an explosion.

'I don't blame him. It was my chance to give back to the family, and I didn't.'

Nandini shut her eyes and took a deep breath. 'Okay! Even if dad wants to help you, he won't be able to convince Akash. He has been asking Akash to bail out the Omkar Group for years, but Akash is too smart to prop up a sinking ship. Try to get your share before it's too late. The Omkar Group can shut shop any day now.'

'My share of the family property?' asked Neil, aghast at the ridiculous suggestion.

'Yes, and then you will understand your family's reality,' Nandini chuckled. 'I haven't got my share yet, and I am the daughter. So let's see what happens to the nephew.'

Neil laughed. 'I already got more from my family than I deserve.'

'Okay! Then stay a loser. Go sit on your uncle's lap.'

The waiter served the soup. Neil ate it in a few moments of quiet reflection.

'If I ask for money, they will ask me to join the business,' he said.

'Grandma wants you to join, but not dad,' said Nandini. 'You should use this to drive a wedge between them. They have different objectives. Grandma wants you to get your inheritance, but she also wants you to stay inside the family. She always wanted to keep the family together. Her biggest complaint against Akash is he listened to his wife and moved out. She discouraged you from playing cricket to stop you from moving out. But dad wanted the benefits to go to his two sons, so he encouraged your cricket. But he did not expect Akash would move out, and that Gagan would drive the business to the ground.'

Even after Nandini's passionate pitch about driving family conflict to extract his share of the family's wealth, Neil knew Akash was at the centre of his problems. Getting his inheritance wouldn't help if Akash stalled him at every step. But how would he make peace with Akash? They had been out of touch for a long time. Akash ignored him whenever their paths crossed during social events. A meeting was impossible—Akash declined even phone calls. Neil had stopped trying two years ago when Akash refused him permission to enter his house.

I thought he is ignoring me because of his high social status, but the hatred is much deeper. Once he had travelled all the way to New Zealand to see me play for India, but now he won't even accept my apology. But I must find a way—plead, beg, grovel, do whatever shameful act is required to appease him. And only Nandini can help.

'Can you talk to Akash?'

Nandini sighed. 'I tried. It did not work.'

'Why?'

'Because I was canvassing for you and not asking for anything for myself.'

Why wouldn't she take Akash's help to clear up her mess?

'Are you too proud to ask?' he asked.

'What's the use?' Nandini looked morose. 'He can't make my husband love me. He can't give me back the last seven years of my life. I don't want Akash to think he can change my life.'

She is impossible! She wants the status quo; she likes the pain, enjoys the same self-pity she accuses me of having. And that's why she is fighting her parents through me.

'You can't expect help from Akash, nor forgiveness,' she said. 'I am not defending him, but why should he care for you? What have you done for him?'

Neil smiled. 'But you did nothing for him either.'

'Exactly! But then I am the sister, and you are only a cousin. We are alone in this world, Neil! Fight for your rights. No one likes it when I fight your battles for you.'

A Billionaire in Thirty Minutes

Next Day, in Gurgaon

The intercom buzzed. 'Sir, we stopped Mr Gagan at the main gate.'
'Good! Let him walk the rest of the way,' said Akash.
A body search and then a one-hour wait downstairs will give him a stroke.
Akash glanced at the review articles and framed pictures adorning his office.

'A Billionaire in Thirty Minutes!' —*The Wall Street Journal*

'The Most Influential Tech Companies in Asia. AlphaX Tops List' —*Forbes*

'Among the Top Five CEOs of India' —*The Economist*

'Top Ten Technology Thought Leaders' —*Harvard Business Review*

There were photographs with Bill Clinton, Warren Buffett and Bill Gates. There was a personal letter from Steve Jobs. There was also an honorary doctorate from IIT Delhi.
Has Gagan seen these? I should chain him here, with his eyelids glued to his skull. Maybe then he will realize the terrible mistakes he made in his life. Incompetence has a price. Today's humiliation will start his new life among the commoners.
The Wall Street Journal had called him 'a billionaire in thirty minutes' after AlphaX's IPO in Nasdaq made his net worth shoot up by three billion dollars in the first thirty minutes of trading. The global media reported it as a triumph of 'Emerging India'.
They missed the real story. It took a lifetime of relentless back-breaking work for those 'thirty minutes' to happen.
After two hours Akash allowed Gagan to enter his cabin.
'Why did they stop me?' fumed Gagan.
Akash ignored him and kept reading a document.
His fuse will blow soon. Fun!
Gagan made a 'hmm' sound and sat on a chair. 'What the fuck! I did not come to read magazines and drink coffee.'

Akash looked up and smiled. 'You read? Since when?'

'You made me wait. Fucker!' Gagan screamed and banged his fist on the desk.

'Why are you not wearing a suit?' asked Akash in a calm voice. For a moment he considered asking Gagan to go back home to change, but decided against it.

Too much pressure too fast will spoil the show. Let me unravel him step by step.

'This is an office, not a bar,' Akash said. 'Next time, wear proper clothes. Otherwise the security will throw you out.' Someone knocked on the door, and Akash shouted, 'Come in.' An office boy dressed in a white uniform entered with a tray, but Akash shooed him away. Akash picked up a report from his desk. 'We made a loss of sixty million last quarter, with no major orders in the pipeline. As the CEO, what's your solution?'

'We need to raise money,' said Gagan.

'How can we get new orders?'

Gagan shrugged. 'I don't know, maybe by throwing money at our political contacts? He shifted in his chair with a squeaking sound, and it sounded like he farted. 'Why should I have all the answers? How about you having some ideas?'

Akash sighed. 'So your solution is to borrow money and then spend it on politicians to get orders?'

'Yes, and also...' Gagan paused and took a deep breath, '...it's an emergency; we will have to shut down without the money.'

'Can't allow borrowing from the market,' said Akash in a stern voice. 'Let it shut down.'

Gagan twisted his lips. 'That's your solution?'

'Improve the operations. Cut costs. Fire useless officers. Take no salary or perks. Go door to door to get business. We will spend money only after new orders,' said Akash.

'To get new orders, we have to spend money.'

'We need credibility, not money, for new orders, which you don't have.'

'Okay! Here's the deal. Why don't you lend us the money? I promise I will give you the results,' said Gagan.

'I don't think you can.'

Gagan looked around the office and whistled. 'You are always spending so much needlessly. Every time I come here, this office looks different. Expensive paintings, furniture, all waste…'

'Am I spending your father's money?' asked Akash in a cold voice.

'My father is the same as yours,' snapped Gagan. 'Help the company or get out. Don't just sit here and lecture me.'

Akash laughed. 'You will stop me?'

'What is your problem?' scowled Gagan, jumping up from his seat.

As Gagan showed his street fighter avatar, Akash used the intercom to get help. 'Ask the security to come in.'

'Why this animosity?' Gagan asked in a calm voice. He sat down and wiped the sweat from his brow. 'How have we harmed you?'

'You don't know?'

'I don't,' Gagan shook his head. 'You hate us. I couldn't find a single photo of either dad or grandma in this building.'

'They helped me?' asked Akash.

'Fucker…you are both insane and ungrateful,' exclaimed Gagan. 'You built this out of thin air?'

'Why didn't you build a company?' said Akash. 'You had the same resources.' Two guards entered the room; Akash signalled to them to wait near the door. He lifted his heavy frame from his chair and approached Gagan. He played with a stress ball as he addressed Gagan. 'You are useless. You dared to flirt with my secretary while waiting outside my office?'

'Who?'

'My secretary, Pooja. You asked her out for drinks?'

'Pure nonsense…' blurted Gagan.

'You will take her to the Gymkhana Club?' Akash hit Gagan with the stress ball. 'How do they admit people like you there? I will get your membership cancelled. You are an embarrassment to that fine institution.'

Gagan hung his head in silence.

'Do you know who her boyfriend is?' fumed Akash. 'Hmm?' One of the security guards walked over to hand him the stress ball. Akash toyed with the ball and walked around. 'He is the founder of crackdeals.com, a real achiever; Harvard-educated, raised 115 million dollars in venture capital.' Akash paused and jerked his head upwards. 'And you? Hmm?'

Gagan gestured with his arms. 'I was just casually talking to her.'

'Listen carefully,' Akash said in a low, menacing voice, standing almost on top of Gagan. 'Don't come near her, ever, or I will cut off your balls. You have no ability; at least mind your age.' Akash grabbed Gagan's hair and yanked it. 'You piece of turd! Instead of working, you are attending cocaine parties and womanizing with that debauched Jayshankar. You can't respect your own sister?'

'Don't lecture me, okay? You are no different,' snapped Gagan. His bloodshot eyes betrayed his seething anger ready to explode. Gagan released his head and moved away from Akash. 'You change secretaries every three months; I know what is going on here.'

'You dare accuse me, you characterless bastard!' Akash screamed and grabbed Gagan's collar. 'I will crush you like a peanut.'

The security guards rushed forward, ready to intervene.

'Now get out,' Akash tilted his head towards the door. 'Don't come back without a plan, otherwise we will throw you out from the gate itself.'

Gagan left, and Akash asked Pooja to come in.

Bastard tried to hook up with Pooja when he has come here to beg for money? Twenty years ago he could pick up any girl he wanted anywhere, but not any more, and not on my watch. He is an extraordinary imbecile who thinks he can pull off impossible stunts all his life. He can't see that the sand had shifted since our childhood and buried him deep. The big prizes in life belong to the more deserving among humans, and he is an ape.

Akash asked Pooja to draw the curtains. He gasped as she walked over to the window with the clip-clop of her high heels and the delicate sway of her shapely butt. The smooth skin of her thighs showed through the split in her blue skirt and reflected light, almost hurting his eyes. He loved how her well-groomed hair covered half her boobs and stopped just before the nipples. The male muscle tightened between his legs.

I had so many all over the world, but this chick is exceptional.

'Anything else, sir?'

Akash casually touched his lips. 'Next week I am going to Spain; come with me.'

Pooja leaned on the desk with a coy smile. 'Just work? Or… something more?'

'A little fun has hurt no one,' she said.

Akash smiled. 'Awesome! And listen, book yourself first-class tickets.'

A Long Dead Career

Next Day, Evening

At precisely 7 p.m., Neil walked into Delhi's Taj Mahal Hotel to meet Mr Jatinder Singh, the chairman of the ICCL Governing Council.

'The chairman is busy,' the hotel staff informed him. 'Please wait or come back another day.'

Neil hated people who did not honour their commitments. But Jatinder was not at fault here. His commitment had collapsed in the absence of respect for Neil. Could anyone refuse Saurabh Goyal? It was not personal. People snubbed Neil because they lacked respect for him, not goodwill. It was the same story in grandma's constant pestering for him to join the family business, in Gagan's lethargy, in uncle's unresponsiveness, in Akash's enmity.

Initially Jatinder had refused him an appointment, and had only relented when Gautam Chatterjee had lobbied Delhi's power circuit to set up a fifteen-minute meeting.

Imploring Akash for forgiveness won't help. Only respect for me can kill his anger.

Neil pulled out a newspaper clipping from his pocket, wondering if the ICCL was his gateway to redemption.

'The Cricket Control Board of India has announced the launch of The Indian Club Cricket (ICCL) League with eight privately owned teams. Cricket legends Justin Prober, Heath Gunn and Saurabh Goyal have joined as icon players. More international and Indian cricketers are expected to join in the coming weeks.'

It was past midnight when the hotel staff escorted Neil to a restaurant on the ninth floor where the chairman was sitting with three gentlemen and a lady. The chairman's generous belly had forced him to sit at an uncomfortable distance from the table, and he grunted every time he reached for a drink.

People who never played cricket in their lives, or any sport, are now running Indian cricket. He looks eight months pregnant; so inspirational for young cricketers.

Neil smiled, hoping his geniality would camouflage his disdain for sports administrators.

'How do you know Gautam?' the chairman asked in a slurry voice.

Neil took his time to settle down. 'Sir, he coached me in the Bengal team,' he said.

'So?'

'I wanted to discuss my coaching ideas for the ICCL.'

Neil produced a document from his folder.

'Why? I am not a team owner,' scowled the chairman.

The lady took the document from Neil.

'Sir, Justin Prober, Heath Gunn and even Saurabh Goyal got contracts, so I thought…'

'They are joining as players, not coaches.'

'But they have retired…'

'They are there more for the glamour factor,' replied the gentleman wearing red suspenders on oversized pinstripe trousers. 'It's a new league, requires big names.'

'They are in great shape,' said the lady, tilting her head. 'Amazing bodies!'

'I train every day…' stammered Neil.

The lady laughed as she read Neil's document. 'You want to focus on the domestic players?'

'They will form the bulk of the teams,' said Neil.

'Who cares? Domestic players come a dime a dozen,' said the chairman.

'Who decides on the coaches?' asked Neil.

'The owners, obviously.'

'But you can always recommend?'

The chairman shrugged. 'I can, but I won't.'

'What's your value proposition?' asked another gentleman.

Neil ignored him and addressed the chairman. 'Who should I contact?'

'The team auction will decide the owners,' the chairman gulped down his drink. 'Unless you are a psychic…'

Everyone guffawed at the joke and exchanged high fives.

Huh! Probably the only thing they know about cricket is the high fives.

'Coaches are very senior players; you don't have the profile,' said the chairman.

'Yes, I do; five years of coaching experience.'

The third gentleman placed his empty glass on Neil's document and joined the conversation. 'You lack glamour, bro. This is showbiz.'

'Who do you coach?' asked the gentleman with red suspenders.

'Anyone who wants to learn…'

The lady looked surprised. 'Not professional coaching?'

The third gentleman laughed. 'Fat kids looking to lose weight?'

'Two of my wards have played for India under-19,' said Neil. 'Fat kids can't survive my class…'

'I must go now,' said the chairman. He grunted as he tried to lift his bulk from the chair, succeeding in the third attempt. 'Tell Gautam you have your answers,' he said in a loud voice.

Fuck! He is leaving without giving me definite next steps.

Neil sprang up from his chair and offered a handshake. 'Sir, you are doing an amazing job—the ICCL will totally change Indian cricket.'

The chairman wiped his cheery red face with a large white handkerchief.

'I want to take part in the ICCL,' said Neil. 'Please help me.'

'Here's the perfect solution for you—buy your own team and become the owner, coach and player—all in one.' The chairman assumed a straight face as his companions burst into laughter. 'I am afraid many old cricketers will try to buy teams to resurrect their long-dead careers.'

Those unkind words reverberated in Neil's head long after the chairman had left. By ridiculing him, the chairman had shown him the path forward. Owning a cricket team seemed like a good business. People who invested millions of dollars must have worked out the financials. Neil couldn't dare to ask for his share of the family's wealth, but he could ask his family to invest in a cricket business managed by him. Uncle loved good deals, and a successful cricket team could revive the family's fortunes and reputation. It was like killing two birds with the same stone—cricket and family business rolled into one venture. Even grandma wouldn't oppose this idea.

Surely, Gautam Chatterjee can find the right person to help me with the business plan, someone who knows the cricket business.

My time will come when I will meet Mr Jatinder Singh again. But first we must have a team.

A Butcher's Fantasies

Three Days Later, Morning

Sudha's booming voice echoed through the speakerphone. 'You can't destroy the business we built with our sweat and blood.'

'What nonsense, grandma!' fumed Akash. 'Should I hang up?'

Ramesh supported his mother over the phone line. 'Don't hate us, son. We raised you…'

'Come to the point,' said Akash.

'It's all over, unless we raise money.'

'From whom?'

The previous night, Nandini had told Akash about Cap Jay's plan to bail out the Omkar Group. Sudha had asked her to keep Cap Jay happy and make sure he did not change his mind. Nandini laughed about Sudha blaming her for Cap Jay's reluctance to help them in the past, but Akash found such loose talk revolting. *Which self-respecting family pawns their daughter for money?*

Ramesh discussed a few ideas for raising money without mentioning Cap Jay and moved on to ramble about how they should work together.

Akash cut him off. 'Dad! Please present this to the board. You can sell me your shares and raise money.'

'Let us all sell in equal proportion,' said Sudha.

Akash lost his temper. 'No! Fire Gagan first.'

'Won't happen,' said Ramesh.

'Then no point wasting time here,' said Akash.

'We may have to sell the farmhouse and become homeless,' said Ramesh in a sad voice.

Akash wouldn't fall for his father's emotional blackmail. 'Yes! It will keep the company alive for another month. Then you will fire Gagan.'

'Your wife screwed your brain,' snapped Sudha.

Akash cursed, twisting in his chair.

Of course they will hate Divya. She foiled their plan to control me. She forced me to break free from dad's slavery. Divya's father funded AlphaX; I owe my success to my in-laws, not to these uneducated goons.

Akash controlled his urge to give grandma a piece of his mind. *Sometimes politeness has more ferocity than rudeness. Let them have their spite; soon they will eat their words.*

'Divya made me successful,' he said in a calm voice.

'Success means nothing if it hurts the family,' replied Sudha.

Gagan is the king's son—destined to sit on the throne. I won't get any credit just because I refused to accept their mediocrity. My contribution to society doesn't matter—I created thousands of jobs, developed world-class technology and earned global recognition for Indian businesses. But grandma's malice is futile; when you spit at the moon, it falls on you. If the lazy and the jealous determined the destinies of men, heroes wouldn't exist in this world.

'Please don't force me to be rude, grandma.'

'Why are you so angry?' asked Ramesh.

Akash laughed. 'Dad! You haven't seen my anger yet.'

'Is that a threat?' asked Sudha.

'Funny! Somebody destroyed the family business with his debauchery. Apart from me no one tried to correct him, yet I am the one who is "screwed up",' said Akash.

'Gagan is not an outsider, Akash! Yes, he has done many things wrong. But destroying him is not the solution, is it? You could force him to change. But why this?' said Ramesh.

Akash couldn't forgive his father for supporting Gagan's nuisance at every step. Calling Gagan a 'stud' and boasting about his popularity with women, paying a hefty sum to keep him from getting arrested when he had impregnated his classmate in college, unconditional support when he had instigated the union to rise against Akash who, as the CEO of Omkar Group, had tried to implement fresh ideas to improve the efficiency and culture of the archaic company...he had done it all! The same conservative family that had forced Nandini into an unhappy marriage had swallowed Gagan's transgressions. How could a father support a bad son against a good one?

Dad probably lived vicariously through Gagan, fulfilling his secret desires through him.

'I am not his father...you are; I won't do your job,' said Akash.

'Come home today in the evening, along with Divya and Rohit,' said Ramesh. 'Let's celebrate Diwali as a family. I promise to listen.'

'Sorry, I can't,' said Akash. 'Sack Gagan from the position of CEO and then we will talk.'

The Omkar Group was too weak to resist Akash's marauding power play, but he planned to wait before a full acquisition. Like a butcher at a meat shop, he relished killing them slowly, cutting one tissue at a time, while whispering sweet nothings into their ears to kindle hope among them, making them feel they would escape.

Let them believe the deal with Cap Jay will work. At the right time I will cut the jugular. Then it will all be over.

The Darkness of Diwali

Same Day, Evening

Ramesh Upadhyay grunted as he tossed the folder on the table. 'Not today, Neil. Will try in the next few days. Just not today.'

'Heard of the ICCL?' asked Neil.

No reply. Ramesh preferred reading the newspaper to a casual conversation with his nephew.

Neil hung around, eager to discuss his business plan. Just a few minutes of uncle's attention would be enough for him to slip in the highlights and trigger a conversation. In the ornately decorated living room of Upadhyay Palace, numerous photographs lined the walls celebrating childhood, graduations, marriages, triumphs in business or sports, babies born, even death. A huge picture of Neil accepting the 'ICC Emerging Cricketer of the Year' award occupied a prominent position on the long wall. Every family member found space on those walls except his father. It seemed he had never existed—no photographs in the house, no anecdotes ever shared during family events, no memorabilia kept as an honour, no anguish about his absence. *What did they do with his sitar?*

Neil regretted never knowing his father. Theirs was not a conventional father–son relationship. Sports, holidays, movies—activities sons did with their fathers never happened in their lives. When not travelling for his concerts, dad had always kept to his room, practising or teaching his students. Mom had been the only link between father and son. She had forced him to spend time in dad's music room even though he had always resented Neil's presence there.

Why was dad so upset with me? Because I had no interest in music? He wouldn't have encouraged my cricket had he been alive.

Ramesh Upadhyay continued reading, and Neil moved out to the garden to kill time. In the fading sun, Upadhyay Palace looked like a decked-up bride ready to welcome the grand Diwali evening. Rows of mini Diwali lights adorned the boundary walls—the red, blue, yellow and green, blinking in a complex psychedelic maze. The manicured lawns had lost the green shoots of monsoons, and the trimmed flower beds had shed the excess weight of the roses and the lilies. Footprints of people and their accumulated memories were missing from the pathways, and the driveway was devoid of dry leaves and tyre marks. A stray cracker being burst somewhere momentarily disturbed the dull perfection of the place, otherwise it presented an elegant and peaceful picture. Diwali was the time for rejuvenation and renewal, but the celebratory lights failed to enlighten the haziness of the path ahead.

Meeting grandma was never a pleasant experience for Neil as their interaction always seemed like an interrogation for crimes he had never committed. He wanted to discuss his plan with uncle and not grandma. She had not yet emerged from her afternoon nap, and Gagan was missing, which made this the best time for a discussion.

But uncle is busy reading.

Neil walked to the kitchen, where his aunt Madhu supervised a small army of cooks.

She smiled. 'Do you want something to eat?'

'No, just water,' said Neil. 'Is uncle okay?'

'No! Very tired and grumpy,' said Madhu.

'Hmm! I wanted to discuss a plan…'

Madhu frowned. 'Oh! Don't bother him; Gagan will help you, or Akash, although I doubt if he has the time.'

A thousand-bulbed chandelier glittered in the central living room of Upadhyay Palace for the special Diwali dinner. Sudha had a regal appearance, unwithered with age. People meeting her for the first time never guessed she was eighty-five. A lifetime of regular walks, yoga, meditation, frugal eating and a disdain for modern medications had delayed her ageing and helped her maintain her posture and mobility. Her sharp features had enduring beauty and grace to captivate any audience.

Sudha's presence unsettled everyone, and Neil was no exception. He couldn't muster the courage to discuss his business plan until she broached the subject after dinner.

'So you want us to buy a cricket team?' asked Sudha. She put her palm on her lips, struggling to chew the warm dessert.

Neil gulped. 'It's good business; here is the financial model…'

Sudha raised her eyebrows. 'Financial model, eh? Impressive!' She smiled as she paused before every word. 'Good, you are learning;

soon you will be ready to join the business.'

Sudha's tone unsettled Neil. 'I discussed the value proposition with experts,' he mumbled.

Sudha studied the printout before tossing it on the table. 'I don't agree. But even if it's a great opportunity, why are you interested?'

Neil stammered, searching for the right answer. 'Well! I can run the cricket part, and someone else can run the business part...'

'Hold on, hold on,' Sudha extended her arms to stop Neil. 'We should spend hundreds of millions of dollars to give you something to do?'

Neil gulped. 'I can create a great team, and...'

'We don't have the money to spare, Neil,' said Ramesh. He looked grave. 'Your ability is above doubt, but we don't have the monetary strength to do it...'

Sudha interrupted Ramesh. 'Oh no! We wouldn't invest even if we had the money.'

'But grandma...'

'Enough!' screamed Sudha, banging her fist on the table. 'You have wasted twenty years of your life on this nonsense. Now help the family.'

'Appoint Neil in the company,' Sudha told Ramesh.

Ramesh sighed. 'We have a hiring freeze; the board, which means Akash, approves new appointments.'

Sudha's face quivered with heavy breathing. 'I will tackle Akash.'

It was slipping away from Neil.

Now or never.

'But I only know cricket,' he said.

'Well then, learn other things,' shouted Sudha. 'How can you live with such incompetence? You were thrown out of the stadium. People are openly insulting us. You have destroyed our prestige.'

Neil hung his head as voices fell silent in the room.

'Yeah! It hurts, doesn't it?' said Sudha coldly. 'Problem is, it doesn't hurt enough for you to act.' She looked at Ramesh. 'Who misbehaved with Neil?'

'It was a Delhi cricket official,' said Ramesh.

'They knew his family?'

'No idea; you should ask Neil,' scoffed Ramesh. 'They offered him another seat. Why fight people more powerful than you!'

'Punish this insolent official,' said Sudha.

'We don't have the power any more.'

'You will tolerate this?'

Ramesh smiled. 'We are tolerating Jayshankar; after how he treats Nandini.'

'That's Nandini's personal matter,' scowled Sudha. 'No one forced her to marry him. We can't interfere unless she asks for help.'

'Neil hasn't asked for help either. Have you, Neil?'

Neil watched in silence as a futile argument ensued, different from the issues burning in his mind. Uncle was right about avoiding confrontation with powerful people, but it still bothered him that unlike grandma, he did not take umbrage at his eviction from the stadium.

Ten years ago he would have moved heaven and earth to avenge this insult. Maybe he has decided not to support my nonsense any more. But he could have at least discussed my business plan. Why are they discussing Nandini and Jayshankar?

'We have to reestablish Neil,' said Sudha in a low voice, as if speaking to herself.

'We will see,' said Ramesh.

'Don't see—just follow instructions,' scowled Sudha.

Ramesh discarded his unfinished dessert and walked away from the living room.

Later, Neil left Upadhyay Palace, struggling to cope with the tectonic shift in his world. Uncle's lack of interest in his plans constituted a new and terrifying reality. Nandini had warned him that uncle wouldn't help, but he had hoped that just like the old times, uncle would ask a few questions and then make it happen. He always found a way to help. Neil wasn't sure if uncle understood his proposal. He rejected it before hearing him out.

He drove through the deserted roads of South Delhi and remembered the night his parents had died. It was a night like this one, dark, brooding, eerie in its stillness. An errant truck driver had strayed from his lane and crushed the car carrying his parents, killing them on the spot. He had been watching a cricket match on TV and had not known about the tragedy for a few hours. No one had told him even after the bodies had arrived in the house. Later, when confronted with death for the first time in his life, he had hidden his face in grandma's sari, not knowing how else to react. He went for cricket practice the next morning and accompanied the bodies for cremation after he returned. Life moved on. Unlike other children orphaned at thirteen, he did not experience the 'sudden coming of age' or 'sense of responsibility' associated with such tragedies. Uncle anyway took care of everyone in the family. Upadhyay Palace was full of servants, cooks and chauffeurs. There was plenty of help available. Neil attended the same school as his cousins, and uncle and aunt treated him as their own son. His parents' death did not create significant turmoil in the family. No one missed them as they had added no value to the family and contributed nothing.

Neil experienced a sudden heaviness in his heart, and for the first time in his life, he felt orphaned. Just like his parents, he, too, had become inconsequential for the family. His plans were dead, and so were his dreams of redemption.

Backchannel Negotiations

Next Day, Afternoon

'Please join us for the class of 1990 reunion in New York City.'

Akash opened the envelope and found inside The Wharton School's class of 1990 graduation photograph. A crowd of 800 wannabe CEOs, with Jennifer flashing her Colgate smile from the second row. That picture resembled an open can of soda that had lost its fizz over seventeen years. Jennifer had encouraged his interest but had backed out just when the relationship had started moving from friendship to intimacy. She had laughed when he had proposed to her. Her laughter had wounded him more than her rejection could ever have. It travelled with him when he moved back to India. He heard it at every step he took towards greatness. It played in his head whenever he received news of her steady march towards degeneration. Life extracted from her the retribution for foolishness: divorced, laid off, depression, drug abuse, no money, no career, no family, no prospects.

Did she laugh when her husband cheated on her with her own sister?

Akash trashed the photo. 'Send a cheque,' he wrote on the envelope and dropped it on the out tray.

The intercom buzzed. 'Sir, your grandma is on Line 2.'

Akash braced himself for the familiar pitch. 'Tell me something new,' he snapped at Sudha's voice.

'Why don't you remove Gagan? You control the board,' Sudha said.

Akash laughed. 'The elders should take such big decisions, not me.'

'I am not impressed by your sarcasm.'

'Won't do your dirty work for you.'

'Ramesh refused.'

They are fighting. Fuck! A crack in the iron frame—the beginning of the end.

'Dad has to pull the trigger,' said Akash. 'No outside investment till then. If the company dies, so be it.'

'Then we will take money from Jayshankar,' said Sudha in a low, halting voice. 'Don't force us to take favours from that horrible man.'

Akash laughed. The rift between Ramesh and Sudha had forced

them to seek help from a person they both detested but never admitted they did.

There is no worse punishment for them than the ignominy of begging Jayshankar for a bailout. Let me rub it in.

'But you forced Nandini to marry this horrible man,' he said.

'Nobody forced her.'

'You stopped giving her money.'

'Why didn't you help her?' asked Sudha.

Grandma's brazen defence of the indefensible infuriated Akash. He felt the sudden urge to crush the phone on his desk.

'I didn't know.'

'Okay, let's come back from conjecture to reality,' said Sudha. 'As per the Memorandum of Association of Omkar Industries, the board can't stop a shareholder with over 10 per cent shares from changing the financial structure of the company if he has overall 35 per cent support for his plan. Jayshankar owns 11 per cent, and with our support, he will have 35 per cent. You can't stop this.'

Such minor complications never flustered Akash, but he knew neutralizing Jayshankar was essential to contain the damage.

'Send Vikram,' he instructed an aide over the other phone.

'I won't stop Jayshankar,' he told Sudha. 'Let him invest and suffer a huge loss—a fitting punishment for ill-treating my sister.'

'Fine! We will also appoint Neil in a senior role,' said Sudha.

What? Neil working in the company? Is she crazy?

Akash cursed under his breath.

Bastard comes back from the dead. I thought he was gone for good.

'Grandma! One imbecile can't replace another,' said Akash. 'What has Neil or his father done for the family?'

'I decide such things, not you,' snapped Sudha. 'Just remember, if he does not get his due, I will give him my shares. Then he will become a board member.'

Sudha's power play stunned Akash. Even with one leg in the grave and the other bent in submission before a nefarious son-in-law, she was still trying to rule the planet. After Gagan, she now wanted to prop up Neil.

'Please threaten someone else,' said Akash in a calm voice. 'Your shares can't make a donkey the king. I will make the company go bankrupt, and he will get nothing.'

'I can always sell my shares and give the money to Neil,' said Sudha.

'Sure, you can. I will buy your shares at a fair market price. As per the Memorandum of Association of the company, the same one you were referring to, you must offer your shares to the major shareholders before selling them to the public,' said Akash.

And then I will slap Neil and force him to cough up the money.

Akash clenched his fists.

This time I will finish him.

'What else can we expect from a master manipulator!' Sudha said aggressively.

'Excuse me!'

'You are scaring away customers.'

Akash laughed. 'Yeah right!'

'You told the Singhals to build their ship hull in Singapore?'

'Yes! Because we can't build their design,' said Akash.

'Don't be arrogant. Your success is not just yours. Sure, your father-in-law helped you, but we gave you the base.'

'Grandma! The base, although significant, cannot hog credit for the huge structure built on it. The base should recognize reality. Goodbye!'

Akash cursed and disconnected the call.

First Nandini, and now grandma. Why do they love Neil? Nandini cared for him more than she cared for herself. Why? Leaving him alone to live out his pathetic life was a mistake. Seems his failures weren't punishment enough for him. Now I will humiliate him in such a way that he will either commit suicide or disappear forever.

Vikram Singh (head of security) informed Akash that Gagan and Cap Jay were planning to buy a cricket team in the ICCL, apart from the investment in the Omkar Group. The same investors in Dubai were investing in both companies.

After he left, Akash walked over to his cabin's window. In the distance, the jagged Aravalli Hills disturbed the perfect uniformity of the metal and glass skyline of Gurgaon.

The world is more imperfect than it should be.

His stomach churned. Was Jayshankar serious, or was he just playing them as usual? With no self-interest, he won't even give candy to a child. Is there a bigger game going on?

Behind Jayshankar's wasted exterior was an adept and shrewd businessman. He was smart enough to avoid a direct confrontation with Akash. He was a guerrilla fighter who relied on posturing and distraction to gain strategic advantage. Jayshankar resented Akash's superiority and aspired for space in his life and business.

Are these mind games to attract attention and balance out our unequal relationship?

Low-Hanging Balls

After One Week, Late Afternoon

Corona beer, fried chicken, grilled fish, prawn tacos, salads and seasoned olives. The Delhi Golf Club indulged Cap Jay's nutrition and hydration needs.

Three waiters hovered around Cap Jay as he examined the cuff of his shirt, struggling to extract a piece of loose thread. The manager came over to supervise, and everyone waited with quiet anticipation as if Cap Jay would pop a baby.

'Are we celebrating something?' Akash asked as he reached the centre of activity. The manager greeted Akash and clicked his fingers to scatter away the fanboy waiters.

Cap Jay gave a side glance and took a large, luxurious sip of beer. He whistled as he examined the cuff, apparently in no hurry to engage with the fifth richest man in India.

Akash wiped the sweat off his face with a napkin.

I must show this debauched motherfucker his place. Can't sit next to him.

He signalled to the waiter to get him a chair. 'Suddenly you are interested in the Omkar Group?'

'Finally we have Mr Upadhyay's attention,' said Cap Jay. He shook his legs to create an irritating flapping sound. Tapping his cheek with his finger, he looked coyly towards the ceiling. 'Let's see—why am I interested? No special reason; just my wish.'

'Why now, suddenly?'

'Don't have to explain.'

'The cricket team?'

Cap Jay ate the chicken. 'I love sports,' he said in a garbled voice.

'Come on; what's the real reason?'

'Is this an interrogation?' snapped Cap Jay and gulped down the beer. 'I have investors in Dubai who want to enter the cricket business.'

Akash smiled. 'I can stop you.'

'You are the new don in town?'

'Stop messing around with Gagan.'

'Yeah! Keep dreaming.'

'Gagan will blow your money…you don't have a lot anyway.'

'I like Gagan,' said Cap Jay with a twinkle in his eye. 'Why are you so jealous of him? He is kind of cool.'

Akash rubbed the throbbing nerve in his temples. 'If you were not my sister's husband,' he said in a low rasping voice, 'I would have killed you long ago.'

'Don't you control your membership?' Cap Jay rebuked the manager. 'I lose my appetite in unpleasant company.'

Cap Jay's guerrilla tactics were tiring Akash. He moved to the couch to be in Cap Jay's face. 'I can outbid you for the cricket team.'

'So you are here for the team?'

'Two per cent of my cricket team, in exchange for not investing in the Omkar Group. Final offer,' said Akash.

'How generous,' mocked Cap Jay. 'Thanks for throwing crumbs at street dogs.'

'You can't afford over 2 per cent.'

'Can you? Why don't I buy the team and give you 2 per cent?' said Cap Jay.

Akash sighed. 'Okay, how much do you want?'

'Who said I want to negotiate?'

'Cut the crap…how much?'

'If you lose this tone, you can be a nice guy,' said Cap Jay. 'Learn how to ask for a favour. Fold your hands, say "please"…and ask for help. Perhaps then…'

'Maybe my bodyguard should talk to you?' said Akash.

'Relaaaax…' said Cap Jay. 'Why are you so uptight? Not getting enough sex?' He laughed and leaned forward to touch Akash's tummy. 'I can help you…but you need to lose this. Does your dick even reach the…' He created a ring with his fingers and blew through it, sniffing like a dog.

A heat wave passed through Akash's body.

That's it. A few hours of treatment by my security team will make him lose his insolence.

He asked a waiter to call the bodyguard.

Cap Jay winked at the waiter. 'Get uncle a beer.'

Akash leaned towards Cap Jay and grabbed his testicles. 'What did you call me, you motherfucker?' he rasped.

Cap Jay gave a sharp cry. 'Sorry! I was just joking...with your IIT nickname.'

The manager rushed over. 'Anything wrong, sir? Can I...'

The waiters watched from a distance as Akash's bodyguard pushed the manager away.

'Do you know what happened to them?' whispered Akash in Cap Jay's ears. 'People who called me uncle...'

He let his warm breath fall on Cap Jay's face and kept pressing his testicles. Cap Jay gasped and howled like an animal.

'They are stuck in mid-level boring jobs, struggling to save a few rupees every day to afford a Maruti 800 or a once-in-three-years holiday to Shimla. And where am I?'

Cap Jay gurgled, his eyes popping out like ripe cherries.

Akash scowled. 'And what happened to the hep girls who liked the sexy, cool, athletic men...of IIT?'

Life returned to Cap Jay's face as Akash relaxed the pressure on his testicles.

'They are bloated after popping babies from arranged marriages with middle-aged men. Now they spend their time taking their kids to schools in autos...kids who fret about becoming "cool",' said Akash, pressing the testicles again.

Cap Jay howled, begging for mercy.

'You dare cross me again, I will cut off your balls...and also your loose tongue,' whispered Akash, pressing again, this time harder. Cap Jay screamed and kicked the table across the room, splattering the exquisite marble floor with Corona and chicken.

Akash released Cap Jay and pointed towards the door. 'Now get out before I kill you.'

The fanboy waiters stayed away as Cap Jay hobbled towards the door, muttering under his breath.

Akash smirked, remembering the spite he faced from his classmates at IIT Delhi. They had rejected him because he was overweight. They tried to dent his confidence, and now they pretended to be close friends, sending him long emails, begging for help.

Do they remember their cruelty towards their 'uncle' when they get no response from him?

Almost a Father

After Five Days, Early Evening

Ramesh Upadhyay hopped and jumped to save his handcrafted leather sandals from the wet soil but stepped right into a puddle. 'Fine leather...ruined,' he lamented. 'Life wets you when you are least prepared. No one can carry an umbrella throughout life.'

Neil escorted Ramesh to a chair and braced himself for the inevitable. Uncle's unexpected visit could only mean a final call to join the family business.

Grandma won. It's all over.

'Finish your work,' Ramesh pointed towards the batting nets. 'I'll enjoy the outdoors.'

Neil panicked at Ramesh's uncharacteristically laidback behaviour. For a man who always placed a high premium on his time, he seemed in no hurry to conduct the business that had caused his first visit to Neil's cricket academy.

Battling traffic for two hours to enjoy the outdoors? The farmhouse is bigger than this ground. Why then?

'I am impressed by how you are shaping young players,' Ramesh drank from a water bottle and belched.

Neil pulled up a chair and waited for the real story.

How come uncle is suddenly interested in cricket coaching?

'Do you agree that I have always helped you?'

Neil smiled. 'Yes, uncle, I am very grateful.'

Ramesh touched Neil on his knee. 'Neil! Helping family members is not a favour, it's a duty.'

Neil felt a dull throbbing in his heart.

First he asked me to accept he has helped me, and then stopped me from acknowledging it. What's the point here?

'Thanks for understanding our limitations,' said Ramesh.

Neil reached out for a bottle of water and used the diversion to withdraw his knee from Ramesh's grip.

'But then I tried to imagine how your father would handle this situation,' said Ramesh. He looked up towards the sky and wiped his eyes. 'Would he let your aspirations die?'

'Yes he would, unless it was related to music,' said Neil. He smiled, impatient with the melodramatic behaviour.

Ramesh clapped his chest. 'But I, as his representative, will support your plans.'

Neil shook his head.

What does he want?

'By buying a cricket team,' said Ramesh in a low voice, as if revealing a secret.

'Oh! Wow,' blurted Neil. 'Thanks, uncle.'

Ramesh patted Neil on his back. 'Jayshankar will be co-owner, and you will be the head coach. But, a small problem…'

Neil came out of his trance on hearing the word 'problem'. It was too good to be true, of course. Nothing in his life came easy, so why would this be an exception.

'Your grandmother wants you to join the family business,' said Ramesh, twisting his face. 'You are dear to her, but…'

Neil pinched his lips.

Of course grandma would play the spoilsport. Fuck! She has nothing else to do!

'So, what will you do?'

'Do I have an option?' snapped Neil.

What nonsense. Grandma's opposition is nothing new. Why start a dramatic conversation, raise hope, only to make it fall flat?

Ramesh held his hand. 'Yes! Satisfy her for now. Tell her you are winding up this coaching business, and you will be ready to join the company in six months.'

'Okay.'

'Once you become the head coach, she won't stop you from continuing with cricket.'

Neil choked as he hugged Ramesh. 'Thanks, uncle. You are my dad!'

'Oh! Come on,' Ramesh stroked Neil's hair. 'Big boys don't cry. You were an excellent cricketer, but today I realize you will do wonders for our team as a coach,' Ramesh said as Neil walked him to his car.

'I won't disappoint you,' sniffled Neil.

'Good! Gagan will keep you posted. Don't discuss our plans with anyone, and be very careful with grandma. We should never contradict each other.'

'Yes, uncle, don't worry.'

Neil wasted no time in planning the next steps. Uncle's benevolence had given him a second chance to succeed in cricket. Gratitude wouldn't repay the family's debt, but performance could. Failure wasn't an option any more.

I have to move fast before others get into the act. Can't wait till the team auctions to sign up key people. The first step would be a list of support staff.

Utsav Narang as batting coach? Absolute lack of ego and the ability to follow instructions without questioning them were his greatest strengths. Nitin Talwar as the assistant coach? Both Utsav and Nitin were successful coaches at the under-16 level. Neil had played with both in the domestic circuit and knew their cricketing skills. Sudhir Yadav as icon player and captain? His aggressive batting technique was ideal for the T20 format.

Sudhir will remember how I helped him when he debuted for India. He is a big star now, but it will work out if I respect his position as a captain. I must consult him before signing up other players and support staff.

I will shut down this academy tomorrow. Nandini won't like it, but I am done. It is not fair that I am ditching these kids without warning, but there is no better way to convince grandma I have moved away from cricket.

Buried Under Stardust

After Four Weeks, Evening

Sudhir Yadav raised his arms in the Titanic pose and caused a mini riot in the hotel. Press photographers jostling for candid pictures, fans penetrating the security cordon, shrieking young girls throwing kisses, autograph-seekers battling for vantage positions, hotel staff lining up with flowers; pandemonium spread as the surging crowd carried the 'icon' inside the hotel.

Neil watched this melee from the coffee shop. 'There is a book launch, sir, of Sheetal Nandkarni...the Bollywood star,' the waiter informed him.

'Even filmstars are now writing books,' snorted Neil.

'Yes, sir...she is famous.'

'They are dating...it came out in the newspapers.'

The waiter grinned. 'She is not the only one. He is a big star, sir...the women change every week.'

'Hmm! Soon he will play cricket. Represent India.'

Sudhir stopped near a big Christmas tree, decked with mini lights, cheap bling and fake gifts. The crowd cheered as Sheetal made her way to the Christmas tree through a human chain, and Sudhir kneeled to receive her, looking cool because of his unshaven face and sunglasses perched on top of his wild hair. The high-definition muscles of his upper body threatened to rip apart his tight-fitting V-neck tee. He twirled her in an intimate dance, making her baby pink gown swirl. The DJ yelled 'Happy New Year', and the revelry moved up a gear, with people gyrating to popular Bollywood numbers.

Neil remembered Sudhir as the humble and hardworking boy who had risen from the slums to play for India—very different from the arrogant asshole he later became.

It's a shame. Couldn't he spare thirty minutes for me?

'Happy New Year...sir,' said the waiter.

'Will he hang around?' asked Neil.

'There is an after-party, sir, upstairs, in Crystal Ballroom. It's a closed event...are you invited?'

'I will be...'

On the dais, Sudhir Yadav opened a package and held up copies of Sheetal Nandkarni's new book, *An Old Man's Fantasies*, to boisterous applause from the audience. Sheetal kissed Sudhir and walked to the lectern. 'This book is about my experience of working with elderly men. Right from a young age, men have told me their fantasies...and have tried to fulfil them through me. It's difficult to be a woman in this industry full of predators,' she said.

The crowd cheered without realizing Sheetal was discussing abuse and exploitation.

'Thanks, Sudhir, for supporting me,' Sheetal said as Sudhir joined her at the lectern.

'As you know, I don't read...' said Sudhir. 'I have not even finished high school...'

The crowd cheered, and the DJ again became hyperactive.

'But this book is one that I will read...to support Sheetal. And if you support her as well by buying the book, you can be one of the five lucky winners invited to a private dinner with us...'

Egged on by the DJ, the fans continued partying even after Sheetal and Sudhir had slipped away.

After Forty Minutes

Neil gatecrashed the after-party and accosted Sudhir's manager. 'You don't have basic decency? For the last one month I am chasing...'

'Who invited you?' the manager asked, signalling to the security guards.

'You did,' scowled Neil. 'Unless you want to create a ruckus.'

The manager shrugged and moved away.

Sudhir Yadav sprawled on a couch surrounded by boisterous hangers-on laughing at his every joke. A steady stream of fans swooned over him, seeking autographs and photographs, offering everything from kisses to sleepless nights and undying love. Sheetal was missing from the room.

A young girl tried to sit on Sudhir's lap. He jumped up, and the girl crashed on the floor with a loud 'ouch'.

'Are you insane?' shouted Sudhir.

'Will you marry me?' she implored. She caught his hand and

hung on for a few moments before crashing again on the ground. 'You can't get rid of me...I will write letters to you in blood,' she screamed and tried to catch his legs, but this time Sudhir was ready. He moved away just in time, and the hotel staff rushed in to remove her from the crime scene.

Sudhir complained but looked happy. 'The problems of being a celebrity—everyone wants a piece of you.'

Neil waited in the periphery for an opportunity to interact alone with Sudhir. When Sudhir went to use the washroom, he occupied the urinal next to him.

'Hello, Sudhir...long time.'

Sudhir's puffy eyes revealed he had consumed a sizable quantity of alcohol. He ignored Neil and focused on finishing his business. He moved to the washbasin and Neil followed him.

'You interested in the ICCL?' asked Neil to test the waters.

'Why do you care?' scowled Sudhir.

Neil clenched his fists. 'Because we are buying the Delhi team. And, I might consider you...'

Sudhir laughed and clapped his hands. 'Man! Are you hallucinating? You will consider me?'

He whistled as he dried his hands. 'Akash is my good friend; who are you?'

'Akash is not involved,' snapped Neil. 'The Omkar Group, my family's company, will own this team.'

'And you are the future spokesman of this future team?' said Sudhir with a coy smile.

Neil ignored Sudhir's sarcasm. 'The head coach; and yes, I will run this team.'

Sudhir laughed again. 'Man! What are you smoking?'

Someone entered the washroom and headed straight towards Sudhir.

'Get out!' Sudhir yelled, forcing him to leave.

Neil swallowed, struggling to calm down. 'Why can't I?'

'What credentials do you have?' asked Sudhir. He leaned towards the mirror and adjusted his hair. 'Accomplished players become coaches. That's how leagues are run; look at football. The Omkar Group is bankrupt, and you are not even a sidekick there. Akash has told me all about it. You are nothing but a smelly fart they try to keep out of their house.' Sudhir laughed again. 'Head coach? Yeah, right! I am surprised by your showmanship. You should consider a career in Bollywood.'

Neil's blood boiled as Sudhir walked towards the door.

Fuck! He is getting away...

'I will fax you my appointment letter,' Neil said.

'Yes! Akash and I will have a good laugh over it.'

Brother from Another Mother

Same Day, Late Night

She squealed 'ouch' as Gagan pulled and released her spaghetti straps.
'It hurts...'
'Then take it off.'
Gagan spanked her butt. 'Get my brother a drink, baby...'
'Tonight...I will fuck her brains out,' he said in a slurry voice. 'Guess how old she is...'
Neil raised his eyebrows, hoping Gagan would note his disinterest in her physical details.
Gagan winked. 'Just turned nineteen, but not a virgin.'
He pulled Neil towards him. 'Want to enjoy eternal youth? Fuck young girls...they add years to your life.'
Neil excused himself to take a phone call from his aunt.
'Did you find Gagan?' she asked.
'Yes, I did, aunty, he called back, and I am with him now at The Ashok Hotel,' Neil replied, wondering why she was so eager to follow up on his plan to meet Gagan. Usually, she ignored his inquiries about Gagan's whereabouts.
Maybe uncle is tracking Gagan. Can't blame him. Gagan and Cap Jay aren't exactly famous for their discipline. And yet, somehow, all our plans depend on them.
He banged his head with his hand.
Fuck! Uncle had asked me to keep my mouth shut. I messed up by jumping the gun. Sudhir will tell Akash and screw us.
We have to buy the team ASAP, before Akash executes his strategy. He cannot do shit once I am officially appointed. Even Sudhir Yadav will apologize.
Uncle monitoring Gagan is good news. I can't tackle Akash without Gagan's help. But we need to move fast. Anybody working on buying the team? Or is it just alcohol, young women and a good life?
The F Bar at The Ashok Hotel buzzed with excitement that night. Florence Ballantino's techno ensemble (for one night only) promised an unforgettable experience for Delhi's rich and famous

and their protégées. The presence of many middle-aged men among fewer young women depicted the real story of Delhi's popular culture. Sleeping with a forty-five-year-old womanizer was probably a small price to pay for a nineteen-year-old eager for a place at the most happening event in the city.

Gagan walked over with two girls hanging on his arms.

'Where's your drink, bro? The bitch didn't get you one?'

'Can we talk?' asked Neil.

'Did dad send you?' smirked Gagan.

Neil shook his head. 'No.'

'Follow me.'

Neil accompanied Gagan to the smoking room.

'We should discuss a few things about the team…,' said Neil.

Gagan lit up and exhaled loudly. 'Which team?'

'Our ICCL team.'

'Where?'

Another girl smoking nearby put on a coy smile and tried to whisper something in Gagan's ears.

'Bitch! I am busy…' snapped Gagan. 'Don't climb on me.'

She registered a feeble protest but fled when Gagan raised his right arm, threatening to knock her out.

'Fucking whore,' shouted Gagan and turned towards Neil. 'What the fuck were you telling me? Which team?'

A drunk and agitated Gagan wasn't the best discussant, and Neil searched for an excuse to bail out. 'Never mind, you enjoy the concert,' he said, moving towards the door. 'We will talk tomorrow. Goodnight!'

Gagan stopped him. 'No…no, talk,' he rasped. 'You called me like two hundred times this evening. Who has died?'

'I met Sudhir Yadav,' said Neil, hoping Sudhir's name would explain the urgency of his calls.

'Who?'

'Sudhir Yadav? The Indian cricketer? The person you see in the Tata Motors ad…'

'What about him?'

Neil gulped, avoiding eye contact. 'I met him to ask him to join our team,' he said in a halting voice.

'Which fucking team?' shouted Gagan. The chatter in the smoking room instantly died, creating an unnerving silence. It seemed everyone had fled, leaving Neil alone with a murderous Gagan. 'Answer me, you idiot!'

'The cricket team we are buying,' snapped Neil.

Faint signs of comprehension on Gagan's face emboldened Neil to vent his frustration. 'I am working day and night trying to set up stuff, and you are having a merry time.'

'Okay, okay, I got it,' said Gagan, looking disturbed. 'So, what happened?'

'Sudhir refused to believe we will buy the team or that I will be the head coach,' said Neil angrily.

'So?'

'Are we doing everything to win?' asked Neil.

Gagan took a large drag and blew smoke on Neil's face. 'We are, no worries...'

'Please release a press statement about my appointment...'

Gagan laughed and made a weird cuckoo-like sound that irritated Neil.

'What's so funny?' Neil wondered if Gagan had dementia.

Asshole! Fooling around with girls his daughter's age.

'You are already talking to people?' said Gagan, consumed by a wild fit of laughter.

'I have to deliver results...'

'Reeeeelllllaaaaxxxx,' said Gagan. 'You have to do nothing; just have fun.'

'We can't all dedicate our lives to alcohol and women like you, Gagan.'

'Then go fuck yourself,' shouted Gagan. He stumbled and crashed into the wall. 'Fuck the team, for all I care. Fuck the press statement.'

Neil grabbed Gagan and pinned him to the wall. 'Is this the alcohol speaking? Why did uncle offer this to me if you are not interested?'

Gagan pointed at a girl on the other side of the glass wall.

'That one is so hot...you can make an omelette on her thighs,' said Gagan, licking his lips. 'I can set you up with her. Get laid—long and hard.' He dismissed Neil. 'Forget about the team and go get a life.'

'Should I call uncle?'

'Yeah...go ahead.'

Gagan stumbled out of the smoking room just as Florence

Ballantino kicked off his show amidst a flurry of flashing lights, loud cheers and bare skin.

Neil chastised himself for trying to deal with Gagan when uncle could have handled that dirty job better. Gagan was a bum, but suggesting sex in the middle of a serious discussion about the team was a new low, even for him.

This team will die a premature death if it needs Gagan's support for survival. Uncle is cursed, having to depend on this imbecile to run his business. I need to bypass Gagan and work with him, otherwise soon this dream will be all over.

Vision Statement

Four Days Later, Afternoon

'The prodigal son has returned home.'

Divya spat on the plush carpet with a loud 'thooo'.

Akash recoiled as Divya's spit landed near his shoes.

Fucking bitch! Ruined the office carpet. Why do I tolerate her?

'Let me explain,' he implored, watching the carpet to avoid stepping on the spit. He tried to hold her, but she pushed him away.

'No more stories!' screamed Divya, shaking hysterically. Her left hand hit a crystal vase, sending it flying across the floor.

She stomped on the vase, crushing it into the carpet.

'I never asked you for anything,' she vented her anger. 'Only wanted you to succeed and screw the people who plotted against you. But you sucked their dicks.'

'Who is feeding you this nonsense?' asked Akash.

Divya turned to face Akash. 'Normally, your father, the great statesman, never calls me. He has been angry ever since we moved out of the farmhouse. But today he called me first thing in the morning, to convey the good news.'

'And?'

'Gagan is buying out Akash's stake in the Omkar Group,' she said, twisting her face to mimic Ramesh. 'Jayshankar is funding the company.'

Akash smiled. 'My father is fantasizing. In three to six months, I will own the Omkar Group.'

'Yeah right. Am I an idiot?' screamed Divya.

Her heavy breathing and flushed face alarmed Akash.

God! She might get a stroke.

'I will make your cousin the CEO,' said Akash. He leaned back on the couch and spread his arms across the backrest. 'Ask him to get ready.'

'Now listen, don't act smart,' snapped Divya.

Pooja entered the room with a stunning smile and a breath of fresh air. But, she committed the cardinal mistake of meddling in Divya's affairs.

'Is there a problem?' she asked, sifting through a stack of papers on Akash's desk.

'Come here,' commanded Divya.

Pooja continued her search as Akash rushed over from the couch. 'We are busy, so…go,' he nudged Pooja towards the door.

'Ah! Here,' Pooja's face lit up as she produced a letter marked "very urgent" with red ink. 'Sir, you saw this?'

'Leave now,' snapped Akash.

Pooja gave a puzzled look and moved just enough to avoid Divya's stiletto flying past her head. The pointy heel shattered a glass-cased memento affixed to the wall. She gave a panicked glance towards Divya and bolted.

'Don't you have manners?' fumed Akash, marching towards Divya. 'This is my office—a professional place.'

Divya leaned on the French window, showing no sign of intimidation or regret. 'You fucking her?' she asked.

'No! Are you mad?'

'Then how come this impertinence?'

Akash banged his head with his hand. 'Oh my God…she was just asking.'

Divya scowled. 'It's okay if you are fucking her…she is quite a shag. But at least admit it like a man.'

Akash hunched over on the couch, struggling to collect himself. 'Come here…I need to tell you something,' he said in a low voice.

Divya smirked. 'What? That you love her?'

'Leave her alone, dammit!' screamed Akash. 'She is just an employee…'

He raised his arms in the air, as though appealing to a higher power. 'I love you,' he panted. 'And, that's why I am buying a cricket team for you.'

His words halted Divya's righteous indignation. Her eyes twitched as she processed the stunning new piece of information.

'Why suddenly this largesse…?' she blurted out.

'Because I love you.'

Akash hugged her, eager to exploit the shift in mood. 'You will be the face of the team. Everyone will report to you...top international cricketers, coaches.'

Her eyes drifted to a distant space...as if imagining a stadium standing up to applaud her...TV interviews, awards, parties, hot cricketers...the possibilities were endless.

'Why did you hide this from me?' asked Divya, looking normal again.

'To surprise you...'

'Hmm, but you are still giving them your shares?'

'Come here...'

Divya joined Akash on the couch. Her persona seemed to have lost its aggressive edge, and she was eager to hear the details without flipping to the dark side again.

Akash tilted his head upwards and looked out of the window. 'My dad played a big game after Neil, the loser par excellence, and asked him to buy a cricket team.'

'Those beggars will buy a cricket team?' scowled Divya.

'Yes, Neil thought so,' grinned Akash. 'And Jayshankar thought he can earn quick money.'

Divya looked alarmed. 'Through match-fixing?'

'Not necessarily match-fixing,' said Akash, impressed by Divya's quick mind. 'Stuff like money laundering, hawala, etc. Jayshankar needed a front company and roped in Gagan. Then my father made an elaborate plan to make Neil the head coach and use it as a bait to prevent him from joining forces with grandma. In return, Jayshankar promised to fund the Omkar Group.'

Divya laughed and clapped.

'So I convinced them to let me buy the team where Jayshankar can be a co-owner,' sneered Akash. 'In return, I promised to sell my stake to Gagan at a later date...which will never happen.'

Divya gasped and moved her jaw, struggling to speak.

'I had no choice, believe me,' said Akash. 'Jayshankar would join them if not for my offer.'

'Why don't you take over the company and throw them out?'

Akash shook his head. 'They control more than 35 per cent shares. They will gang up to deny me the controlling stake.' He snorted and closed his eyes. 'No point without a controlling stake. Plus, the share price is still too high.'

'So, we will tolerate Jayshankar just to save money?'

'Don't take money so casually,' rebuked Akash.

Divya hyperventilated, and Akash softened his voice. 'Sorry, I was too harsh on you. How would you know!'

'What exactly do you mean?' snapped Divya and stood in front of Akash. She adopted a menacing posture, resting her hands on her hips. 'That I am brainless?'

'Don't put words into my mouth,' said Akash. 'I love you…and it's just a matter of a few months.' He grinned. 'It will be a lot of fun, trust me, slowly shattering their plans.'

Divya paced the room and Akash hoped he had enamoured her by the gory picture of revenge he had painted.

'Okay! But he should not get into my face…' she said, releasing Akash from the tension.

'He won't,' babbled Akash. 'Jayshankar will disappear after the first season…maybe even before that. So don't worry.'

'And Neil?'

'For now, we will tolerate him.'

'I hate the loser.'

'Me too—but he can become a pain in the ass with grandma's support. He is like a child—easily satisfied. So we throw candies and watch him crawl.'

'Hmm.'

'Get ready for fun,' gloated Akash. 'They are making elaborate plans, expecting the money to come in a few months.' He paused for effect. 'I will send people to them with business proposals… and encourage them to spend before they get the money. When the proposals don't work out, they will go bankrupt. Then I will buy their shares for peanuts. They will have to sell.'

'And Jayshankar?'

'He won't dare to oppose us. If he does, then…God help him.'

Missed by a Mile

Two Weeks Later, Early Morning

The hazy fog confined Delhi to small personal spaces of cozy existence warmed with room heaters and thick quilts. With anxiety and excitement juxtaposed in a new dawn, Neil awoke early to prepare for the big day—the scheduled announcement of the ICCL team auction results.

He called Gagan, but, instead of enthusiasm, he got a cold recorded message: *We are sorry. The number you are trying to reach is unavailable right now. Please call again later.*

He cursed the phone company and sent a text: *They will declare the auction results on TV? Which channel?*

After a few minutes, he texted again.

```
Wake up, bro. We have to make plans.
```

Neil showered, thinking of his talking points for the media interaction.

Online contest for deciding team name
Play aggressive cricket intending to win every game
Give back to the game as a coach by nurturing young talent
Grateful to the family for supporting cricket

He reviewed his to-do list. There was a lot of pending work. Complete the list of support staff by tomorrow, first staff meeting in one week, decide player auction strategy, connect with Nandini's friends for team jersey and logo, discuss team budget with uncle or Gagan or Cap Jay.

Over breakfast, Neil checked his phone every few seconds. No new messages arrived; Gagan was probably still sleeping.

Bloody fool. What will I tell the media?

He called Gagan again—no response; called uncle—no reply; called the farmhouse landline number—call answered by a servant who had no clue about anything.

What's happening? No one is interested.

He borrowed his neighbour's newspaper, and found that he had missed the ICCL media briefing the previous night. The headline on the first page hit his eyes like a bullet fired at close range.

'AlphaX Technologies win ICCL bid. Team named 'New Delhi Royals'. South African cricket legend Pattrick O'Donnell appointed head coach. Sudhir Yadav named icon player.'

Neil collapsed on the floor like a sack. His felt dizzy as he read the whole story.

> In the ICCL team auction held yesterday evening, AlphaX Technologies won the bid for the New Delhi-based franchise. The company stated in a press release that Mr Akash Upadhyay's emotional connection with the city where he has lived and worked his entire life drove this bid. Mrs Divya Upadhyay decided the team's name, 'New Delhi Royals', to honour the 5000-year-old royal legacy of Delhi.
>
> According to anonymous sources familiar with the Upadhyay family, Mr Neil Upadhyay, a former Indian cricket player and Mr Akash Upadhyay's first cousin, had lobbied for the position of head coach. Neil was so confident of his appointment that he offered contracts to potential players and support staff before the team auction. But Mr O'Donnell was appointed the head coach because a former cricketer of his stature would bring in world-class expertise and international following to the team.
>
> Irrespective of the reasons behind the appointment, Neil Upadhyay's premature solicitation of players and support staff raises questions about the fairness of the team auctions. Were the team auctions rigged? Or was Neil Upadhyay just operating out of turn? Prematurely strategizing for a team that existed only in his imagination?
>
> AlphaX Technologies' spokesperson later clarified Mr Neil Upadhyay was never in contention for the position of head coach and he had no authority to solicit people on behalf of the company...

But, I, as his representative, will support your plans...

Uncle's pompous words reverberated in Neil's consciousness as he sat on the floor with the newspaper on his lap. With misty eyes, he cursed the grand posturing and false hopes that had transformed him into a dreamer with visions of an illustrious future.

But why the lies? I had reconciled with my failures.

Ambition without resources is a curse. Desires need talent, and a resourceful father...a real father.

Eventually, he found the headspace for rational thinking. Uncle was evading his calls. That man had never risen later than 5 a.m. in his entire life. Did he no longer have the guts to face him? But why had uncle fooled him? Was Nandini right? Was there a conspiracy? Or, was uncle in trouble? Blackmailed by Cap Jay or Gagan?

I need to meet him ASAP in the farmhouse.

Neil dressed and rushed to his car. His phone rang just as he fired the engine.

Ramesh Upadhyay gave brief instructions over the phone. 'Stay calm and don't talk to anyone. Meet me in an hour at the Gymkhana Club. Will discuss everything there.'

Gratefully Numb

The usually boisterous coffee shop at the Delhi Gymkhana Club wore a forlorn look that morning, the brutal cold forcing the loyal chatterati to prefer the isolation of heated homes over the alluring company of political gossipmongers, fixers and retired public servants. The cooks prepared meals for empty sofas and unopened newspapers, soaking the air with aromas of brewed coffee, freshly baked bread and fried eggs. Neil stepped out to avoid empty greetings and irrelevant offers for breakfast from the overenthusiastic waiters. Outside, the fog engulfed unwilling spectators in a seamless mass of white ecstasy, numbing senses and freezing thoughts, temporarily suspending the need to tackle catastrophic incidents.

The brain freeze sheltered Neil from the irreparable circumstances of his hopeless life.

After Twenty Minutes

Ramesh Upadhyay tapped on Neil's shoulders, yelling at the top of his voice. 'Are you deaf? I was calling you from across the lawn.'

His breath condensed in the cold air and hit Neil on his face like a jet stream.

'What's the matter with you?' asked Ramesh.

Neil scoffed at Ramesh's convenient aggression, designed to put him on the back foot. Even amid a catastrophe, Ramesh had dressed up as if it was just another day in the office, appearing prim and proper in black trousers and a brown tweed jacket, complemented by a black muffler wrapped around his neck and tucked inside his collar. His clean-shaven face showed no sign of remorse for his lies.

Beside him Gagan looked barely awake in worn jeans and a faded black hoodie, his bloodshot eyes protruding out of a dirty cap covering his head. He reeked of whiskey, probably consumed at a party the previous night to celebrate his big brother's success in the ICCL auction.

Akash elbowed us out, but Gagan did not notice. How does he live with himself? Forever the loser; forever betraying people.

'Come on, let's go in before we die in this cold,' said Ramesh, moving towards the coffee shop.

Neil collided with Gagan while trying to follow Ramesh, crushing him flat on the ground. He smirked at Gagan's extended hand before moving on without helping towards the coffee shop.

'I convinced Akash to make you the assistant coach,' said Ramesh as the waiter served coffee. 'You will play an important role in the team. So, nothing has changed, and no need to get angry.'

'You said I will be head coach,' said Neil, maintaining stern eye contact. 'Bombastic statements...representing my father...'

'Hey, listen,' Ramesh shook his finger. 'I helped you...more than your father.'

'False hope is unkind,' said Neil in a soft voice.

'No, I didn't give you false hope,' shouted Ramesh, spilling coffee on his shirt. 'Even I have limitations. You can't doubt my intentions.'

Gagan suddenly came out of his comatose state. 'What's the problem, man? Just be with the team, have fun...and...'

Ramesh's penetrative glare forced Gagan to back off from an ill-timed intervention.

'The family business is in trouble,' Ramesh looked downcast. 'We need external investment to survive—and Akash can help. He wanted the team. What could I do?'

Neil assumed a poker face.

Ramesh shuffled in his seat, looking unsettled. 'I forced Akash to make you assistant coach,' he mumbled.

'Why didn't you tell me?'

'Because you would have backed out and lost a good opportunity.'

Neil smiled. 'Good opportunity? Really?'

'Well...you get the chance to work with a great player—learn from him—and prove your credentials for the role. Don't see how it is bad.'

'Do I have the credentials for head coach?'

'No idea.'

'But Akash has an idea?'

'Ask him.'

'I was dealing with you.'

'You can stay and fight or just follow your grandma.'

'Maybe I should. At least she is transparent.'

'Fine! Do as she says. Join the business, become a clerk,' said Ramesh.

Neil rose to leave. 'Sure! Will do.'

Ramesh caught his hand. 'Sit, Neil.'

Neil withdrew his hand and sat down with a sigh.

'Don't take this personally, Neil. Akash believes a famous overseas player will be good for the branding of the team and help it get international fans,' Ramesh said. He paused briefly to clean his glasses. 'Be patient, and one day you will become the head coach.'

Neil grinned. 'You promising that, uncle?'

'I don't deserve your sarcasm; I made your cricket career.'

'Okay, thank you,' said Neil and rose again to leave.

Again Ramesh stopped him. 'Don't make a hasty decision, Neil. Please trust me.'

Neil collected his car keys and walked away with no further courtesies.

Ramesh called after him. 'Think this through, Neil. This opportunity won't come again…this can redeem your career.'

After Neil left, Ramesh sent a text to Akash.

```
Neil did not agree. Will try to stop him from
meeting ma. You make sure Nandini does not brainwash
him.
```

Akash promptly replied,

```
Don't worry, I will force him to agree. Will
distract Nandini. She won't have any time to worry
about Neil.
```

Schadenfreude

Hello, head coach. When will you send the contract?

Neil read from the long list of messages—most of them sarcastic, others mocking and downright nasty, and a few conveying untrustworthy concerns for his debacle. People were enjoying his embarrassment rather than lamenting his inability to help them get a place in the team. Mediocrity was a self-sustaining ecosystem that celebrated the defeat of people who tried hard to escape the boundaries of their possibilities.

No one cares about my fight for relevance. They should fight the same battle, but they don't. Strange world!

'You can't expect help from Akash, nor forgiveness,' Nandini's words reverberated in his ears as he realized Akash had once again nixed his plans. Her words sounded like a priest's sermon to a sinner in a confession box. Akash resembled an omnipotent God condemning him on judgement day for the cardinal sin of failing in his career.

Akash won't back off even if I give him a blowjob. If uncle wouldn't have surrendered, I would have outfoxed him this time. What now? Stay and fight or take the honourable stand and walk out? Go where?

Nandini's sudden preoccupation with urgent matters at home deprived Neil of a sounding board that always produced gems of profound truth. He missed her unique voice born out of her utter disillusionment with the world. When she did not return his calls, he refused to move forward and resisted the unprecedented pressure Ramesh had mounted on him by calling him three times a day for a decision.

Pull of the Umbilical Cord

Five Days Later, Late Evening

Nandini's long overdue phone call shook Neil out of his hibernation.

'Thanks for sparing five minutes in five days,' snickered Neil. 'Generally, you comment on everything in my life. How did you decide this was not important? What's your formula?'

'There is a problem; so...sorry!' replied Nandini. Her worry-laden voice did not counter Neil's abject sarcasm.

Neil dropped civility for a caustic tone suitable for venting his pent-up anger. 'Yes, the endless family conspiracies. I know! But my more immediate concern is...should I take this position?'

'Look at you...and your endless problems with cricket,' shouted Nandini. 'Others have problems too, but do you care?'

Nandini's verbal volley stunned Neil. Before he could recover, she fired again. 'There was a threat to Abhi's life. Last five days... were hell!'

Neil reeled from that sudden blow to his virtuousness. 'What? Threat from where...is it serious?'

'No, it was just a casual, friendly conversation.'

'I am sorry; why didn't you tell me?'

'Why? What would you have done?'

Nandini's blunt assertion about his uselessness slaughtered Neil's fragile self-esteem. He skirted the question, fighting hard for validity in a conversation that had turned his resentment against him.

'What happened?' he whimpered like a puppy.

'Not now; I am too tired.'

'Please! I want...'

Nandini interrupted Neil. 'Five days ago, I got a phone call... threatening to kill Abhi unless my motherfucking husband behaved himself.'

Neil tried to act surprised, as though Cap Jay and misbehaviour were not synonymous with each other. 'Behaved himself where?'

'God knows. They terrorized me, calling almost every hour for five days. Jayshankar did not care. So I asked Akash for help. He got a few armed guards posted outside my house.'

'Who were they?' asked Neil, walking out to the balcony just when the skies opened and sprayed his face with dirty rain. Traumatized by the muck, he lost focus on Nandini's fears that had failed to impress him anyway. Blatant insensitivity followed, disguised as a casual remark meant to assuage her concerns. 'Nothing happened, right?' he said. 'Relax! It seems like it was a prank.'

'Yes, right. A prank. For five days. Involving a five-year-old child,' snapped Nandini. Her cold voice felt like an icicle penetrating his ears. 'For you nothing is worth worrying about other than cricket.'

'Sorry, I...'

Nandini cut him off again. 'What did you want to discuss?'

Reeling from the fallout of the faux pas, Neil struggled to engage Nandini in a focused discussion about his dilemma. Her fury terrified him, but he couldn't wait for her mood to swing the other way.

She might disappear again, and I can't hold off uncle any longer.

'Should I accept?'

Nandini laughed. 'You are considering it? Seriously?'

'Maybe I can redeem myself.'

'It's a trap, to stop you from claiming your share of the family loot.'

'Ramesh uncle promised I will be head coach next year.'

Nandini's firm voice again stopped Neil mid-sentence. 'Really? You are still trusting dad?'

'The question is, can I work in this team?' said Neil, desperate to change the context of the discussion from Nandini's abject hatred for her family.

'Yes! As long as you are ready to carry drinks. But you won't coach anyone.'

'But I can show my capabilities and...'

'Sure, go ahead,' said Nandini. 'I can't penetrate your unidimensional thick head.'

'Hey, listen! You can't...'

'Do what you like, Neil,' said Nandini in a calm voice. 'Talk to grandma; you will be surprised.'

'Grandma? She is now making team decisions as well?'

'Not everything in this world is about cricket, Neil!' screamed Nandini. 'There is a significant family business share up for grabs, in a game much bigger than cricket.'

'Yes, you told me countless times,' said Neil, laughing.
Nandini killed that inconsequential conversation.
'Goodbye Neil; will talk again in a few days.'

Enforced Pride

Same Day, Late Night

```
Neil! Let's meet and get ready before Pat shows up
next month. Let me know when.
```

Sudhir Yadav's unexpected text startled Neil. Why this sudden outreach? For reconciliation, or again a setup to mock him?

Soon, a barrage of messages followed from Sudhir.

```
Also wanted to thank you for convincing your
family to appoint me the icon player. Thanks for
showing faith in my abilities.

Congrats on Pat's appointment as head coach.
You gave excellent advice to your family. Pat is
a great statesman of cricket. The team will benefit
a lot from his coaching.

Just like you, I am very excited about the ICCL.
Looking forward to getting started.
```

Those kind words were unexpected from a man who had insulted him a few weeks ago. Maybe Akash asked him to send those—to create the right environment for the team. Or, was it a facade for something sinister?

Can't trust this guy.

Neil's phone buzzed again—this time because of Sudhir's call. Those friendly texts had cajoled Neil to reciprocate.

'Hey, Neil! Did I wake you up?' said Sudhir in a merry voice.

Neil's heart sank. The excessive bonhomie in Sudhir's demeanour wasn't good news. He was behaving as if a close friend was trying to mend a strained relationship through an overdose of good behaviour.

'Hello!... Hello! Sudhir...can't hear you,' said Neil, planning to disconnect the call after pretending the connection was terrible.

Sudhir laughed. 'Listen! Can we meet sometime next week? I want to discuss a few players and support staff I have identified.'

'Okay!'

'Is your role formal?'

Neil coughed to avoid the question.

'Neil?'

'I will be the assistant coach,' blurted Neil, unable to hold off any more. 'And hopefully, head coach next year,'

'Oh! Congrats,' said Sudhir, sounding happy. 'Everything will go well, I am sure.'

'Yes, hope so,'

'Okay, great! Looking forward to the official announcement of your appointment. Talk soon. Ta ta.'

'Bye.'

'In the meantime, I will inform people about your role,' said Sudhir. 'It will thrill everyone that you are on board.'

After this call, Sudhir sent a text to Akash.

```
Did as you asked. He said he is assistant coach
of the team and will become head coach next
year. Is that the plan?
```

Akash ignored the text. After a few minutes, Sudhir pinged him again.

```
I still don't understand why you want to hire
this asshole.
```

This time Akash replied.

```
Don't understand; just follow instructions and
focus on cricket. I do the future planning. Will
instruct you going forward.
```

```
Don't send me any more messages. I am busy.
```

Later, Akash sent a text to Dhananjay Rawat, the Head of PR at AlphaX Technologies.

```
Release the announcement about Neil's appointment
```

to the press. And tell the background story to the correspondents off the record and make sure they include it in the news articles tomorrow. Handle it carefully and make sure it is OFF THE RECORD and not traced back to us. I don't trust these journalists.

Mr Assistant Coach

Next morning, the report appeared in every important newspaper in India.

New Delhi Royals Appoints Former Indian Cricketer Neil Upadhyay As Assistant Coach to Mentor the Domestic Players

In a press release yesterday, AlphaX Technologies, the owners of the New Delhi Royals ICCL team, announced the appointment of former Indian cricketer Neil Upadhyay as the assistant coach of the team. He will report to the head coach, Mr Pattrick O'Donnell, and will mentor the uncapped domestic Indian players.

Sources close to the Upadhyay family have told this correspondent, off the record, about the hectic lobbying in the family for finding a suitable role for Neil in the team. After his retirement from international cricket, Neil was running a small cricket coaching academy, which shut down a few months ago. Family elders were concerned about his unemployment and forced the team to create this junior role to keep him 'engaged'. Neil's appointment was thus the outcome of nepotism and not meritocracy as he has no experience of coaching cricketers at the first-class level.

The New Delhi Royals are now expected to hire another assistant coach with direct coaching experience at the state/national level...

Part 2

DESPERATION

'When the waterholes were dry, people sought to drink at the mirage.'
—Evelyn Waugh, *Brideshead Revisited:*
The Sacred and Profane Memories of Captain Charles Ryder

Rottweiler Turned Pug

Nine Days Later, in London

'It was a googly—the king of deliveries. You need the eyesight of a Bengal tiger to read it in the air. Even the best batsmen cannot survive its many variations,' Pattrick O'Donnell yapped on his phone about the just-concluded India–Australia series.

Pat's impudence to dress in track pants and tee for their first meeting warned Akash about his headstrong personality. Akash loved dealing with stubborn men—they didn't bend easily—but once they fell in line, they delivered better results than the friendly ones did.

The Amaranto lounge of the Four Seasons Hotel wore a forlorn look that afternoon, providing Akash little distraction from Pat's insolent usage of a mobile phone in his presence.

Business class tickets from South Africa, thousand pounds per night suites and fifty-pound high teas for a blasted lecture on spin bowling. Making a person of my stature wait. Let me tame this horse, and then I will ride his ass all over London.

'You don't wear suits?' asked Akash after Pat finished his lengthy discourse.

'Why? Casual dressing not allowed in this hotel?' said Pat, looking amused. Akash winced as Pat crossed his legs, revealing his fluorescent orange tennis shoes and frayed navy blue socks.

'They should impose a dress code,' fumed Akash. 'This is a business hotel, and we have a business meeting.'

'I am a sportsman. This is my business dress,' snapped Pat and examined his phone again. He lifted his glasses to read messages and took his time replying to them.

'But you are now a business professional.'

'How?' asked Pat, squinting his eyes.

'You are the head coach of a privately owned cricket team—a business enterprise. Thus, you are a businessman.'

'I handle only the cricket, not the business. That makes me a sportsman.'

'Let us then discuss your deliverables as a sportsman,' said Akash, surprised by Pat's bravado. In the last fifteen years, no one had had the courage or the ability to challenge his words at every step like Pat was doing. He gritted his teeth.

I need to cut this bastard to size. Legend of the game, my foot!

'What deliverables?' asked Pat, twisting his mouth. He shrugged and returned to his phone. 'The team must win; I get it. Why make it so complicated?'

'Simple or complicated, I decide, not you.'

Pat shrugged and gave Akash a lazy half-glance.

'Now note your first deliverable—manage Neil.'

'Manage?'

Akash sighed. 'Stop him from operating; prove he is useless.'

'He can be invaluable for the Indian players,' said Pat.

'No, he won't.'

'Then why have him?'

'Not your position to ask questions,' scowled Akash.

Pat smiled. 'You want me to manage the team or Neil?'

'Follow my orders.'

'You hired me for coaching the team.'

Akash struggled to keep calm. 'I paid extra...for this piece of work. Think of it as a side assignment.'

'But...'

'Don't question me at every step,' shouted Akash. 'Follow orders or get the fuck out. I can easily find another coach.'

Pat's phone buzzed, and he took the call.

Akash snatched Pat's phone with a small cry and broke it into two by using the sharp edge of the table. 'Here, play with this,' Akash said, flinging the broken pieces onto Pat's lap. 'Never ignore me again. This time it was your phone; next, it will be your career.'

A flash of anger crossed Pat's face. 'Fucking lunatic,' he blurted out and flung the broken phone on the table. 'You can't treat a world-famous player...'

'Yes, I can, because I am rescuing you from bankruptcy.'

Pat gasped and paled as if he had seen a ghost.

'I know how much you owe the Stevenson brothers,' said Akash, grinning. 'They will kill you if you don't pay. Your horse-breeding business has collapsed. You will lose your house. Family problems—

wife filing for divorce, kids in college. Only I can prevent your world from falling apart.'

'How do you know?' asked Pat in a croaking voice.

'My staff digs up such information before I appoint people to important positions,' said Akash. 'Good coaches come a dime a dozen; every damned retired cricketer is a coach. I chose you because I could use your situation to control you.'

Pat nodded, looking downcast.

'Your job is to follow instructions,' continued Akash, pointing his index finger towards Pat. 'Never forget I am the boss and you are my employee.'

Pat shrugged and uncrossed his legs. 'Sure, boss!'

Akash smiled. 'Good! Now we are on the same page. You have a free hand to recruit the players and support staff. But I decide the targets for you to deliver.'

'Ok, boss.'

'Three things; first, we must win the tournament. I always win, so cricket cannot be an exception. Second, respect my wife. She loves this team, and I want her to get the importance she deserves. Indulge her if she interferes with the cricket but you have the final say. For everything else just do what she says. Manage her tactfully,' continued Akash. 'Don't want to hear complaints.'

Pat nodded. 'Okay, and for Neil?'

'Neil's case is simpler. Be cordial but firm. Allow him to hang around the team without a role and no scope for impact. Let him express his ideas, but don't accept them. Don't allow him to coach the players. Use him to fetch balls and carry drinks.'

Pat smiled. 'Forgive me for questioning you, boss, but how can I reject his good ideas?'

'You come up with better ideas,' scowled Akash. 'Is he better than you? Should I appoint him as head coach?'

The faint smile disappeared from Pat's face.

Akash rose to leave. 'Oh! And please ignore the co-owner, Jayshankar Pandit. Block his access to the team. Everyone should refuse his invitations for parties. I will immediately fire anyone who talks to him. Ask him to contact me if he complains.'

The Guru's Disdain

Two Days Later, Morning

'Only a few succeed. Not everyone belongs to a rich family like you. Most cricketers die in poverty.'

Neil tried hard to look interested in the stories Gautam Chatterjee's wife told about her children and grandchildren, how they had made the wise decision to pursue careers other than cricket. He wished she would realize that being born in a wealthy family does not necessarily make a person rich. Her sermons blighted the gigantic achievements of Gautam's career and she refused to acknowledge his excellence in the domestic circuit just because he had never played for India.

Mrs Chatterjee continued her tirade against professional cricket while Neil zoned out, taking refuge in his memories of his four-year stint with the Bengal cricket team under Gautam's tutelage. Neil had transferred to Bengal when the Delhi players and coaches had accused him of elitism after he had spent one year in Australia to rehabilitate his broken ankle. The Bengal players had treated him like family, and Gautam Chatterjee had corrected his bowling action to help him return to the Indian team. Kolkata was a second home for Neil, and he was the city's adopted son.

Great people and excellent sports culture. They adore me.

Gautam Chatterjee strengthened his reputation for punctuality by arriving in the living room exactly at the appointed time of 10.30 a.m. He looked regal in his well-pressed, starched white kurta-pajama and neat back-brushed silver hair.

'Should we go out, sir?' Neil asked as Gautam hugged him. 'I have already taken too much of madam's time.'

'No, stay here for lunch,' said Gautam's wife. 'I will cook your favourite prawn curry.'

'Oh! No ma'am,' replied Neil with a fake smile. 'I am in a hurry today.'

'No, no, you must stay,' she insisted, jumping up from her chair.

Neil hallucinated about wild conspiracy theories, brain-fried by Madame Chatterjee's mindless chatter. Her shrill voice would give him nightmares for a long time.

Maybe Gautam wanted to rag me. He could have arrived earlier; but he waited inside just to show he is punctual.

Gautam seemed to have realized his discomfort. He glared at her, and she fled the room.

'Now, Neil...what made you fly all the way to Kolkata to meet me?' asked Gautam, raising his eyebrows. 'Anything confidential?'

'Actually, sir, I wanted to discuss...'

'The ICCL circus?'

Neil fumbled for words, unsure about Gautam's stance.

'Neil—I know your family situation and the story of the ICCL bid. Why did you get into this mess?'

'Coaching is wrong?' asked Neil.

'The ICCL is downright immoral. Sports teams should belong to the public.'

'With all due respect, sir, I disagree.'

'I won't hold it against you,' said Gautam, smiling. 'I know the industrialists who bought teams. They are very ambitious and successful but with one fatal flaw—they don't know how to lose.' Gautam laughed. 'Sports is a great leveller; it doesn't care for wealth or pedigree. Everyone loses in sports. They won't be able to handle failure. Watch out when that happens.'

You may theorize as much as you want, sir, but you will never understand what I am going through. I have had enough; first your wife's lectures and then yours. These Bengalis talk too much. Let me try one more time and then I will leave.

'Please give me some ideas for coaching a new team,' said Neil. 'You were a genius coach...you transformed my game.'

'Go back to coaching kids, Neil,' said Gautam. 'Return to where you belong and forget about this showbiz.'

'Okay, sir, thanks! I will take your leave now.'

Gautam looked surprised. 'You won't stay for lunch?'

'Sir, I have another meeting.'

Before Gautam could react, Neil touched his feet and walked out of the room.

Gautam Chatterjee's dismissive attitude motivated Neil to seek help elsewhere. Later that night, he made arrangements for a two-week stint in the UK with the coaches and players of the county of Kent.

He believed the UK's strong cricket league system would provide him with invaluable insights for coaching young players and prove to be a game changer for his role in the New Delhi Royals team.

Test Team for T20

After Three Weeks

New Delhi Royals Creates a Test Team for T20, Buys Senior Players for a Young and Fast Format

At the ICCL player auction conducted yesterday, the New Delhi Royals franchise bet on 'experienced' players for a young and fast format. Of the 10 foreign players they purchased, 4 are over 35 years old and at the fag end of their international careers. Jeffrey Beer (South Africa), Kyle Slinger (Australia) and Antonio Charles (South Africa) are strong Test cricketers who have not played limited overs cricket for their countries in the last 2–3 years. The heavy bidding for these cricketers drove up their price and surprised everyone. Evidently, other franchises also saw value in their experience over their youth (or lack of it).

The New Delhi Royals franchise also did not buy other Indian international cricketers, apart from Sudhir Yadav (their captain and icon player whom they purchased before the auction) and Dinesh Singh (right-hand batsman), with the latter being 38 years old and retired from international cricket.

Late yesterday evening, they declared their list of support staff. Stuart Bronte (physiotherapist), Kieran Bresson (mental conditioning coach) and Laurence Cranmer (data analyst) are all South Africans who have never worked with any major international team. The owners gave a free hand to the head coach Pattrick O'Donnell to buy the best international support staff for the team, but he chose his friends from South Africa over other available professionals with superior credentials.

Neil stared, horror-struck, at this news report, wondering why Pat and Sudhir had deliberately crippled the team.

'*Can't tell you—its confidential,*' Pat had said when he had enquired about the player auction strategy during their meeting two days ago.

Why did they refuse to take me to the auction?

Pat had berated him for going out of line.

'Neil, Akash has instructed you can't go there. Don't you have self-respect?'

Pat's refusal to even discuss his recommendations, let alone accept them, troubled Neil. He expected contempt from Akash but couldn't cope with the same behaviour from Pat. Sportsmen share strange chemistry; on the field they are fierce competitors, but off the field they are cordial and respectful. Pattrick O'Donnell was senior to Neil and way more successful. They had competed on the field and had got the better of each other on different occasions. Pat had praised Neil when he had debuted for India and expressed disappointment when he had retired without realizing his full potential. Neil couldn't understand why such a generous man had become petty and arrogant.

Akash should know Pat ignored my suggestions. My presentation to Pat and this news report will act as evidence. Should I contact him?

But what if Pat had sidelined him under pressure from Akash? In that case, complaining to Akash would destroy the little sympathy Pat might still have for him. Akash was too impressed with Pat's credentials to take this complaint seriously. Neil realized that he should depend on Pat and their mutual respect for each other to prove his value in the team. He must work with Pat, and not against him.

He sent Pat a text.

```
Congratulations on the successful player auction.
Looking forward to the training. Can you please send
me the full list of players we bought?
```

His text did not elicit a response, and he realized it would be a slow and painful process for him to climb up from the deep hole of irrelevance.

I have to be patient and believe in myself, look for small wins without rushing things, take one step at a time towards my goals.

Hell Hath No Fury

Seven Days Later

A beautician pedicured Divya's feet perched on the desk, while Pattrick O'Donnell, a world-famous sportsman and global legend of cricket, waited outside her cabin in a navy blue suit and red tie. She had summoned Akash and Pat for a meeting in the new 20,000 sq. ft office of the New Delhi Royals but seemed in no hurry to start the proceedings.

Divya whistled and examined her hair in a handheld mirror. She made funny faces that looked hideous on her botoxed skin. 'Maybe I should get a curly perm and blue highlights,' she said to nobody in particular, thrilled as though she had unlocked the secret to eternal youth.

'Can we call Pat?' asked Akash, perturbed about the Belgian delegation waiting in his office. A joint venture in Europe was in jeopardy because an attention-seeking imprudent woman had forced him to abandon his guests in the middle of serious discussions.

'Let him wait till I finish my pedicure,' said Divya, without looking up from her mirror.

Divya's tendency to throw a massive fit whenever Akash missed a team-related event had convinced him that buying peace would cost less time than direct conflict with his vitriolic wife. But he had not factored in the possibility of unexpected delays caused by Divya's mood swings and mind games.

Akash regretted buying this team. He couldn't understand why it was necessary to host events for trivial activities such as unveiling the team uniform or announcing the cheerleading team. Divya's insistence on his presence in every event created an unsustainable burden on his time and patience. He would have complied if she invited him only to the special events as the guest of honour. But Divya just insisted on his presence while she hogged the limelight, wasting time posing for photographs and making inconsequential speeches.

'I am feeling unwell,' said Akash, touching his forehead. 'Either we start now or reschedule; I have to see a doctor soon.'

'Should I call an ambulance?' smirked Divya and asked the beautician to leave.

Akash ignored her scorn and rushed to the door to call Pat. 'Please lower your legs,' he said. 'Your panty is visible.'

Divya scowled but did not budge. Akash watched in despair as she adjusted her hair and moved her legs only after Pat had entered the room.

Pat shook hands and sat without waiting for an invitation. Although he smiled, he looked edgy.

Divya rocked in her chair and avoided eye contact while she browsed through the contents of a file. 'So, Test team for T20?' she said.

Pat shook his head. 'Excuse me?'

'You read Indian newspapers?'

'Don't have the time.'

'What's keeping you so busy?'

Pat mumbled, and Divya cut him off.

'But first we should discuss this,' she said and threw a printout towards him which floated around before landing on the desk.

He looked irritated as he scanned the paper. 'Yes, what about it?'

'Jesus Christ! Do I have to spoon-feed you?' screamed Divya, banging on the table. 'Why did we buy old players? We wanted a young and hep brand image. Bastard! People are teasing, calling me a grandmother.'

'Relax!' Akash moved in to calm her down. 'Pat will explain.'

Pat smiled. 'I have played international cricket for twenty years; I know more about cricket than this journalist.'

'But why did we not buy cool young international players?' asked Divya.

'Sudhir is young.'

'Why not the Australian captain...what's his name?' Divya scratched her head. 'Guy with the ponytail...uff.'

'Dan Trivoli.'

'Yes! Why didn't you buy him?'

'He has failed in Indian conditions,' said Pat in a self-assured tone. 'Experience matters more than youth in cricket. It's a new team and a new format. The senior players can mentor the junior Indian players.'

'Dan is young and sexy. My friends wanted to meet him.'

Akash winced at Divya's reference to her parasitic friends who treated this team as a never-ending party funded by a man whose stupid wife believed she could become 'cool' by throwing money at everything. How had they made her so hungry for their approval? He hated them for eliminating his influence on Divya, and for using her gullibility to avenge his indifference towards them. They had persuaded her to hire hundred-plus people and lease a posh office in Gurgaon for a team that would operate only two months in a year. She was sponsoring an all-expenses paid holiday for them during the tournament, with travel in private jets, boarding and lodging in five-star hotels and access to parties and promotional events. In return, all they had to do was be in sync with Divya's moods. She did not care for the expenses, as for the first time in her life she had emerged from Akash's shadow and attracted the limelight she had always craved for.

Hopefully, this nonsense won't give her the time to question my moves in the Omkar group. A silver lining, perhaps.

He sent Pat a text.

```
Produce sound cricketing reasons for your decisions
to convince her. And make it fast. I don't have
all day.
```

'They can meet Dan in the after-parties,' said Pat.

Divya shook her head. 'Not the same. We want to spend the next two months with these cricketers.'

Pat looked confused. 'Spend two months? Cricketers are very busy...'

Divya frowned. 'Oh! We will be there in the dressing room, in the dugout, during practice. We will go wherever they go.'

Pat read Akash's text and tilted his head towards him.

'Not possible; against the rules,' said Pat.

'Ha! We make our own rules.'

'Owners can't break the rules.'

'We can't?' Divya asked Akash. 'We own the team...'

'Let's discuss this separately,' Akash said, trying to wriggle out of an inconsequential discussion. 'Finish with Pat first.'

Akash grimaced as Divya rechecked her papers.

Oh! Fuck, more. Will I have to kill one of these two for this meeting to end?

'Do you guarantee success?' Divya asked Pat.

Pat shook his head. 'I guarantee the best effort...'

'How many matches will we win?'

'Maybe nine or ten out of the fourteen...'

'Why so few? After spending so much money we should win every match,' said Divya.

Pat glared at Akash but Akash did not intervene, to make sure Pat could manage Divya without his help.

Pat seemed to get the message. 'Why guess anything at this stage? Let the league start first.'

'I won't pay if players don't perform,' declared Divya.

'That will ruin our reputation forever,' said Pat. 'Fans will desert us; good players will boycott us next season.'

'Okay! Meeting over for now,' said Divya with a dismissive wave of her hand. 'My team will contact you for endorsement-related events.'

'I won't have the time. Sorry!' said Pat and established strong eye contact with Divya. She was about to explode, but Pat's calm determination made her reconsider it. 'And one more thing,' he leaned towards Divya. 'Never ask me to explain my decisions. Akash has assured me of a free hand. I can't work any other way.'

Pat knocked on the desk with his knuckles and left the room without waiting for Divya's response.

Halley's Comet

Four Days Later, Late Evening

'Please welcome Miss Kanika Suri, representing International Sports Management Inc. as the director of operations of the ICCL. This pretty lady is a celebrity in sports management…who makes elite sportsmen dance to her tunes.'

Neil and Nandini exchanged glances as Kanika appeared on stage looking sexy in a short skirt and a tight-fitting black sleeveless blouse. The crowd cheered as she danced a small jig, matching her steps to the beats of Roy Orbison's 'Oh, Pretty Woman'.

'Let's have great cricket…and some serious fun. Here's to a great first season of the ICCL…I love you all,' she said, blowing kisses to acknowledge the boisterous applause and whistles.

Neil dreaded meeting his former girlfriend at a time when he was struggling with his life and career. When they had parted, he had been at the top of his game in the Indian cricket team—a big star adored by fans all over the world. Now, thirteen years later, he was struggling to claw his way back to significance. He had no wish to become an object of her sympathy.

She will get a kick from knowing how my life crashed after she left me. She will feel very important.

Nandini hugged Neil. 'Go talk to her; use her connections.'

'God! Hell, no; never! After so many years…'

'Don't want to meet her?' asked Nandini, smiling.

'Yes, I have to, professionally.'

'Right! She means nothing to you,' Nandini chuckled and moved away.

Neil loitered around, pretending to enjoy the show, while his eyes constantly searched for Kanika. Glitz, glamour, fashion, fake smiles, money power, unreal pleasantries, false show of friendship, best-catered food, high-end alcohol flowing like water, drugs in hidden corners, unbridled debauchery—the ICCL launch party celebrated the world of the elite. Pasty-faced models walked for a fashion show on a revolving stage, admired by guests segregated by nationality, status and special interests. The foreign players, coaches and support staff from various teams occupied one corner of the lawn, while Akash huddled together with other elderly men engaged in serious discussions. Divya and her friends behaved like excited teenagers, drinking with abandon and loud 'cheers'. The senior Indian cricketers and celebrity ex-cricketers obliged the photographers and autograph-seekers. The junior Indian players, overwhelmed by their first exposure to the big league, stood in another corner like obedient children eager to please the headmaster. Other stray people, not belonging to any of the groups, focused on the abundant supply of good food and expensive alcohol. Cap Jay was not visible, but people had seen him arrive at the premises a few hours ago.

Someone tapped Neil on his back. He turned and saw Kanika Suri standing behind him.

She grinned. 'Hi there! I was looking for you.'

It took Neil a few moments to collect himself. 'How have you been?' he blurted out. 'Congratulations on your new position.'

'Thanks!' she said with a toothy smile. 'I am in India after ten years. I was working out of Singapore.'

'I had no clue,' Neil shook his head.

'Care for a drink?' asked Kanika.

Neil hesitated, but Kanika pulled him towards the bar. 'Let's go.'

Although a little awkward about meeting a woman whose memories had troubled him over the years, he lacked the will to refuse her company. Kanika couldn't be ignored. She stood out in a gathering of top Bollywood stars and global supermodels and turned heads as she walked across the lawn. It was impossible for ordinary mortals to resist her magnetic personality.

'You look the same, except the hair,' he said.

Kanika laughed. 'And you look different somehow. Maybe your eyes...'

Neil rubbed his eyes and made a funny face. 'My eyes?'

'They have matured—seen a lot.'

Neil wondered if Kanika was nudging him to discuss his life. He was not ready to tell, and she did not deserve to know.

After ignoring me for thirteen years, she can't behave as if we are close friends catching up over a drink.

'Why did you cut your hair?'

'It was difficult to manage. And then...' Kanika smiled and looked away. 'And then, you can't satisfy people all the time.'

Neil detected traces of profound sorrow on her face, but he had no interest in exploring further. He changed the subject. 'In Singapore, did you work as a celebrity manager, or...'

'Yes, but for athletics and soccer. I led a team of thirty in five countries.'

'So why this change?' Neil raised his eyebrows.

Kanika sighed. 'For a change of scenery...it was suffocating in Singapore.' She winked. 'I wanted to meet new people...some old...'

Kanika ordered a glass of Cabernet Sauvignon at the bar while Neil opted for a Heineken. Two elderly gentlemen dressed in expensive suits hugged Kanika, and she transformed into the flirtatious and cheerful sweetheart everyone adored.

Is she unhappy, or am I just hoping I am not the only one with a shattered life?

Neil marvelled at the mind's ability to project a person's deepest emotions as reality.

Do I want Kanika's life to be miserable, as a divine justice? he asked himself but couldn't get a clear answer. The murky world of conjecture with contrasting end goals and infinite possibilities zapped his mind.

Why should I care?

He watched the Bollywood dance show to block Kanika from his field of vision.

I won't get involved again. She has caused me a lot of damage. I can't allow history to repeat itself, especially when I am fighting for survival.

After a while, Kanika again tapped on Neil's shoulder. 'Hey there; sorry I made you wait.'

'Not a problem,' said Neil, looking at his watch. 'Unfortunately, I will have to leave now. It is well past my bedtime.' He smiled and looked around. 'But where is Nandini?'

'Guess I will run into you during the league,' said Kanika.

They shook hands, and she did not offer a hug.

So, it will be business-like and formal? Good! She has been a serial hugger all evening, hugging everyone.

A commotion erupted in the area as Cap Jay arrived, accompanied by two girls young enough to be his daughters. He smooched those hapless victims as they supported his heavy body through the lawn.

'Hey there, Captain,' Kanika called out. 'Where were you?'

'Right by your side, darling,' said Cap Jay, looking flushed. 'Entertaining these two beauties. But now I am all yours.'

Cap Jay stumbled and collapsed on the floor with a low cry. The crowd laughed at the clown's antics. As Kanika and the two girls could not lift his bulk, two able-bodied men volunteered from the crowd and hauled Cap Jay into a chair.

Cap Jay tried to pull Kanika towards his lap, but she thwarted him by using her elbow. 'Captain, you naughty boy,' she said and lightly slapped his face, hiding her disgust under a smooth smile. 'Go home! Where's your wife?'

'I will go with you,' Cap Jay said in a gurgling voice. He struggled to keep his eyes open but continued the buffoonery. 'Long time no see. Let's do it.'

'Did you find Nandini?' Kanika asked Neil.

Neil smiled and shook his head.

'You with him? Again?' Cap Jay pointed at Neil and made his finger droop with a funny face. 'A spent force; drained.' He laughed and punched his chest. 'Try me. A real man.'

Neil rushed forward to confront Cap Jay, but Kanika pulled him away. 'Don't bother about him. We are good friends, so he jokes. You have bigger fish to fry in the ICCL.'

Neil realized Kanika meant well. A clash with the co-owner would have finished his prospects in the team. She probably knew how the events of the last few months had shaped his life. He worried about the bad impression she may have formed. The man she was meeting was surviving on the largesse of his family and bore no resemblance to the star cricketer she had dated. And yet, she was interested in his plans. Why? To make up for the lost years?

Kanika stared at him with kind eyes, and he forced a smile, alarmed by his audacious hope of a reconciliation.

She knows my fears. What will she do about them?

She held his hand and kissed him on his cheek. 'Don't worry—it will all work out. Go home now. I will see you later,' she whispered and walked away.

Thanks for Not Helping

Two Days Later

Pat looked annoyed as Neil boarded the team bus.

'Too big to wear the team jersey?' he asked Neil. 'The media will cover the first day of practice. You are not part of the team?' Next, Pat gave the administrative assistant a dressing-down. 'You forgot to give Neil the team kit? Move him into the team hotel. He will travel and stay with the team for the whole tournament.'

Neil relaxed as the ice broke between him and Pat.

Thank God Pat clarified about my stay and travel. It would have been embarrassing to push for it.

He exchanged pleasantries in the bus, and his uneasiness disappeared when he found everyone cordial and responsive to his outreach. Earlier in the day, he had waited for six hours in the hotel lobby to board the team bus as he did not know the team's schedule. Nervous about the team dynamics, he had analysed every scenario and fine-tuned his game strategy and training plans to create a strong impression in the first team meeting. But Pat's public endorsement of his place in the team eased his fears. He was confident once the team settled down to play cricket, the ego clashes would stop, and mutual respect for cricketing skills would take over. There was a tournament to be won, after all. Pat couldn't reject his suggestions without solid reasons. As a professional, why would he deliberately hurt the team? Plus, Sudhir and Dinesh would not go against their own intimate knowledge of Indian conditions and side with Pat if he was unreasonable.

On reaching the stadium, the team assembled for a meeting in the dressing room.

Pat rose to address the players. 'Welcome, everyone, to the New Delhi Royals,' he said. 'Players who perform will get more opportunities, and those who fail will carry drinks. Sudhir Yadav is your captain. During the match, his word is final. Off the field and during training, my word is final. Clear?'

Everyone nodded, and Pat continued, 'We will divide the team into three groups—batsmen under the guidance of Dinesh Singh, fast bowlers under Antonio Charles and spinners under Kyle Slinger. I will be the overall in-charge, and Neil will help as and when required. Questions?'

Neil panicked as Pat's plans almost eliminated his role in the team. 'Oh! Excuse me, Pat...' he said, raising his hand like an eager student in a class.

'Yes?'

Eager to use his last chance to get a foot in the door, Neil broached a safe topic Pat couldn't refuse.

'We should discuss game strategy in Indian conditions,' he said.

Pat looked puzzled. 'As in? How to play in Indian conditions?'

'Yes, and train accordingly. We can't bark up the wrong tree.'

'Why do you think we haven't discussed it?'

'If you have, please share the insights. It will help everyone,' said Neil in a calm voice, trying to appear humble and eager to learn. He looked around to garner support but found nothing but noncommittal poker faces.

Pat sighed. 'Everything in good time, Neil. Not wise to overload the team with too much analysis.'

'We also don't want everyone to become thinkers,' said Sudhir. 'There will be total chaos—everyone running in different directions. Only the coach and the senior players will analyse. Everyone else will just follow orders.'

'I should train the fast bowlers,' said Neil and turned towards Antonio Charles with folded hands. 'I know the Indian conditions better than him.'

'Antonio has toured India seven times,' said Pat with an evil grin, looking like a sadistic teacher eager to cane a pupil. 'He has been very successful here—and overall, in his career, he has been much more successful than you. He knows what to do, don't worry.' Pat surveyed the silent dressing room. 'Antonio will play every game. He should assess and train the bowlers who will bowl with him.'

Neil couldn't believe his ears.

Play every game? Antonio is well past his prime and in poor shape; his bowling is wayward, not suitable for T20.

'Your suggestions are welcome,' Antonio told Neil in a husky voice.

Neil realized opposing Antonio would end the only feeble opportunity he had of coaching the team, and held back his comments. Antonio's willingness to listen gave him a platform to showcase his knowledge.

Antonio has Pat's ears, and if he provides good feedback, Pat will realize my value.

'So, sorted?' said Pat, clapping his hands. 'Now can we practice? We can't win by sitting around in the dressing room.'

Square Peg in Round Hole

Five Days Later, Afternoon

'Come on, Snoopy, give us a six!' screamed Divya, as Antonio charged in to bowl during the afternoon training session. The cheering reached a crescendo till Antonio's vicious bouncer hit Snoopy on his chest and knocked him down like a sack of potatoes. After a moment of stunned silence, panic-stricken players, staff and friends rushed inside the practice net where Snoopy's wiry frame lay squirming in pain.

'Oh my God...he is dead,' shrieked Divya, pushing through the crowd. 'Call the police, and get this brute arrested...' she said, pointing at Antonio who was standing with his head bowed like a felon.

'Don't worry, he is alive...maybe a couple of fractured ribs... that's all,' said Pat, hauling up Snoopy. He gently slapped his face, and Snoopy stirred, muttering under his breath. 'You want water, son? Don't feel bad. Few people can face a bowler of Antonio's calibre.'

'Call a doctor and clear this area,' Pat instructed Somoresh Basu, the team manager. 'Resume practice right away. And don't let this nonsense happen again.'

Divya's friends accosted Antonio after the support staff carried away Snoopy. 'Showing your strength, man? Body-line bowling?' they said, pushing Antonio. 'Want to fight? Come outside the stadium...'

'Keep off him,' shouted Pat, stepping in front of Antonio. 'I requested you to stop your friends from practising with my players,' he told a distraught Divya. 'This is professional cricket...not a picnic.'

'Why did he bowl so fast?' shouted Divya. 'This is an assault; I will cancel his contract.'

'Your call; I won't be responsible for the consequences,' said Pat in a cold voice. 'We are sorry for the injury, but please understand it is unsafe to play here.'

He shook his head and sighed. 'We appreciate the enthusiasm, but please stay at a safe distance and let us do our job.'

From the seclusion of the dressing room, Neil watched Divya's friends wrap up their showbiz and fade away to the sidelines. No one could have fun at the cost of a severe injury. He laughed at how a single blow on the chest produced the result Pat's constant pleading, negotiating and threatening couldn't achieve. Over the last five days, this evil gang had terrorized the team—instructing the players, commenting on batting and bowling techniques, controlling the sequence of activities and interjecting themselves into the play at every step. Pat and the support staff hadn't been able to stop their ostentatious display of power and entitlement. These imbeciles disrespected men, better and more accomplished than them, and fled for their lives after one blow on the chest. Professional cricketers took such blows almost every time they played.

Neil had shared with Kanika his frustrations about Divya's friends disturbing the team. Her hectic travel schedule had prevented them from meeting since the ICCL launch party, and they had depended on phone calls and text messages to restart a relationship that had abruptly ended thirteen years ago. He was left with nothing to do after Pat denied him direct responsibilities in the team. So Neil started looking for engagement with Kanika. He was aware every thought or stimulus would revive emotions he had consigned to the trash bin of consciousness, but he was helpless. Somewhere inside him burned the desire for closure, even though moving towards it posed the inherent risk of self-destruction.

Kanika is no ordinary woman. No ordinary man can stop himself from falling for her.

In the New Delhi Royals training camp, a disaster was waiting to happen. Antonio allowed Neil to voice his suggestions but refused to accept them, nullifying his impact on training. He rejected Neil's suggestion that in Indian conditions fast bowlers should bowl a good length on the off stump and asked the fast bowlers to bowl full length on the middle stump. When Neil pointed out that the batsmen would hit the full-length ball if the bowlers failed to control the line, Antonio claimed that making the bowlers practice the same delivery over and over again would solve that problem. Pat did not encourage the batsmen to practice shot improvization and pinch-hitting, which were strategies crucial for the T20 format. The foreign players avoided fielding practice by complaining that they would get injured on the rough ground. The running between the wickets of the whole team lacked speed and coordination, and the head coach seemed unwilling or unable to make a difference. Pat's training plans defied common sense, but Neil had no say. He withdrew from the practice sessions when he tried to point out his concerns to Pat but got nothing but a cold shoulder in return. Thus, he decided to wait until the team failed in the first match, when everyone would realize the value of his ideas.

Outside the cricket field, Neil also worried about the impact of the daily parties on the young cricketers who did not understand the value of moderation. Day after day, they suffered from alcohol-induced sickness. Even there he couldn't intervene beyond a point as the young players were unamenable to his advice.

Instead, Neil spent his time providing a blow by blow account to Kanika of the buffoonery of Divya's friends, the late night parties, promotional events and media interactions. He discussed everything with her except his role in the team as he did not want to put off Kanika with his sob stories. He hoped good sense would prevail on Pat and Antonio after the first match.

Neil also wanted to prevent Kanika from dominating his mind. Telling her about his situation would have compromised his position as far as she was concerned. She had always influenced his decisions when they had been together, and controlled everything, right from his social interactions, endorsements and friends to the decision to move out of Upadhyay Palace into his own apartment. He had been so dependent on her that everything fell apart when she left.

I won't allow the same thing to happen again.

Hara-Kiri on the Horizon

Ten Days Later

'Please applaud Antonio, Kyle, Sudhir and Dinesh for training the junior players,' extolled Pat, slowly raising his hands like a priest conducting mass in a church.

Pat frowned as the applause died in the dressing room. 'I have here, with me, a team list prepared by Neil for tomorrow's match,' he said, showing a piece of paper. 'Neil, care to explain your thoughts?'

'There are two important criteria for team selection,' said Neil, enjoying the rare opportunity to display his cricketing knowledge. 'First, we can play only four foreign players, and second, we should play five batsmen, one wicket-keeper, three bowlers and two all-rounders.'

Neil walked to the blank whiteboard and grabbed a marker.

Sharing the team list before this meeting was a smart move. Now he can't deny me the credit. I was right...finally he can see my value.

He wrote names on the whiteboard.

Batsmen: Sudhir Yadav, Dinesh Singh, Ismail Abdullah, Travis Robins, Benjamin Roister

Bowlers: Manuel Cyclic (MF), Neeraj Dara (S), Baldev Madan (S)

All-rounders: Aarush Burman (S), Divit Verma (MF)

Wicketkeeper: Harish Bhasin

'This is an interesting proposition...' said Pat and exchanged smiles with Sudhir. 'Bold...almost radical.'

'Spinners and medium-fast bowlers will be more effective than the fast bowlers in the low and slow Delhi pitch. So that's why this... as Pat said..."radical" approach,' said Neil.

'Bullshit!' Pat snatched the marker from Neil. 'Fast bowling is the key to win against Indian players who can't play anything faster than 120 kmph.' Pat laughed, looking at the foreign players as though Neil had cracked a joke. 'One spinner will be enough. And the two all-rounders you have chosen can't bat or bowl. An all-rounder is someone who can play both as a bowler and batsman.' He slowly joined his cupped palms. 'A player who is a half-bowler and half-batsman can't become an all-rounder by combining two inadequate skill sets.'

'Your assessment of Aarush and Davit is wrong,' said Neil. 'Not playing them will be a huge mistake.'

Pat smiled and shook his head. 'They won't play.'

Why this show if he had to reject my recommendations? To humiliate me...because I had dared to prepare a list? Fuck!

Pat pointed towards an empty seat, but Neil ignored him. In the audience Dinesh grinned without showing which way he tilted, while Sudhir seemed frozen, joining ranks with the poker-faced players and support staff of the New Delhi Royals.

'How did you choose the batsmen?' asked Pat. 'Sudhir and Dinesh are obvious selections, but why Ismail, Travis and Benjamin?'

Neil crossed his arms and sighed. 'Because they are young and fit T20 specialists. They will save at least 10 runs each in every match, which makes a big difference in T20 where the margin of victory is generally very slim.'

'You think T20 is a slam-bang format with no need for genuine batting skills?' asked Pat. 'Right now the team needs more experienced players to anchor the batting. Please return to your seat now.' Pat pointed again towards an empty seat. 'Ismail, Travis and Benjamin won't play because we have better foreign players. Sudhir, Dinesh, Rodney Wyatt and Jeffrey Beer will be the main batsmen in the team, supported by Kyle Slinger—a genuine all-rounder—as the fifth batsman. Among the bowlers you suggested, I will select only one— the spinner Baldev Madan.'

Neil shook his head as Pat replaced the names he had written on the whiteboard with his own list. Both Rodney Wyatt and Jeffrey Beer were struggling with fitness, and selecting them over Ismail, Travis and Benjamin was insane. Kyle Slinger was a decent bowler, but an atrocious batsman who had scored over 20 only once in the last ten innings.

What is Pat doing? This is hara-kiri.

'These are also Sudhir's recommendations,' said Pat, and stepped away from the whiteboard. 'No one knows the conditions here better than him. Right, Sudhir?'

Sudhir made a gurgling sound and cleared his throat. 'Yes, I agree. Let's see how things go,' he said in a halting voice, not sounding very enthusiastic.

Sudhir's strange reaction surprised Neil. Was Pat's team selection really based on Sudhir's recommendations, or was he using his name to add credibility to his own decisions? The otherwise ebullient Sudhir was unusually quiet during the meeting and spoke only when Pat prodded him to comment. Was Pat arm-twisting Sudhir to make him fall in line?

Pat rambled on about the Chennai Chettinads team, their opponent for the first match of the ICCL, and read individual statistics of all the players from a notebook. Neil zoned out in the wake of the inconsequential barrage of numbers. How come Sudhir and Dinesh supported Pat? Anyone with a basic knowledge of cricket would know this team selection was stupid. But why was Pat deliberately selecting a bad team? A person of his calibre wouldn't make rookie mistakes, so either he had gone mad, or he was facing pressure from people more powerful than him. But who could pressurize him? At the end of the day he would have to defend the results.

'It's important we focus on our individual roles and nothing else,' said Pat and tilted his head towards Neil. 'So, stuff like team selection, training plans, etc. are the responsibility of the team management. Clear? Now let's get ready to kick ass tomorrow. Move!'

Pat's unnecessary final attack after he had already established his supremacy on the team made Neil drop his plan to discuss the team selection with Sudhir and Dinesh in private. They were anyway too smug to value his opinion. Pat had done him a big favour by giving him the opportunity to present his ideas in front of the team. People had seen Pat rejecting his recommendations, so what was bad for the team would be good for him.

Tomorrow there will be deliverance, and then I will speak again.

Room Service

Later That Night

'We are going to create history tomorrow. Let's celebrate tonight—just the two of us.'

Kanika leaned on the door frame and flashed a naughty smile as she clinked a bottle of wine with two glasses. 'Special Sangiovese wine; all the way from Florence, for you.'

Neil gaped at Kanika. 'No after-party?'

'Won't you ask me to come in?' quipped Kanika and gently pushed Neil into the room. She peeped inside and smiled mischievously. 'Who are you hiding there?'

Neil smiled. 'Just soiled clothes and dirty dishes.' He stepped away from the door. 'Come in, please! Sorry for the casual dress.'

Kanika sat on the couch and adjusted her short skirt. She grinned. 'I have seen you in pyjamas before.'

Neil moved the wine bottle and glasses to the centre table. He sat on the couch at a close enough but not-so-intimate distance from Kanika.

'Had enough parties,' Kanika played with her hair. 'I wanted to meet you, so I told people I am going to rest for the long day tomorrow.'

Neil opened the wine bottle using a corkscrew from the minibar.

First, she ignores me for three days despite staying in the same hotel, and then she skips a party to meet me. She loves parties. So why is she here? Interest in me?

He poured the wine into the two glasses and took one to his lips.

'Wait! Let's toast, at least—to this wonderful tournament, and to our friendship,' said Kanika, leaning over to clink glasses. 'Smell the wine. There is a hint of olives and lavender—they grow on the same farm with the grapes.'

Her eyes closed as she drew a long whiff from her glass while Neil got nothing but the strong odour of her perfume. He feigned interest in smelling the wine, his mind in a tizzy from the small talk of this dicey woman who was avoiding a discussion about his situation in his team.

She really does not know? Or is she waiting for me to say it?

'Anything bothering you?' asked Kanika, holding his hand. 'Don't worry about the team.'

Neil smiled. 'Right! Why should I care?'

Kanika crossed her legs and displayed the delicious contours that had stoked his passion for eternity. He seemed unfocused, and the sudden surge of ecstasy subdued the embarrassment of his ungentlemanly behaviour.

'You can look...don't feel shy,' Kanika winked. 'You still blush like a teenager—so cute. Your face has turned red.'

Neil grinned, unable to defend the indefensible.

Fuck! Who cares why she is here! I am having a good time.

Kanika walked to the window and lit a cigarette. Neil sipped wine ensconced in the couch, heady from the dreamy silhouette of her perfect body in the contrasting light and dark of the hotel room. She took deep drags of her cigarette and exhaled slowly towards the ceiling in a reflective mood.

Is she thinking about my role in the team? What can I do; it is what it is.

She returned to the couch and refilled her glass. 'You know what intrigued me about the texts and calls we exchanged in the last two weeks?'

Neil gulped down his third glass of wine.

Here it comes.

Kanika smiled. 'You never asked about my personal life. I am sure you don't have expert-level research on me as I have on you. Is it because you are not interested?'

Neil sighed, shaken by the replacement of one uncomfortable topic with another in his mind. 'I was afraid it will give me nothing but pain,' he said, reeling from the wine-induced loss of self-control. 'I mean...don't I already know you are in high demand? Men run after you—as though one smile or touch from you would save them from a terminal illness. Beyond that, how does knowing the graphic details of your affairs do me any good?'

'Really? You think my life is a chick flick?' snapped Kanika. 'I live in fairyland, while you are languishing in a dungeon?'

Neil sat up, the haze clearing from his brain. 'You don't? Aren't you God's chosen child, with superpowers to shape the destinies of men?'

'Yes, a superwoman with two failed marriages,' said Kanika in a halting voice. Her eyes glistened with tears ready to stream down her smooth cheeks.

'Two marriages?' exclaimed Neil. 'And children?'

'Thank God, none. It's very hard on kids when parents divorce. My vagabond lifestyle wouldn't have helped.'

'I am sorry to hear this.'

'Oh! Don't be,' said Kanika, waving her hand. 'There are advantages to living without roots. I don't have to please anyone…'

'Weird! We broke up because you did not want commitment. Eventually, you committed twice,' said Neil.

Kanika gave him a fleeting glance but avoided his gaze. 'It's about timing. You do it when you think you are ready. And it falls apart when you least expect it to,' she said. 'My first marriage collapsed because I had no time for the relationship. We married after two years in a live-in relationship, and my ex-husband was familiar with my schedule, but he still couldn't handle it.' She looked distraught. 'Maybe marriage makes us weird. We think we own people.' Kanika lit another cigarette. 'My second husband was very accommodative of my schedule, and I thought I had married the right man. Then I understood why he was so nice.' She smiled and took a deep drag from her cigarette, blowing out a cloud of smoke towards the ceiling. 'Because he was cheating on me.'

Neil wondered why Kanika was giving him a tour of the dark alleys of her life. Few people would be privy to this stuff.

Then why me?

'I could have cheated,' snapped Kanika. 'I always had the opportunity—but I didn't. Not as a favour to my husband, but he never appreciated my honesty.'

Neil nodded but kept silent to avoid intervening in a contentious matter.

'Hope you don't mind my smoking?' asked Kanika.

'No, I don't.'

'You were dead against it at one time.'

'Times have changed, and so have I,' said Neil and walked over to the balcony. 'As you grow older, you realize it is silly to have firm opinions about things.'

'I know you are upset, but trust me, you would not have been able to handle my hectic professional life,' said Kanika.

Hectic professional life...what hogwash! As a professional cricketer, I was busier than her.

Neil looked away to hide his disdain. 'Why do you think I am upset?' he asked. 'Sure, I felt bad for some time, but I moved on.'

Kanika joined Neil in the balcony. 'I am happy you are not holding a grudge.'

'You took a decision that affected both of us without discussing things with me.'

'I tried, but you did not listen,' said Kanika. 'You insisted on marriage. And I was not ready to commit and give up my career, and so I did the difficult but necessary thing.'

Neil went inside the room and slumped on the bed with a 'hmm'.

'Any idea what "hmm" means?' asked Kanika.

'Nothing,' said Neil, biting his lips. 'It happened at a wrong time in my life. After you left, I wasn't able to handle it; my career collapsed and I never recovered.'

'I am so sorry,' said Kanika, and hugged Neil. 'It was a strange time. I wish I could roll back time and make better decisions.'

Neil smiled. 'I am not blaming you, Kanika. I should have managed myself better.'

'Awesome, Neil,' said Kanika, beaming. 'My respect for you has quadrupled in this last one minute.'

'I don't need respect from you, Kanika,' said Neil in a cold voice. 'From you I only wanted love, which you could not give.'

Kanika touched his arm. 'Sorry! I was just...'

'I wanted respect from other people...for my cricket, which I never got,' said Neil, taking a few steps away from her. 'Now I am fighting a desperate battle for survival...'

Kanika hugged Neil from behind. 'You are not alone in this battle. This time I will stand with you.'

Neil dissolved into her hug and connected with the only human who really understood what he was trying to do.

She understands without explanation. We have a strange bond. It seems we never parted.

'Thanks,' he said, choking. 'I find strength in your support.'

'What happened in the team meeting today?' asked Kanika, leading Neil back to the couch and the Tuscany wine. 'Don't tell me the team list, as that's confidential, but did you play a significant role in the proceedings?'

'Nope,' said Neil, finding no reason to hold back the truth from her. 'Pat and I don't agree about the team selection...and he rejected my recommendations.'

'Did he say why?'

'Yes, he did, but his reasons are wrong. Everyone knows it, but no one opposed him.' He hesitated for a moment. 'How should I tackle him? At present I am doing nothing in the team.'

'It's a tough situation, I must admit,' said Kanika. 'Akash does not realize his ego will destroy the team. For now, I suggest you hang in there. You are doing your job by voicing your opinion. There is nothing more you can do. The good news is, it's a dynamic environment, and things will change quickly. Let's decide on the next steps after the first few matches.'

The Lady in Purple

Next Day, Evening

'Mr Akash, finally we have a level playing field,' said K. Gopal (owner of the Chennai Chettinads team) in a nasal voice. 'You can use political power to destroy competition in business, but not in sports. Anybody can win here.'

Akash detested Gopal's irritating habit of coming too close to the people he addressed. He recoiled and wiped away microparticles of Gopal's spit from his face. 'There is only one winner here, Gopal—me!' he said, thumping his chest. 'Don't be delusional. Cricket can't erase the status difference between us.'

Akash gasped as Kanika appeared dressed in a short one-piece purple dress. She bent, struggling to stop her high heels from penetrating the soft soil of the Feroz Shah Kotla Stadium, and the perfect roundness of her hips hit him in the eye.

Fuck! She is getting hotter with age. What a figure! What extreme confidence!

He remembered how, during a visit to Upadhyay Palace, she hadn't bothered to adjust her dress even after she had seen him looking at her panty through the gap between her uncrossed legs. Her defiant smile had forced him to look away, but she hadn't moved. What did she see in Neil? Maybe he was good in bed...sportsmen sometimes had unfair advantages.

Unbelievable woman!

On the other side of the ground, Neil and Rohit practised with the junior New Delhi Royals players. Akash worried Rohit would imbibe Neil's loser attitude. Why was Rohit spending time with Neil when he had access to much bigger players?

Is Neil using my son to impress me? Bastard!

Before Akash could reach Rohit, Pat gave the group marching orders. 'Don't want to get dehydrated before a major match. Enough practice already; everyone go inside,' he shouted, pointing towards the dressing room door. 'And Neil, you will consult me before organizing an impromptu practice session again.'

Akash smiled as the players rushed inside, leaving Neil to collect the cricket gear. Only a man with no self-respect could accept such humiliation. Or was the lure of fucking Kanika stopping him from quitting?

Can't blame him—she is a bomb. Good for me. She will keep him where I want him to be in this team. Later, I will fuck her just to rub Neil's nose on the ground.

Cap Jay emerged from the dressing room and abused Somoresh Basu (team manager) who tried in vain to calm him down. Dressed in a sweat-scarred white linen shirt and trousers with a blue scarf hiding his bloated neck, Cap Jay looked like a joker applying for a job in a circus.

'Even here you are high? Shameless character,' said Akash.

'Cut the crap,' scowled Cap Jay. 'Pat removed me, the co-owner, from the dressing room. And you are having fun? Any idea what's happening in the team?'

'I don't need to know; Pat's in charge,' replied Akash in a calm voice.

'But one of the two owners should watch the team,' said Cap Jay, softening his tone. 'Pat won't let me. You tell him to correct his behaviour.'

'Never! I won't curtail Pat's autonomy,' said Akash.

Kanika walked towards Akash, caressing her long hair flying in the breeze. His body temperature rose to boiling point.

'But I won't interfere in the cricket,' snapped Cap Jay. 'Just make sure nothing fishy happens.'

'Is something bad happening there?' said Akash, struggling with his heavy breathing. 'They are just playing cricket...for God's sake. Somoresh will watch them.'

'Do you want trouble?' asked Cap Jay and sat on the ground. 'Remember the match-fixing shit? It happened in unmonitored dressing rooms.'

Akash watched Kanika as she stopped to talk to someone else.

'So I should make the biggest criminal the prefect of the class,' he asked. 'Don't violate the rules, Captain. Focus on your wine and women and let the professionals do their jobs.'

'Balls to the rules,' growled Cap Jay. He smeared his white linen trousers with mud while getting up from the ground. 'They can't treat me like shit. Yesterday I invited the team to my farmhouse for a party, and they refused. Why? Visiting my farmhouse is not against the rules. Pat is not allowing me to see the team practice, while Divya is around all the time with her friends. The players don't talk to me or join me for a drink…'

'They are not here to party,' snapped Akash. 'I heard you offered,' he made virtual quotations marks in the air with his fingers, 'an endless supply of women.'

'Are they are not fucking around?' snapped Cap Jay. 'Partying every day in the hotel…'

'After-parties are a part of ICCL.'

'It's your doing, isn't it?' asked Cap Jay, smiling. 'You asked them to ignore me…to insult me.'

'I don't have time for nonsense,' said Akash.

'Soon you will have time…' smirked Cap Jay, shaking a finger. 'When I invest in the Omkar Group.'

Akash smiled. 'No, you won't. You know the consequences.'

'I don't fear you.'

'Fine, try me.'

'Ok, I will.'

'Now fuck off.'

Cap Jay tried to respond, but Vikram Singh pulled him away just as Kanika arrived.

'Hi there…long time!' said Kanika, flashing her signature smile which was a sexy amalgamation of confidence and coyness.

'No time to meet me, huh?' asked Akash, shaking her hand. A current of thrill passed through his veins as he stroked the back of her palm with his thumb. 'What have I ever done to make you treat me so disrespectfully?' he asked, mimicking the famous line from the movie *The Godfather*.

Kanika pulled back her hand and bowed. 'Forgive me, Don Upadhyay.'

'So, what brought you back here…my passionate cousin or my enigmatic brother-in-law?'

'Neither! Just trying new things in life,' said Kanika. 'Congrats on buying a cricket team. It's visionary to invest in sports.'

'I wanted to draw you to India,' said Akash, smiling.

Kanika blushed. 'So refreshing to see your funny side.'

'Yes, it provides relief from the heat...which you have increased,' Akash said, looking at the sun. 'How do you maintain your awesome figure?'

Kanika laughed, punching Akash lightly on the chest. 'Yoga, and...'

Akash winked. 'And...lots of sex? Your ex-boyfriend has lost his fizz...carrying kitbags for my team,' he smirked. 'He can't perform; but you can help him...'

The sudden change in Akash's demeanour wiped the smile from Kanika's face.

Akash put his hand on her shoulder. 'Think whether your friends are useful—especially that drunkard joker, Cap Jay. Will he cause problems for you and Neil? Should you dump him and join my team?' Akash smiled as he hugged Kanika. 'Let's meet to discuss this. I will satisfy a gorgeous woman like you—I promise.'

The New Delhi Royals won the first ICCL match by a narrow margin that evening. Akash left soon after the last ball. He refused to meet the players or attend a felicitation ceremony the ICCL Governing Council had planned for him. He switched off from the match and analysed Cap Jay's next steps. Cap Jay's investors would skin him alive if he didn't provide information about the team. How would he gain access? Fund Gagan? Promise to help Neil? Maybe use his friendship with Kanika to influence Neil? Would Neil's love for the game survive against the force of his unfulfilled desires?

Newspapers Lie

Next Day, Late Evening

The excessive celebrations within the New Delhi Royals team worried Neil. He feared the fluke success in the first match had blinded the team from reality. A lousy strategy might produce short-term success but wouldn't help them win the ICCL. By the time people realized their mistake, it would be too late.

He had felt violated by Pat and Sudhir's arrogance during breakfast that morning. *'Read and learn about confidence and a positive attitude. You coach kids; learn how not to screw up their attitudes,'* Sudhir had said, throwing the newspaper towards him.

'Your doomsday prophecies did not come true,' Pat had said when Neil pointed out Antonio had performed below par by leaking 47 runs in 4 overs. *'Do you have a personal problem with Antonio? He softened the batsmen with pace, which helped other bowlers get wickets,'* Sudhir added.

Neil feared Sudhir's support would encourage Pat to play Antonio in all the matches.

Neil scanned the newspaper report.

> NDR won the toss and batted first even after the cricket pundits said it was more prudent to chase in an unfamiliar format. They created an experienced batting unit comprising players with extensive international experience, and in the bowling department, they bet on a pace attack, going against the conventional wisdom of using a spin attack in India. They made a slow start, with the openers Dinesh Singh and Jeffrey Beer scoring only 13 runs in the first 4 overs and they lost quick wickets when they tried to score at a rapid rate to reach a final score of 136 runs in the allotted 20 overs. Kyle Slinger was the highest scorer, with 42 runs in 33 balls, and none of the top order players scored over 15 runs.
>
> In response, the Chennai team started well, with the openers Callum Hawkes and Eshan Acharya scoring 38 runs in the first 4 overs. The Australian fast bowler Antonio Charles bowled a wrong line and conceded 47 runs in 4 overs. But

an unfortunate run out in the fifth over triggered a collapse, and they lost 7 wickets in the next 6 overs. The late order tried to recover from the situation, but Baldev Madan took 2 wickets in the eighteenth over to choke Chennai and win the game, with 7 balls to spare.

In the post-match interaction with the media, the belligerent Sudhir Yadav praised the coach Pattrick O'Donnell for the creative team selection and match strategy. He said the team could take its own decisions and did not need the advice of the so-called 'experts' who criticized others when they had achieved nothing significant in their own careers.

Neil sighed. The atmosphere in the team had changed in the last twenty-four hours. Even the junior players with no chance of ever playing a game behaved as if they had won the tournament. What were they celebrating? They wouldn't get credit for the team's performance. Shouldn't they rather hope others didn't do well, so they had the opportunity to play?

Conflicting loyalties traumatized Neil. Did he really want the team to win? What would he prefer—the team's success which would prove him wrong or its failure which would prove him right? He indulged himself with visions of an ideal world where he became the head coach when the team won after following his advice. Sadly, the real world was far removed from the tantalizing world of his dreams.

Later in the evening, Neil met a former girlfriend who had hounded him for a date since his arrival in Bengaluru that morning for Delhi's second match. Although desperate for a release from his mental cage, he declined her invitation for a night of guilt-free sex.

'After you, I have met no one with such a great body. Please!' she had said, pleading for a dalliance for old times' sake. But Kanika's attraction prevailed over the romantic mood created by the large whiskey sours and the retro pop music in The 13th Floor's lounge. Neil's quarrel with Kanika the previous night had cast a dark shadow on his consciousness. He had blasted Kanika when she had advised him to align with Cap Jay to gain leverage in the team.

'Why are you canvassing for him? He wants to sleep with you. I can't become friendly with a lecherous womanizer who misbehaves with Nandini and lives only to drink and fuck every woman who crosses his path,' he had said.

'I don't need your permission to sleep with anyone. No one can arm-twist me. When you tried the last time, I left. Again you are doing the same,' she had said before slamming the door on his face.

Should he call Kanika? Would an outreach forever compromise his autonomy in their relationship? Maybe she was right about working with Cap Jay, but she couldn't expect him to forgive the insults Nandini and he had faced from that slimeball.

Kanika cannot dictate my approach to life. I would rather perish than take Cap Jay's help. She will have to apologize if she wants to restart our relationship; otherwise it's goodbye.

He checked his messages once more before switching off the phone for the night.

The Prodigal Son

Three Days Later, Morning

'Rohit never visits me,' cried Madhu, burying her wet face in Akash's chest. 'You are coming here after so many years. I am dead for you...'

'Don't cry, ma, we will come...' said Akash. 'Now get me your famous ginger tea and coconut cookies.'

Akash felt hollow inside for making empty promises, but what could he do? The poor woman lived in this soulless house with criminals who didn't care for her well-being. He adored her. She was the only person who had supported Divya when she had moved to Upadhyay Palace after marriage. Everyone else had tried to control how she dressed, ate and talked, as if she had grown up in a jungle.

These retards didn't know Divya's dad could have bought them out with loose change from his bank balance.

Madhu's emotional outburst over the phone had forced him to rush to Upadhyay Palace that morning. Was dad using her for emotional blackmail? She had never imposed on him. Then why this sudden outreach?

I haven't visited this damned place in four years.

He walked through the expansive corridors of the once-bustling mansion and noticed the decoration on the walls had not changed since he had moved out. Grandma's fortress had no new stories to tell. The negative vibes in the air choked his senses. The chronic jealousy and desperate sighs of the inmates screamed out from the walls. Apart from his mother, there was nothing valuable there.

Sudha clapped as Akash entered her home-office. 'The prodigal son returns home. A rare honour for us to welcome a person of your stature in this humble place.'

Akash ignored the smirks from Ramesh and Gagan. 'Can we discuss? I need to leave ASAP.'

'Please don't mind your mom's call,' said Ramesh, smiling. 'She has done a lot for you and deserves...'

'Let me worry about her, dad!' snapped Akash. He realized dad had forced mom to call him that morning. An emotional pitch was the last resort of the incompetent; it wouldn't work.

Driving mom against me? How much lower can you fall, dad?

'We need urgent funds for our new projects,' Sudha gave Akash a printout. 'Look; we can turn the fortunes of the company around.'

Akash smiled and tossed the printout. 'Yes, I know...I gave you the projects. What's Jayshankar's timeline for funding?'

'Should take another two–three months,' said Ramesh.

'Has he started the paperwork?' asked Akash.

Sudha scowled. 'He is busy with his "diverse" activities...' She fumed at Ramesh. 'I had warned you...'

'So, what were we supposed to do?' shouted Ramesh. 'Let the company die?'

'We had an alternative,' said Sudha in a calm voice.

'Bullshit.'

'Can we focus on this meeting?' intervened Akash. 'Please fight after I leave. The industry minister is...'

Ramesh stopped Akash. 'We want to borrow money from the market. We are growing, so no reason for you to object.'

Akash frowned. 'I won't allow new liabilities while I am the biggest shareholder. Please buy out my shares before you borrow money.'

'But we can't till Jayshankar invests,' said Sudha.

Akash smiled as a deafening silence enveloped the room. Their never-say-die attitude impressed him. They wanted him to help them borrow money in his name so they could buy him out with the same money.

What are they, hippies? Living in la la land?

'Give us a personal loan,' said Ramesh.

'I can, but I will need collateral,' said Akash, amused by his father's pretentious behaviour.

He wants to coax me into doling out my hard-earned money by feeding me ginger tea and coconut biscuits.

'How dare you!' scowled Gagan, clenching his fists.

Akash moved his chair away from Gagan.

If he attacks me, I will finish him for good. The police will break his bones in the lockup.

'What collateral?' asked Ramesh.

'Shares of the company,' said Akash. 'I can give you a small personal loan without collateral. You won't have to repay it. You and grandma have always taught me to follow the due process in business.'

Ramesh smiled and shook his head.

'I will send a few more clients this week and more next month,' Akash told Sudha. 'Does this prove my loyalty?'

Sudha rose from her chair and pinned Akash with her stern gaze. 'Send us the paperwork for the loan, and we will see,' she said, and rushed out without added courtesies towards her illustrious visitor.

On his way back from Upadhyay Palace, Akash learnt his marketing team had hired the Bollywood star Sheetal Nandkarni as the brand ambassador of AlphaX Technologies.

He sent a text to Jagatjit Puri, the head of marketing at AlphaX.

```
Good work, Jag. Organize the first meeting tonight
at the Amrish farmhouse. Ensure privacy and SOP
suitable for such meetings.
```

He relaxed in the back seat of his Bentley and wondered how Sudhir Yadav would react if he found out his girlfriend was sleeping around to gain lucrative endorsement contracts. Maybe he wouldn't care. After a person becomes part of upper-class society, he loses the 'middle-class morality'.

But I can use this to deflate his ego if he ever challenges my diktat.

Divya had created a ruckus when a newspaper had published a photo of Akash hugging a model five years ago. But she had forgotten his infidelity when she had seen the large diamond ring he had got for her. She did not care even after it was clear he was sleeping with the model. Now he had given her a bigger diamond—a cricket team. The secret to controlling people was to engage them in things much bigger than their understanding so that they were never able to focus on the real issues.

Our politicians have mastered this art long ago. We can learn a lot from them.

He flipped through the Sheetal Nandkarni book.

So she has described the fantasies of old men. Now she will learn about the fantasies of business tycoons.

The Edge of Compromise

Two Days Later, New Delhi, Late Morning

A rasping voice rang out from the darkness as Neil entered his hotel room.

'Two losses in a row; explain this, Mr Assistant Coach.'

'Who the fuck!' Neil shouted. Reeling from the adrenalin rush, he produced a bat from his kitbag. 'Stop! Don't you dare…'

He switched on the lights and saw Cap Jay on the couch. 'Fuck! How?'

Cap Jay peered over his glasses with his hands clasped behind his head. 'We are losing,' he said in a low voice, 'while the coach, assistant coach, manager, physiotherapist and other highly paid halfwits are farting away to glory.'

'Ask Pat, not me,' said Neil and collapsed on the bed. After three hours of bowling in the sweltering heat, he couldn't take bullshit from an angel, let alone from this imbecile.

Cap Jay poked Neil on his chest. 'Why are we losing? I want the truth,' he shouted. 'No bullshit, no passing the buck, just the truth.'

Neil struggled with extreme fatigue. His career had just touched its lowest point. Apart from carrying drinks for players who were toddlers when he had played for India, he was also explaining the decisions of an arrogant coach and his cronies. Cap Jay behaved as if he was unaware of the power structure in the team.

Bastard!

Cap Jay charged toward Neil. 'Hey! You won't answer?'

'Don't you know I am just a ball boy?' snapped Neil. He rose from the bed and opened the door. 'Now please leave.'

Cap Jay sighed and sat on the couch. 'Trust me, I didn't know Pat has become a dictator. He should use your experience. No wonder we are losing.' He patted the seat next to him. 'Come, sit. Tell me the whole story.'

Neil closed the door. 'The team lacks cohesion and players don't have defined roles,' he said. 'The junior Indian players lack training for this level. They are not treated with respect and thus they are afraid and demotivated. Antonio's strategy for the fast bowlers is wrong, but he won't listen. Pat is not asking the batsmen to improvise their shots or adjust the pace of the game according to the situation. Our fielding sucks, but Pat does not even discuss fielding in team meetings. I don't think he understands the T20 format. He is still playing his favourite foreign players even after they have failed in every match. He is not interested in the Indian all-rounders who can add a lot of value…'

'You train the junior players,' said Cap Jay.

'Pat won't let me,' snapped Neil.

Cap Jay paced the room. 'Hmm! I must tell Akash.'

'Isn't Divya running the team?' asked Neil.

'Nonsense! That bitch is trying to be a TV celebrity.'

Neil ignored his fears of Cap Jay and hoped for a breakthrough. 'So, what's your plan?'

'Build a strong case for Akash,' said Cap Jay. 'Use solid evidence, otherwise Pat will escape the blame.' He snorted with eyes closed. 'Sportsmen always get the benefit of the doubt. But now we will expose their bluff.' Cap Jay hugged Neil. 'Help me rescue this team from Pat's tyranny. Will you?'

'Yes!'

Cap Jay bounced with joy. 'Great! Give me real-time information about the team.'

Neil wondered how he would stall Cap Jay's orders for 'real-time' information. It was a delicate situation that required a compromise, a middle path. Finally he had ditched the idealism Kanika had flagged as the biggest obstacle to his success. He smiled. 'Ah Captain! I will tell you everything except give information for the upcoming match. That's confidential; there will be serious trouble if it leaks.'

'How will it leak? I am a team owner, not an outsider.'

'But still, it is against the rules—instructions of the anti-corruption unit.'

'Are you interested in helping the team?' shouted Cap Jay.

Neil spread his arms to protest. 'Do I have to answer?'

'Yes! Everyone, including you, is under the scanner. Seems like you are not ready to become the next head coach.'

'I will give information after the match.'

'How will it help?'

'Why not? It will be current data.'

'After the match, Pat can always explain his decisions. We must stop him before the match; otherwise we will lose,' said Cap Jay. 'You can show Akash how your plans differed from Pat's only if you speak out in real time. After the match, anyone can appear intelligent.'

Neil excused himself for a bathroom break to think through the matter. Had Kanika sent Cap Jay to his room? Why? An indirect way of making them meet? Why did he need real-time information? Match-fixing? Did Akash suspect Cap Jay? Is that why he had ordered Pat to sideline Cap Jay?

'I can give Somoresh Basu my suggestions,' said Neil as he emerged from the bathroom. 'Later he can tell Akash.'

'Now don't get smart with me,' snapped Cap Jay. 'I will throw your ass off the team. From a ball boy you will become a security guard at the stadium.' He sighed. 'Sorry, bro. I am just sad the team's losing. Can't blame you for not trusting me here.' He hugged Neil again. 'Sorry for my bad behaviour. Please forgive me.'

Cap Jay's odd mix of threats, abuses and apologies convinced Neil his analysis was correct.

The bastard is trying to fool me by dangling a lollipop. Let him shove the lollipop up his own ass.

'I'll leave—let you think this through,' said Cap Jay. 'Please cooperate to help the team…otherwise you can't convince Akash to make you the head coach.'

'You want to grab a drink at the bar?'

Cap Jay got no response; he shrugged and left the room.

Coach or Ballboy?

Next Day, Morning

You tried to sabotage the team by playing the victim? Did you consult the PR manager before talking to the media? I need an explanation.

Neil realized this terse message from Pat written on a newspaper cutting was a fallout of rejecting Cap Jay's overtures. No other human being other than Cap Jay had such perennial spite for decency and civilization. He read the newspaper article.

New Delhi Royals Assistant Coach Is Now a Ball Boy

Former India player Neil Upadhyay works as practice bowler; carries drinks for the team. It is never a pleasant sight to see a former sportsman who has represented India compromising his dignity for trivial gains. Sportsmen are role models and when they lose their self-respect and pride, it destroys everything we hold dear in a civilized society.

Neil Upadhyay's family owns the Omkar Group of Industries. While other cricketers struggled under challenging conditions, Mr Upadhyay's wealthy and influential family propped up his career by providing expensive equipment, state-of-the-art facilities and the best coaching for him in England and Australia. A dedicated set of people worked on his bowling action, diet, exercise regimen and physiotherapy. He would never have played for India had his powerful family not lobbied for him.

Neil Upadhyay had a semi-successful career at the international level. He got repeated chances—and the jury is still out about how many of those chances he deserved—but he did not give the Indian team a dependable fast bowler. He repeatedly got into trouble with the cricket board and the team management, and eventually, this sorry saga ended with his retirement five years ago. Indian cricket would have been better served if more serious, diligent and down-to-earth cricketers got the opportunities he wasted. If he was not serious about cricket, then why did he become a cricketer? He could have enjoyed his wealth without troubling the country with his cricket.

For the ICCL, Neil Upadhyay lobbied hard in his family to secure a coaching position in the New Delhi Royals team owned by his cousin, Mr Akash Upadhyay, a highly respected global businessman. They appointed him as assistant coach to mentor the junior Indian players in the team. But the head coach, Mr Pattrick O'Donnell, did not use his skills, which led to their defeat in three successive matches. Instead of using him to train the fast bowlers, Pat made Neil a practice bowler and a ball boy, which are roles generally given to junior players. Reliable sources in the team have informed us off the record that the team can benefit a lot from Neil's experience, but Mr O'Donnell is an obstinate individual who refuses to change even after his strategy has failed.

Against this backdrop, we again question why Neil Upadhyay would accept such humiliation if he is a serious cricketer. His compromise reflects poorly on the other cricketers who have represented India at the highest level, and humiliates Indian cricket.

Why is Neil Upadhyay not resigning? He owes an explanation to this country where cricket is a religion and cricketers are 'Gods'.

Neil knew Pat could use this article to oust him from the team unless he exposed Cap Jay first. The article mentioned Pat's role in the team's poor performance, so maybe he could use it to implicate both him and Cap Jay. He pondered about his options and decided to inform Akash through a text message.

```
Hi, please read the article in today's IA newspaper
about why our team is losing. I can help the team.
Let's talk.
```

No reply. After an hour, he messaged Akash again.

```
BTW, Cap Jay met me yesterday. Wanted information
about the team to persuade you to remove Pat. I
refused to give info. Just wanted to let you know.
```

Again, no reply from Akash. What now? Should he contact Divya? She was staying in the same hotel. How would he do that? Barge into her room? She would scream, but he had no other choice. She wouldn't give him an appointment if he called her. He should exploit her anger about the team's performance. A bold approach might create a place for him in her plans.

Neil saw a 'Do Not Disturb' sign hanging from Divya's door and dithered about ringing the doorbell. But soon the hotel staff arrived to deliver breakfast and solved his problem. She couldn't blame him any more for disturbing her sleep; the hapless busboy would weather the storm. He would appear only after the busboy had entered her room.

'Excuse me, sir!' the busboy knocked on the door. 'Breakfast, sir! Room service.'

Sir? Why is he calling her 'sir'? Is this the right room?

'This is Divya Upadhyay's room, right?' he asked the busboy.

'Yes, sir! An Iranian delegation has booked all the suites, so she is staying in this room for now.'

The locks clicked, and Francis Hale (junior cricketer from New Zealand) opened the door, struggling to wrap a towel around his otherwise naked body.

Shocked beyond belief, Neil peeked inside and saw Divya lying face down on the bed with her bare arms exposed over the sheets. She stirred and turned as the busboy placed the tray on a table.

Divya screamed and covered herself. 'What are you doing here?' she shouted at Neil. 'You mannerless asshole…barging into my room.'

Francis Hale hurried over to the door. 'Leave, mate! Give us some privacy,' he said, pushing the door on Neil's face.

'Please! I found the door open. Can I talk to Divya? Just five minutes…'

'No, you can't,' snapped Francis Hale. 'Fuck off, or we will call security.'

'Sure! Call security and explain what you two are doing here,' said Neil. He smiled and shook his head. 'I won't tell if you don't. You have more to lose than me…so chill.'

'Never again should I see that bastard near my room,' screamed Divya, as Francis Hale shut the door. 'Ask the hotel to post a guard outside my room.'

'Fucking a player her son's age, while giving sermons about teamwork and high standards,' muttered Neil as he walked away. He awoke to a new reality about his environment. The owners didn't care about winning, and their standards and opinions changed as per convenience. Fair play, sportsmanship and good personal conduct were lofty concepts only for brand-building, not for driving the team's culture. He had been naïve to follow Pat's orders like a loyal dog. The owners were in no position to fire him after this article exposing Pat had been released. The media would ask questions, and the fans would rebel if they punished him. All gloves were off now. He would speak out about the team's problems. Working as a practice bowler was also out of the question. After losing every match, Pat wouldn't have the nerve to face the public.

Pebble in the Shoe

Later That Morning

Akash read the newspaper article and admired Neil's resilience.

The bastard has integrity; gets kicked in his face every day, but still fights.

So, how would the game of cat-and-mouse play out between Jayshankar and Neil? The debauched motherfucker would unleash Kanika on Neil. Every man had a fatal weakness, a breaking point. Did Kanika still have the power to persuade him?

Neil will get screwed if she succeeds. If she fails, Jayshankar will go with Gagan, and then he will get screwed.

'Jayshankar did this,' he told Somoresh Basu. 'Neil and Pat are not fools; won't fuck their own asses.'

'But it's true, sir,' said Somoresh, standing like a statue near Akash. 'Pat has sidelined Neil, just as you wanted.'

'And Jayshankar?'

'Sir, he is now staying in our hotel.'

'Why?'

'I don't know, sir. He will also travel with the team.'

'Why are we losing?' snapped Akash.

'Sir, the players are not performing. We included two players Neil had suggested in the last match, but even then we lost.'

'Why?'

'Bad atmosphere in the team, sir; there are groups...'

'Neil's doing this?'

'No, sir; it does not involve him.'

'Then?'

'Sir, please ask Pat. He always tries to deflect the blame. Now he is using this article to accuse Neil of spoiling the team's culture.'

'He barged into my office this morning without an appointment,' scowled Akash. 'Tried to arm-twist me into sacking Neil. I sent him packing...the asshole. Fled when I asked him to guarantee we will win if we remove Neil.'

Akash's competitive DNA couldn't accept the ugly reality that success in business couldn't guarantee success in sports. He imagined his competitors mocking him for his loser team and vowed revenge. Life was not fair; the other team owners didn't have a fraction of his net worth. Yet, they were winning, and his team was fighting about newspaper reports. This should not have happened to him, but it did because he had been foolish enough to import a dinosaur all the way from South Africa—a tired old guy who had no original ideas and who wore tracksuits to official meetings. Pat had cheated him. One day he would make him pay dearly for his betrayal.

'Ask the PR team to dismiss this report,' said Akash. 'You, Pat and Sudhir should solve the team's problems. If Divya complains about the results, or anyone else disturbs me…then heads will roll. I will fire you first.'

Somoresh Basu was too shocked to speak. His eyes popped out as if he was having a stroke.

'Now get out before I kick your ass. Leave!'

'Call my father,' Akash ordered his assistant on the intercom.

On his desk lay a letter from the chief financial officer of the Omkar Group.

Thank you for your offer to extend us a business loan.

Upon a careful review of the proposed contract, we find the following terms and conditions in violation of basic norms of decency and goodwill expected from an organization owned by a member of the Upadhyay family.

- *Reduction of loan period from the agreed upon 2 years to 6 months*
- *Valuation of the Omkar Group using 25 per cent of the market value of shares is juvenile, bordering on idiotic*
- *Inclusion of a full ratchet clause and the provision for seizing the personal assets of the signatories in case of loan default*

Since we are no longer in need of financial help, we reject your loan offer and express our disinterest in any further renegotiation of this contract.

Akash worried about his father's survival instincts and singular ability to change a game in his favour. Had they won the lottery? Or was it some other scam? The aggressive tone of this letter showed they had a concrete plan. Was this Jayshankar's way of warning him he meant business?

The intercom buzzed. 'Sir, your father is on Line 1.'

'Hello, Akash beta, how are things?'

Ramesh Upadhyay's cheerful voice rang alarm bells in Akash's mind.

'Beta'? I have never heard such a word of endearment in the last ten years. What is the deal here?

'You don't need the loan any more?' Akash asked in a stern voice.

'Beta, I want to share fantastic news. We will get Jayshankar's money in about six weeks.'

Akash gasped as his heart pounded in his obese chest like a sledgehammer. How had Jayshankar bypassed him? He had made a big mistake by underestimating that slimy womanizer. How would he stop the investment at such short notice?

'Congratulations! Finally Jayshankar has delivered,' said Akash.

'Yes, beta, by the grace of God...'

Akash flinched on hearing the 'beta' again and prayed his father would stop mocking him with excessive endearment.

The poor man does not realize that one day it will come back to bite him.

'What is he offering for my shares?' asked Akash.

'20 per cent over the market rate. I hope you will settle and not create a problem.'

'I might get better value in the market...'

'We will match it, don't worry. Take one week and come back to us if you have a better offer.'

Ramesh Upadhyay's overuse of the collective 'we' amused Akash. His father was feeling tall by standing on Cap Jay's shoulders. Partnering with Cap Jay was like riding a roller coaster without a safety belt. It would thrill him till it dumped him in the next turn.

'What are you paying the other shareholders?'

'None of your business,' snapped Ramesh. 'They can decide for themselves. Don't interfere.'

'I can easily find out.'

'Go ahead. But it won't help you. Over 40 per cent shares are with the public. They will sell if we offer a good price. So, even if you don't sell, we will become the majority shareholders and take control of the board by buying from the public.'

'Send me the papers, and I will see,' said Akash.

'You will have the papers today and then one week to respond,' said Ramesh in a cold voice. 'We won't allow you to delay...'

'I don't want to delay anything, but my team has to review and plan,' shouted Akash. 'God! What's got into you? This is a major transaction...I can't hurry.'

'After one week we will buy from the market.'

'Okay.'

'Even a world-famous businessman like you can't throw me out of my house so easily,' said Ramesh, laughing. 'Remember I made you, and not the other way round. Show humility and grace sometimes.'

'Who is throwing you out? Are you daydreaming?'

'Yes, right, beta...as if I understand nothing. Anyway...the tide has turned now. You are already out of our lives. So, beta, take this offer and get out of the company as well,' said Ramesh and disconnected the call.

Burning with anger, Akash smashed his phone on his desk.

He took a few deep breaths to calm down and then analysed the matter. Surrender was out of the question; he would defeat the dark forces ganged up against him. They had not seen his real power and did not realize he could do anything to protect his interests. No more discussions, negotiations or compromises. Jayshankar's time was up. He would fall into a bottomless abyss and pull everyone down with him.

Enjoy your happiness while it lasts, dad. It will be over soon.

Booze and Brawl

Two Days Later

'Rome was not built in a day, my friend,' Arif Khan doffed his hat. 'No one cares for an ex-cricketer. I sucked the dicks of important people for a long time to avoid oblivion.'

He laughed and patted Neil on his back. 'For example, look at my career as a TV commentator. Former cricketers who can talk come a dime a dozen, but I got the job because I knew the broadcaster. Simple!'

Freshly imported from South Africa, Jeffrey Beer's curvy blonde girlfriend ruled the dance floor at the post-match party that night. The twirling skirts and shaking bellies pumped the deflated spirits of the boys. The revelry snowballed, riding on tequila shots and champagne cocktails, buoyed by the choicest world music, ranging from Shakira's 'Whenever, Wherever' to Daler Mehndi's 'Bolo Ta Ra Ra Ra' and Enrique Iglesias' 'Bailamos'. Bollywood starlets and guests of sponsors shed their inhibitions and saturated the air with fluorescent lipstick, expensive cologne, lace and lycra, balancing the testosterone-heavy bunch with hot pants, mini skirts and spaghetti tops.

'The head coach of Mumbai? How?' Neil asked Arif, his voice slurry from consuming four large whiskey sours in twenty minutes. He envied Arif more than anybody else in this world. Why was he so adored when he had achieved nothing significant as a cricketer? Neil had been more successful as a cricketer, yet Arif became a head coach, and he didn't.

'Perception management—my friend,' said Arif, frowning. 'Even after sixty years of independence, we are still in awe of the white man. Please tell me why most of the franchises have hired foreigners as coaches. Don't we have great cricketers in India?' Arif thought for a moment and gulped down his drink. 'It makes me furious Indians don't value their own people. So I fought it…'

'How?'

'By manipulating the owners to make them believe they will lose out if they don't hire me. It wouldn't have worked had I applied for the job, so I used people they trust to prove my credentials as a coach.'

Neil shook his head. 'Does it work?'

'It does,' said Arif. 'We have played together for India, and I know you are talented. But who else believes in you? Absolute reality is a myth, my friend; perceived reality is everything. If the perception about you is wrong, the reality does not matter, does it?'

'This is not my way,' said Neil, shaking his head. 'I enjoy simplicity, and maybe that's why I am a cricketer. Sports is unambiguous; performance is not subject to interpretation…or, as you will say, "perceived reality".'

'Fair enough,' said Arif, smiling. 'But what would you enjoy more—your simplicity, or beating a team owned by one of the richest men in the country and coached by a great white man, a South African legend of cricket? We dismissed you guys for 49 runs today. For me, the opportunity to create such a debacle makes all my backdoor maneuvering worthwhile.'

Harmony and cohesion prevailed in the New Delhi Royals dressing room despite the ignominy of a crushing loss against The Brave Marathas of Mumbai. Coaches, support staff and players, both junior and senior, foreign and Indian, drank and danced with their wives and girlfriends till the wee hours of the morning, creating an atmosphere of camaraderie never seen before in the team.

'Four losses in a row—not looking good for you guys. None of your batsmen reached double figures today. But no one is bothered,' Arif pointed towards the frenzy on the dance floor. 'Do they work so hard at the nets?'

'We can only go up from here,' said Neil, succumbing to alcohol-induced optimism. 'This loss can inspire us to fight.'

'Did you meet Kanika?' asked Arif.

Neil snorted. 'Yeah.'

'So…?'

'So what? Nothing!'

'Not trying to get back together?'

'Naah! Relationships are complicated. I am happy that even after thirteen years we have at least kept our friendship.'

Arif laughed. 'So, you do want a relationship. As they say, *never believe in anything till it is officially denied*. You are a terrible liar, my friend.'

Neil twisted his face. 'I have no interest…'

'Where is she?' Arif looked around the room.
'No idea; maybe in Jaipur for the earlier match…'
'And your colourful brother-in-law?'
'Cap Jay? I heard he is in Dubai.'
Arif grinned. 'He is the life of a party; a truckload of fun.'
'Oh! He is your friend as well?' asked Neil.
'You bet! But why haven't you used his connections?'
'I can't; I prefer to keep my dignity instead.'

The sound of a scuffle drew Neil's attention towards the dance floor.

'Bastard!' yelled Jeffrey and rammed his knee into Vineet Srivastav's stomach. The music stopped, and a hush engulfed the room as Vineet doubled up and fell.

Jeffrey charged towards Vineet again, but Antonio and the other foreign players pulled him away. 'He was molesting my girlfriend. Bloody native—has forgotten his position.'

Vineet writhed in a foetal position on the floor while Jeffrey Beer continued his tirade from a distance. 'Motherfucker! Wants to play cricket. He should wash toilets,' shouted Jeffrey and tried to break free from Antonio's grip, but the veteran Australian fast bowler was too strong for him.

Neil rushed over and supported Vineet into a sitting position. 'Stomach hurting?' he asked in a cold voice.

Vineet shook his head but looked dazed as the physiotherapist checked his eyes. Neil tried to haul him into a chair, but he fell back with a groan. He clutched his stomach and puked all over himself.

'Take him to his room and make sure there are no internal injuries,' Neil instructed the team's physiotherapist. 'Call a doctor if needed.'

The party was over. Within minutes the crowd thinned out, leaving the New Delhi Royals behind to manage their crisis.

On the other side of the room, Pat, Sudhir and a bunch of foreign players surrounded Jeffrey Beer who breathed like a steam engine. Antonio poured a bucket of water on Jeffrey to cool him down.

At a distance, Jeffrey's girlfriend stood cross-armed, looking apologetic for the commotion she had caused. 'He was not doing anything,' she said. 'Why do you drink so much?'

'Yeah! Wasn't doing anything—just making out with you?' screamed Jeffrey. He took off his wet shirt and showed a maze of psychedelic tattoos on his pink skin. 'Always a whore wherever you go. Didn't I ask you not to mix with the natives here? But you can't help being a slut, can you?'

'Now calm down,' Pat said in a condescending voice. 'I will have to manage this shit—so don't create any more trouble. Go back to your room and don't talk to anyone till you hear from me. Understood?'

Pat summoned Somoresh Basu after Jeffrey and his entourage left the room through the back door.

'Impose a gag order on the team,' ordered Pat. He pointed towards Neil. 'And watch him. He is a high-risk category.'

Somoresh looked terrified of the impossible task imposed on him and tried to mumble a faint protest, but Pat dismissed him. 'Do your job. Earn your salary. You are not here to drink free booze. Call the PR manager to my room. We have to work on this tonight.'

Rebel with a Cause

Next Morning

The Jeffrey–Vineet brawl did not feature in the newspapers, radio or TV news the next morning. The only ICCL news the TV channels reported were the results of the previous day's matches and footage of promotional events attended by the glitterati. The New Delhi Royals had blanked out the embarrassing incident from the media.

Neil derided the media's unethical conduct. The phony journalists would go after defenseless people like him but let the high and mighty off the hook. They would sell their souls for a bottle of whiskey, or a free pass to a cricket match.

Bastards!

The immunity enjoyed by a foreigner who had assaulted an Indian player in India outraged him. The foreign players were making tons of money in an Indian tournament but they refused to respect the Indian players. Jeffrey had assaulted a teammate and deserved to go to jail, but here he wouldn't even offer an apology. Arif Khan was right. Indians still lived under the boots of the white man.

Not fair. I must help Vineet get justice.

The atmosphere was tense as the New Delhi Royals assembled for a meeting in the dressing room before the afternoon practice. No casual chit-chat, jokes or cricket analysis—players and staff sat in awkward silence, waiting for a catalyst to break the ice.

Pat walked in dressed in a brown sports jacket on top of the team's sky blue practice uniform. He peered through designer glasses perched low on his nose and looked like a lawyer ready to demolish his opposition in a packed courtroom. 'Our performance is pathetic so far,' he said. 'Our batting would embarrass even a school-level team. Please realize who we are and whom we are representing. The lower batting order, especially the number 4, 5 and 6 batsmen, have to take more responsibility. It cannot be business as usual.' Pat pulled out a printout from his hardbound leather folder. 'We will play the same team in our match against Punjab tomorrow. When the whole team has failed, we can't penalize only a few players. This is our best team and our best chance to win. Questions?'

Neil didn't question Pat's strategy as he did not want an argument about team selection to divert attention from the bigger issue at hand. Pat behaved as if nothing wrong had happened the previous night. He tried to brush the ugly incident under the carpet by selecting both Vineet and Jeffrey for the next game. How could they play together unless they resolve the matter?

'Come on, let's play,' Pat gestured towards the team to move. 'Today I will monitor the batsmen, so get ready to show me your A-class game.'

The team filed out of the dressing room, but Neil and a group of junior Indian players including Vineet Srivastav stayed in their seats.

'Pat—a word?' Neil called out as Pat reached the door.

'Sure!' said Pat, looking irritated. 'Can we talk while walking to the nets? We are already late.'

Neil shook his head, patting the seat next to him.

Pat walked towards Neil, cursing under his breath. 'What's this, Neil? I don't have the time…'

'Oh! Make the time,' said Neil. 'Jeffrey Beer will have to pay for his crime.'

Pat looked confused for a moment before light dawned on him. 'Oh! I see. You mean last night's party?' He snorted and shook his head. 'Such minor things happen when people spend so much time together. No big deal!'

Neil rose from his chair. 'Would it be a minor thing if Vineet had been at fault?'

'How is it not his fault?' Pat pointed towards Vineet. 'He misbehaved with Stella. I should have kicked Vineet out of the team, but I supported him as he is a good player and important for the team. I talked to Akash, managed the press and convinced Jeffrey to forgive him. But instead of being grateful, you are organizing a mob here?'

Neil approached Pat with his hands on his hips and stood almost on top of him. 'We were there, Pat,' he smiled. 'Stella said Vineet is innocent. Only you and Jeffrey claim it was Vineet's fault,' smirked Neil. 'Is it because Vineet is an Indian?'

'Will you shut up!' shouted Pat, and slid his chair back, away from Neil. 'You are the big protector of Indian pride here? This is not an Indian versus foreigner thing. Everyone was drunk, having a good time. Something unfortunate happened, which should not have happened. A misunderstanding, perhaps. Should we drag it on? For

God's sake, we have a match to play tomorrow.'

'No one will play the match,' said Neil, looking at his cohort. 'I warned you about the importance of maintaining mutual respect, but you favoured a coterie. The toxic culture you created has now blown up in your face. Now we can't move forward unless Jeffrey apologizes to Vineet in front of the whole team.'

Pat looked pensive. 'Hmm! Otherwise what happens? A rebellion?'

'Yes! An unfortunate but necessary thing to improve team dynamics,' said Neil. 'But we can avoid it with a sincere apology. I assure you neither the news of the fight nor the apology will ever leak out. It is my commitment to you.'

'I will get back to you on this,' said Pat. 'Give me a few hours.' Pat shook his finger at Neil and addressed the cohort. 'You have more to lose than he has. His career has long been over. So please come over for practice.' He smiled, but his eyes looked evil. 'This rebellion might satisfy your ego, but it will hurt your reputation and your future in both Indian and franchise cricket. Think! Should you make the enemies you are making?'

With those ominous words, Pat walked out of the room.

The New Delhi Royals practised that afternoon without the rebelling Indian players. Neil waited the whole day for an outreach from Pat or Somoresh, but nothing happened. By night, he became worried when they ignored his calls. He drank to soothe his nerves frayed by Pat's laidback approach to a major crisis in the team.

He felt sick in his stomach and struggled with extreme anxiety. Was there politics happening behind his back? But Pat could only delay the process, not stop it. He would have to negotiate before the match against Punjab. The team wouldn't be able to play the match without these players.

Pat might hate me, but he needs my help to get these boys back in the team.

Maybe Pat was buying time to cool down tempers and create the right environment for a compromise. His optimistic reasoning was probably far from the truth, but Neil could not find any other explanation for this impasse. He let the matter rest for the night.

No need to worry. There will be a solution first thing in the morning tomorrow.

A Goat Is the Leader of Sheep

Next Morning

    Meeting at 8.30 a.m. Conference room. Be on time.

Somoresh Basu's terse message irked Neil. He was relieved good sense had prevailed, but they needed a lesson or two in politeness. Such arrogance was not acceptable after committing the greatest sin in a cricket team. Players got life bans for assaulting teammates. Here they were not even ready to apologize.

'Why this false ego?' he muttered to himself while walking towards the conference room. 'They could have resolved this yesterday. We have better things to do on match day.'

Kudos to the boys for sticking to their stand. I won't compromise, won't let them down.

Twenty Minutes Later

'Come in...welcome,' Pat jumped up from his seat as Neil entered the conference room.

He escorted Neil to a chair. 'Made travel plans yet?' he grinned. 'You need a long vacation after having worked so hard. Very soon you will go far away from here,' Pat waved goodbye. 'Far, far away... from where you cannot see us...or brainwash our players.'

Somoresh Basu dropped a bombshell before Neil could make sense of Pat's jibes. 'So, Neil, Pat has complained you have incited the players to rebel against the team management.'

'Absolutely false,' shouted Neil, edgy about the abrupt shift in the situation. He tried to put up a brave front. 'Call the guys here; let them say this on my face.'

'Your buddies backstabbed you,' said Pat in a cold voice. 'They gave a written statement that they have no complaints against the team management, and that you forced them to rebel.'

Somoresh handed Neil a piece of paper. On it was a signed

statement by the six players, including Vineet, on whose behalf Neil was fighting.

Neil quickly analysed a few strategies for compromise but found nothing to offer in exchange for mercy. He cursed himself for lacking the foresight to preempt this coup and braced himself for the inevitable death sentence. They had screwed him while he had been chilling in his room. Only a brain-dead person lacking common sense would expect junior cricketers with no credentials to withstand the pressure from Pat and Somoresh.

I deserve this for trying to lead a herd of sheep.

'You are fired.' Pat shook Neil by his shoulder. 'Look at me when I talk,' he snapped. 'You are fired. You understand? Get your ass out of here, now!'

Somoresh pulled Pat away from Neil. 'I informed the hotel you will check out in the next thirty minutes,' he said. 'They will arrange a taxi to take you wherever you want to go in Delhi.'

'And you can keep the kitbag as a memento,' smirked Pat. 'You can see it every day...' he closed his eyes in a meditative pose, 'and dream.'

'I want to talk to the boys,' said Neil.

'No! Leave at once,' screamed Pat.

Somoresh pointed towards the door. 'The exit.'

'This is coming directly from Akash, in case you want to run to your uncle again,' said Pat. He snorted and twisted his mouth. 'How do you live with yourself? No gratitude for the family that feeds you?'

Neil had neither the energy nor the interest to argue his case any more. He was done. After meditating on his situation for a few moments, he walked out without speaking another word.

Fire, Smoke and Then Water

'Naivety and attitude problem have hurt your career,' Kanika's words rang in Neil's ears as he packed his luggage, eager to leave as soon as possible. He should have known everyone had sold their souls in that blasted setup. No one stood for the truth any more. But fools like him never learnt. Getting involved in someone else's fight? All his efforts had been flushed down the toilet by a foolish act.

He was ready to leave in fifteen minutes, but the hotel was late with the checkout formalities.

'There are six bags. Should I carry them myself?' he asked the help desk.

'Sir, there is a small problem we are trying to solve. Please wait. Can we send you a complimentary drink in the meantime?'

'No! I can't wait any more.'

'Sir, I promise to help you in the next ten minutes.'

Another thirty minutes passed, and Neil couldn't take it any more. *Assholes! And this is a five-star hotel.*

The doorbell rang as he carried two bags to the door.

'Thanks for your prompt service,' Neil scowled at the busboy. 'Now get going. Is my taxi ready, or will it take another hour?'

Instead of an apology, the busboy offered him a mobile phone. 'Sir, please take this call.'

Neil guessed the call was from the hotel's manager to inquire why he was leaving. He decided it was more prudent to finish the call quickly than risk a delay by refusing the exit interview.

'Hello?'

'Neil, it's Cap Jay—we need to talk. Urgent!'

'But why are you calling on this phone?'

Neil walked back into his room, and the busboy closed the door and left.

'Because I was not sure you would take my call. We have trust issues, and I am not in the country.'

'Okay! Fine. I am listening.'

'I heard what happened. Why didn't you inform me about the fight?'

'Pat had put a gag order.'

'So, becoming Pat's faithful dog has led you where?'

Comparison to a 'dog' hit his self-esteem, but Neil did not fire back, as Cap Jay was right. 'How would you have helped?'

'I would have asked you to take sworn affidavits from the players and use them to blackmail Pat.'

Neil smiled. 'Blackmail? I am not a criminal.'

Cap Jay laughed. 'You aren't, and that's why you are a dog, and that's why you need me.'

Cap Jay's jibes shocked Neil and enlightened him at the same time. He was beating himself up for intervening in someone else's fight when the real problem lay in his mishandling of the matter.

Neil sighed. 'You are right. I didn't think it through.'

'I can save you...'

'Thanks, but not interested.'

'Shut up! You are not a quitter,' scolded Cap Jay.

Neil felt Cap Jay's fury through the phone line, but he didn't care any more.

Cap Jay sighed. 'Neil! I always admired your resilience. You never gave up—despite all odds. Now you are quitting after all the hard work.'

'Didn't I tell you they fired me?' said Neil in a stern voice. The events of the morning and Cap Jay's overbearing attitude had exhausted his patience, pushing him to the brink of an explosion.

'I can help you,' said Cap Jay.

'No!'

'Neil—don't be a fool. And don't quit on your responsibilities.'

'Excuse me?'

'It's your family's team. Sure, you made a mistake, but you can't let the team perish in someone else's hands. What happened to your commitment to the game?'

Neil laughed. 'I have paid the price for my commitment. Why me—ask other people to commit.'

'Neil! If you leave, no one will remember it after two days. Only you will remember it for the rest of your life. And, I guarantee you—not a day will go by when you won't regret it.'

Even with a mindset bordering on delirium, Neil realized Cap Jay was right. The decision to retire from the Indian team taken in haste had created a lifetime of agony and regret for him. This decision would have the same result, especially after Cap Jay was offering him a way out of the mess.

He decided there was no harm in hearing Cap Jay out. He could always back out later.

'Okay! What's your plan?' he asked.

'Just save yourself for now. Later you can screw them,' said Cap Jay.

'How?'

'I made a deal with Akash; they will excuse you if you apologize.'

Neil tried to find a middle path between his anger and his ambitions. Compromising would lead to a loss of face, but Cap Jay's advice offered him a shot at redemption.

'Fine! I will do it.'

Neil knew this decision would make Kanika very proud.

I must apologize. Poor girl tried to help me. Why do I always drive away people who love me?

'Great! Let's work together going forward.'

Neil squeezed out a feeble reply. 'Okay.'

'You still don't trust me?'

'I am sorry. I trust you now,' Neil said, realizing he was again mishandling the situation. 'Completely!'

'Good! I will be back tomorrow. Meanwhile, call me directly if there is any issue. Don't even pee without asking me.'

Never Say Never

Same Day, Late Night

'Care for a drink? Nashik, not Naples…be Indian, drink Indian.' Neil examined the bottle of wine in his hand. 'Sula?'

Kanika leaned on her door, looking radiant in a chic black off shoulder evening gown. 'Peace offering…huh?' she asked.

'Promise of good times too,' Neil winked. 'Can I come in?'

Kanika flashed her famous toothy smile and moved back from the door. 'Sure! Make yourself comfortable.'

She walked to the bathroom with her phone. 'Just give me five minutes, and then I am all yours.'

Neil sat on the couch and examined her room. A huge bouquet of red roses in a crystal vase occupied the prime spot on the centre table, accompanied by an ice bucket containing a bottle of champagne. Scented candles burnt on a side table near the well-made bed, saturating the air with lavender and sandalwood. A few gift-wrapped packages lay in one corner of the clean, clutter-free room.

What is she celebrating? Perfect room, flowers, champagne, candles, sexy dress. Who sent her flowers?

Kanika returned, preoccupied with her phone, and sat on the couch, seemingly oblivious to his presence there.

'Expecting someone?' Neil asked, hoping she wasn't.

She put her phone away. 'Was there trouble in the after-party?'

'Cap Jay told you?' asked Neil. The couch creaked as he crossed his legs.

'Heard rumours…'

'Like what?'

Kanika picked up her phone but put it away without using it. 'About a fight…but I didn't enquire about it as it did not involve you. I have seen a lot worse.'

Neil wondered how to tell her his embarrassing story without destroying the little respect she might still have for him.

'Wine or champagne?' she asked. Without waiting for an answer, she uncorked the bottle of wine and the air was filled with a strong fruity aroma.

Kanika leaned forward to pour the wine, and her delicate cleavage peeped through her low-cut gown.

Neil breathed heavily as she gave him a glass. 'Twirl the wine before drinking,' she said and closed her eyes. She smelled the wine and groaned after the first sip. 'This is awesome. India produces such good wine?'

'Not just wine; some of the Indian whiskeys are also world class,' said Neil.

Kanika nodded and sipped the wine. 'So, you were not involved, right?' She put down her glass, suddenly looking alarmed. 'Please tell me you weren't.'

'Not in the fight, but later…we refused to practice until Jeffrey Beer apologized to Vineet.'

'"We" as in, the players?'

Neil nodded. 'Six junior Indian players.'

'But why?' asked Kanika, exasperated. 'When your own ass has no protection?'

'It was the right thing to do,' said Neil.

He noticed Kanika's irritation and tried to play it down. 'Not a big deal; it got sorted…'

'You blackmailed Pat?' she asked in a cold voice.

Neil looked down at the floor.

Fuck! She will hate me for this.

'Neil, what happened?'

'They fired me,' he avoided eye contact.

Kanika gasped.

'Relax! I survived. Cap Jay helped me,' Neil said, shaken by Kanika's reaction.

God! She really cares for me.

'I apologized to Pat and Jeffrey Beer.'

'In private?'

Neil smiled. 'In front of the whole team. But that's okay…' he tried again to lighten the matter. 'I realize now Pat doesn't care about winning matches. It is a game of controlling the team. Results be damned.'

'Who are you—a union leader?' snapped Kanika.

She jumped up from the couch and her abrupt movement toppled the wine bottle. 'Look at me when I am talking,' she shouted. 'How was this your business?'

'As a former India player and a coach, I thought it was my duty to guide the youngsters,' Neil tried to counter Kanika, without conviction.

'What nonsense!' Kanika said, raising her hand. 'They drink and fight, and you defend them? Who are you? Mother Teresa?'

Neil knew he had to come clean before Kanika. He would never get a better setting for sharing his motivations. She required information to understand him. 'I guess…deep inside me…I wanted to be the person they look up to.' He took a deep breath. 'People ask me why I am doing this.' Kanika watched in stoic silence, and Neil continued. 'Because I underutilized my privileges—a rich family and an uncle who cared for me like a dad.' He looked up with a sigh. 'I lost focus, rubbed people the wrong way, had bad luck, got injured at the wrong moments. I couldn't achieve greatness. And I don't want to give up without leaving a legacy in cricket.'

Kanika hugged Neil and buried her face on his neck while Neil reeled under the emotional backlash of his own words.

'Sorry for judging your friendship with Cap Jay,' said Neil.

'No worries,' she kissed him on his cheek. 'I also lectured you,' she said, leading him back to the couch. 'Please use Cap Jay. He is an ass, but you two share the same interests. They have also sidelined him in the team.'

'He's asking for confidential information.'

'Again the idealism,' Kanika smiled and leaned on the couch. 'What happened when you tried to do the right thing?'

'He is a shady guy.'

Kanika refilled his glass. 'A super-rich man like him won't get involved in match-fixing. He just wants to help the team.'

'You are right,' said Neil, feeling energized. 'The ICCL does not specifically bar the team owners from getting information. Pat had imposed this rule on us. Why do I have to listen to Pat any more?'

'True! Cap Jay can't help you if you don't trust him.'

Neil smiled. 'He will blast me for losing again today. He's passionate!'

'Let's go out for dinner…change the mood,' said Kanika.

'Sure! Also, stop by at the after-party,' said Neil, trying to accommodate her needs.

'Fuck the after-party,' Kanika winked at him with a naughty smile. 'Not today…not when we finally have a way forward. We are together after a long time. Let's not include anyone else in our celebration.'

Blast from the Past

An Hour Later

'Girlfriends?'

'Yes, but never long-term.'

'Your family did not force you to marry?'

'They tried but failed.'

'You didn't want to marry?'

'Never met the right person…apart from you.'

'Really?' giggled Kanika. 'Delhi's women are so stylish and beautiful. I am nothing compared to them.'

'Now you are fishing for compliments,' Neil smiled. For a few moments he played with the breadsticks. 'Don't believe me? Do a survey about the most desirable woman in the ICCL. I will donate a kidney if you don't win hands down.'

Kanika blushed and took a break from having her soup. 'Remember that girl who stalked you in London?' She covered her mouth with the napkin and laughed.

'Yeah! Threatened suicide,' Neil grinned. 'What a nut.'

'Wrote letters to you in blood,' said Kanika, struggling to control her glee. 'Or was it red ink?'

'God knows.'

'I think you would have fallen for her if I wouldn't have been there,' said Kanika, laughing again. 'She was beautiful. I don't buy your…"looks don't matter" crap.'

'Yeah, right!' Neil grinned. 'Never said looks don't matter…but you know…' he closed his eyes and moved his palms in the air as if conjuring a magic trick, 'the complete package—looks, fun, personality, charm…'

He opened his eyes and frowned. 'There is no one like you.'

'Do you still live in the apartment we had taken together?' asked Kanika, after a few moments of awkward silence. 'It had a gorgeous view of Connaught Place.'

'Naah…I moved out after you left,' said Neil in a halting voice. He avoided eye contact to prevent his overflowing emotions from ruining a perfect outing. 'Too many memories. It was painful.'

'Sorry, Neil,' Kanika held his hand. 'I was selfish to leave and screw up your life.'

Neil saw nothing but sincerity and remorse on her pretty face. 'It's okay,' he said, patting her hand. 'We were both immature.'

'We can't turn back the clock, Neil,' Kanika looked deep into his eyes. 'But we can try to make sense of the future.'

Neil nodded, unsure of what she meant.

Does she want to get back together? Or is it just friendship?

They returned to her room after a refreshing dinner and conversation. Neil wondered if her invitation for a nightcap meant something more than just sipping good wine. Fiery passion built up in his body as she reclined on the couch with a dreamy expression on her face. Was she waiting for him to make a move? Or would this be too soon?

I must take it slow. She might slap me.

'There is something on your nose,' Kanika unfastened her top bun and shook her hair free. She crossed her legs and watched him clean his face. Leaning on her side, she moved close to his face as if to inspect it and kissed him on his lips. She caressed the back of his neck and moved on to his lap as they exploded in a passionate duel with their tongues. They broke apart for a moment before melting into an intimate embrace, the touch of her skin creating a tornado of desire blowing through his breath. He sucked her ear, and she moaned like a distraught animal pleading for mercy. She unbuttoned his shirt, slowly, one button at a time. He laid her on the couch and sucked her toes—a homage he had always reserved only for her. He kissed the fern tattoos on her beautiful feet and thought about the payals he had once tied on her ankles. '*I wouldn't allow anyone else to do this,*' she had said.

He lost his intensity. She noticed the ebb and folded her legs to draw him towards her, on top of her, tilting her head with a small moan urging him to go on. Poor sexual chemistry with other partners had dented his confidence, and he added a touch of drama to camouflage his panic. He tore away her delicate gown with brute force and went down to pleasure her first before satisfying himself like he always did. But Kanika stopped the intricate sequence she had once established as a pathway to mutual bliss.

So how do I satisfy her? Or does she not need it any more?

She turned her face down on the couch, and he moved in on her back and ripped away the lone piece of satin from her hip—the last physical barrier separating their bodies. As he struggled for strength to penetrate, he knew it was impossible to experience ecstasy while trying to control the underlying emotions.

You can't control it when trying to lose control. Let nature take over; just let it flow.

Kanika turned on her side and climbed on top of Neil. She stroked him between his legs and guided his throbbing muscle to its ultimate destination. She moved in perfect rhythm and gradually raised the tempo to cause a final violent eruption that emptied him in cascading gouts of wet ecstasy.

They lay together on the narrow couch and rested in blissful silence, lulled by the lullaby of their hearts throbbing in synergetic harmony.

'I owe you a new dress,' he said.

'Just one?' she panted. 'Won't you tear more?'

Till Death Do Us Part

Two Days Later, Morning

'Something bad has happened; I have a very uncomfortable feeling. Like I told you last night, no one has seen him in the last twenty-four hours.' Nandini accosted Neil in the hotel's lobby when he returned from the morning practice and irritated him with her concerns for a man she had loathed all her life.

His patience ran out as she rambled on about Cap Jay's plausible disappearance. It seemed everyone had suddenly fallen in love with Cap Jay. The man lived the high life. He was probably lying somewhere with a few women, sleeping off his intoxication. Why was she troubling him with her useless worries?

'Let's check his room now.' Nandini looked distraught. 'I have been waiting here for the last two hours.'

'Why didn't you check his room by yourself, or ask the hotel guys to help you?' asked Neil, peeved with her selfish attitude. Suddenly, she had no mental space left for anyone else other than her great husband. She couldn't spare two minutes to ask him how he was doing.

'I didn't want to enter his room,' said Nandini hesitatingly. 'God knows who is there with him…and in what condition.' She shook her head. 'The hotel guys know what happens in his room…but I didn't want them to spread the 'spicy story' about how I caught my husband with his pants down.' Nandini rushed towards the elevator, but Neil stayed put. She turned to check on him after a few steps and gave him an angry look. 'What happened? Let's go.'

'Can I change first?' Neil scowled, holding his wet shirt away from his body.

'When did you become a model?' snapped Nandini. 'Fretting about clothes, huh?'

Kanika appeared in the lobby, accompanied by two young girls who were evidently ICCL cheerleaders. He passed them en route to Cap Jay's room and took a sneak peek at the fern tattoos adorning her ankles.

God! I love this woman.

Maybe he had never stopped loving her. No wonder he had never had a serious relationship after she left. The body's memory was stronger than the mind's. It remembered the ecstasy of her touch.

The other night was something special. I can't imagine life without her any more.

He itched to propose but feared undue haste might prompt her to run again as she had done thirteen years ago.

I will take her on a nice vacation after the ICCL, get her in the right mood and then make her mine.

Nandini knocked on Cap Jay's door, but got no response. She stepped back and gave Neil the spare key.

'He's not here,' said Neil.

'He is inside,' said Nandini, pointing at the 'Do Not Disturb' sign hanging from the door.

'Let's ask the hotel to check the CCTV cameras.'

'Go in,' shouted Nandini. 'He might be unwell. Go!'

Neil entered the room and Nandini waited outside. The self-closing door shut behind him. Cap Jay's room was empty but in a state of mess. The bedsheets had fallen on the floor, leaving behind mutilated pillows on the backrest. Dirty plates rested on the bed with their contents on the mattress. Cigarette buds and empty beer bottles littered the floor while a heap of clothes covered most of the couch. A pile of luggage occupied one corner of the room, but the walk-in wardrobe was empty. A strong smell of sweat, tobacco and alcohol permeated the air, causing nausea. This room could not have belonged to anyone other than Cap Jay.

But where is he?

Neil checked the bathroom and found the situation there as obnoxious as the bedroom. Toiletries strewed the platform around the washbasin, and dirty underwear and towels covered much of the floor. Small mounds of white powder lay scattered on the towels near the wall.

So much talcum powder? Some kind of sexual fetish? Fucking animal!

A separate enclosure on the far side of the bathroom housed a large bathtub. Through the translucent partition, he noticed an odd reflection on the water and walked over to check it.

And there, floating naked, face down, with his head submerged, was Cap Jay. He was dead. No one could be alive in such a position.

Neil froze in a state of denial. After a few minutes, he stepped inside the tub and hauled out the body to the bathroom floor. Cap Jay's closed eyes and bloated cheeks made his face almost unrecognizable. He pumped Cap Jay's chest, but got no response. He checked his pulse; it was absent.

Fuck! He is gone. Just when he could have helped me.

One Step Forward, Two Backward

Later That Night

'He died of a cocaine overdose,' said Kanika as Neil entered her room. She lit a cigarette and exhaled smoke towards the ceiling. 'This is now an unofficial murder investigation.'

Neil raised his eyebrows. 'Unbelievable! Wasn't he the most loved man in Delhi?'

Kanika's smoke rings created a haze around her face which she cleared with her hand. 'Oh! Many wanted him dead.'

'Like who?'

'Like your cousins Nandini and Akash,' said Kanika. 'And till recently, even you.'

She took a deep drag from her cigarette. 'You were in the same hotel.'

'Are they suspecting me?' mumbled Neil.

'No, silly,' Kanika laughed again. 'I am teasing you.'

'The police said he died of a heart attack,' said Neil in an animated voice.

Kanika shrugged. 'He might have overdosed on his own.'

'Yeah!'

'How is Nandini?'

'Fine now, but she was crying a lot after we discovered the body,' said Neil. 'Strange she is so upset; he was an animal.'

Kanika smirked, but did not comment.

'I have a better reason than her for being sad,' said Neil, grinning. 'He was supposed to be my saviour. I have mixed feelings—I am happy for Nandini, but sad for myself.' Neil sighed. 'Now I am back to square one.'

'Many people loved him,' said Kanika.

'The same man—villain to one, god to somebody else, a great friend to others,' said Neil.

'You lost a strategic partner,' said Kanika. 'What he was to others shouldn't matter to you.'

'True! Must say the obituaries surprised me,' said Neil. 'After sidelining him, Sudhir and Pat almost said he was their guiding light. We live in a hypocritical world.'

'And Akash's statement?' smirked Kanika. 'He called him a brother who shared his vision of supporting cricket in India.'

Neil fetched a miniature Chivas Regal from the minibar. 'When is the cremation?'

Kanika burst out laughing. 'You're asking me? He was your brother-in-law.'

'Will they stall the ICCL till they solve the murder mystery?' Neil took a large sip of the Chivas.

Kanika shook her head and paced the room. 'The ICCL is supposed to restart in three days.'

'Hey! Maybe Nandini can help me. She is the new co-owner of the team,' said Neil.

'She can't fight Akash,' snorted Kanika.

'Yeah!' Neil nodded. 'Anyway, she always discourages me. Like last night, when I told her about working with Cap Jay, she blasted me without hearing me out.'

'Why?'

'No reason, apart from warning me not to trust him, as the issue is very complicated.'

'Hmm, weird,' said Kanika and stubbed out her cigarette in the ashtray. She lit another one and watched the space outside through the window. 'Don't worry. Something will come up. Just have patience.'

Is something bothering her? She is smoking so much; and I have never seen her so tense. I think she knows more about Cap Jay's death than she is telling me. Yesterday, Nandini was also doing the same. What's wrong with these women?

'What's bothering you?' asked Neil.

'Oh, nothing,' said Kanika. 'Just ICCL issues…'

'Cap Jay?'

Kanika hesitated for a moment. 'He was murdered,' she blurted out. 'And it might be related to the New Delhi Royals.'

'What!'

'Just a hunch. Doesn't concern you, so don't worry.'

Kanika refused to elaborate. Later, as they lay in bed, Neil couldn't get her words out of his head.

Cap Jay was murdered? And it's related to the team? How does she know? And why does she refuse to discuss it? She wouldn't have said it without having authentic information. What's going on here?

From Ass to Ash

Four Days Later

Cap Jay's dead body lay ready for cremation at Delhi's Nigambodh Ghat crematorium, and the city's elite arrived to pay their last respects to their beloved 'friend'. Prominent businessmen, politicians, out-of-work movie stars, Page 3 models, former and current Indian cricketers, representatives of ICCL teams, relatives—distant and close, friends of friends, all lined up in their perfect whites, wailing their hearts out.

Akash smirked at this deluge of affection.

Maybe they are worried about how they will continue their debauchery without him.

Dressed in an off-white sari, with her head covered, Nandini was the perfect picture of a grieving widow. The untimely passing of her loving husband seemed to have emptied her life energy. Akash felt the family elders had brainwashed her into putting up this show. They had cut her off from the world, and asked her to move back to Upadhyay Palace. Nandini was vulnerable as she faced turmoil at a much deeper level. Her life had suddenly opened up, with various possibilities, which is paralysing in its own way. She would be afraid of making a mistake again after seven years of torture. Status quo has a certain level of comfort. People yearn for change but struggle when it finally arrives.

Grandma and dad will exploit her confusion. She will inherit a significant amount of money. They must have already planned how to use her to bail them out. They will suck her dry, those parasites, and then throw her out again.

Akash loved Nandini like a daughter. He fumed at her blatant exploitation but couldn't do much till he got the chance to talk to her. But how would he break in? Those bastards were guarding her like snakes around a pot of gold.

Maybe late in the night, after they fall asleep. I will persuade her to meet me outside her house.

Everyone stood up as Abhishek moved to light the funeral pyre amidst the frenzied chanting of hymns and mantras.

Good riddance, Jayshankar. A man like you had no right to live.

Akash stood looking at the fire that became a roaring inferno, consuming body and wood alike.

I did this world a lot of good by getting rid of you. Hope you rot in hell.

A Question of Loyalty

Later That Night

The driver held the door open for Nandini and moved away after she sat in the back seat next to Akash.

He noticed the white sari and absolute absence of jewellery on a person who always loved to dress up. Her tear-laden swollen eyes seemed ready for another downpour.

'Why so sad?' he asked. 'Don't be a cow; it doesn't suit you.'

'I am not grieving for Jayshankar,' Nandini said in a low, halting voice. 'Seven years of my life just went down the drain.'

'So, *the* Upadhyay Palace will rescue you?' snapped Akash.

'Stop lecturing me,' Nandini glared at Akash. 'What have you ever done for me? At least they are trying to help. Your wife, on the other hand, is pissed I stopped the blooming cricket tournament.'

'When did you ask for help? Huh!' asked Akash, jerking his head upwards.

Nandini's cold, fidgety eyes looked puzzled.

'Don't listen to dad,' said Akash. 'Claiming Jayshankar's money will be a huge mistake.'

She shook her head. 'Why? It is my money.'

'Nandini! Jayshankar's extended family and business partners in Dubai are co-owners of many of his businesses. Don't mess with them.'

'Dad and Gagan will sort this out.'

'Yeah, right!' Akash smirked. 'They will sell you for a penny.'

'So I should become poor again?'

'Claim the assets where he was the direct owner,' said Akash. 'The bungalow in Delhi, the trading company and the malls in Gurgaon are enough for you to lead a very lavish life.'

'And his shares in your cricket team?' asked Nandini.

She smiled as Akash fumbled for an answer.

'It's complicated. Owned by a conglomerate...'

'Nonsense! You are misleading me because I spoke to Pat about Neil.'

'That was so silly,' snorted Akash. 'You can't control the team, even if you own 7 per cent shares. I don't control anything even after owning 93 per cent.'

'I want to see the legal papers.'

'Forget the papers. I will buy your 7 per cent.'

'I won't sell.'

'Don't be foolish, Nandini. You can't control the gang that has funded this stake.'

'I will take my chances…'

'Is Neil forcing you?'

'Accommodate Neil, and then buy me out at the end of the season.'

'Never! He is a freeloading incompetent imbecile.'

'Your golden boy Pat has failed.'

'Form is temporary, Nandini, but class is permanent,' said Akash. 'Pat brings prestige to the team which Neil can't. Sure, he has faltered, but who knows if Neil can succeed!'

'I cleaned up your mess,' snickered Nandini. 'Reimburse me by helping Neil.'

Akash smiled. 'What?'

Nandini adjusted her glasses. 'Jayshankar's bathroom was full of cocaine. Someone had forced him to overdose. I cleaned it up before the police arrived.'

Akash laughed. 'Really? So?'

'The police might be interested to know you threatened Jayshankar,' Nandini glared at Akash. 'Plus, the CCTV cameras near his room were not working.'

'Tell them,' smirked Akash. 'They will book you for tampering with evidence.' He sighed and turned in his seat to face Nandini. 'Don't blackmail me, Nandini. Only I care for you. Don't give the money to dad. It won't be good for you.' He held her by the shoulder and established stern eye contact. 'This is neither a threat nor friendly advice—I am ordering you as an elder brother not to do it. And, irrespective of how Jayshankar died, always remember you benefitted from his death. Be grateful to the people who helped you.' Akash squeezed her shoulder and gave her a hug. 'Good luck, sister. Don't be foolish, and you will be safe.'

Faint Light of Dawn

Two Days Later, Late Morning

Gagan barged into Neil's room and helped himself to a beer from the minibar. He looked around and burped. 'Ah! Nice room. I should become a coach.'

'Anything important?' asked Neil in a cold voice, having no patience for the shenanigans of a perennial backstabber. But Gagan behaved as if it was business as usual. He lounged on the couch with a cigarette in one hand and a beer in the other.

'Come here,' Gagan patted the couch. He belched loudly. 'Order some fish and chips. It goes well with the beer.'

'I don't have the time.'

Gagan sat up, looking surprised. 'Oh my my, what a beauty,' he teased. 'Our little boy has found a voice. He jumped up from the couch and kissed Neil on the forehead. 'Don't be so angry.'

Neil struggled with his anger as he remembered how Gagan used to kiss his forehead when they were young to show he was the elder brother who would always be there to protect him. But, over time, Gagan's failures had made him emotionally bankrupt and incapable of caring for anyone. The once-youthful Gagan had aged rapidly in the last few months. He now looked old and haggard, with a head full of grey hair.

Gagan evaded eye contact and turned away from Neil. 'Akash promised to accommodate you as an assistant coach, and I thought it was fine. And you know my lifestyle, right? What with my wild parties and women, I forgot to tell you. Sorry!'

Neil was in no mood to engage with Gagan, nor was he ready to forgive. He wanted to get rid of him as soon as possible. 'Okay! What do you want today?' he asked in a curt voice.

'Correct the wrong, nothing more.'

'How?'

Gagan led Neil to the couch. 'Relax! Everything will be fine now.'

Neil realized hearing Gagan's pitch was the only way to get rid of him. He sighed and sat down. 'Okay! You have my undivided attention.'

'So, how is your relationship with Mr Pat?'

Gagan's atrocious question stunned Neil. Why was he asking a question whose answer was public knowledge? Was Gagan trying to taunt him? But he wasn't the taunting type.

Neil played along, hoping the torturous conversation would end soon. 'Bad! Everyone knows, so…'

Gagan drank his beer with a loud 'aaahhh' and farted.

Neil twisted his face, disgusted with the smell.

'I have solid evidence against Mr Head Coach,' said Gagan, and raised his eyebrows. 'You want it?'

Neil snorted, smiling cockily.

Bullshit! Fucker has gone totally mental.

'Video and audio of abusing Akash, extensive footage of taking money from the foreign players to buy them at a high price in the auction, videos of conspiracy against you, etc.'

Neil smiled and rose from the couch. 'Okay! We had a nice chat, you had your beer, now time to go.'

'You don't believe me?' asked Gagan. 'No problem. Look at these videos and then judge me.'

Gagan produced a mobile phone from his pocket. The first video showed Pat in his hotel room, discussing money with someone on the phone. The time stamp showed the day before the player auctions.

'We have the phone recording with Antonio Charles and Jeffrey Beer as well,' said Gagan. 'He was negotiating the kickback for buying them.' Gagan stopped the video midway and played the next one. 'Here is the meeting of his core team, discussing how to fuck you, analysing politics in the team and expressing what they feel about Akash and his wife. Some highly uncharitable stuff about her ass and how if she lost weight she would be a sex bomb… And here is the one about the rebelling players.' Gagan grinned. 'Interested?'

'How did you…?' Neil couldn't find words to complete his sentence.

'Don't bother about "how",' said Gagan. He fetched another beer from the minibar. 'Just let me correct my past mistakes.'

Neil was tempted to expose Pat and claim his rightful place as the head coach of the team, but those videos did not feel right, and he couldn't understand why they were making him nervous. Maybe Gagan's history was shaking his confidence.

How can I trust Gagan? Nandini has promised to help. I would rather work with her.

Neil shook his head. 'I can't.'

'Are you crazy?' snapped Gagan.

'I don't want to destabilize the team.'

Gagan laughed and rolled over on the couch. He shook his hands and legs like a madman and crashed the beer bottle on the floor.

'What's so funny?'

'You are, man, you are,' Gagan said, holding his stomach. 'Hilarious! You sucked everyone's dick to become the head coach. Everyone screwed you, and now you are refusing the only chance you have to unscrew yourself.'

Neil smiled. 'You won't understand this, Gagan. Some people have pride. They want to win, but not by screwing others. For them, the team is more important.'

'Oh you poor bastard!' said Gagan. 'Soon you will come to your senses.'

'Let me deal with my situation,' said Neil and walked over to open the door. 'Now please excuse me, I have a meeting.' He waved his hand, showing Gagan the way out. 'Leave, please!'

That night Neil received a text from Nandini soon after the New Delhi Royals lost their match against the Rajasthan Rockers (their sixth successive loss after having won the first match).

```
Hey, I couldn't convince Akash. There is a
complication about the investor group that funded
Jayshankar's 7 per cent stake, so, at present I have
no leverage on the team. I know you were depending
on me, but please understand I tried. Sorry!
```

Nandini's text dashed Neil's last hope of overcoming his problems through a fair and dignified approach. He thought about the disastrous turn of events leading to the ICCL and realized neither mercy nor miracle would change his situation. Whenever shoots of hope sprouted within him, the vagaries of life mercilessly devoured them at every step.

Then there was the question of Kanika, whose sudden reemergence in his life had created goals bigger than cricket. How would his professional struggles impact his personal life? Why would she choose a loser when she had successful men queuing up to woo her? Her love wouldn't survive without respect. A loser gets sympathy and pity, but only a winner gets the beautiful girl.

Only a bold attitude can change my destiny.

Faint hearts have never won the fair lady. He remembered the famous quotation as he picked up the phone to call Gagan.

Akash is blind with spite, and Pat with arrogance. Half the tournament is over. We are facing elimination. It's now or never.

The Greasy Pole

Two Hours Later

Using a mix of snide remarks and veiled threats over SMS, Neil cornered Pat for a meeting in his room. Seeing Pat's panic-stricken eyes he felt a little sorry for a man he had admired as a great ambassador of cricket. But, Pat had washed mutual respect and goodwill down the toilet through blatant impropriety and arrogance.

Now it is his turn to pay.

The high-pitched sound of a girl screaming in ecstasy filled the room as Neil played a video of Pat having sex with a cheerleader.

'Is this allowed?' Neil peered at the screen. 'Go slow, man. She might die.'

Pat sighed. 'Cut the small talk…'

Neil played another video. 'Oh! This is interesting.'

'We can arm-twist those poor fuckers to sign a statement against Neil,' Pat's voice rang out from the screen.

'So, evidence of the conspiracy against me. Awesome! The media will love it,' mocked Neil. 'But the next one is even better…'

Neil played a video of Pat and Antonio conversing over a beer.

'Fat bitch…Divya…very tight ass. A great fuck if she slims down.'

'Yeah! She is just my type. I like big asses.'

'Should I send these to Akash?' asked Neil with a serious face. 'He should know how you fucked the team by buying fat, retired players and taking kickbacks…'

'How did you get them?' asked Pat in a cold voice.

'None of your business,' snapped Neil. 'Your job is to just follow instructions…so go get a piece of paper and take notes.' Pat did not move, and Neil chided him like a school principal talking to a disobedient student. 'Go on, boy…sharpen your pencil…take notes…learn.'

Neil clicked his fingers and Pat hurriedly grabbed a notepad and pen from the desk.

'I am now the boss of this team,' said Neil. He stood with his hands on his hips in a menacing pose. 'You and your cronies will blindly follow my instructions. At the end of this season, you will credit me in the media for the team's success. Then you will ask Akash to make me the head coach and leave the team.'

Pat smiled. 'But, only if the team succeeds?'

'You will take the blame if we fail and tell the media you made a big mistake by ignoring Neil's strategies, and thus he should become the head coach for the next season.'

'You seem to have figured it all out,' said Pat. 'How long were you planning this?'

'Tomorrow we will discuss your speech for the team meeting,' said Neil.

'And Akash?' asked Pat.

'He won't mind, as officially you are still the head coach. Convince him I can help the team.'

Pat shook his head. 'I can't. He won't listen.'

'Well then, I will release these videos.'

'Akash forced me to misbehave with you,' Pat looked distraught. 'I took some liberties as I do not plan to return next year. Sorry!'

Akash asked Pat to misbehave with me? Did he make me an assistant coach to insult me? Fuck! This easily beats the worst I could ever imagine he would do. Nandini was right, but I can't back out now. I can't allow these assholes to win.

'You were one of my idols, Pat,' said Neil in a calm voice. 'I expected you to honour our cordial relationship, but you got carried away.'

'Akash tied my hands,' Pat showed his hands, looking sorry.

'You rejected my ideas when you knew I was right.'

'They made no sense,' Pat shook his head. 'Sorry!'

'Really?' smirked Neil. 'Your excessive greed has made you senile, old man!'

'Excessive greed...did you say?' Pat smiled. 'What do you know about poverty? I did not grow up in a palace like you did; my father was a poor potato farmer who couldn't even provide enough food for his family. And yet I rose from abject poverty to dominate world cricket for twenty years. But I never made money. Cricket then did not have a river of cash flowing in through endorsements and lucrative coaching assignments. If I had been born ten years later, I would not have been so desperate. So please be a little gentle while judging me.'

Neil laughed, shaking his head. 'Every crime has a sob story justifying it. You think I am rich? Sure, my family was rich...but I became an orphan at thirteen. I depended on my uncle to help me at every step. Trust me, it did not feel good...but I did not sell out.'

'You gotta be joking,' Pat let out a shrill laugh. 'You are judging me for selling out while blackmailing me using videos recorded on the sly. Care to practise what you preach?'

'It is all for the team, Pat,' said Neil in a halting voice, a little rattled by the word 'blackmail'. He reeled as the scope and nature of his actions dawned on him. But Pat's unrepentant attitude soon snapped him out of the passing attack of righteousness. 'Here, the end justifies the means,' he said. 'And you deserve to have your snooty nose rubbed on the ground.'

'I always loved you, Neil...God's honest truth,' said Pat. 'Please understand, my financial situation forced my hand. Again, I am sorry— let's move on now; come, join my group and share the profit.'

'Everyone is not for sale, you asshole,' shouted Neil and kicked the table in front of him. Two glasses flew from it and shattered on the floor. 'You deserve a kick in your butt,' he fumed. 'You are no sportsman...you are a businessman...a manipulator...a schemer.'

'Don't do this...you will get into trouble,' said Pat, looking unperturbed by Neil's harsh words. 'Whoever is helping you now will backstab you later. Such is the nature of life. People use you and then dump you.'

'No, they won't,' mumbled Neil, unable to support the bravado in his voice with inner conviction about his actions. Pat's confident voice felt like a sledgehammer crashing on his head, but he couldn't analyse right versus wrong any more. He dismissed Pat's dire predictions as his last desperate attempt to survive the coup, and resolved to seize the best opportunity for redemption life had presented to him after years of misfortune. 'I am backed by very powerful people, so I will be fine,' he said. 'Don't worry about me. Just do your job without asking questions.'

Coronation

Two Days Later, Late Afternoon

Two hours before the match against the Bangalore Bulls, Pattrick O'Donnell dropped the bombshell in the team meeting. 'I have an important announcement to make,' he said, looking glum. 'Four weeks ago, we came together as a team, but it has not worked out for us.' Pat paused for a moment as a death-like silence engulfed the room. 'So I sought new ideas to improve the team,' he said in a halting voice. 'Neil will now be a part of the team management. He will help in strategic planning, training, player selection and deciding the batting/bowling order for every match going forward.'

Sudhir fidgeted in his chair. 'Does Akash know?' he asked with a grunt. 'You didn't tell me...?'

'No major change—we are just pooling our resources,' replied Pat. 'But to answer your question, I don't have to discuss this with Akash. He gave me a free hand.'

'What can Neil do?' Sudhir asked Pat, looking irritated.

'Neil, you want to answer?' asked Pat, yielding the floor to him.

Neil rushed to the front of the room. 'We must re-imagine our strategy and take drastic action if we want to avoid elimination. So I've developed a plan based on my conversations with the coaches of the other teams...'

'So you are leaking information?' interrupted Sudhir. 'No wonder we are losing.'

'No, no...silly,' snapped Neil. 'I have played with these coaches and know how they think. So please respect my integrity.'

'Okay! Let's discuss the team selection,' said Pat, looking at his watch. 'Gotta go for pre-match drills...'

Neil produced a piece of paper from his pocket. 'Manuel Cyclic will be...'

'Who the fuck are you to decide the team?' shouted Sudhir and jumped up from his chair. With a twisted face, he rushed towards Pat. 'Why didn't you ask me?'

'That's the drastic action Neil was talking about,' said Pat in a cold voice. 'Our approach hasn't worked, so he has selected a new team. Better get used to this change.'

'Fuck you,' Sudhir screamed and kicked a chair, which crashed into the wall.

'Your suggestions are welcome, Sudhir…but for this match we don't have time for a debate,' said Neil. 'We have lost six matches in a row…so why not try something different for one match? What can we lose?'

Pat and Dinesh persuaded Sudhir to stand down, but not before he had mouthed the choicest expletives.

'Manuel Cyclic is the only foreign player we are keeping from the last match,' said Neil. 'And we are replacing Rodney Wyatt, Jeffrey Beer and Kyle Slinger with Ismail Abdullah, Travis Robins and Benjamin Roister. Sudhir Yadav will remain captain, and Dinesh Singh will also play.'

'So, you will decide if I will be captain?' mocked Sudhir. 'Akash appointed me. Have the owners changed overnight?'

'Talk to Akash if you have a problem with me,' snapped Neil. 'He will remind you that you scored 43 runs in the seven matches so far. If performance alone was considered, you would not be in this team. I am doing you a favour by keeping you here. Go ahead, call Akash; we will wait…'

Sudhir cursed and stormed out of the room.

Neil regretted his bravado as soon as he saw Sudhir using his phone.

Fuck! He is calling Akash. Now what!

He took a deep breath and surrendered to destiny.

Anyway, it is too late now to worry about Akash. Pat will explain his decision, not me. Akash won't be happy, but he will not complain if we win tonight. I have to motivate the players to play well.

After a few minutes Sudhir returned to the dressing room looking deflated. Evidently he had failed to contact Akash. As the meeting resumed, Neil noticed a bearded man clicking photographs on the porch outside the dressing room.

Is he a reporter? Isn't this a restricted area?

With his dark sunglasses and straw hat, he looked like a villain straight out of Bollywood movies from the 80s.

'Okay, let's wrap this up,' said Pat, clapping his hands.

Neil bumbled around, worried about the unprecedented breach of security in a tournament where everything was supposed to function like clockwork.

Is he here to report the story? Did Pat leak it? Why? Does he want to distort the facts by planting a story?

'Neil! Finish please,' said Pat.

'Oh yes,' Neil smiled, embarrassed about being distracted. 'So our wicketkeeper in the earlier match, Harish Bhasin, will play today, but his batting position will change to number 3. Davit Verma and Vineet Srivastav will play, but Baldev Madan and Prabhu Subramaniam will make way for Aarush Burman and Neeraj Dara,' he said. 'This is almost the same team I had suggested for the first match, but no one listened. Our complacency killed us. Please understand that this is professional cricket and not one big party. We have to train hard and be match-ready, so parties won't be allowed anymore on the night before a match,' said Neil. 'No one in this team has a guaranteed place in the playing eleven. Team selection will depend on how you perform and our assessment of the opposition. We have to think on our feet and modify our game according to the situation of the match. I have defined your roles, so please take responsibility for your game and don't depend on me to send you instructions from the outside.'

Pat sighed, shaking his head.

'Any suggestions or comments?' asked Neil, looking around the room.

Only Manuel Cyclic spoke up, while the rest looked on, poker-faced. 'Sudhir should open the batting as he is our best batsman, and Dinesh should come towards the end to finish, as his experience will be valuable in case we lose quick wickets.'

'An excellent suggestion—good work, Manuel,' said Neil, feeling happy about the team warming up to him. 'We must have a culture of respect in this team. Everyone is at the same level—no one is boss.' Neil raised his arms, like a political leader rousing his followers. 'Please come forward with your suggestions—my door is always open for you. Ask for help if you have a problem. Although I can't improve your technique overnight, I can certainly help you play the best cricket you are capable of playing. Starting today, our fortunes will change, and we will do this together. We have seven more matches, so let's make them count. Come on, let's play!'

The team moved out of the dressing room, but a group of junior Indian players stayed back inside with Neil.

'Neil, sorry we let you down,' said Vineet Srivastav. 'They threatened to fire us. I hope...'

'Don't worry, I understand,' said Neil in a calm voice. 'I should have protected you guys. But it's cool now. Only your performance matters.' Neil called out to Vineet Srivastav as he left the dressing room. 'If you are really sorry then do well in the match. That's all I want.'

First Blood

Later That Evening

The New Delhi Royals beat the Bangalore Bulls by 32 runs after Sudhir scored 67 in 28 balls, which included five sixes, two of which sent the ball out of the stadium. The fire in his batting prompted the TV commentators to declare that he had silenced the detractors who had criticized his poor form in the ICCL.

Neil eulogized the positive attitude of the team in the after-party and showered extravagant praise on Sudhir who was absent from the ballroom. He became belligerent after getting drunk, and made grandiose predictions about the team's fortunes. 'Read my lips...we will win the ICCL,' he said to loud cheers from the junior Indian players who seemed to have found a leader to look up to in Neil. 'Celebrate all you want tonight...because tomorrow we will wake up to a new life. We will beat any team on any ground in India on our road to victory.' Thumping his chest with his fist, he yelled, *'Bring it on!'*

Instant success and the enthusiasm for his leadership among the players encouraged Neil to believe his career path had taken a definitive turn towards success. But his upbeat mood changed to a sombre one when he entered his hotel room in the early hours of the morning and noticed faint footprints on the bathroom floor, open drawers and luggage and cricket gear moved from their original positions, as though someone other than the friendly folks of the housekeeping department had entered the room. Someone had been there...someone careless, looking around. Or, was this just his overactive imagination? Alcohol-induced insecurity? Paranoia? Was Pat planning a coup? He couldn't be happy about losing power, but he had partied with his cronies till the wee hours of the morning. The win was a slap on their faces. They should have been burning with misery, but instead, they had behaved as if everything was fine.

How are they so relaxed?

The surge of emotions exhausted Neil, and he missed Kanika who was in Kolkata to cover another match. He read her congratulatory message and realized that apart from the players no one knew of his role in changing the team's fortunes. Was Pat planning to hide the shift in power within the confines of the dressing room and take credit for the team's success? He could impose a gag order on the team, arm-twist Somoresh to hide the correct picture from Akash, remain the face of the team in front of the media and enjoy the fruits of someone else's talent.

Wow! Genius.

Neil searched his room for cameras and listening devices but found nothing. He walked out to the balcony to relax in the fresh air, but the atmosphere outside was still and eerie, although dawn was about to break in the distant sky. Stray birds living in the gardens had not yet started their pre-morning rituals, and their unusual silence compounded the desolate ambiance of the bustling property. The main road near the hotel was dark and deserted, and the hotel staff had not risen from the slumber of the long night. He felt a shortness of breath and reeled from an odd and ominous intuition about an impending catastrophe.

But why am I so nervous when today is one of the greatest days of my life? Nothing wrong can happen now. Be confident and deal with Pat.

Neil was frustrated at his inability to recreate the euphoria he had experienced a few hours ago.

Someone was in this room tonight...I am 100 per cent sure...plus the bearded guy outside the dressing room seemed out of place...a plan is definitely taking shape behind my back. Is Akash involved? This time I won't allow them to surprise me. I will preempt their moves by leaking my story to the media. Then I will arm-twist Pat to support the story, and their game will be over. Even Kanika won't believe me unless the media reports this story. Then I will meet her as a winner. It will be fun to see her surprised. For now, let her believe that Pat is king.

The Writing on the Wall

A Day Later, Morning

The following report appeared in *The National Times*:

> 'Performance' wins over 'reputation' in the New Delhi Royals team. Pattrick O'Donnell cedes power to Neil Upadhyay after a string of poor performances. Neil guides the team to their first victory after 6 losses.

Akash summoned Pat when he read this report. He told Akash that Neil's position as the unofficial head coach was not only irreversible but also desirous to the fans. He refused to issue a statement contradicting this report and challenged Akash to fire him if he so wished.

Akash did not know how to control a man whose defiance was far more significant than his fear of material loss and vented his frustration on Somoresh Basu. But even Somoresh advised him against firing Neil as it would demoralize the team and upset 'Divya ma'am' who was fascinated by Neil's persistence. It might even lead to a revolt by the fans.

Akash had never felt so powerless in an entity funded with his own money. As a businessman, he willingly conceded power to the customers as they paid for his products, but pandering to the will of fans was new to him. He couldn't acknowledge fans as customers who indirectly paid for his team through tickets and endorsements. Neil's rise to a leadership role in his team caused him unbearable embarrassment, for which he vowed never to forgive Pat. Although he was not ready to acknowledge Neil's talent, he appreciated his single-minded focus in chasing his dream.

But how did he convince Pat? Something has happened between them.

He thought of calling Sudhir whose calls he had been ignoring for the last two days.

But what will I tell him if he asks me to remove Neil? I can't show that I am powerless.

'Locate the source of this news,' Akash instructed Somoresh. 'Talk to Sudhir and find out what happened between Pat and Neil. Use whatever method necessary, but I need results. Remember—I might not be able to fire Neil, but I can always fire you at any time.'

A Cat and Mouse Game

Congratulatory messages and calls flooded Neil's phone post this news report. Ramesh and Gagan called, followed by former teammates, coaches, friends and acquaintances—people seemed to have found an unlikely hero in an unassuming, quiet man fighting a lonely battle for relevance. Neil's resilience in the face of extreme adversity, boldly rebooting the team by replacing non-performing big stars with low-profile effective players to orchestrate a turnaround, made this the story of a loyal man who wouldn't allow pillaging outsiders to ruin his family's team by their incompetence. Television, print, radio, the Internet—commentators criticized the trend of hiring foreign coaches and called it the colonial hangover.

Neil reflected on the media coverage of his story en route to Mumbai for the next match and loved his fans for supporting him once they got proof of his talent. This significantly reduced the deep sense of victimhood that had surrounded his thought process. After more than a decade fans again approached him for autographs. People who had misbehaved with him, who had made him wait for hours for a meeting, would now line up for five minutes of his time.

Cricket is as much a mental game as a physical one. The team was intimidated by Pat's domineering personality. Our players showed their true potential once I gave them the confidence to play fearless cricket. Pat's hands-off approach to coaching is absolutely unsuitable for the league cricket format where players come from all over the world. A modern coach must get his hands dirty and train with the players to help them gel as a team.

Amidst the euphoria of victory and the expectations of a bright future, three points of concern threatened to mar the near-perfect picture of Neil's life. Akash had not yet reacted to the news report, and his enormous ego could still cause unforeseen complications. Even a win did not seem enough to convince him that things were fine. The second complication was because of Sudhir, who had still not accepted him as the head coach. Sudhir and Akash were quite united in their hatred for him, and they could gang up to bring him down. And then there was the curious case of Kanika who had not shown a lot of excitement after the news report had exploded in the media. Why this lack of interest when she was generally very curious? Was she just busy, or did she suspect foul play? Her suspicion could only stem from a high level of information about his deal with Pat.

I will know more when we meet tonight. Her questions will tell me what she is thinking.

Abrupt End to the Honeymoon

Same Day, Mumbai, Evening

Neil relaxed with a drink in his hotel room, excited about renewing his friendship with Gagan that had withered off in the last few years. They were staying in the same hotel and planned to party in Mumbai that night. He felt tender about his family, especially Gagan, who always came up with new plans to help him. Although lazy and spoilt, he was big-hearted and caring. He chuckled as he remembered how Gagan had once roughed up a neighbour's kid just because he had hit Neil for a six in a cricket match. That kid was so terrorized, he had come to Upadhyay Palace to apologize to Neil.

Gagan fucks up because of his lifestyle, not because of malice. He won't ever intentionally harm me.

The jarring note of a phone ringing snapped Neil out of his dream world. He checked his phone and realized it was not *his* ringtone that he was hearing, and followed the sound to the bathroom.

Someone else's phone in my room? Strange!

He discovered a cheap Nokia handset tucked in between the stack of towels.

Maybe the housekeeping guys left it here by mistake.

His heart palpitated without reason as he saw that the call was from an undisclosed number. He disconnected the call, intending to return the phone to the hotel staff. But before he could leave the bathroom, the phone buzzed with a text message:

```
We know your secret. Take the call, or else...
```

The phone rang again, and he froze. Was someone in the team playing a prank on him? With shaking hands, he replied to the text.

```
Who is this?
```

Within moments, he received a reply.

```
Your father from heaven.
```

Neil gave it back to the caller, convinced someone was playing the fool.

```
Tell that to the police when they arrest you.
```

Again, the reply arrived almost instantaneously.

```
Will also tell them how you became head coach.
```

'Ah! So it is Pat,' Neil mumbled, frustrated with Pat's juvenile attempt to rattle him. Just as he was about to power off the phone, it buzzed again with a message.

```
Check the CD we have placed in your room. Below
the TV, top drawer.
```

Neil dashed to check the top drawer and found a CD there, neatly packed in a transparent plastic case. He played it on his laptop and found in it a full video recording of his conversation with Pat from two nights ago.

Fuck! Pat recorded this? To reverse blackmail me? He knew I had some proof against him. We met in his room; he had the time to set this up...unless it was someone else.

Neil rechecked the phone, weak and out of breath. There was a new message.

```
Checked?
```

Neil texted.

```
So what? I also have proof against Pat.
```

The reply was immediate.

```
We provided the proof.
```

Was this Gagan? Had the asshole suffered brain damage because of a drug overdose? Neil sent another message.

```
Stop this, Gagan. I don't have time for such nonsense.
```

Again, the reply came in nanoseconds. This was followed by a rapid exchange of texts.

```
Gagan who?
What do you want?
Information.
What kind of information?
```

> Take my call, and I will tell you.

The phone rang again, and this time Neil took the call.

'Listen, you bastard—and listen carefully,' a gruff voice spoke at the other end of the line. 'We don't represent Pat or Gagan or whoever. We have proof you became head coach through blackmail. So, you cooperate; otherwise it will go to the press and the police. What will Akash do when he finds out?'

Neil realized he couldn't pretend any more. 'What do you want?' he mumbled.

Fuck! Gagan has screwed me again. Fucking asshole!

Mr Gruff Voice laughed. 'Relax! We are not asking for your kidney or liver. At least not yet. Just simple information about the pitch, toss, team selection, batting, bowling order, etc. will do.'

'That's against the rules,' said Neil in a halting voice.

'So is blackmail.'

'I don't always have the information.'

'Oh yes, you do. We have empowered you. Now it's your turn to deliver. Enforce your will on the team and get the information you need.' The marauding Mr Gruff Voice trampled Neil's feeble protest. 'We will contact you when needed. Write down nothing; don't discuss this over the phone. Never try to contact us, or tell anyone, especially your girlfriend. You won't get into trouble if you cooperate.' After a brief silence, Mr Gruff Voice continued. 'Switch off this phone after this call and leave it where you found it. We will collect and destroy it. And try no tricks. We are monitoring you round the clock. We even keep track of when you go to piss.' Mr Gruff Voice panted as if he was doing cardiovascular exercises. 'Don't believe me?' he asked. 'Here's proof. After you arrived at the hotel today, you went to the bathroom in the lobby. Right? And then you sat in the coffee shop and ordered a club sandwich. Am I right?'

Neil did not respond.

'Am I right?' Mr Gruff Voice hollered.

'Yes,' mumbled Neil.

'Good! Now we are on the same page. Your code number is 5426. That's what our agents will use to identify themselves. Remember the number.'

With that vague piece of information, Mr Gruff Voice disconnected the call.

Face Behind the Mask

Neil rushed to meet Gagan and heard low-pitched female moans emanating from his room.

'Open up, fucker,' he screamed. 'Playtime is over. Get rid of your whore.'

The woman's moans intensified into mini-screams as Neil banged on the door. Gagan opened it, dressed in a crumpled white dressing gown, his hairy chest heaving. Unshaven and stinking, he looked as if he had not bathed or seen sunlight in days.

'What the fuck...' scowled Gagan, rubbing his eyes. He looked uncharacteristically calm even after Neil had disturbed him while performing the holy act. 'Its too early for us to go out, bro. Don't worry, I will take you to the party,' he continued in a condescending voice as if he was scolding a tantrum-throwing ten-year-old. 'Just go. Chill!'

Neil barged in as Gagan tried to close the door. 'Ask her to leave,' he snapped, pointing towards the scantily dressed woman sitting on the edge of the bed. 'You have a lot of explaining to do.'

Gagan maintained a straight face, but Neil detected a faint sign of triumph in his body language.

How is he so relaxed? He usually explodes with anger when challenged.

Gagan reached for his wallet and threw a bundle of currency notes at the woman. 'Ask Nirmal to send someone with more meat,' he said, pointing his palm towards his chest. 'You are too flat for my liking.'

The woman left and Gagan turned to face Neil.

'Now...what's your problem?' Gagan asked with a serious face, but his eyes betrayed his mirth. 'Pat bothering you again?'

Gagan's mocking voice shook Neil to the core.

Fuck! He knows what happened. It was a trap, not the mistake of a bumbling fool. He told me to show Pat the videos only in his room, where they had installed the recording device.

'You double-crossed me!' screamed Neil and pushed Gagan on to the table behind him. The thud of his head hitting the table barely masked the loud splintering noise of breaking wood.

Before Gagan could recover, Neil jumped on him and pinned

him down by his throat. The table collapsed under their weight. 'You trapped me, you bastard!'

Gagan's face turned pink as he struggled to breathe. Neil relaxed his grip for a moment, fearing that he might die, and Gagan used the reprieve to bang his left knee against Neil's groin. As Neil cowed with pain, Gagan escaped from his grip. He rushed to the bed and pulled out a shiny silver revolver from under the pillow. Gagan pointed the gun towards Neil and unlocked the safety catch. 'Please cooperate,' he said in a cold voice. He moved forward and put the gun on Neil's forehead. 'You become emotional, you die.'

Neil screamed as Gagan kicked him repeatedly on his stomach.

'This was so unnecessary,' Gagan yanked Neil off the floor and helped him to the bed. He popped a can of beer. 'Want one?' he smiled. 'It will ease the pain…'

Neil grimaced with pain. 'You knew?' he rasped, almost choking with the effort.

'Everything has a price, brother,' Gagan belched and patted his uncouth belly.

'I thought you were helping me.'

'And I did; I elevated you from a pathetic existence.'

Neil forced a smile. 'I can't betray cricket.'

'Was blackmailing Pat not betraying the game?' snapped Gagan. 'You were ready to work with Cap Jay. What's different here?'

Neil gasped. 'How do you know?'

Gagan hugged Neil. 'Oh! My innocent little brother…we are all in this together.' He squeezed Neil's cheeks. 'You thought people help you because they love you? Ah! Sweet.'

The Slippery Slope of Adulation

Neil drove around Mumbai, furious with the world for betraying him at every step. He sobbed, thinking about how Gagan had defended him from bullies when he was a kid. Now the same Gagan, the same elder brother who had made sure he never felt like an orphan, had put a gun to his head.

He considered his options. Should he leave the team? But what if they released the tape? People would believe the allegations. He had made a big mistake by leaking the story to the media. The media would unearth the truth. But what if he ignored these goons? Blackmailers gain nothing by executing their threats. They might quit when they saw he was fearless.

Should he discuss the situation with Kanika? Using evidence of misconduct to depose Pat was no crime, and Kanika would surely give him the benefit of the doubt. But could he trust her judgement? She was a know-it-all with poor ability to assess people. She had convinced him to work with Cap Jay, which was the worst advice he had ever received. Sometimes people screwed others even with the best of intentions.

Divya and her gang barged into his room immediately after he returned to the hotel. They had brought bouquets and wine. She surprised him with a kiss on his cheek. 'Congrats! You as now the official head coach. Here's your appointment letter,' she said, handing over a sealed envelope.

A wiry-looking man accompanying Divya kneeled and kissed his hand. 'Please save this team,' he said in a sing-song voice, as though he was addressing a messiah. Following his cue, a woman with purple hair tried to kneel, but changed her mind when she was halfway down.

Neil mumbled a few words of thanks, stumped by the circus.

Divya frowned. 'You look horribly stressed.'

Neil smiled, shaking his head.

'Guys...we need some privacy,' Divya raised her hand. 'Please wait in my room.'

Divya's gang reluctantly moved out, and she closed the door. 'What's troubling you?' she asked. 'You can be frank with me.'

Neil couldn't avoid her questions any more, so he settled for a safe issue. 'Akash appointed Pat...so...'

'Let me handle Akash,' snapped Divya. 'I will screw anyone who disturbs you.'

Divya's support made Neil relax. He wondered if she could tackle Gagan and his buddies. Her support meant the entire might of Akash's business empire was available at his disposal. She hated Pat and wouldn't care how he was toppled. Only the team's performance mattered to Divya.

But I should wait till we win the next match. Then my credentials will become rock solid.

'Thanks, Divya. This means a lot,' he said.

Neil was well aware her support would vanish if they didn't continue winning. Cricket was a cruel and unpredictable game, and he required an exit option in case they fell out. His official appointment as head coach would tie him to the team and prevent him from bailing out if the need arose.

'We should postpone my appointment till the next season,' he said.

'Why?'

'I wanted the role more than the designation,' said Neil. 'So let's not humiliate Pat any more. Let him stay the titular head.'

Divya's face flushed with emotion. 'Wow! My respect for you just doubled.'

Neil laughed and forgot his troubles.

'Let me know if there is anything you need,' said Divya. 'You now have full authority to run this team as you think fit.'

'Sure.'

'We will win?'

'Absolutely.'

Someone knocked on the door, and Neil rushed to check who it was. Kanika entered, carrying flowers and champagne.

'Oh! Celebrations?' she asked with a naughty smile.

'Just talking...' Neil said in a feeble voice.

Fuck! Hope Divya and Kanika won't fight. They are not great friends and I can't afford to make either angry.

'I should leave...not become the third wheel,' said Divya with a coy smile and hugged Neil again. 'Enjoy your evening...' she winked and left the room.

The End Justifies the Means

Kanika shook her head. 'Newfound love for the prodigal cousin?'

'Yes! Made me head coach,' Neil smiled. 'But I postponed it to next year.'

'Why?'

Neil thought of telling Kanika the real story but couldn't muster the courage. 'They will screw me again if we lose. So I protected myself with a bailout option.'

Kanika nodded. 'But Pat hasn't denied the story.'

'Yes! But we haven't acknowledged it as true either.'

'Impressive,' Kanika kissed Neil. 'Let's celebrate. That bitch appreciating you is no small achievement.'

Neil poured the champagne into two flute glasses and passed one to Kanika.

'How did Pat suddenly flip?' asked Kanika, massaging her feet.

Neil shrugged. 'After six losses he had no option.'

'But he could have just used your ideas?'

Neil tried to find a suitable explanation for his story but drew a blank. 'Divya's pressure perhaps. Didn't ask; just did my job.'

Kanika stared at him, wide-eyed. 'So, he just asked you to take over?'

'Not exactly,' said Neil in a halting voice. 'He wanted me to meet him halfway—partially implement my ideas. I refused because it wouldn't work. So he said, fine, you take over. But you will take the blame if it fails.'

Kanika's eyes almost popped out of her head.

'I had nothing to lose,' said Neil. 'It worked out...so there's no turning back.'

'Cheers to the new head coach,' Kanika said, raising her glass. 'I was confident you will get there. Didn't I tell you something will come up?'

Kanika's reaction to his story buoyed Neil. He had expected her to grill him and had prepared to confess, but her trust and happiness in his success melted his heart.

Maybe I will tell her at the end of the season. But now I must focus on the next match and the threat looming over my head. One more win and Gagan will see the full force of Akash's empire going up his arse.

'I heard something shocking today,' said Kanika. 'ICCL matches are being fixed.'

Neil froze; his throat suddenly became dry. 'Really? How do you know?'

'The anti-corruption unit told us during the coordination committee meeting that the betting mafia has recruited somebody important in one of the teams,' said Kanika. 'We will now meet all teams and discuss the dos and don'ts.'

Fuck! Now they will monitor everything. I will get caught.

Neil laughed to hide his panic. 'No one is involved in my team, I can bet. Our poor performance is not because of match-fixing.'

'There are many forms of fixing...'

'I know,' said Neil with a dry smile. 'Been a cricketer for twenty-five years.'

Kanika nodded. 'But be cautious. This is nasty business.'

'Why do you always think I will fail?' snapped Neil, breaking under the stress.

'Just be careful...'

'I'll be careful,' shouted Neil. 'Don't repeat it a hundred times...'

'Okay...sorry!' said Kanika and put her head on his shoulder. She kissed him and caressed his chest, but Neil moved away when she tried to sit on his lap.

Kanika followed him to the window. 'What's wrong?'

'I can manage my team without your help,' said Neil, wiping his brow. 'Anyway, your advice is bullshit...like asking me to talk to Cap Jay.'

'Why? He tried to help you...' said Kanika.

'He was a fucking criminal,' snapped Neil, gesturing with his hand. 'If he would have been alive today, that alert would definitely be about him.'

'How do you know?'

Neil was tempted to tell Kanika how Gagan had trapped him using Cap Jay's master plan, but he controlled his anger for the larger goal of protecting himself. 'Forget it; doesn't matter,' he said, rubbing his hands. 'Oh! I went around Mumbai in the evening today...to the places we used to visit—Pizza by the Bay, Crawford Market, Haji

Ali…it was a trip down memory lane.'

Kanika peered into his eyes as if trying to read his thoughts. 'You sound as if I left you again,' she grinned. 'Let's go there again—for a quick drive. It will cheer you up.'

Neil shook his head. 'I am exhausted.'

'Okay! Let's sleep then,' said Kanika and led him by his hand to the bed.

As Neil lay on the bed, Kanika undressed quickly and climbed on top of him. For a moment he worried about hidden cameras recording their intimate moments, but Kanika evoked a rush of uncontrollable passion in him and swept away his awareness.

Later, while Kanika slept, Neil re-evaluated his options. The anti-corruption alert had totally changed the situation on the ground. Since the ICCL would now monitor every team very closely, he could no longer ask Divya to tackle Gagan and his mafia friends. If she went after them, the ICCL security team would surely notice the fallout and learn the whole truth. Then they would accuse Neil of not only using the mafia's help to topple Pat but also of compromising the matches the team played under his watch. So it was best to silently manage the problem. Anyway, all they wanted was low-level information, which wouldn't impact the matches. Since the owners and the fans were appreciating his work, everything else was inconsequential.

Let them have their damned information. I will just honestly work to help the team win.

Part 3

REDEMPTION

'Any fool can be happy. It takes a man with real heart to make beauty out of the stuff that makes us weep.'

—Clive Barker, *Days of Magic, Nights of War*

Overdose of Emotions

Five Days Later

'It is such a relief to have an elder brother supporting you,' Neil stammered as Akash congratulated him over a call. 'The entire fucking world is full of backstabbers.'

Neil's morose words startled Akash. Coming after two successive wins against Mumbai and Chennai, his sombre mood seemed at odds with both his general nature and the recent upswing in his fortunes.

Who has backstabbed him? Gagan? Somoresh is right—something big is disturbing him.

'Which incident are you referring to?' asked Akash in his usual commanding tone designed to force out secrets. 'Be frank with me.'

'Nothing! Just a general comment,' stammered Neil. 'I'm sorry I opposed you during the union problem. Please forgive me.'

'Aah! That's ancient history,' said Akash.

This bastard always surprises me with the most unexpected behaviour. Newfound humility? Wow!

'I did not realize it then...the sorrow of being betrayed by a brother,' said Neil, sounding emotional, as if dealing with an existential crisis. 'Now I can empathize with your feelings.'

Akash loved winners who showed initiative to create opportunities for themselves. Although initially furious about Neil's impudence, he had come around to appreciate his leadership in seizing control of the team from the South African dinosaur. Neil's gloomy mood and reports of his recent meetings with Gagan had, however, alarmed him about potential manipulations happening behind his back. Neil was angry when Gagan ditched him, so how come the newfound camaraderie? *Did Gagan help him topple Pat? And was he now fucking with him?*

Long years of experience as a businessman had taught Akash that abrupt change does not occur without compelling undercurrents. Pat was unsuccessful and frustrated, but he wouldn't dare to elevate Neil without asking Akash first, and thus, his defiance was a clear sign that he had succumbed to forces much more powerful than him.

I have to unravel this mystery, otherwise people will take me for granted. But it has to be done gently—Divya won't forgive me if I screw up her team just when it has started doing well. So, for now, let Neil think I got his back.

Milk and Cookies

The New Delhi Royals returned to Delhi for the home game against Kolkata, with Neil fluctuating between fear and denial about the evil forces that had gatecrashed his party. At the hotel he dithered about going to his room, fearing the mafia would have delivered the next set of instructions there. Should he move out of the hotel and disappear? he wondered. But Gagan could help the mafia trace him. Also, Pat might become suspicious if he was missing, and spread rumours.

Fuck!

But a security cover could prevent the mafia from contacting him. How would Somoresh react if he told him he was afraid of match-fixers and needed round-the-clock protection? What would he tell Akash?

I need to think this through.

Neil dragged himself to his room to change for the afternoon practice. He opened the door and tentatively looked inside, half expecting to find the mafia waiting there. Slowly closing the door to not alert his imaginary visitors, he peeked under the bed and checked the walk-in closets before walking into the bathroom.

And there it was—a printed note stuck to the mirror.

> Don't include Davit, Aarush and Neeraj in the next match. Instead, select Vineet, Prabhu and Rajiv. Open the bowling with Vineet. Make Dinesh face the first ball.

Neil's head reeled. He pressed against the wall, sweating like a marathon runner at the end of his race.

This isn't low-level stuff…it's match-fixing. We will lose if I make these changes.

Vivid images of his public humiliation flooded his mind as he sat on the edge of the bathtub.

Are they aware of the repercussions? Won't they make more money if we win? Maybe they will understand if I explain. I have to force a discussion.

He scribbled, 'Call; need to discuss' on the note and left it on the bathroom mirror for easy visibility.

The housekeeping staff is definitely involved in this racket. Hope the right people see it.

Neil returned to his room late in the night and found the note undisturbed on the mirror. Before he could wonder what had happened during his absence, a busboy arrived with a tray containing a glass of milk and a placard, with 5426 written on it. He instantly recognized the significance of 5426 and stood aside to let him in.

'Call room service and order some hot milk,' said the busboy curtly as he placed the tray on the table.

Neil rushed to the intercom, his heart pounding in his chest like a hammer. When he returned, the busboy showed him a text message on his phone.

'Read this. I know nothing more than you do.'

Neil peered into the phone without taking it from the busboy's hand. The sender's name was saved as 5426, and the message was the same, word for word, as the one on the mirror.

Is 5426 just a random code or something specific?

'I can't do this; they are the same players I had thrown out of Pat's team,' Neil said.

'You have to manage.'

Neil sighed, shaking his head. 'What is 5426? Who is behind this? He must understand…'

'Should I tell them you are asking questions?' snapped the busboy. 'It won't be pleasant…'

'Is my room bugged? They told me I will give information… but this has…'

Without any warning, the busboy grabbed Neil's arm and knocked his forehead with the phone. 'What are you—a dork?' he cursed, twisting his mouth. 'Why don't you understand—you can't ask questions!'

As Neil grimaced in pain, the busboy walked to the bathroom and ripped out the note from the mirror.

'You have memorized this?' he asked.

Neil nodded.

'Great! Now drink the milk and go to bed like a good boy,' the busboy said, switching off the lights.

A Game of Glorious Uncertainties

Neil tried to contact Gagan, but found him missing from the hotel, and his phone was dead. Next morning, he learnt from the service manager that the busboy who had visited him the previous night had gone on an unplanned leave for three weeks. He tried to attract attention during breakfast by placing a paper on his table with 5426 written on it, but no one responded to his advertisement. The mafia's operating model had blocked all avenues for negotiation and seemed tailor-made for getting unpleasant work done easily. Before leaving for practice, Neil left another note in his room.

> *If we select the players you suggested, we will get eliminated from the tournament. You want that?*

When he returned, he found his question had been answered.

> *Just follow instructions. We control the result of every match. It is fixed that you will reach the finals. Some players in your team are working for us. We are watching you, so don't try anything silly. BTW, we know of your lunch meeting with the ICCL commissioner today. What did you discuss? If you squeal, we will throw acid on your pretty girlfriend's face. Think about it the next time you fuck her.*

How do they know who I met? If everything is fixed, then what's the purpose of this stupid tournament? I should have listened to Gautam Chatterjee and stayed away. Fuck! How do I keep Kanika safe now? I can't put her in danger for my foolishness! I will do what they are asking.

That evening, the New Delhi Royals lost their first match since Neil had taken over as head coach. The Royal Bengal Tigers of Kolkata hit Vineet Srivastav for 18 runs in the first over, scoring 203 runs in 20 overs. Later, they clean-bowled Dinesh Singh in the first ball, restricting Delhi to just 165 in 17 overs, with no batsman scoring more than 15 runs.

Be Warned

Next Morning

'Exciting team selection yesterday,' said Pat, taking the empty seat next to Neil for the flight to Mohali. 'The media reported it as a brain fade.'

Pat prodded, and Neil lazily opened his eyes. 'Let them write whatever they want. It is easier to criticize than to do something.'

'But why change a winning combination?'

Neil slapped his head with his hand. 'To shock the opposition. Didn't work, but we will try again.'

An airhostess stopped by to take orders for breakfast. 'Would you like coffee, sir?'

Neil ignored her, but Pat didn't. 'Yes, black coffee for me.'

The airhostess tried again with Neil. 'And for you, sir?'

Neil waved his hand to dismiss her. She disappeared with no further courtesies.

Pat opened the sports page of the newspaper. 'Forgive me...but isn't this a bad time for experimentation?'

'Relax! We will win the remaining matches.'

'Neil! Let me ask you...' said Pat. He paused with a questioning expression, as if seeking permission to continue.

Neil nodded.

'Is everything clean?' whispered Pat, leaning towards Neil. 'Things don't add up.'

'What are you suspecting?'

'Too much is happening, which can't be a coincidence.'

Neil sat up and fiddled with his phone.

Does he have specific information or is he just fishing for some? I need to know.

The airhostess arrived with Pat's coffee and smiled at Neil again. 'Are you sure you need nothing, sir? Coffee, water, juice, tea?'

This time, Neil dismissed her for good. 'Please don't worry so much. I will live.' The airhostess fled, and Neil faced Pat. 'Speak clearly, Pat.'

Pat looked around him and lowered his voice. 'You fixing matches?'

Neil laughed. 'That's preposterous! You know my passion for the game.'

Pat's glare stopped Neil. 'Sometimes ambition gets the better of our passions,' he said. 'No one imagined Hansie Cronje could become corrupt—such intensity and passion...'

I have to defuse this bomb; his suspicions can reach the media or Akash.

Neil moved Pat's coffee cup from his hand to the table. 'Pat... look at me.' He pointed a finger towards his chest, breathing heavily to show his agitation. 'I am better than Hansie Cronje. This is my family's team, and I don't have to defend myself before an outsider. Understood?'

'Be careful, man,' Pat said, rolling his eyes. 'When the shit hits the fan, no one will support you.'

Is this a veiled threat? I have to put him in his place. Can't risk a loose cannon.

Neil picked up the newspaper. 'Very powerful people support me, Pat. Anyone who disturbs me will suffer. So you be careful as well.'

Accident or Attack?

Akash rushed to Nandini's house after her son met with an accident on his way to play school. A speeding truck had veered to the adjoining lane and crashed the car against a tree. The son, Abhishek, had luckily escaped with minor injuries, but the driver had died of severe head trauma.

'I had asked you not to allow Abhi to go out unless it's an emergency,' shouted Akash. 'Is play school absolutely essential? Why don't you listen to me, Nandini!'

'Fuck off! Who are you, my guardian?' shouted Nandini.

Akash ordered his men to guard the entrance of Nandini's house. 'Since you are irresponsible, I am taking over,' he told her.

'Is this house arrest?' snapped Nandini.

'Yes, for your own protection.'

'Bullshit! You caused this accident to scare me.'

Akash couldn't believe he had to defend himself before a person he loved like a daughter. Somehow she misunderstood him whenever he tried to help.

Why do I care any more?

'Nandini...careful!'

Nandini snorted, crossing her arms. 'You aren't exactly clean...'

She is using Jayshankar's death against me. The bastard kicked her face every day for seven years. Ungrateful bitch!

'I helped you, damn it!' he shouted.

'And you had nothing to gain from it?' mocked Nandini.

Akash realized Nandini would never give him the benefit of the doubt. And without her trust, his affection was irrelevant. He needed a quick and honourable exit from her life.

Nandini wiped her eyes with her sari. 'He could have died today.'

Just then, the entire Upadhyay clan arrived in Nandini's living room.

Ramesh hugged Nandini. 'How is Abhi now?'

'Oh! You don't have to worry about him,' said Akash and pulled Ramesh away from Nandini.

Ramesh frowned. 'Akash! Never tell me what to do, son. I changed your nappies; it was not the other way around.'

Gagan and Ramesh surrounded Nandini, but Akash did not intervene. She wasn't his problem any more.

She does not deserve my help.

Gagan put two fingers together and touched his forehead. 'Be careful. Cap Jay's family is dangerous.'

'Don't worry; we will sort it out,' said Ramesh, patting Nandini on her back.

Nandini held her head with both hands and screamed. Everyone rushed towards her, but she staggered back as if to dissociate herself from that artificial show of sympathy. 'I need nothing from you or Jayshankar's family,' she sobbed. 'I don't care for any business or cricket team. I am moving back to the US. Hopefully, after that I won't see any of you ever again. Now get out and leave me alone.'

She stormed into the bedroom and slammed the door shut.

Family Comes Last

'She can always move to the farmhouse and feel safe,' said Sudha, wrinkling her nose. 'Why this over-the-top reaction to a minor accident?'

Akash had expected Sudha to blame him for Nandini's decision. He had started the rebellion by moving out of the family business, and now she was following in his footsteps. Nandini's genuine disgust never touched Sudha's conscience. After ruining her life, she still believed the solutions to Nandini's problems lay in the farmhouse—the damned fortress where she was the queen without an empire.

No crisis was big enough to stop the Upadhyays from indulging in 'living room' business. Sitting in posh environs, they discussed, debated, plotted, argued, conspired and abused, but did no actual work. Akash sensed the atmosphere ripe for new developments and stayed back in Nandini's house to watch the fun.

Everyone looked at Sudha as she cleared her throat. 'I will sell my entire stake in the Omkar Group and go away,' she said in a quivering voice. 'Family members are free to bid, but I will sell to the highest bidder.'

Akash maintained a poker face and enjoyed the tension engulfing the room. Gagan and his father had thwarted his move to acquire the company, but now it was all over for them. With grandma's shares in his kitty, he would force them out.

'You should also sell,' Sudha told Ramesh, who showed no visible sign of distress. 'If you do, I will give Gagan 25 per cent of what I make.' She turned towards Gagan. 'You will get a good corpus—a sufficient one—if you ditch your bad habits.'

Gagan fumed like a Rottweiler being teased with a piece of meat. His patience looked ready to snap at any moment.

'The company is collapsing, and we can't raise the money to buy out Akash,' said Sudha, caressing her eyebrows. Although her words were polite and businesslike, her face displayed her pain of defeat. 'Soon your shares will be worthless. So, get out.'

'Grandma, we weren't exactly waiting for divine intervention,' said Gagan, vigorously shaking his right leg resting on the left. 'Jayshankar wasn't our only financier.'

Ramesh nodded. 'We will buy your shares.'

'Right! Money grows on trees,' scowled Sudha.

'Even a witch spares her own family,' said Ramesh. 'After building this business, I will now have to pay to own it. Strange!'

While Ramesh ranted, Akash cursed the failure of his overpaid fat-ass security team to detect this new game. Who were the new investors? Cap Jay's friends? This must be a money laundering scheme.

'Who is funding you?' he asked.

'You don't need to know,' said Ramesh.

'Of course I do,' snapped Akash. 'Can't allow dirty money…I will go to jail.'

Ramesh smiled as he sat beside Akash. 'Please! Have some respect for your father. Don't worry; it's clean money.'

'Then reveal the source.'

Ramesh patted his left knee. 'Come on, son, don't be naïve. We can't destroy our competitive advantage by revealing our sources. This is a basic business strategy. You are an MBA from—what's the name of that place again?'

He looked towards Gagan, trying to remember the name of Akash's alma mater.

'Wharton.'

'Yes, *the* Wharton! Didn't they teach you…?'

Akash backed off from the argument, in spite of the deliberate attempt to mock him by adding the unnecessary 'the' before his alma mater's name. They were trying to provoke him to misbehave in front of Sudha and fall out of favour. She would forgive no one who insulted an elder of the family, and Akash was too smart to allow his temper to harm his business interests.

'Why do you need the money? Planning something?' Gagan asked Sudha.

'None of your business,' she snapped.

'You never liked us…God knows why,' blurted Gagan. 'Only Neil…'

Sudha's eyes flashed with anger, but she controlled herself. 'No favourites; the highest bidder wins. Buy me out if you can.'

She walked towards the door but stopped midway and spoke again. 'Any attempt to pressurize me won't work.' She grinned but couldn't hide the tension on her face. 'I know some very powerful people. So, in case you...'

'So, grandma, Neil gets your money?' asked Gagan, breaking into a devilish smile. He tried to hug Sudha but stopped, as her body language resembled that of a coiled rattlesnake, ready to strike. 'Oh! Don't worry, we will take care of Neil.'

'I will buy your shares, grandma,' said Akash. 'I will exceed the highest offer you get. So let me know when you are ready.'

Sudha nodded. 'Also, I want to give some shares to your son.'

'Thank you, grandma, but Rohit doesn't need your money,' said Akash. 'Let's have a purely commercial transaction. Please contact me before you sell the shares to anyone else.'

2 + 2 is not 4

Next Morning

'It was an attack, Neil...not an accident,' Nandini's high-strung voice rang out from the portable CD player as Vikram Singh pressed the play button.

'We recorded this last night, sir,' Vikram grinned. 'We tapped Neil's phone.'

'Very impressive,' mocked Akash, pointing to the door of his cabin. 'Get out. I am very busy.'

'Sir, Nandini ma'am is moving to the US in two days, and she invited Neil to go with her, but he refused,' said Vikram Singh in a high-pitched voice that trailed off when Akash glared at him. 'She was applying for jobs in the US over the last one year, and last month she got an offer from a university in New York.'

'You mean...New York University?'

'Isn't it strange, sir...she was applying for jobs in another country while being in a happy marriage here?

'Happy marriage?' scowled Akash. 'You idiot...Jayshankar could make any woman commit suicide in one day. And she spent seven years with him; she was mad to do so.' Akash twisted his face. 'Or maybe not; she retained her green card. Maybe she is deeper than I think.'

Vikram fast-forwarded the CD. 'Please hear this part, sir...'

Nandini: *So why did Akash suddenly make you head coach?*
Neil (stammering): *He did not...but later he supported it...*
Nandini: *Later? This happened without his permission?*
Neil: *I spoke to Pat, and he agreed...*
Nandini: *Wow! I am impressed by your ability to negotiate.*
Neil: *I used the skeletons in his cupboard...*
Nandini: *What skeletons? Akash knows about them?*
Neil: *I don't know...*
Nandini (sounding agitated): *What did you have against Pat?*
Neil: *It's nothing—don't bother.*
Nandini: *You won't tell me?*

Neil (snapping at her): *Oh, drop it, will you? It's nothing you will understand.*

Nandini: *Neil! Are you doing anything illegal?*

Neil (in a halting voice): *Relax! I will be fine…*

Nandini: *You were talking to Jayshankar. Are you now working with his friends?*

Neil (stammering almost inaudibly): *Not exactly.*

Nandini: *Because if you are, then God help you. There are many things you don't know, and I can't tell you, but remember, you are in grave danger if you get involved with this gang.*

Neil (snickering): *Don't worry…people like my work. Akash supports me…*

Nandini (shouting): *You fool! You are dead if Akash supports you.*

Neil (panting): *Nandini, please! Allow me to use my own judgement…*

Nandini: *Sure! You are a very wise man. I shouldn't waste my words on you.*

Neil (shouting): *Who the fuck cares! A person who couldn't manage her own life thinks she can run the whole world. Ha ha!*

Nandini (in a soft voice): *Really, Neil? Even you will blame me for Jayshankar? That witch has screwed with your mind. It's amazing what free sex can do to a man.*

Neil: *Yeah? The same thing you did to that writer in New York? Screwed with his mind? Dumped him to marry this debauched motherfucker?*

Nandini (in a cold voice): *You know what you are saying is not true, and yet you are using it just to win an argument. Scoring points. What has she done to you? … We are over, Neil. I decided to end all contact with my family here, but I wanted to include you in my life. Now you are also out. Go hide in Kanika's skirt.*

Neil (shouting): *I will; unlike you, she doesn't find new ways to insult me every day. She uplifts me, while you have only demoralized me all my life. Goodbye and good riddance!*

Vikram Singh switched off the CD player. 'A few things to note here, sir—first, Pat's skeletons, second, how Neil learnt about them, and third, the most important part—he did not deny it when Nandini ma'am asked if he was doing anything illegal. And sir, my sources in the underworld say that the cricket betting mafia is using the code 5426 for their main guy…'

'What's 5426?' asked Akash.

'Don't know, sir,' said Vikram in an apologetic tone. 'Must be related to Neil...'

Akash stopped Vikram Singh and churned the information in his head. Cap Jay supporting Neil, Pat suddenly yielding power to Neil, Gagan hanging around the team, Neil lamenting about backstabbing, an anti-corruption alert, controversial team selection in the last match, 5426...what was the story connecting all this? He squeezed his eyes as reality dawned on him. 'Oh fuck! Gagan got Neil involved with the mafia. It makes sense now,' he exclaimed. 'His current financiers are the same ones who were backing Jayshankar, and they had interest in betting. After Jayshankar's death dashed their plans, they reached Neil through Gagan. They helped him topple Pat and then fucked him.'

Vikram Singh offered Akash his hand. 'Sir, you are a genius. Nobody can analyse situations like you...'

Akash ignored him and continued his monologue. 'Aah! That's why Gagan is meeting Neil. This also explains his confidence about raising money. But what is 5426? Is it related to cricket? Or something else?'

'Sir, it must be cricket. Mr Neil has nothing other than cricket in his life.'

'Or it can be a random code,' said Akash, massaging his head.

How to find out? Maybe travelling to Mohali can provide answers. I can force a loose comment from Gagan. Sudhir is desperate to talk. Maybe he has inside information.

'Find Neil's connection to 5426.'

'Yes sir. One more thing...'

'What? Make it quick.'

'Another conversation we recorded, sir, between Neil and Sudha ma'am...'

'I know. Grandma is giving Neil her money, right?'

Vikram Singh gaped. 'Yes sir. But how did you know?'

Akash shrugged. 'I just do. But instead of asking questions, do your job. Find out about Pat's skeletons. That's the key to the whole conspiracy.'

5 for 26

Later in the Day

Outside the team hotel in Mohali, a group of pretty women performed aarti while bhangra dancers in traditional outfits led by an incredibly energetic drummer greeted Akash with loud cries of 'balle balle' and 'swagat hai'. Overenthusiastic hotel managers had spared no effort to accord a grand welcome to a man of his stature.

Akash felt as if a hammer was banging on his eardrum. He glared at Somoresh who tried to make way to the porch, but the bhangra dancers refused to budge. The police snatched the drum, which abruptly stopped the dancing, and then created a corridor for Akash to pass through the crowd.

Three Hours Later

'It is easier to meet the prime minister,' said Sudhir as he entered Akash's suite. 'You made me wait outside for two hours. Why? What's my mistake?'

Akash frowned at Sudhir's bloodshot eyes and sarcastic smile.

The bastard is drunk in the middle of the day, creating a ruckus. I should have allowed the police to arrest him.

'Sometimes even prime ministers have to wait for my appointment,' he said. 'Cricketers like you get bought and sold if I fart. And you thought I am your friend.'

Sudhir lurched forward and parked himself on the couch opposite to Akash.

'So what's happening in the team?'

'I have the same question,' said Sudhir in a choking voice.

'We are winning...'

'We lost the last match.'

'That's a blip. We will recover...'

Sudhir laughed, clapping his hands. 'Now I know why you allowed this coup...'

Akash raised his eyebrows. 'And why?'

'You fell for the slander campaign against Pat,' said Sudhir.
'We lost six matches in a row under Pat,' Akash said curtly.
'It is a new league…'
'But Neil turned it around.'
'No he didn't, damn it!' shouted Sudhir. 'You are so demented.' He took a deep breath. 'I am sorry…'

Akash crushed his beer can, spilling the beer like a fountain. 'How many runs have you scored?'

Sudhir sighed, bowing his head. 'Pat is a superb coach…'

'The results don't agree with your words,' said Akash. He noticed how his calm attitude had rattled Sudhir. People feared his serenity more than his aggression.

Good! He should now expect a big bamboo up his arse soon. I will keep him guessing.

'We have to think long term,' Sudhir stammered. 'The good players won't play under Neil. The fans won't support us as Neil wasn't a star cricketer.'

'But Pat appointed Neil.'

'The media pressurized him,' snapped Sudhir. 'And you allowed Neil a free run.'

Sudhir looked nervous as Akash sat next to him.

'How did Neil convince Pat?' asked Akash.

'It's a mystery,' Sudhir shrugged.

'Maybe they have a deal…'

'Impossible…'

Akash grunted a few times in quick succession. 'You are canvassing for Pat without knowing the whole story. Why are Indians the biggest champions of white men? Seems we haven't recovered from the effect of two hundred years of British rule.'

'What British rule?' asked Sudhir, rubbing his forehead. 'Are you okay?'

'Why are you so impressed by Pat?'

'Because of the same reasons he impressed you,' said Sudhir, raising his voice. 'His achievements, ideas, approach…'

Akash smiled. 'The truth is, you like him because he ill-treated Indians.'

'Bullshit!'

'We Indians love foreigners who ill-treat our countrymen. We lack self-respect.'

Sudhir tried to speak, but gave up with a sigh.

'Do you know I forced Pat to sideline Neil?' asked Akash.

'Really?'

'Yeah! So don't take Pat seriously.'

'That still doesn't justify Neil becoming head coach.'

Akash put his left arm around Sudhir's shoulders. 'Then prove it; find out how Neil toppled Pat; point out his mistakes.'

Sudhir grinned and moved away from Akash's embrace. 'You want me to be a spy?'

'Moral dilemma?' snapped Akash. 'Then just accept the situation. Even I am not happy, but I can't ignore his performance...unless... you give me a bigger reason...'

'Okay, I can try...but I might not find anything.'

'What's 5426?'

'5426? No idea.'

'Is it some score related to Neil or Pat?'

Sudhir shook his head.

'A nickname?'

'How will I know? Am I a trivia collector?' snapped Sudhir.

'Find out if you want to retain your contract next year,' ordered Akash, like a school teacher chiding an errant student. 'If you don't, I will assume you are jealous we are winning despite your pathetic performance.'

Sudhir shook like a frail branch shaking in the strong wind, but Akash did not soften the final blow. 'Other teams also won't dare to buy you.'

'I don't fear you,' scowled Sudhir and sprung up from the couch. He stood almost on top of Akash. 'Don't forget I am a top star. If I tell the media you are harassing me, then you will be gone, Mr Corporate Honcho.'

Akash barely concealed his excitement, as Sudhir's flaming eyes showed character and defiance befitting a top sportsman.

I just have to rub him a little more, and he will squeal.

'Oh, you don't fear me? But, your texts tell a different story,' said Akash, picking up his phone. 'Let's see...'

He opened a text message and read it aloud.

```
    Are you upset with me? I am sorry if I made a
mistake. Please forgive me.
```

Akash chuckled. 'You were shitting bricks when I ignored your calls. Here is another one.'

```
    Please tell me what you want? I will do anything
4 you.
```

Akash froze as he read that message again.
Anything 4 you; the 4 means 'for'. So the 5426 might mean 5 for 26.

'Wait a second—how about 5 for 26?' he said. 'Any connection to Neil?'

Sudhir took a moment and then nodded. 'Yes! The other day we were discussing the best Indian bowling figures, and this came up—Neil's best bowling performance is 5 wickets for 26 runs, against Australia.'

Sniffer Dog

That night the ICCL appointed 'special anti-corruption officers' for every team to counter the match-fixing threat. In a blatant conflict of interest, Akash forced the ICCL to appoint Sanket Singh (former Deputy Commissioner of Delhi Police) to the New Delhi Royals. Sanket was on Akash's payroll as a serving police officer, and post-retirement often worked as his consultant on projects of 'strategic' importance.

'Report directly to me and don't talk to the ICCL jokers,' Akash told Sanket when he reached Mohali by a chartered flight that night. 'Neil is guilty, but we don't have proof. Push him to confess, but don't use the third degree. My family is emotional about this team, so be careful.'

Akash visualized his hands around Neil's neck.

After sending him to jail I will ask Nandini why she loves him.

The Smell of Information

Next Morning

'He caught Hansie Cronje—exposed the match-fixing racket.' Somoresh Basu gave Neil a wicked smile, pointing towards a grey-haired gentleman in a navy blue suit sitting on the other side of the restaurant. 'Don't be fooled by his gentlemanly looks. He is a former DCP—expert at squeezing out information. You will soon see...'

Neil shrugged and tried to look casual, although he was rattled since the previous night when the mafia had alerted him about Sanket's appointment. 'I have nothing to say. The team's security is your job, not mine.'

'Sir! Please complain to Mr Akash if you want,' said Somoresh in a grim voice. He signalled to Sanket and walked away.

Neil shivered internally as Sanket walked towards him.

Someone trying to scare me and force a mistake? But how do they know? Pat?

Sanket extended his hand. 'Mr Neil...pleasure meeting you.'

Neil smiled and shook hands with him. 'Mind if I finish my breakfast first?'

'Sure! So, the conference room in fifteen minutes?'

After Thirty Minutes

Sanket peered at Neil through rimless glasses, as if examining his soul. 'Did you see anything suspicious?'

'No; but ask Somoresh,' said Neil.

'We will.'

'Great! I'll head for practice.'

Sanket signalled with his hand for Neil to sit down. 'How did you suddenly become the head coach?'

'Owner's decision.'

'Oh! Come on...Mr Akash never approved this. You and Mr Pat settled it among yourselves.'

'It is our internal matter; I don't have to explain it to an outsider.'

'How did you convince Mr Pat?' asked Sanket in a stern voice.

Sanket's eyes gleamed with spite and Neil smiled to diffuse the tension. 'Pat realized we required urgent changes. I admire him for dropping his ego for the team.'

'What happened in the last match?' asked Sanket.

'I am guilty as charged by the media,' said Neil. Sanket's eyes lit up and Neil indulged him. 'I made some really bad decisions. But hey, sometimes it works, sometimes it doesn't.'

'What's 5426?'

Fuck! How did he find out about the code? I have to quickly throw him off the scent.

Neil frowned, countering Sanket's penetrative glare. 'It's five thousand four hundred twenty six...or six thousand minus five hundred seventy four.'

Sanket sprang up from his chair. 'Mr Neil, this is not a joke. We are...'

Neil banged on the table with his palm. 'And I am trying to save my team here. I've a million things to worry about. But why should you care? You can ask me the same thing a hundred times, but if I don't know something, how will I talk about it?'

'Sir, you are not being singled out,' said Sanket in a soft voice. 'We are asking everyone...so please cooperate.'

Neil stuck to his aggressive stand to press home the advantage. 'I will be the first to report anything suspicious,' he said, slapping his chest with his left palm. 'I have some credibility, right? This is my family's team,' he shouted, thumping the table again, 'for God's sake!'

'Okay, fair enough,' said Sanket, collecting his papers. 'We will meet again once we have more details.'

'Again?'

'This is an ongoing investigation...'

'Somoresh will talk to you.'

'Very well, but please be available if we need you.'

'I can't. I am swamped...'

Sanket raised his hand to stop Neil. 'If you don't, we will expel your team from the ICCL.'

Neil backed off, realizing Sanket had the authority for making such threats. 'Okay, sir! Will do. Now may I go?'

Sanket smiled. 'What are you hiding?'

'No, no, no,' screamed Neil, holding his head in his hands. 'The same question, again and again...'

'Mr Neil, I was a senior police officer,' said Sanket, unfazed by Neil's melodrama. 'I have interrogated thousands of hardened criminals—tough nuts who wouldn't break even under extreme torture. But I always broke them. You know why? Because my instinct always alerted me if they were hiding something. So I persisted...and they broke. Eventually they all do.'

'So? Why should I be interested in your illustrious career?' snapped Neil. 'Should I talk about my achievements?'

'Because...my instinct is alerting me now...that there is information hidden in this room,' said Sanket. He closed his eyes with Zen-like calm. 'I can sniff it...it is fouling the air.' Moving his palms around his face he squeezed his nose, as if having an unpleasant experience. 'But I will persist...and it will come out.'

Between a Rock and a Hard Place

Same Day, Early Afternoon

Select Neeraj, Baldev and Antonio for the next match. Choose to field after winning the toss. Open batting with Dinesh but not with Sudhir. Send Sudhir fifth down or later. There will be spot-fixing, so make sure no one messes with our guys.

These instructions arrived in his room as a note hidden inside a newspaper. The new busboy asked him to memorize the instructions and then flushed the paper down the toilet.

Neil wiped the sweat from his forehead. Neeraj and Baldev had become friendly when he had taken over as head coach, so they were probably involved right from the beginning. Fuck! When did this game become a money-making operation? Young cricketers risking their careers for a few bucks!

Neeraj was a preferred player, but selecting Antonio and Baldev would guarantee the team's loss in the next match and fuel Sanket's suspicions. *Can anyone tell me how to demote Sudhir?* Neil was talking to himself. *He is the captain, an international star. And how do I stop anyone from messing with the spot-fixers? The captain is in charge on the field.*

I can't do this. Let them expose me if they want to.

What could the mafia do? Apart from the blackmailing bit, they had no other proof against him. Blackmailing Pat did not connect him to match-fixing. Pat's exit at the end of the season would anyway neutralize their threat. Thus, refusing to follow their orders would force the mafia to negotiate, while ignoring Sanket could cause immediate and permanent damage. Akash would never tolerate an external agent screwing around with his team unless he himself wanted an investigation. But why was he suspicious? Had Gagan told him something during one of his drunken fits? Fucker! Akash wouldn't have camped in Mohali for two days unless he had a bigger objective.

I can't risk getting caught. Akash is more brutal than any mafia in this world.

That evening, Neil left a note for the mafia hidden inside a magazine in a drawer. He placed an old cricket ball on top of the magazine to make sure the message was noticed.

> *I can't follow your instructions. Another loss will raise suspicion. Sniffer dog is asking questions. Who is leaking information? Please help.*

Polite Enquiries

Two Hours Later

'Congrats, Neil...very proud of you.'

Ramesh Upadhyay never indulged in casual chit-chat. But that afternoon he surprised Neil with a seemingly purposeless call right in the middle of practice.

Neil grunted, a little unnerved by uncle's playful voice.

'Relax! Don't take it personally. Compromise is good...'

'What compromise, uncle?'

Ramesh laughed. 'Nothing! I was pepping you up...'

Neil couldn't decipher uncle's odd comments. Had Gagan told him as well?

Fuck! This will destroy my reputation in the family.

After screwing him, the bastard was educating the world about his exploits.

'Did Gagan update you, uncle?'

'No! Gagan is too busy with work and parties.'

'Is that true? Then why is he here?'

'To help you.'

'Oh, he has been of great help,' said Neil, clenching his fist. 'More than I expected from an older brother.'

'That's nice,' said Ramesh. 'Consult him, but above all, be patient. Don't take hasty decisions that you will regret later.'

'Is this pep talk again?'

'I'll go now,' said Ramesh. 'Take care; you have my blessings—and you need it.'

Neil couldn't understand the strange behaviour of his family members. Why had everyone become weird after he had saved the family's team from ruin? First Akash and now uncle—taunting tone, sly remarks, advising him to be patient, hinting at some unknown 'compromise'... What compromise was he talking about?

Surely not my involvement with the mafia? Or is that it?

Hormone-Struck Teenagers

Later That Evening

'Switch on the TV and go to a news channel, any news channel,' shouted Somoresh Basu over the intercom as Neil returned to his room after practice.

Neil slammed the phone down. Was Somoresh raking up the last match again? Someone famous must have enlightened the world with a comment. A former cricketer, perhaps?

God! It's just cricket, not the end of the world. Now let it go! I will see the stupid news later. Let's first check if they replied to my message.

He found his note untouched in the drawer and checked his watch. It was 9 p.m., and time was running out for a discussion. After Kanika arrived, he wouldn't even be able to fart without arousing her suspicion. He was confident of convincing the mafia if they would give him a chance to explain.

Everyone loses if we don't qualify for the playoffs. They are not dumbasses, after all.

Neil switched on a news channel and saw the breaking news about a 'sex scandal'. A team of anchors and self-styled experts dressed in tasteless attire educated the public in their unique animated style about the unholy mix of sex and money in the ICCL. He flipped channels and soon realized the story was about them. Someone had posted his intimate photos with Kanika on the Internet.

Who clicked these photos? Uncle and grandma will see them. Shit!

Before he could analyse how it had happened, Somoresh called him again.

'Please explain,' he asked in a curt voice.

'No idea; maybe someone secretly photographed us.'

'Hmm, but who? You are responsible...this is a cricket team, not a...'

Does he have a problem with the photos or my affair with Kanika? I have to show this clerk his place.

'Somoresh—don't lecture me about my personal matter.'

'You tarnished the image of the team.'

'And losing six matches didn't?'
'Was Kanika responsible?'
'Go ask her.'
'Divya ma'am is very upset; she might ask for an explanation. Drop this aggression when you talk to her. And stop your extracurricular activities till the league is over. This is a cricket team, for God's sake, not your honeymoon.'

Somoresh ranted on about maintaining disciple and setting a good example, but Neil switched off the intercom, wondering who was responsible. Gagan again, or Akash?

Thank God…at least they don't show us naked.

'They posted these on a blog,' Somoresh said.
'Whose blog?'
'Sanket Singh will investigate…'
'Why Sanket?' stammered Neil. 'This isn't match-fixing.'
'Might be pressure tactics.'
'Impossible.'

Somoresh laughed, producing a weird nasal sound like a dog's bark. 'Let's see what he finds. We will try to remove this from the Internet and the news channels ASAP. It will die soon if you behave.'

After Somoresh hung up, Neil strolled to the bathroom with that devilish laughter ringing in his ears. A note posted on the mirror made his blood freeze.

You saw the trailer? Should we release the whole film?

Neil leaned on the wash basin, lacking the strength to react.

Oh shit! They leaked the photos. What more do they have?

He splashed water on his face, wishing he could disappear into the wilderness where no one knew him.

Why didn't they discuss this with me? Sanket will now nail me.

The doorbell rang and he hastily destroyed the note. Moments later, Kanika walked in, whistling a jaunty tune. 'What's up, coach? Get me a drink, please!'

Drink? She doesn't know? Ridiculous!

Neil shook his head, pointing towards the TV. 'What happened here?'

Kanika twirled a hanky around her fingers. 'Oh! It was a prank, nothing serious. Hormone-struck teenagers who have a little "something" for older women. They are upset I am dating you.'

'Who are these so-called "hormone-struck teenagers"?' asked Neil.

'Don't know; they send me love letters, emails, postcards and messages written in blood or red ink. What's the big deal? They are not showing us having sex...just kissing,' said Kanika. She changed into a black negligee. 'Don't worry; I told the press they are morphed photos—and not real.'

In normal circumstances, the sight of Kanika's shapely legs would make his pulse race like a Ferrari on full throttle, but that day the embarrassment of having his private life paraded on national TV seemed to have made his male hormones hibernate. How can a woman be so casual about her compromising photographs appearing in the public domain? he wondered. And why was she so eager to dismiss this as trivial? Was the mafia blackmailing her as well?

Fuck! They are surrounding me for the kill.

'Someone secretly photographed us, and you are not worried?' asked Neil.

'Morphed photos—not real, remember?'

'They are real,' shouted Neil. 'I can recognize our faces.'

Kanika sighed. 'It doesn't matter. A denial kills the story.'

'Tomorrow more might leak out.'

'The more reason there is to deny it. After my clarification to the media, every photo or video automatically becomes useless.'

Lying on the bed, Kanika lifted her leg and pointed her toe towards Neil. 'Are you going to just stand there and watch me? Or will you come to bed?'

Hiding in Plain Sight

The mafia's threat broke Neil's resistance to their demands. So, next morning, he accepted their orders through a note scribbled and kept inside a magazine in the top drawer. As usual, he placed a cricket ball on top of the magazine for easy identification.

At breakfast, he faced sarcastic smiles and knowing glances, but no comments or oblique references about the embarrassing incident. Neither the newspapers nor the TV channels carried the story any more. New Delhi Royals had used all forces under its command to protect the dignity of their prized coach.

'Decided the team?' Sudhir asked with a sly smile.

'It is a fast wicket, so maybe we should play Antonio,' said Neil.

Pat laughed. 'Really? After you declared him as toxic waste?'

'Who will he replace? asked Sudhir.

'We will see,' said Neil, burying his face in the newspaper.

Pat and Sudhir walked away, shaking their heads, but Neil had bigger things to worry about. Kanika had left early in the morning without waking him up, which was highly unusual. Her casual reaction to the leak continued to bother him. Why had Sanket not questioned him that morning? He shivered as the fork dropped from his hand and made a clanking sound on the plate. Where is Somoresh? Were they searching his room?

Fuck! I must save myself.

Neil rushed to the elevator and almost elbowed people to board the first available lift. He ran to his room and saw the door ajar. A group of men were combing the furniture.

'What the fuck!'

'Relax!' stammered Somoresh, rushing towards Neil. 'It's standard practice...'

Sanket checked his watch, looking surprised. 'You lost your appetite?'

Neil saw the open top drawer and almost lost his balance.

Shit! They have the magazine. But have they seen the message? Maybe not, otherwise they would have charged me by now.

'You couldn't wait for me to return?' he asked in a pseudo-agitated voice. His guilty conscience failed to muster the indignation for a strong protest.

'No time—lots of rooms to check,' said Somoresh, shaking his head.

'There is personal stuff here.'

Sanket's men had taken apart the room; the closets were empty, with his clothes and cricketing gear piled on the floor, and the bed was dismantled, with the mattress and pillows on a table. A ladder was installed to check the false ceiling, and fingerprint powder covered the table and mantle. Two agents with flashlights checked the closets and the minibar, while a group worked in the bathroom.

'Go finish your breakfast,' said Sanket.

'Absolutely not,' said Neil. 'I can't allow you to plant evidence against me.'

'But I am here...' said Somoresh, looking surprised.

Neil smiled. 'Exactly the reason I should be here. A team that doesn't trust its own coach is capable of anything.'

Somoresh shrugged and turned away to supervise the investigators.

Neil loitered around the room looking for the magazine, but couldn't locate it.

Maybe the mafia took it before these assholes arrived. But it is unlikely that I have such good luck.

'Mind if I borrow this?' asked Sanket from behind him.

Neil turned and saw Sanket holding the magazine. He felt the floor collapsing under his feet.

Fuck! Remain calm. He won't know if I don't panic.

'It's hotel property,' Neil said, hyperventilating.

'Are you reading it?'

'Yes! Reading helps me relax.'

Sanket smiled. 'You read *The Economists*?' he said, raising his eyebrows as he flipped through the magazine again. 'World affairs, China, The IMF. Heavy stuff. Wow! You surprise me every day, Mr Neil.'

Suddenly, Sanket looked towards the ceiling as if drawn towards an apparition. 'Something is wrong,' he sniffed the air. 'The air is foul. Uff!' He discarded the magazine. 'Any comments, Mr Neil?'

'What nonsense!' Neil said in an aggressive tone, determined to show confidence and establish his innocence. 'There's cricket gear here. Obviously it will smell. But how will you know!'

'No, no, that smell is pure,' Sanket sniffed the air again like a dog. 'I know; I've played cricket for Haryana.'

'And then you were thrown out?' smirked Neil.

'Not everyone is rich like you, Mr Neil.'

'Listen—don't taunt me,' shouted Neil. 'And you don't have evidence against me, so stay out of my way.'

The Tragedy of Passionate Fans

'Sir, their modus operandi is very sophisticated,' said Sanket, moving in front of Akash in the VIP box. 'Mr Neil has no digital trace—only the number 5426.'

Akash scowled and pushed Sanket away to watch the army of fans that had arrived in Mohali that afternoon carrying drums, bugles and trumpets, wearing fancy dresses and with faces painted in the team's lemon green colour.

These poor bastards expected their team to fight hard and win, but my fat-assed investigators can't stop a small-time thief from betraying their trust. That's the unfortunate reality of life. People we support the most are the first to betray us.

'You are sure about Neil?' asked Akash.

'Without doubt, sir! I am an expert...'

'Shut up...asshole,' Akash snapped and sprayed Sanket with coffee. 'Stop praising yourself. He's mocking me every day, and you are scratching your balls?'

'Sir, we can catch him only if he makes a mistake,' said Sanket in a meek voice. He wiped his suit, unflustered, as if accepting the punishment. 'I am trying, sir, please have patience.'

The crowd roared when Sudhir won the toss. 'We will bowl first,' he said to the TV anchor. 'Two changes in the team—Baldev Madan and Antonio Charles will replace Davit Verma and Manuel Cyclic. We had an off day in the last match, but we are confident of winning today.'

Akash cursed as the TV commentators criticized both the decisions, of choosing to bowl first in boiling hot weather and including Antonio Charles in the team by dropping a star performer. 'Put a camera in his room,' he said.

'The hotel won't allow it, sir.'

'How are they talking to him?'

'Maybe through the waiters, or Mr Neil is using someone else's phone, or through visitors at the hotel or the stadium...'

'But your man is shadowing him?'

'Yes sir, 24 × 7, but we can't go into the washroom with him, or...'

'Monitoring the waiters?'

'Yes! But the team is constantly travelling, so it's difficult.'

Akash scowled. 'In the last thirty minutes, I have only heard excuses. Are you a real man? Or one of those fags? Do you have children?'

'Yes sir, three...one son and two daughters.'

'Are they yours? Hmm?'

'But sir...'

Another roar went off in the stadium as the New Delhi Royals team entered the ground, led by their captain Sudhir Yadav.

Akash pointed at the crowd. 'They love this game. And we are cheating them.'

Sanket bowed his head. 'Did Mr Sudhir say anything?'

'Sudhir is absolutely worthless,' said Akash, cursing under his breath. 'I will fire him next season—doesn't score runs, doesn't give information; a freeloader.'

'Sir, we should force Mr Neil to confess.'

'Are you mad?' shouted Akash. He pointed towards the second VIP box from where Divya and her friends were cheering the team. 'Will *you* explain things to her if the team gets screwed? It would be fine if we were not doing well, but not any more. We must trap him naturally and then negotiate with his backers. Understood?' he said, pushing Sanket's forehead with his palm. 'Or should I give you the third degree treatment?'

'No, sir,' said Sanket, looking away.

'Why did they leak his photos?'

'Because he refused to follow orders.'

'But eventually he did?' asked Akash in a soft voice, touched by Neil's resilience.

The bastard is fighting, despite all odds. It was a mistake not to appoint him the head coach right at the beginning.

'He had no choice,' said Sanket.

'So, they can put up cameras but we can't?' snapped Akash.

'Those photos are from a few weeks ago,' said Sanket. 'And honestly, sir, even installing cameras won't help any more. He knows he might be recorded, so he will be careful.'

'How about a listening device?'

'Yes, sir, we did instal one, but he keeps changing shoes and clothes. He's smart.'

'Hmm! So, why did Pat resign?'
'Mr Neil blackmailed him.'
'How do you know?'
Sanket smiled. 'I heard rumours...from my network...'
'What?' Akash waved his hand to urge Sanket to continue.
'That Pat took kickbacks from the foreign players,' said Saket.
'Can we pressurize them to give a statement?'
'No, we can't, sir. Their embassies will object, and this will become a diplomatic situation. Anyway, we cannot connect their testimony to Mr Neil's blackmail.'
'Hmm!'
'Mr Gagan must have helped him...'
'Did you search Gagan?' asked Akash.
'Found nothing, sir,' Sanket smiled. 'His computer is full of porn. It's interesting...both of them have reformatted their laptops recently. They are not novices, sir! Mr Neil is being advised by experts—otherwise, by now we would have nabbed him.'
'His girlfriend is involved?'
Sanket sighed. 'No sir. We are monitoring her as well—she looks clean.'
'Can we use her to trap him?
'How? Unless Mr Neil tells her something?' said Sanket, throwing up his hands. 'We installed a listening device in her bag, but nothing happened. She warned him about the alert...and he acted as if it doesn't concern him.'
'So what's the solution?' snapped Akash. 'You're just parroting the situation...'
'Sir, I have a plan. Please give me a few hours...'
'How few?'
'Six hours max.'
Akash frowned, looking at his watch. 'It's 4 p.m. now. If I don't get a credible plan by 10 p.m., your career is over. Is that clear?'

That afternoon, Punjab scored 206 runs batting first. New Delhi's opening bowlers Antonio and Baldev were hit for 46 runs in the first

4 overs. The brutal heat led to wayward bowling, missed catches and other fielding errors. New Delhi's loyal fans supported their team through their disastrous bowling performance but rebelled when Sudhir did not open the batting with Dinesh, and stopped play for a full fifteen minutes. When play resumed, Dinesh and Harish exploited the insipid Punjab bowling and scored 123 runs in the first 10 overs. The succeeding batsmen maintained the high scoring rate, and the match was almost over by the time Sudhir came out to bat, with New Delhi requiring only 7 runs from 2 overs. The TV commentators eventually changed their stand about New Delhi's match strategy and praised the team's unorthodox batting order that exploited Punjab's weak bowling.

The Great Escape

Late That Night

The incessant ringing of the doorbell forced Neil out of his sleep, but he found no one waiting outside when he answered the door. He stumbled back inside in a semi-awake state and stepped on an envelope on the floor. Inside was a message from the mafia.

> *5426, go to the third stall from the left in the men's washroom in the lobby—near Mansur restaurant. You will get a call in the next ten minutes. Don't leave fingerprints on the phone. Turn it off after the call and drop it deep inside the trash bin.*

Neil groaned about his unknown master's unnecessary penchant for drama and washed his face to get rid of the lethargy. He reread the note and felt that the last two lines were unusual. The mafia had stopped instructing him about how to handle hazardous material after the first call, so why give these instructions again? Was a new person in charge? Or had something changed?

Neil walked towards the hotel lobby, relieved that Kanika had slept through it all. Did they not know she was with him? What would he have told her had she woken up? Those stupid assholes had left a note when they knew he was being monitored. The messenger could have whispered the instructions to him—like they generally did. Why had things changed this time? Were they planning something big that required a conversation? Or maybe it was a tip-off to save him from Sanket?

He leaned against the wall to catch his breath, immobilized by terror.

Fuck! Will I get caught?

The hotel bustled with activity all day, but at night the deserted passages and lifts looked eerie, as if hiding demons waiting to spring out from hidden corners without warning. The reception area was empty, relieving him of the compulsion of exchanging unnecessary greetings and courtesies from the hotel staff. Neil entered the washroom and got a shock on seeing his hunched-up dishevelled reflection in the mirrors. He rushed to the third stall and found the phone taped to the backside of the commode and kneeled with his face close to it to extricate the phone, using a handkerchief to avoid fingerprints.

The call came through immediately after he switched on the phone, as though the caller had real-time information of his movements. He covered the phone with his hand and answered in a low voice. 'Hello.'

'Open the bowling with Manuel Cyclic and Baldev Madan in the next match,' the caller said in a muffled voice. 'Demote Dinesh Singh in the batting order and open the batting with Benjamin Roister.'

What? Open the bowling with Manuel when he is injured and out of the next match? They usually track the team's activities. Something is off here.

Neil reeled as the caller spoke again. 'You there? Speak up…'

They only give instructions, never entertain a discussion. Who is calling? This is a setup—a trap.

Neil smiled, a little surprised by his presence of mind. 'Who the fuck are you?' he snapped. 'And how dare you tell me what to do?'

'I am the master of your destiny,' the caller snickered. 'Seems the photos were not enough. Next time bedroom scenes; promise!'

'I will take your ass for this prank, asshole! Disturbing me in the middle of the night!'

'Then the videos will leak.'

'I don't fear your threats,' shouted Neil. 'Just wait; the police will shove a baton up your ass.'

Sanket did this to frame me. Bastard! Now I will fuck him.

Neil pocketed the handkerchief and smeared the phone with his fingerprints before switching it off. He rushed out and bumped into Sanket Singh by the washroom door. 'Oh! How come you are here?' Neil asked, startled. Sanket's presence so close to the crime scene reassured him he had made the right assessment. 'I am officially reporting to you that match-fixers have approached me. I have, of course, turned them down. Here is the phone they used to contact me,' said Neil, pushing the phone into the top pocket of Sanket's dark grey jacket. He smiled as he smoothed the wrinkles on the jacket and then produced the note from his pocket. 'And they used this to bring me here.'

'Mr Neil…may I ask why you responded to this note?' asked Sanket, adjusting his glasses. Even after his plan had bombed, he looked in control of the situation. 'After all, it is not normal for you to attend a phone call at 4 a.m. in a bathroom five floors below your room.'

Neil coughed to clear his throat and then frowned. 'Mr Singh... two things to note here; firstly, although I am not as educated as you are, I am aware it is bad style to address someone by his first name after the title "mister". So, you should either call me "Neil" or "Mr Upadhyay". Please don't call me "Mr Neil" any more.' He closed his eyes in mock horror. 'Please! I request you...'

Sanket's eyes flashed, but he did not retort.

'And, secondly, Mr Singh...please understand that I am a sportsman, not a policeman.' Neil shrugged with a wry smile. 'I didn't know how to handle this. I was barely awake. You can accuse me of foolishness perhaps, but not of impropriety. And since I have reported this incident myself, I have followed all the ICCL rules.'

Sanket Singh mumbled a few incoherent words and suddenly looked very uncomfortable.

'By the way, what are you doing here at this odd time?' asked Neil. 'Were you expecting this to happen?'

Neil leaned on the bathroom wall and grinned as Sanket Singh walked away, with no further courtesies.

Reboot

Next Day

'Keep making grand plans...while they show me the middle finger,' said Akash, after Sanket narrated the story from the previous night to him. 'An IPS officer? Amazing! You don't deserve to be a constable.' Akash rushed towards Sanket and gave him a tight backhanded slap on his face. 'You destroyed my reputation...son of a bitch,' he gasped as his heart slammed against his chest like a sledgehammer. 'They are laughing at me—the globally renowned businessman who can't even tackle a small-time crook. Fuck!'

'Sir, please give me one more opportunity,' pleaded Sanket, crawling on the carpet to find his glasses which had been dislodged by the slap. 'Kill me if I fail, but please, sir...'

Akash collapsed into a chair and analysed the matter again. Was Kanika involved? She was the only unexplored link. Maybe she was the go-between; after all, she had unrestricted access to Neil and knew people in all the teams. She had been close to Jayshankar who was involved with these goons. But how would he coax her to sell them out? She was a tough nut; wouldn't bend easily. Threatening her would annoy the cricket board whose members drooled when she gave them her attention and shagged every night thinking of her. Gagan had protection from grandma. Grandma would use her shares as leverage to defend him. Divya would get upset if they threatened Neil.

Fuck! Everyone has someone important backing them. Why do people care so much about others?

'Okay! What's your new plan?' Akash braced himself for another overdose of confidence from Sanket. He had zero faith in Sanket's ability to deliver, however, since other options lacked promise, he didn't have an option but to let Sanket take one more shot at cracking this puzzle. 'But make your case in two minutes or less; otherwise you are out.'

'Sir, our main problem is that the mafia has local contacts in the hotels where the team is staying,' said Sanket, enthused by Akash's interest.

'Don't we know that?' scowled Akash.

'Sir, we should change the hotel in Kolkata...at the last minute. No one will know. Somoresh can book another hotel, pretending it is for a conference. And when the team lands in Kolkata, we will take them directly to the new hotel.'

'Hmmm! And if this fails then I will assume either you or Somoresh is involved,' said Akash, smiling. 'Fair?'

'I won't fail, sir, trust me,' mumbled Sanket, looking unsettled. 'We will lose some money, sir, but...'

Akash noted Sanket's ingenuity and wished his execution was as good as his strategy.

All good plans, but poorly carried out.

'Money isn't a problem,' he shook his head. 'But how will it help catch Neil?'

'We will place several guards outside his door—check every visitor and parcel; they will accompany him round the clock. Sir, the betting in every match is for hundreds of crores. If they can't talk to him, they will become desperate and make mistakes.'

'Neil will protest, but I guess we can force him...' said Akash, with a wicked smile. He tried to imagine how Divya would react before he gave Sanket the go-ahead. It would depend on how it was sold to her.

Hopefully this constable won't screw up and get me into trouble.

Sanket laughed for the first time in that meeting. 'Sir, he won't protest...after he voluntarily reported the incident today. We will tell him we are trying to protect him from the mafia.'

Prisoner's Dilemma

Two Days Later, Early Afternoon

'Why so much security?' Gautam Chatterjee chuckled on entering Neil's room. 'Kolkata is very peaceful—no one will kill you here.'

'It's not for me, sir…they want to protect the game,' said Neil in a low voice. He was still preoccupied with the startling event of that morning. The mafia had used Dinesh Singh to deliver instructions during practice. He couldn't believe a senior cricketer like Dinesh would fix matches. The bastard didn't even flinch while speaking to him. Changing the team hotel and having twenty guys to guard him wouldn't work when the entire goddamn world was corrupt.

They are five steps ahead of Sanket. Fuck! Cricket is doomed.

'But why inside your room?' asked Gautam, sounding like an authoritative landlord with his booming voice and crisp white dhoti-kurta. 'Something wrong?'

'Today is our last match, and we must win to qualify,' said Neil in an apologetic tone. 'They come inside only when I have a visitor, sir…not otherwise.'

'Maybe as a status symbol,' Gautam smiled. 'We Indians are experts in show-off. First they humiliated you…now they are treating you like a VIP.' Gautam hugged Neil fondly. 'Well done, my boy…proud of you.'

'No…sir,' Neil cringed from Gautam's embrace, feeling unworthy.

Gautam looked admiringly at Neil. 'I shouldn't have discouraged you. Sorry!'

'You were right in calling this a circus, sir,' Neil said absentmindedly.

He again thought of Dinesh. This time the mafia only wanted minor changes in the batting order, but the larger purpose was to assure Neil that they would qualify for the playoffs.

Is every match fixed? Then why are we playing?

Dinesh probably knew the answer, but he couldn't ask him. He had learnt it was impolite to ask questions his invisible bosses did not want to answer.

'Why are you so negative about the ICCL?' Gautam raised

his eyebrows. 'The quality of cricket is fantastic. Plus it is giving opportunities to youngsters…helping Indian cricket.'

'I agree, sir,' said Neil hesitatingly. 'But like you had said, when individuals own cricket teams, it causes complications.'

'Oh! You are still upset about the initial phase,' Gautam shook his head. 'Everyone is praising you for having motivated your team to excel. Your precise match strategies have outfoxed all the other teams. You are now the undisputed king of the ICCL. Feel it! Breathe in your stardom; imagine what you can achieve next year…'

'There won't be a next year,' muttered Neil.

Gautam looked shocked. 'What? Why? You can't give up like this. Tell me what's bothering you…'

'There are just too many moving parts, sir,' said Neil. 'My interest is only in cricket. I don't want to deal with the nonsense that's part of the job.'

Gautam sighed, rolling his eyes. 'But you won't have to, any more. Next year, I will join you as an assistant coach. Apart from my experience of coaching, I will bring my extensive network in the media and the cricket bureaucracy on board. I will handle it all, don't worry.'

Neil gaped, stumped by Gautam's unilateral plans for *their* future.

'Don't look so shocked,' said Gautam, sitting next to Neil on the bed. 'I don't mind becoming your assistant.' He put his arm around Neil. 'We'll be a great team. And you owe it to me, right?'

Their eyes met briefly as Neil cringed at the sight of the idealist guru succumbing to the glamour and money of the ICCL. After championing 'pure' cricket all his life, he now wanted to become a clown in the circus. Idealism was born from the lack of opportunity; it wouldn't be able to survive the chinking of coins. He probably wouldn't mind fixing matches as well.

Don't know about next year, but for now I have to get this hypocrite off my back.

Neil stood up to ease the sickness in his stomach. 'Sure, sir…it will be a pleasure,' he smiled. 'Let's connect after this season is over.'

A few hours later, Sudhir Yadav scored his maiden century in the ICCL, and Neeraj Dara took 3 wickets for 16 runs to help the New Delhi Royals qualify for the playoffs. Neil noted a few aberrations in the performance of both teams—3 wides in succession from Baldev Madan, Kolkata's Ronit Guha bowled a no ball in every over and Dinesh Singh defended the first ball of every new over he faced, which enhanced Neil's fears about widespread corruption in all teams of the ICCL. Maybe they were coincidences, or maybe not, but he couldn't worry about them any more. Too much water had flown down the Ganges since the time he had joined the team, aspiring to create a legacy.

I just have to get over with this, somehow, without going to jail. Then, never again!

Nothing Succeeds like Success

'I always loved you...believe it or not...but now I also respect you,' Kanika whispered in Neil's ear during the presentation ceremony. 'Without respect love can't survive. You know it more than anyone else, striving for respect all your life.'

She smiled as Neil looked on, startled, her eyes twinkling like a fiery star on a cloudless night. He knew that expression well; it only graced her face on those rare occasions when she was genuinely impressed.

'Why suddenly?' he asked in a playful tone, urging her to elaborate the obvious. 'Surely not because of the playoffs? My record playing for India is way bigger.'

'It's not just your achievements, silly, it's your attitude,' Kanika squeezed his hand. 'I admire your fight. It wasn't easy; a lesser man would have quit ages ago.'

Neil gave himself the benefit of the doubt buoyed by Kanika's endorsement. This rare accolade from Kanika meant more to him than even the congratulatory phone call he had received from Akash. The team had reached the playoffs from an impossible situation. Nothing he did had hurt the team long-term, so it was all fine.

I did the best I could under the circumstances.

'My attitude was never a problem, Kanika...it's the attitude of my bosses,' said Neil. 'It was the cricket board and coaches when I played for India, and now it is the owners of this team...who never miss an opportunity to snub me.'

'You mean the security cordon around you?' asked Kanika in an impatient voice.

'In Mohali, they tried to trap me by posing as match-fixers on the phone,' blurted Neil. 'Around 4–5 a.m.; you slept through it.'

'Fuck! That explains a lot,' Kanika crossed her arms. 'Akash called me yesterday...I didn't overthink it...because...you know...' she covered her mouth, giggling. 'He's always silly with me. But now it kind of connects...'

'What?'

'Well, he was asking me about the match-fixing alert...if we have any leads related to his team. And he also offered me a job...to manage his sports business.'

Neil grinned. 'Really? Congratulations!'

'Yeah, as if I will join him... Please!' Kanika rolled her eyes. 'But I am puzzled why he suspects you. I mean...'

'He thinks everyone is trying to steal his kingdom,' said Neil, laughing. 'His blue-eyed boy failed. Now he can't accept someone he rejected has become the hero.'

'Hmm. And what about *her*?' asked Kanika, tilting her head towards Divya, who stood at the presentation party beaming like an excited teenager.

'Oh! She is cool—became very supportive once I proved myself,' said Neil. 'She is better than my family members who can't look beyond their politics and elephant-sized egos.'

'There is a huge party tonight—lots of big people—nothing less than the IPL launch party,' said Kanika. 'She invited me...'

Neil grinned. 'I thought you guys hated each other.'

'We are getting by...thanks to you.'

'How?'

'See, everyone knows Akash wants to sleep with me, but he can't... because I don't want to,' Kanika threw back her head. 'Divya relaxed when she saw I don't care for her husband. Also, I am important to you, and you are important to her. So...'

They watched Sudhir Yadav collect the Man of the Match award. 'He apologized as well,' Neil said, pointing at Sudhir. 'Finally he has realized my worth.'

'His problem is the same as Akash's...one of pedigree...which assumes only some people are entitled to succeed and others aren't,' said Kanika, kindness pouring out of her big brown eyes. 'But isn't it fun to prove such people wrong?'

Neil nodded and experienced an unprecedented surge in self-worth. After a long time he had finally achieved something of value. Redemption was just round the corner. Kanika preferred him over a billionaire like Akash—surely he must be worthy of her love.

I have achieved my target. With Sanket's guards, the mafia can't harass me. Just two more matches and I will be done. Next year I will call the shots. Gautam was right...I can't quit after reaching the pole position.

Fait Accompli

Three days later, the New Delhi Royals beat the Kingdom of Patiala (Punjab) in a tense semi-final in Mumbai to enter the finals of the ICCL. That night, Akash instructed Sanket to end his operation against Neil. 'Divya feels it's an insult to the team, and even I support Neil now.'

'Some of our players are also involved, sir...' pleaded Saket. 'Please give me one more day. I will catch the whole gang.'

'Our players won't dare to betray me,' snapped Akash. 'I think this match-fixing shit is mumbo-jumbo.'

'You think Neil is innocent, sir?'

'I can't ignore the results,' said Akash. 'Qualifying for the playoffs after losing six matches isn't exactly a joke.'

'Sir...all the betting is against you when you are losing. We won because the mafia fixed the other teams. Mr Neil deserves no credit.'

Akash tried hard not to insult Sanket. 'Your work is done. Immediately withdraw the security cover, and stop whatever the hell you were doing. Send me your bill, and I will clear it.'

The Visitor

Next Day Morning

> *5426, go alone to your Gurgaon apartment today to meet a special visitor, at sharp 4 p.m.*

The mafia's message was at the usual place—on the bathroom mirror in his hotel room. The withdrawal of Sanket's security cover in New Delhi had once again exposed Neil to direct interaction with the mafia.

He shattered the mirror with a cricket ball. The broken glass looked like a spider web with the note in the centre—an apt representation of his situation vis-à-vis the mafia.

Fuck! I asked Divya not to remove Sanket. Bitch! Too pompous to listen!

He ran the shower and dunked his head into the cold water.

Why suddenly this meeting in Gurgaon? Sanket's men are gone, so why not meet here? Or is this Sanket's trap?

Sanket's security cover had protected Neil from having to interact with the mafia and he had started believing that the worst was over and the ICCL trophy would be theirs in a few days. But by forcing an unexpected meeting in a remote location, the mafia had suddenly shattered Neil's sense of security and well-being.

That afternoon, Neil went to his apartment after two months of travelling and felt like a stranger in his own house. A lot had changed in a relatively short time; from wallowing in self-pity, he had fought his way to his goals. The cricketing world was going gaga over how he had orchestrated New Delhi Royal's meteoric rise in the ICCL. A leading newspaper had reported this on their front page that morning:

From Man to Superman: How One Man Transformed the Fortunes of a Cricket Team

Neil had spent countless hours holed up in this apartment fretting about his failed career and dreaming of opportunities to impact cricket. Those motivations for heroism and glory now seemed grossly out of place in his new world where the thick solid line separating right and wrong had blurred into a shapeless porous mass of gut-wrenching compromises. He soon realized that he couldn't live there any more. The isolation and negative energy of that place screwed with his mind.

I should maybe live with Kanika, if she makes me the offer. She might; after all, we are officially lovers now.

Almost two hours after the appointed time of 4 p.m., the doorbell rang, announcing the arrival of The Visitor. Neil dithered for a few moments, looking for an escape route, before surrendering to the inevitable. Outside the door stood a tall bearded man wearing dirty looking khaki trousers and a blue shirt. He carried a large rucksack, typically used by courier guys, on his shoulder.

'Why all this drama?' asked Neil, eyeing the rucksack as The Visitor entered his apartment.

What's in the bag? Sanket can use contraband to trap me. Fuck!

'We should have met in the hotel. It's safe there—I don't have bodyguards any more.'

'I didn't want to be photographed,' The Visitor said in a gruff voice. 'This is a low-end apartment. No CCTV cameras here.'

'Why? What's so special about you?' Neil retorted absentmindedly, trying to think where he had seen that man.

Oh, fuck! He's the same man who was clicking photos outside the dressing room in the stadium.

In a flash, The Visitor put a gun to Neil's head, choking him with the other arm. 'You bastard...' he hissed, 'never question me again.'

'What do you want?' Neil rasped, fighting to breathe.

The Visitor pushed him on to the couch, pinning him with his leg. 'Lose the final...'

Neil sucked in air, struggling to clear his hazy vision. He peered at the gun pointed at his face, wondering if he was hallucinating. 'I am only a coach,' he croaked. 'Can't force eleven cricketers to play badly. They are monitoring us...at every step. It is impossible to pull it off; we will get caught.'

The Visitor grunted as he clicked open the safety latch of his gun. 'Did I ask you for your opinion?' he asked in a low, calm voice. He stabilized the gun using both hands and fired. With a loud cracking sound, the bullet ripped through the backrest a few inches from Neil's head. The fabric and wood were burning, emitting foul black smoke.

Neil lay terrified as The Visitor sprayed water to douse the fire.

'Now listen carefully, so I don't have to fire again,' said The Visitor, hitting Neil with the empty water bottle. 'Don't use your head...just follow instructions.' He paused, touching his temple with his finger. 'Otherwise I will bore a hole into your head. Got it?'

One look at The Visitor's stoned lifeless eyes convinced Neil the game was over; nothing would move that maniac to reconsider his demands. He wiped his face, nodding to show he agreed.

The Visitor fiddled with his beard. 'Good! But just in case you stray from the line...apart from killing your family we will kidnap your girlfriend and sell her as a sex slave in the Middle East. She will be in high demand both before and after she dies. Some customers pay big dollars for the experience of doing a dead body.' He licked his lips. 'And her kind of body will get high premium. Enough incentive for you to comply?' The Visitor grinned, hauling Neil up by the collar. 'Do you understand?'

Neil managed a feeble yes.

'I can't hear it. Louder!'

'Yes!' shouted Neil.

The Visitor dropped him on the couch and left the apartment.

Neil lay cold and shattered, with his face dunked in a toxic sludge of bile, dust and burnt leather. The bullet hole on the couch emitted the odour of gutted self-respect and fractured morale.

Fuck! I just wanted to coach the team. That's my big crime—I tried to help the team win. Couldn't bear to see it become a victim of hustlers and looters. But I failed, just when I thought I would succeed. I failed. Eight months of getting my ass busted for this godforsaken team...the humiliation, struggling to hold up my head. Twenty years of international cricket has come to this. A goon almost shoots at me, threatening to kill and rape unless I sell out the team I built, betray the game I lived for, abandon my only chance at redemption.
I need help.
I surrender.
Akash!

Surrender

Thirty Minutes Later

Akash clapped as he entered Neil's apartment, accompanied by Vikram and Sanket. 'So, finally, the truth has come out. Mr Smartypants thought he will fool me—a person of my calibre.'

Neil slouched on the couch, only half listening to Akash's tirade.

'Haul him up,' Akash ordered Vikram. 'Come on…we need to talk.'

Neil sat up as Vikram moved towards him. 'I was only helping the team,' he pleaded, feeling exposed after telling Akash the whole story over the phone. Akash looked more happy than angry; instead of blasting Neil he was offering a discussion. The glee in his voice rattled Neil more than The Visitor's threatening tone had.

Akash looked around for a place to sit. 'Who asked for your help?'

'We lost six matches.'

'So?'

'You refused to listen.'

'Who gave you the authority?' fumed Akash. 'You betrayed me; instead of giving me evidence against Pat, you helped my enemies.'

'Vikram, get a clean chair for me.'

Vikram arrived with a chair, and Akash called him and Sanket for a private discussion. They whispered among themselves for a few minutes before Sanket took charge.

'We will seal this apartment,' Sanket told Neil. 'Before that, we will record your statement both on camera and on signed affidavits. A magistrate will act as witness.'

Sanket grinned and adjusted his glasses. 'Oh, how did they communicate with you in Kolkata? We were guarding you 24 × 7; so, how?'

Neil coughed and spluttered, trying to decide if he should reveal the names of the compromised players.

Maybe I should; show I am not the only villain. But then they will do a witch hunt and demoralize everyone in the team; we don't need that before the final.

'They could not contact me...' said Neil.

'Really?'

'Yes.'

'Oh, I don't believe you,' smirked Sanket. 'I will grill you with circumstantial evidence.' He rubbed his hands, laughing like a hyena. 'Oh, this will be fun.'

Fuck! This is a big mistake. Instead of trying to save the final they are screwing me.

'Are you going to say again that you have smelled foul air?' shouted Akash.

'Sorry, sir...I was just...' Sanket looked embarrassed.

'Mr Neil, give us the tapes you used to blackmail Mr Pat, and any other evidence you have,' said Vikram. 'Where have you kept them? They are not here, or in your hotel room.'

'I don't have them; they asked me to delete everything,' said Neil.

'He is lying,' screamed Akash. 'Search Nandini's house, search his friends.'

'Sir, that's not a good idea,' said Sanket. 'The news will spread. With the final around the corner...'

'Okay, but grill him...use third degree.'

Akash scowled and moved towards Neil. 'You are fired. Pat's in charge.'

Neil jumped up from the couch. 'Akash, please! I've worked so hard...let me be the coach for just one more match.'

'No! I don't trust criminals.'

'Please, Akash!' Neil joined his palms. 'You think I will fix the final? Then why did I come to you for help?'

Akash shook his head. 'We may lose the final, but at least it won't be fixed.'

'I want to win, Akash,' Neil held him by the shoulders. 'Please trust me—I won't compromise our family's team or our team's glory.'

At Akash's signal, Vikram Singh pulled Neil away from him.

Akash rubbed his shoulder as if it had become dirty with Neil's touch. 'Listen, you son of a cunt—the New Delhi Royals is not your team, nor are you a part of my family,' he said in a cold voice. 'You got it?

Neil saw Vikram and Sanket cowing around Akash and realized servility wouldn't work with him. His aggression could only be met with counter-fire.

'I will tell the media you are forcing me to fix the final,' Neil said.

'You asshole...how dare you!' screamed Akash, rushing towards Neil.

Sanket stopped Akash. 'Sir, please...calm down. It's a delicate situation...'

Akash's bloodshot eyes showed the trauma of being hustled by an underling who, just a few minutes ago, had been begging him for mercy. But he soon calmed down, and Neil capitalized on the small window of opportunity Sanket's intervention had created.

Neil paced the room. 'You don't have proof against me, and I won't help you build any...so no recording will happen.'

'I control the media,' said Akash in a calm voice that rattled Neil. But there was no scope for backing out; Akash would crush him if he showed weakness.

'By the time you block the story, the damage will be done,' said Neil. 'People believe what they want to believe.'

Akash made a gurgling sound, his face twisting, and he seemed to be choking.

'I don't fear you,' Neil grinned. 'You can't imprison me, as Divya will beat the shit out of you. You can't kill me because I am the only proof against Gagan.' Neil raised his eyebrows, looking at Akash. 'So what can you do?'

'You want to fix the final?' asked Sanket.

'Only an arse like you can ask that,' snapped Neil. 'Why did I call Akash?'

'What do you want?' asked Akash.

'Your asshole brother trapped me. A goon fired at me...threatened to rape Kanika,' shouted Neil. 'I rescued your team from doom—I expected you to protect me...' He pointed towards Sanket and Vikram. 'But I just replaced those terrorists with these. Fuck!'

'We can't protect you, Mr Neil,' said Sanket. 'We can't trace them.'

'Yes you can, if you try in the right places,' said Neil in a defiant voice. 'Go arm-twist Gagan, and I'm sure he will talk.'

'I need some time to work this out,' said Akash, looking unusually calm, as if he had just climaxed in his pants. 'I'll meet you tomorrow morning. Till then, don't talk to anyone.'

Neil smiled. 'Sure!'

'It is not safe for you to be here or at the team hotel till I sort this out,' said Akash. 'Check in at another hotel. Vikram will wait there with you till I give the green signal. They will come after you when I do what I am about to do…so be extra careful. Do you get me?'

Et Tu, Dad?

Later That Night

Four policemen, led by Rohit Manwal (Deputy Superintendent of Police), ambushed Gagan immediately after he entered Akash's living room.

Akash had ordered Gagan and their father to come to his house for a meeting. Initially Gagan dragged his feet but later complied when Akash threatened to expose his liaison with Neil.

'You are under arrest, Mr Gagan,' Sanket Singh pointed a revolver at Gagan as the constables handcuffed him after a minor scuffle. He turned the gun towards Ramesh and adjusted his rimless glasses. 'And you, sir, are a senior citizen. I don't want to misbehave with you. Please cooperate. Take a seat.'

Akash grinned. 'Thanks, Rohit. Wait outside, but be alert. These are dangerous criminals.'

Rohit dumped Gagan on the couch beside Ramesh and saluted Akash before marching out with his men.

'Someone shot at Neil today,' Akash told Ramesh. 'Oh! I forgot... would you like some tea?'

Ramesh gulped. 'Where? Is he all right?'

'Dad! Please stop playing this concerned uncle's role,' said Gagan. He scowled, fighting his handcuffs. 'Neil is fine. They just roughed him up a bit to make him fall in line.'

'Why doesn't he follow instructions?' Ramesh shook his head. 'Obstinate ass!'

Akash smiled at his father. 'So you are also involved? No wonder Gagan is suddenly getting such bright ideas.'

'I am just trying to survive,' said Ramesh. 'You haven't left us with anything.'

'What's this nonsense about arresting me?' shouted Gagan. He aggressively jerked his head upward. 'Hmm? There is no proof against me. No one will believe Neil.' He struggled against the handcuffs like a chained bull. 'I will send you to jail...just wait and watch.'

'Na na...you don't understand...I don't want to prosecute you,' said Akash in a cold voice. 'I will just imprison you till the final is over. In the meantime, I will protect Neil and ensure a fair match. Later, your bosses in Dubai will skin you alive.'

'You can still lose the match,' said Gagan in a cocky voice.

'No, we won't lose. We will play against either Rajasthan or Chennai in the final. The owners of both these teams will do anything to please me,' said Akash. 'We are a strong team...even if they slightly manipulate their game, we will get home safe.'

Akash smiled as Gagan and Ramesh turned pale. Finally, he had caught them by their necks. They had believed his lies about manipulating the final.

That's the value of having a formidable reputation—people take your threats seriously.

'You can't...I will...be dead,' mumbled Gagan, looking lifeless.

'You want our shares in the Omkar Group, right?' asked Ramesh in a halting voice. 'Tomorrow we will sell them to you. I hope that's enough compensation for your help.' His pain showed though his twisted flushed face. He had fought all his life to control the Omkar Group for Gagan, and now it was slipping away from him forever.

'I am not giving up my shares,' screamed Gagan, violently clanking his handcuffs. 'He gets the cricket team and I keep the company; that was the deal. He can't go against it.'

'Gagan, shut up,' admonished Ramesh. 'Trust me. I am doing the best for you.'

'It seems they have offered a lot of money,' Akash grinned, overjoyed at being able to force his father to compromise. 'I don't care for your shares. They are not worth much, and after Gagan is gone, I will get them anyway. So, what's my incentive to lose the final?'

'What will change your mind?' asked Ramesh, looking distraught.

'Maybe the truth can help,' said Akash. 'Gagan, did you instigate the Omkar Group union to revolt against me?'

'Are you still thinking about it after so many years?' asked Ramesh, smiling. 'It was a small incident. A big man like you shouldn't bother about such things.'

Akash shook his head. 'Not small at all, dad! It was the main reason why I left the Omkar Group. You and grandma never stopped criticizing Divya for taking me away from the company, when it was never her fault.' He clicked his fingers to attract Gagan's attention.

'Now Gagan! It's time to tell the truth. Did you do it?'

'Yes, I did...and I'm not sorry about it,' snapped Gagan. 'You deserved it.'

Akash smiled at Ramesh. 'Here's the truth you never accepted.'

'Truth?' screamed Gagan. 'It was his idea. He directed it from start to finish.'

Ramesh slouched on the couch, covering his face with his hands.

'Really, dad? You wanted me to fail? Why?' asked Akash, throwing his arms in the air. 'All my life I wanted your love, Nandini's love, but never got it. You loved Gagan. Nandini loved Neil. You loved Neil more than me—and yet you always expected me to help the family. Even today you are doing the same. Unbelievable!'

'I am sorry, son,' Ramesh sat next to Akash. 'At that time I was very upset about your father-in-law controlling you. You moved out of the house after marriage. You ditched me after I did so much for you—made you the man you are. As the CEO, you were doing whatever you wanted, without listening to anyone. The Indian business conditions differ from what you learnt at Wharton, son. I thought that the union problem would make you a better leader. Please forgive me.'

Akash smiled. 'I admit I was immature as the CEO, but you stabbed me in my back, and that I can't forgive.' He stood up and pointed towards the door. 'Get out.'

'Akash—please save your brother,' said Ramesh, with folded hands. He collapsed on his knees, crying. 'Don't do this. We have already spent the money. We are falling at your feet, asking for forgiveness.'

As if acting on his father's cue, Gagan rose from the couch with a jerk and fell flat on the ground with a loud grunt. 'Please forgive me,' he said in a muffled voice. 'I will do anything...'

Ramesh touched Akash's feet. 'Don't kill your brother, I beg you.'

'Please, dad! Don't embarrass me like this,' Akash hugged his father as a reflex. Growing up, he had idolized his father as a guru before their contrasting philosophies and life choices had driven them apart. Even after a rapid degradation in their relationship, Akash had always treated him with respect. In that dramatic moment, the shock of his guru touching his feet reduced his spite, and drove him towards a compromise.

'Okay, dad, let us work it out peacefully,' said Akash, escorting Ramesh to the couch. 'Sanket, ask Rohit to remove the handcuffs from Gagan. It seems that unless we lose the finals, Gagan is dead,' said Akash. 'It won't be easy to convince Neil.'

'Sir, Rajasthan has just won the second semi-final,' Sanket informed Akash. 'They're a terrible team, sir. It is a miracle they won today. It will be tough for us to lose unless Mr Neil helps.'

'Use the family trick on him,' said Ramesh. 'Tell him everyone will die unless he loses. That will work; it always does with him.'

'The share transfer must happen first thing in the morning, tomorrow,' said Akash. 'Only then will the rest of the processes start.'

Ramesh nodded. 'It will be done. Don't worry, I've learnt my lesson.'

Akash re-evaluated the situation after Ramesh and Gagan left his house.

We can't protect Gagan without fixing the final. If they kill him, grandma won't give me her shares. Her connections can also cause real damage to my business. Plus, I am getting dad's and Gagan's shares—so fixing is a good deal. Later I can blackmail both Neil and Gagan. When they become beggars on the street, I will ask Nandini what she thinks of Neil.

Volte-Face

Next Morning

Akash smiled as Neil toyed with the food on his plate.

'The breakfast spread here is better than the other hotels. I love their croissants; heard they have a special French pastry chef,' said Akash.

Neil cringed at Akash's pathetic attempt at small talk; politeness and casual chit-chat suited him as much as a poorly tailored suit.

What's so bad that he cannot tell me about it? I am wasting time holed up here. No idea what's happening in the team. All kinds of rumours must be flying around about me. Fuck! Kanika has sent me fifty messages since last night. But I can't respond. She doesn't deserve to be treated like this!

'I want you to continue as coach,' said Akash in a nonchalant voice. He held Neil's hand. 'Can't be unfair...'

Neil heaved a sigh of relief. 'Thanks! There is no problem you cannot solve.'

Akash frowned and withdrew his hand. 'I wish you had come to me earlier, but now we've a big problem. Our family, including Kanika, is in grave danger; we can't take risks.' He raised a finger as if disciplining a child. 'You must correct what you screwed up; so please follow their instructions and lose the final.'

Neil gaped. 'You are joking, right?'

'No! It is a very dangerous situation.'

Neil knew this wasn't the real Akash speaking. A big shot like him wouldn't worry about the safety of his family. Something else has happened.

What should I do?

'How come this volte-face?' Neil asked.

'Because I won't risk the safety of my family,' said Akash in a stern voice. He sighed and avoided eye contact. 'Look...coming second in such a tough tournament is not a bad outcome at all. And we will always have next year.' He held Neil's hand again and smiled. 'Next year you'll be the head coach, promise! It will be your team, your players, your captain, your support staff. You will be *the man.*'

Neil recognized the lies of a hyper-competitive man who had never made compromises in his life. What game was he playing? He was suddenly so worried about the family he had never cared for.

Has he patched up with Gagan? Does uncle know?

Neil wanted to plead with Akash to reconsider his stand but suddenly remembered how the previous evening his servility had had no impact on Akash. He listened only when Neil threatened to expose him to the media.

'I am disappointed, big brother,' he said. 'You lack the balls…'

Akash seemed he would burst like a volcano. 'Don't you listen? For the last ten minutes…'

Neil jumped up from his chair. 'Akash! Everyone knows you love winning. You wouldn't give up so easily, unless…'

'Shut the fuck up,' snapped Akash. 'You don't know what I know, so give your pea-sized brain a rest. I am your employer, right? I am ordering you to lose…'

'I won't do it,' Neil shook his head. 'I won't betray cricket.'

Akash laughed. 'When you blackmailed Pat, fixed matches, what happened then? Had you shoved cricket up Kanika's ass?'

'Akash! Please treat Kanika with respect,' Neil said in a sombre tone, with folded hands. 'What I did was wrong…but Gagan had trapped me; I would have never done it otherwise…'

Akash caressed his unshaven face. 'Maybe Vikram Singh can convince you.'

Neil smiled at that blatant threat from a bully who, just a little while ago, had been trying to fool him through small talk and niceties. Arrogant assholes like Akash thought they could fool anyone by throwing crumbs. But they revealed their true selves when someone opposed them. Akash and the mafia were the same—they used the same language, applied the same pressure tactics, had the same nefarious intentions. He just claimed to be on the right side of the law when he really wasn't.

I must fight!

'Yes, sure; let's meet Vikram,' Neil said. 'But later I will tell Divya the whole story, and then I will go to the media. You haven't told her yet, have you?'

Akash made a gurgling sound. His eyes looked ready to pop out, but Neil did not offer any help. He knew Akash's trauma was mental, not physical. He was just not used to being opposed. How could a lowly cousin squeeze his balls!

'Come to the farmhouse in the evening, and we will discuss with dad and grandma,' Akash said in a rasping voice. 'Till then, please hide in this hotel.'

Blood Is Thicker Than Water

'I told you not to play cricket; now see what has happened.'

The living room of Upadhyay Palace resembled a Khap Panchayat meeting that evening where the elders pronounced the verdict without conducting a trial. By connecting the present crisis with Neil's twenty-year-old decision to play professional cricket, Sudha had effectively demolished his hopes of garnering support through logical arguments.

Neil felt unsettled by Sudha's hostile body language. Akash had brainwashed her with a false threat to the family, which had led to this over-the-top reaction.

But who convinced him? What happened last night?

'Once again they tried to screw me,' said Akash, moving his hands towards Neil and Gagan. 'First the Omkar Group and now this team.'

'Screw you?' Neil grinned. 'We reached the final.'

'Through what means?' scowled Akash. 'Winning is not everything.'

'I agree it isn't. But I won't deliberately lose a game,' said Neil. 'Fire me if you want…match-fixing won't happen under my watch.'

'What nonsense!' fumed Sudha, hitting Neil on his head. 'You'll run away after creating a big mess?'

'Oh! It is my fault? Gagan trapped me…' screamed Neil, frustrated by grandma's unwillingness to examine the details of the issue.

Grandma's thinking is so predictable: Cricket is evil; family members involved in cricket are the greatest sinners.

'Great! Blame me for helping you,' clapped Gagan. 'You are ungrateful like your father—it runs in your blood.'

'Sure, Gagan…if you say so,' smiled Neil. 'You put a gun to my head and admitted you are involved. Why were you travelling with the team? Why was your best friend Cap Jay asking for information?' He turned towards Sudha and pleaded. 'Grandma, don't you see how…'

Sudha was unmoved. Neil's voice trailed off.

'You loved him like a son; see how he is paying us back,' Gagan shouted at Ramesh, pointing towards Neil. 'I am facing a death threat, and he doesn't care.'

'Why do you hate us, Neil?' asked Ramesh. 'I have always treated you like a son. Don't make me regret it.'

'Gagan is lying,' Neil appealed to Sudha. 'This life threat is nonsense.'

Sudha did not respond, and Neil turned to Akash. 'Doesn't he need a lot of money for the company?'

'The financial matters of the company are sorted,' snapped Akash. 'So don't exert your limited intelligence on things you don't understand.'

'Is that why you turned?' asked Neil.

He noticed Ramesh's furtive glances towards Sudha and Gagan and realized Akash had made a deal with Gagan. They had sorted the family dispute at his expense.

But it can't happen without uncle's involvement. The whole family is a family of fixers; maybe grandma as well.

'No, you asshole—I worry about the safety and reputation of my family,' shouted Akash. 'But how will *you* know…loser!'

'You are right, I won't,' said Neil. 'Nandini had warned me that blood will always be thicker than water. I don't matter. After all, I am the outsider…'

Sudha slapped Neil hard on his face. 'How dare you!' she fumed. 'This family did everything for you.'

Neil stroked his cheek and fought the urge to break down under intense emotion. The family was dead—the final pillar of the crumbling building had collapsed. He looked towards Sudha and produced a sarcastic smile. 'Sometimes I wish I had grown up in an orphanage…and not here.'

'Do you see why I had warned you not to pamper him?' Sudha asked Ramesh. 'You encouraged this indiscipline. It's the same story with both him and Gagan; they get involved in shady activities, and then they get angry when we question them.'

Ramesh nodded. 'All your life you lived on the family's money—and contributed nothing,' he told Neil. 'Same as your father. You should be ashamed…miserable scum.'

'Ramesh, stop this…I didn't mean…' started Sudha.

'Are we your father's servants?' asked Ramesh, sweating and breathing heavily.

'I am not responsible for my father's actions,' said Neil in a cold voice.

'Yeah?' scowled Ramesh. 'But are you responsible for yourself? Without our support...with your demented brain, you would have become a coolie somewhere. You ungrateful piece of shit...not ashamed to take grandma's shares for free. How dare you refuse when we need your help?' He paused and then spoke in a low voice. 'I don't care any more about what you feel. I helped everyone...all my life; but no one will help me.'

The bickering stopped as Madhu arrived, accompanied by servants carrying cups of tea and plates of vegetable cutlets and sandwiches. 'Now stop talking and eat,' she admonished, unaware that she had entered a war zone. 'Are you ill?' she asked Neil, looking anxious. She touched his forehead to check his temperature. 'You should eat properly. How can you coach if you don't eat?'

'I'm fine. Just stressed,' said Neil.

'Stay here for a few days when this tournament is over.'

'I will, aunty,' said Neil, as Madhu smiled and walked away.

Both of us know I won't, yet she makes me feel like I belong here. Uncle and aunty were the parents I never had. But uncle's words just destroyed everything.

The war resumed the moment Madhu exited the living room.

'They will kill Gagan if you don't help,' said Sudha.

'That's a lie to scare you,' said Neil. He was about to pick up a sandwich, but he stopped himself. He couldn't eat their food any more. 'But if it is true, isn't it proof Gagan is guilty?'

'No, it isn't,' shouted Gagan.

'Please help me,' said Ramesh. He joined his palms, looking teary-eyed. 'The issue here is my son's life.'

'Uncle, I thought you helped me because you loved me,' Neil grinned. 'But it seems there was an agenda...'

'After enjoying my patronage for forty years, only a halfwit like you would say such a thing,' snapped Ramesh.

'I am grateful, uncle,' said Neil and sat beside Ramesh. 'You and aunty are more than my parents. I want to help you, but what you want is unethical. It will kill me as a person...destroy everything I value in my life. Don't you care how I feel?'

'What happened when you blackmailed Pat?' sneered Akash. 'Did your ethics go up your ass?'

'The mafia will screw up your reputation,' said Gagan. 'Come on…no one will know. You have already done it in parts.'

'Yes, but never to lose a match,' said Neil in a halting voice.

Gagan laughed. 'Yes, you did…'

'How do you know this?' Neil looked around to draw attention. 'Isn't it clear he is guilty?'

'I don't care who has done what,' snapped Sudha. 'The family…'

'How much money do you want?' Gagan cut Sudha off.

Neil gasped. 'You think this is about money?'

'They will kidnap Kanika,' said Gagan with a menacing expression on his face. 'Rape her…then leak real videos from hormone-struck teenagers. Remember them? You saw a sample in Mohali. The real ones are yet to come.'

Neil sat hunched over, struggling with nausea. Gagan was threatening Kanika, but no one opposed him.

They care for nobody; they won't hesitate to kill her. I can't put her life in danger.

'Pour acid over her pretty face,' Gagan said casually, and caressed his cheeks. 'Imagine her skin peeling off…'

'Please save Gagan's life and the reputation of the family,' said Sudha.

Neil covered his ears with his hands and screamed. 'Okay! Okay! Stop. I will do it.'

He ran out of Upadhyay Palace as fast as his legs would carry him.

Epiphany

'Get me a drink first,' Neil told Kanika, burning with the need to unburden himself, his mind and his emotions tangled in a thousand simultaneous conflicts.

Who will listen? Nandini? Nah! She is gone. Kanika, yes...but she will judge me. It will be the end; I will have nothing to live for...nobody to live with.

She was waiting in his room when he returned to the hotel. She had been agitated about his disappearance since the previous night. He knew he would have to come clean. He owed it to her.

Kanika poured scotch from the mini bar into two glasses and gave one to Neil. She raised her eyebrows. 'So, what's the big secret?'

Neil gulped the Scotch down, unnerved by the prospect of losing Kanika.

What the hell—when my family can ditch me, what can I expect from her? She will leave one day anyway.

He walked over to the minibar to refill his glass, feeling Kanika's penetrative gaze drilling through his back.

I will just say it—I can't hide this ugliness any longer.

He sat on the couch at a safe distance from Kanika and raised his glass to toast. 'I will fix the final on Sunday; we will lose,' he said in a halting voice.

Kanika laughed out loud. 'Yeah, right! What's this...a test of my love? Stop playing games please and tell me the truth; come on, be serious.'

'Your love will evaporate when you hear what I have done.'

Kanika smiled first and then frowned. 'Seriously?'

Neil hung his head. 'Gagan trapped me...helped me blackmail Pat...'

'I knew something was fishy...everything suddenly falling into place,' blurted Kanika. She held her head and screamed. 'Fuck! I trusted you.'

'I was desperate, and they used me. By the time you warned me it was too late. I tried to resist...' He moved to the bed. 'But now I can't fight any more,' he covered his face and lay down. 'Please leave me; complain to the ICCL or whoever you want to.'

'But why is it suddenly troubling you now?' asked Kanika. 'You were fine doing this so far.' Neil uncovered his face and saw Kanika standing at the edge of the bed, almost on top of him. 'You have suddenly developed morals?' she asked.

'No, I am too covered in muck for the morals to stick.'

'I was asking…' Kanika stopped and banged hard on the bed. 'Get up, you!' she screamed. 'Talk to me.'

Neil rose hurriedly and sat on the edge of the bed. 'Sorry; I'll tell you…'

'Go on, I am listening.'

Neil gulped one drink after the other and recounted his story of desperation, deceit, compromises and epiphany. He started from how he had regretted his unfulfilled potential every day after retiring from cricket, and described how his coaching venture with Gagan did not take off, and then his 'moment of awakening' when he was thrown out of the stadium after he had received an award. 'I realized I had let myself and my family down, and I had to redeem myself by creating an impact, a legacy…and that's where I was wrong. It became an obsession, and I kept compromising,' he said. 'I sucked it up when uncle ditched me, and became the assistant coach even after Nandini warned me against it. I stayed in the team even after they treated me like a dog…everything added up. It was like losing money in a casino…you keep playing with the hope that you will recover what you lost, and then you lose more. The team's poor performance under Pat gave me a good reason to persist. So, when Gagan approached me with the evidence against Pat, I was too far down the hole to resist. And they trapped me. I was so messed up I didn't know what to believe. Gagan beat me up when I resisted and put a gun to my head, claiming it was Cap Jay's plan. I tried to resist in every match…trust me…but every time they subdued me. They leaked our photos in Mohali and yesterday threatened to throw acid on your face. Gagan repeated the same threats in front of the whole family, and no one stopped him. They are all in this together.'

He described blow by blow the events of the last twenty-four hours, starting with the bearded visitor in his apartment, his interaction with Akash and his cronies when he asked for help, Akash's stunning change of stance the next morning, and then finishing with the life-changing meeting in Upadhyay Palace that evening.

'How come your uncle has suddenly gone against you?' asked Kanika. She looked sympathetic and her tone had softened considerably. 'Has someone brainwashed him?'

'Oh! No need to brainwash him, as he is the "brain himself",' smirked Neil. 'They have worked out a deal with Akash. And grandma is something else; too headstrong to understand she is being fooled. Once people convinced her that the family is in danger, she shut her mind. Can you believe that she blames my decision to pursue cricket twenty years ago for this mess?'

Kanika shook her head, looking dumbstruck. 'Wow! This is demented.'

'No one accepted Gagan is the real villain here—although the evidence is right in front of them,' said Neil, pacing the room. 'No one cared how I felt. No one mentioned once the torture I had gone through to redeem myself. No one appreciated my dedication to the game. No one acknowledged that I had saved this team from doom and taken it to the final. So I said fuck it, I will do what they want and get out of here. Why should I care for this fucked-up team and this fucked-up game? No one is bothered other than me. I have become a pawn in the family's never-ending internal wars. I always thought they sidelined me as they did not respect me as a cricketer. I was eager to prove my worth, and I did prove my worth, but did anyone acknowledge it? My wish to win my family's respect and leave a legacy was very dumb and out of place. It matters to no one—not my family, not to Nandini, not to the public. It is all in my head; no one cares. Was I ill-treated because I had not proved myself? No! They screwed me because I was Neil—an orphan with no backing.' Neil hung his head. 'I wish uncle had done nothing for me, and loved me, instead of hating me after doing so much for me.' Kanika hugged Neil, opening the floodgates of his bottled-up emotions. 'Actually I was trying to prove to myself that I am capable,' he said, crying like a baby. 'And since I wasn't able to, I was masking it under the ambition of proving my worth to others.'

'You have to prove nothing to nobody,' said Kanika, holding Neil as he sobbed. 'Even before the ICCL, you had achieved more than most people.'

'I am fucked.'

Kanika led him to the couch. 'Don't be so hard on yourself. You are a victim of circumstances. You weren't trying to make money—which is the main motive in match-fixing.' She sighed. 'Your past actions were wrong. We can always judge our actions on hindsight. But under the current circumstances, losing in the finals will be the right decision.'

'What? Betray the game?'

Neil watched, dumbstruck, as Kanika explained her rationale. 'Intention always matters more than action. This is a club, not the Indian Test team. As an employee, you can't oppose the owner's instructions. I mean, let's not pretend this is your team. So you can only do that much. Plus, we can't ignore our safety. We shouldn't die for cricket. I mean…why die like this? This is such a waste. Join the army and make your death count…kill the enemy and then die.'

'Hmm.'

'The money involved is huge—they will do anything to get their way,' said Kanika. 'You got a flavour yesterday. Why did they rough you up when you were already following instructions? It was to show you what happens if you don't. They have already killed Hansie Cronje and Bob Woolmer. See, Akash and the others will protect themselves. They have the wherewithal, and even if they can't, why should you care? So protect yourself and protect me. We are commoners. Is it worth giving your life for a stupid match of a privately owned team when the owner does not give a shit?' asked Kanika in an agitated voice. 'Leave the team after the final. Come with me to Singapore—I can help you start a coaching academy there. There is a lot of interest in cricket—with plenty of Indians in the region—in Hong Kong, Malaysia, Indonesia…'

Neil nodded, realizing her advice was coming from cold rationale instead of foolish passion. He felt dizzy and overwhelmed by a surge of emotion.

Fuck cricket; I just want to spend my life with her. Only a person who loves you can accept your mistakes and give you the benefit of the doubt when it matters the most.

The End of Innocence

'Sleep! Tomorrow morning we'll make love in the bathtub,' Kanika flashed the famous toothy smile that made a million hearts flutter. 'You'll need strength to tackle the buoyancy. Take a sleeping pill. I'll go meet friends.'

Neil's intoxication dropped as the night aged, and he once again felt guilty about betraying cricket. These people had arm-twisted him right from day one. Should he allow them to get away with it? Match-fixing was a big deal; it would destroy everything he ever valued. How would he live with himself? It was easy for Kanika to advocate a compromise when she had never been a sportsperson. Their priorities didn't match at the deepest level. How could she propose sex when he was battling the biggest crisis of his life?

He felt uneasy about something weird Gagan had said earlier in the evening to threaten him, but he couldn't recollect the exact words or the subject.

I heard it somewhere else. Related to Kanika?

A cold uneasiness enveloped him.

I need another opinion. Nandini! Obviously. But will she help? Fuck! I insulted her.

Thirty Minutes Later

Neil drove to Khan Market where he used the maze of shops to lose Sanket's men following him from the hotel. He walked to a friend's house near Lodhi Gardens and used his landline to call Nandini's office in New York University.

Nandini's secretary put him on hold for an eternity and he thought she wouldn't oblige. Her soft voice came through just as he was about to hang up.

'Yes, Neil, what can I do for you?'

Nandini's formal tone dashed his hopes for a quick reconciliation. Thus, he skipped the small talk and used the limited time to update her about his situation. He begged her for advice, but she wasn't interested in his affairs any more.

'Never contact me again,' she said in a firm voice. 'I'm lucky I could escape from that toxic environment, so please…for Abhi's sake.'

Nandini's rebuff rattled Neil to the core, and for a moment it seemed larger than the existential crisis he faced. He had hoped his plight would break through her anger and draw out her natural caring instincts. Her indifference shattered what was left of the delicate relationship he shared with his beloved friend.

'Okay.'

'Also, I can't help you settle in the US any more…' she said. 'I can't risk complications with Gagan, Akash and the lot. They're evil…'

'I understand,' said Neil in a halting voice. 'Don't worry; I will disappear from your life forever.'

After an awkward silence Nandini cleared her throat. 'Don't worry about Kanika. She's safe.'

'How do you know?' asked Neil.

'She was Jayshankar's partner in crime,' she said, pausing between words. 'After his death, I read through his emails. He got her the fancy position in the ICCL. They used to regularly discuss your team. His phone was full of her text messages. Once I overheard him arguing with his partners in the Middle East. He had failed to fix the team. I tried to warn you the night before he was murdered. Remember? But you ignored me because your girlfriend told you he is a saint. I thought the problem was solved when he died. But they trapped you. I knew you were involved—I asked you, but you said no. So I moved on…'

'Fuck!'

Nandini sighed. 'Jayshankar's partners trapped you through Gagan. He knows them well. They were investing in the Omkar Group.'

'Yes, Gagan told me with a gun pointed at my head,' said Neil.

'Well, then Kanika is an integral part of that gang. I wish I could show you Jayshankar's emails. Kanika and Jayshankar go back a long way. How can a woman like her rise so rapidly in the sports management business? Not just by fucking around, right? She is so smart she can chew and spit you out without your knowledge. And she has already chewed you. After the final she will spit you out.'

Again, Nandini's wild imagination. She had always hated her. Kanika involved with the mafia? No way!

'One final thing. Akash will never let his team's reputation get tarnished. His wife will skin him alive. Don't worry, he won't expose you. He's just putting pressure on you.' She cleared her throat again. 'Goodbye, Neil.'

Neil had a million unresolved issues to discuss, but there was no time. So he asked one final question before hanging up. 'Did you say Jayshankar was murdered? Or…'

'Yes! He was murdered…but I don't have the balls to tell you who did it,' said Nandini. 'But it was someone you know well. Think who has the power to do it and also suppress the investigation.'

Neil sighed. 'I think I know.'

'Finally you see the reality of this world. Stay well, Neil. You are a good person, so I helped you one last time…just because you are in such deep shit. But not any more. Please allow me to live my life in peace now.'

Cutting the Cord

Neil oscillated between belief and suspicion on his way back to the hotel. Was Kanika the mafia's mole? She had the best view in the house, with direct access to his thought and plans. It was impossible for them to have live information about him without her help.

But she had also warned him about the anti-corruption alert. Why? Unless she was genuinely concerned about his safety?

Bullshit! I can't suspect the only person who supports me. Kanika loves me. There is no direct proof of her involvement. She never hid her friendship with Cap Jay from me. As usual, Nandini is overreacting. She is mad. Suffered seven years in a bad marriage and then suddenly moved back to the US after Abhishek had a minor accident.

Then he remembered Kanika saying Cap Jay was murdered. How had she known, when there was no proof? It was normal for her to be sad about the death of a friend, but why had she been so worried?

Weird! So worked up about something that did not concern her, and yet so relaxed about things that directly impacted her...like when they had leaked our photos. She dismissed it as the mischief of 'hormone-struck teenagers'.

Right then enlightenment struck and the clutter disappeared to reveal the reality. Gagan had used the phrase 'hormone-struck teenagers' to threaten him earlier that evening. How had he learnt that phrase? Kanika had used it in private; in public she had always denied those were her photos. Gagan was barely educated and incapable of producing delightful phrases to explain straightforward criminal activities. Sanket had combed their hotel room for bugs and listening devices, and thus there was no chance the mafia had something planted there. The only listening devices possibly present were the ones planted by Sanket himself. He may have heard Kanika talk, but why would he tell Gagan? Akash and Gagan now had a common interest, but till recently Akash had been trying to catch him. They had not been sharing information at that time, at least not such trivial information. So how did Gagan know?

Only one person could have told him how she made a mockery of the threat I was facing and probably laughed about it. The same person who encouraged me to work with Cap Jay—the original lynchpin of this conspiracy; the same person who innocently asked me questions about the team's strategies; the same person who cleverly manipulated me to accept Akash's instructions to fix the final, first by showing indignation towards my faults and then by showing sympathy for my emotions.

Kanika!

The Last Supper

Next Day

Kanika looked embarrassed when Neil asked her for a dance. 'A new Neil?' she smiled. 'Where was he hiding all these years?'

Neil ordered fresh lilies and ice-cooled champagne for their 'romantic' dinner in The Garden Restaurant, Lodhi Road. A local band played her favourite tunes. The chef cooked a special menu consisting of her favourite dishes. Like a pig is fattened before slaughter, this extravagant celebration was a fitting facade to their game of smoke and mirrors. The end of a close relationship was like death. Something had died within Neil with the discovery of Kanika's reality.

'How are you holding up?' she asked.

Neil sighed. 'Very relieved, actually. Thanks to you.'

Kanika shrugged. 'We are small fry...'

'I am finally free!'

'Do you have a plan for tomorrow?'

Neil shook his head. 'I just follow instructions.'

'We can discuss...' Kanika rubbed her nose. 'If you are comfortable...'

'See...Dinesh, Neeraj, Baldev and Antonio were already fixing matches...'

Kanika casually played with her hair as though she was reading the food menu.

Fuck! No reaction. Isn't knowing the names of match-fixers hot news? She isn't surprised as she already knows about them.

'Dinesh will manage them,' he said.

'How will it work, since Sudhir is captain?' asked Kanika. Her eyes bulged and she covered her mouth. 'Oh! Shit! Is Sudhir involved as well?'

Neil smiled at Kanika's false show of surprise. 'No, he is too big a cricketer for match-fixing. So they will just remove him from the final.'

'How?'

'No idea. Hopefully they won't harm him...'

'No! Don't worry,' said Kanika.

Again, Neil noticed her assured tone—possible only from a person involved in the background play. Normally he wouldn't have noticed her speech and body language, but in the last one day, he had lost his innocence for good. It had taken forty years of getting kicked in the butt for him to finally grow up.

'Any guesses...how they will remove him?' he asked.

Kanika hesitated for a moment before letting her guard down. 'No idea...maybe he will fall ill, or get injured.'

'Wow!'

'So Dinesh will be captain? When will they announce it?' asked Kanika.

'Just before the match,' Neil laughed. 'To not scare away the gamblers, I guess.'

'Who's talking to the other players?'

Ah! Seems she has a list to check for her bosses. Well! A great opportunity for me to plant information and fool those bastards.

Neil pretended to clean his eyes.

I will try my best to win the final. But even if we lose, my conscience will be clear. Only that can be true redemption.

'Neil? You okay?' asked Kanika.

Pull yourself together, man! She will become suspicious; come on, play the game. You haven't changed the rules, she has; now use them against her. Everything is fucked anyway...nothing left to save between the two of you.

'I spoke to a few players.'

'Who?'

'The opening batsman, Chander Bajwa, Sudhir's replacement. And then the two all-rounders, Aarush and Divit, and the wicketkeeper, Harish Bhasin.

'And?'

'They agreed,' said Neil, lying through his teeth.

'Do you trust them?'

'I don't worry about these things any more,' Neil shrugged. 'They respect me as I gave them opportunities to play; hopefully they won't expose me, out of gratitude if not for anything else.'

Kanika sighed and gulped down the champagne. She looked relaxed as if a huge weight had been lifted from her shoulders. 'What did you tell them?'

'The same thing you told me,' Neil grinned. 'This is not real cricket, and we have to obey the owner's instructions. And Akash wants to lose the match as a favour to the owners of Rajasthan.'

'That's cool,' said Kanika. 'But remember you have survived so far because you were paranoid about safety.' She joined her palms and begged. 'Please be careful.'

'Who will catch me?' laughed Neil. 'Everyone is now on the same side.'

'Don't become complacent,' snapped Kanika.

'Their planning is brilliant,' said Neil. 'The players can't discuss it among themselves as they don't know who else is involved. So everyone is guarding his own secret and thus won't talk.'

'Superb!'

'Let's go to Privee after dinner,' said Neil. 'Enjoy ourselves while we still can…' Kanika gave him a confused look and he explained, 'It's the nightclub in Shangri-La.'

'How about the foreign players?' she asked.

'Can't involve them,' said Neil. 'Apart from Antonio they are all batsmen—so we will manipulate the batting order to reduce their impact.' He laughed. 'They have assured me we will win the toss. Did you know there is heavy betting on the toss?' He threw his arms in the air. 'How can they fix the toss in front of the TV camera?'

Kanika assumed the caring expression she always used to establish trust. 'Don't worry, it will be fine,' she said in a soft voice. 'I am with you, all the time.'

Neil smiled and silently cursed the smooth-talking bitch.

The band played the country song 'She don't know she is beautiful'.

'What a great song,' said Neil. He held her hand and kneeled. 'I love you.'

Kanika blushed. 'I need a proper proposal…not in this shoddy restaurant with a childish song.' She giggled. 'Take me on a romantic holiday, and maybe then I will…'

'How about Hawaii? Immediately after the final?' asked Neil, heady after the false declaration of love.

Never thought I was capable of such games. But she deserves it. Ideal slap on the face of an evil person who thinks the world revolves around her.

Kanika nodded, blushing like a teenager on her first date.

Neil went to the bathroom and stopped midway on the way back to admire her stunning figure against the under-lit shrubbery of the Lodhi Gardens.

She is no ordinary woman. Hell! She dominates even a monster like Akash. I shouldn't regret what happened too much. At least I had good sex. A woman like her who gives celebrities a hard-on with her smile wouldn't fuck someone like me. But I had her; so not a total loss.

He tried to overcome his grief by objectifying Kanika, but deep down he knew his troubles originated not from naivety, but from residual feelings for her that had survived thirteen years of rejection. When she had empathized with his situation and shared her grief about her failed relationships, he had believed her sudden re-emergence in his life when he was fighting a desperate battle for survival was part of a 'divine plan' to rebuild his broken life. But she had led him on and played games behind his back. Maybe the concept of love clashed with her free-spirited personality.

She has no problem living with a person she trapped. How could she ask me to move to Singapore with her? Will she continue pretending even if we win the final?

'By the way, I finally understood the meaning of 5426,' said Neil, on returning to their table.

Kanika looked dazed. 'What's 5426?'

Amazing! Her ability to lie without batting an eyelid. She's truly remarkable.

'It is a code they were using for me.'

'Ah!'

'It is actually 5 for 26—my best-ever figures as a bowler.'

Neil smiled as Kanika's blank look betrayed her absolute lack of interest in the subject.

She's probably busy preparing a report for her boss. Why will she be interested in my achievements? She did not care even thirteen years ago when I was the star of Indian cricket.

But 5426 is a significant part of the puzzle. Why isn't she interested in knowing about it? Maybe she knows Akash told me about it. Maybe he told her while they lay exhausted in bed after passionate sex.

This dinner has set up the final and removed whatever little doubt I had about her guilt. Tomorrow she will realize I am not as dumb as she thinks I am.

'Whoever is running this racket must be a cricketer,' he smiled. 'Who else will care for such information? He has found a unique way of both honouring and screwing me at the same time.'

Femme Fatale

Next Morning

'He has turned a new leaf, as they say.'

Akash watched Sanket Singh announce his verdict with a grand flourish and feared he would again hear a fairy tale about the most incredible deductive powers ever possessed by man.

'Who the fuck cares!'

'Sir, last night he had dinner with Kanika madam in The Garden Restaurant.'

'So? Has he never been in a restaurant before?' scowled Akash. He struggled with an uncontrollable urge to throw his coffee on Sanket's face. 'Leave! Before I...'

'Sir! Please let me explain. Yes, nothing special about going to a restaurant. But a custom menu, champagne, flowers, a special band? What was he celebrating? Just two days after he was attacked? And he is not known to be a very romantic person.'

'Why is he so happy?'

'Exactly my point, sir. Why?'

Akash clenched his fists. 'Is there an explanation? Going by your awesome deductive powers?' he asked in a low voice.

'Sir, maybe he proposed to Kanika, and she said yes. Or...'

Sanket paused, and Akash lost his patience. 'Asshole! Come to the point,' he screamed.

'Or, sir, she might have convinced him that match-fixing is good. She has a lot of influence on men. You noticed, sir...the way she walks?'

Akash took a deep breath and looked out of the window into the faraway sky. 'Yes...she has a way about her. I must meet her after the final.'

Sanket grinned. 'I can talk to her, sir. As you know, I can be very persuasive.'

'What are you, a pimp now?' scowled Akash. 'So why do I need to know this? How does it affect us?'

'Sir, if she has convinced him, then she believes in match-fixing.

But we have recorded conversations where she repeatedly warned him against it. So why did she change her stand?'

'Hmm! Interesting,' said Akash.

'Sir, I think she's working for the mafia.'

Akash clapped his hands as he paced the room. 'That does explain a lot of things. She was close to Jayshankar; she tried to create a friendship between Neil and him; she had unrestricted access to Neil—she could watch him 24 × 7 and report to these criminals.'

'You are right, sir. Her warnings to Neil were just a facade to prevent him from suspecting her,' said Sanket. 'She might have convinced him to accept our plan. I didn't expect him to agree so easily.'

'So she is helping our cause...' said Akash. 'Can we make her give a statement against Neil, now that he has confided in her?'

'Sir...I don't think she will admit she knew about the matter.'

'Ha! She's a superwoman we can't fuck?' snapped Akash. 'Bring her here, and I will show you.'

'Sir, please wait till the final is over. Disturbing her now might disturb Neil. She's providing valuable information about Neil to the mafia, which is coming to us through Gagan. Let us not disturb this valuable resource just yet.'

Akash nodded. 'Okay! But make sure she does not leave India before we get her statement. Once she leaves, we cannot do anything. Find out about her travel plans.'

'I will stop her, don't worry,' Sanket grinned. 'And then you can "meet" her in your farmhouse.'

Akash fumed at Sanket's audacity but let it pass this one time. They had more important things to focus on. 'How will we frame Neil and Gagan?' he asked.

Sanket produced a note from his pocket. 'Sir...here's the plan.'

Akash quickly reviewed the note.

1) *Isolate corrupt players after the match and force them to give statements against Neil*
2) *Force Neil to confess; take Kanika hostage if necessary*
3) *Force Pat to give a statement about the blackmail*
4) *Sanket, Vikram and Somoresh will monitor and record everything on the ground*
5) *Somoresh will coordinate with Neil during the match to*

ensure he follows the plan and also pass on last-minute instructions

'What happens if we accidentally win the match?' asked Akash. It's cricket after all...unpredictable.'

'Sir, then God save Mr Gagan.'

'How can we save him?'

'Difficult to predict how it will pan out, sir. There are many people involved—and we can't control everyone. They rarely forgive people who betray them. Fear ensures compliance.'

'Give him security for the next few months, so that grandma doesn't blame us for any mishap,' said Akash. 'Once I have her shares, I don't care what happens to Gagan.'

Sanket nodded. 'Yes sir.'

'Make sure nothing leaks to the media. If we win, we will celebrate it as a great victory. If we lose, we will blackmail Neil and Gagan. But we won't destroy the team. Either way, the reputation of the team should stay intact. I owe this to Divya.'

Gone for a Toss

Early Evening

New Delhi Royals' fans had created a festive atmosphere inside the Feroz Shah Kotla Stadium to support their home team in the finals. Sporting lemon green coloured clothes and carrying the team's banners, they sang the team anthem, egged on by an overenthusiastic DJ. The East European cheerleaders gyrated to Bollywood music while hungry spectators mentally undressed them, lapping up every move of their scantily clad bodies. The cheerleaders had the best deal in the house. Unlike the fans, they had no stake in the proceedings. Match-fixing couldn't prevent them from having fun while dancing to songs they didn't understand, in a game they didn't care for.

Delhi's elite arrived to patronize the game with their holy presence. The VIP boxes were chock-a-block with bureaucrats, politicians, businessmen, friends and families of the owners, and other hangers-on who had beaten tremendous competition to bag a seat on the house. The celebrities made cricket almost an inconsequential sideshow to a garish display of designer clothes and expensive jewellery on out-of-shape drunk bodies. The entire Upadhyay clan was present, except Nandini and Gagan, to cheer for a team they had conspired to defeat.

The celebrating fans amused Neil. Why did they expect a fair game when corruption in cricket was a well-established fact? Or didn't they care, as long as it was fun? Ironically, they were hailing him as a hero in the same stadium from which he had been thrown out less than six months ago. No one remembered that incident any more; public memory was short and focused on current distractions. No one realized how it had triggered a search for redemption that had led to this present conundrum. Neil felt proud about his resilience and had no more regrets about his actions. He wanted to win the final, but he feared neither the result of the match nor the outcome of resisting the mafia. He was free from the pressures of achievements and legacy, free from the threats of the criminals sullying cricket, free from the approval of people he had worshipped without knowing their dark reality.

Sudhir's absence in the razzle-dazzle of the closing ceremony forced the New Delhi Royals to declare his unavailability for the final. Everyone associated with organizing the match had known about it since early afternoon when the team bus had arrived without Sudhir, but somehow Somoresh had managed to prevent this hot news from leaking on air till it was no longer possible to do so.

The TV commentators reported Sudhir was unavailable because of food poisoning and thus Dinesh would lead the team in the final. They played down the impact on the New Delhi Royals by highlighting Dinesh's extensive leadership experience and the batting depth in the team which would prevent them from missing Sudhir.

At the toss, Arif Aziz and Jitendra Sisodia, the two former cricketer-turned-commentators, focused on Sudhir's health rather than the health of the team.

'It must be something he ate. But Sudhir is fine now, resting in his room,' said Dinesh, looking at his watch.

'Is he allergic to something?' asked Arif.

'Don't know...ask him,' said Dinesh and pointed towards the coin. 'Shall we?'

'Who replaces him?' asked Jitendra.

'I will say after the toss.'

'Sure!'

The match referee Mieki Odongo gave the coin to Nitin Dalmia, captain of the Rajasthan Rockers.

'Heads!' yelled Dinesh as Nitin tossed the coin.

'Heads it is,' said Mieki and picked up the coin. 'New Delhi has won.'

'What will you do?' asked Arif.

'Oh! Bowl first,' said Dinesh. 'Easier for us to bat if we have a target.'

'And your team composition?'

'Chander Bajwa replaces Sudhir, Antonio Charles in place of Manuel Cyclic and Baldev Madan for...'

'But Manuel was man of the match in the last match...'

'We can only have four foreign players. Considering the pitch and the opposition, we thought Antonio is a better fit.'

After Dinesh returned from the toss, Neil and Somoresh met him in a secure space outside the dressing room to review the final plan.

'Did we really win the toss?' Neil asked Dinesh.

Dinesh grinned. 'We will bowl first—that's all that matters.'

'Okay, let's focus…we have no time,' said Somoresh, referring to a notepad. His professional demeanor resembled that of a business leader working on a complex corporate project. 'Let's go over the bowling instructions first. Dinesh, please take notes.'

'Are you crazy, old man?' Dinesh laughed. 'You expect me to look at notes in the middle of the match? I'll get banned.'

'So how will you remember?'

'I will remember, don't worry.'

'Okay, Neil here is a witness. You screw up…you pay.'

'Just bark, old man,' scowled Dinesh. 'The match is about to start, and I have to change.'

Somoresh read from his notes.

» *Open with spinner—Neeraj or Baldev.*
» *Use 3 different bowlers in the first 3 overs.*
» *Rajasthan should score at least 30 runs in the first 3 overs.*
» *Restrict Rajasthan to less than 100 runs in the first 10 overs.*
» *Antonio will bowl 2 no balls in his first over—the third and fifth balls. Remind him at the beginning of the over.*
» *Do not allow Rajasthan to score over 170 runs in 20 overs, otherwise all the bets in favour of Delhi will shift to Rajasthan. Keep the score high but achievable.*
» *Antonio will bowl the third and fifth overs.*
» *There should be a no ball at the beginning of the eighth and ninth overs.*
» *Drop at least 2 catches.*
» *We will communicate other instructions during the innings.*

'Yes, got it,' confirmed Dinesh.

'We will review the plan for the second half during the break,' said Somoresh. 'Let Rajasthan make a good total, but not over 170. While batting, we have to keep the match well balanced till the fifteenth over when the window for switching the bets will close. This is most important.'

'I understood,' shouted Dinesh. 'How many times will you repeat the same thing?'

Deception

Neeraj Dara bowled a series of short balls in the first over and Rajasthan's Jon Lopez hit him for two sixes and a four. Divit Verma checked Rajasthan's onslaught in the second over by conceding only 6 runs, before Antonio bowled 2 no balls in the third over to push the score to 32 runs—2 runs more than the 30 runs' minimum limit set by the mafia. Rajasthan capitalized on a catch dropped by Chander Bajwa to take their total to 62 for 1 at the end of 7 overs.

Neil took Dinesh aside for a chat when the umpires called the first 'strategic timeout'.

'Bowl Baldev and Neeraj now—let their best batsmen score as many runs as possible,' Neil said. He tried to look anxious about implementing the mafia's plan, when he was actually trying to convince Dinesh to save the best bowlers for the death over. 'Let the all-rounders and Antonio bowl in the end as anyway the batsman will try to hit everything and it won't matter who is bowling. This will ensure the most runs.'

'Yes, good idea,' said Dinesh. 'Good you briefed Chander. Rajasthan is playing safe, so his dropped catch helped a lot.'

'No worries, everything is under control,' Neil grinned. 'Just reminding you—we need no balls at the beginning of the eighth and ninth overs.'

Dinesh nodded and walked away.

Sanket Singh was monitoring the match from the porch beside the dressing room using a pair of binoculars. Neil felt nervous about Sanket's deduction abilities. He had the nose of a German Shepherd for sniffing out trouble. Vikram Singh was also present on the ground, reporting on a wireless device from directly behind the dugout.

I have to make them believe we are following the script. Only then will my plan work.

Baldev and Neeraj leaked 48 easy runs in the next 5 overs to help Rajasthan reach a score of 139 for 1 in 15 overs. It was a precarious situation for New Delhi—with 9 wickets in hand, Rajasthan could cross 200 and take the match out of their reach. The second strategic timeout was an opportunity for Neil to instruct his loyalists Divit and

Aarush, but how would he talk to them in front of Dinesh?

I have to convince Dinesh to slow the scoring rate. Even a slight check will keep us in the game. The match-fixers have finished their quota of overs, but he might still use part-time bowlers instead of the all-rounders.

'Remind Dinesh to drop one more catch,' Somoresh told Neil as he walked out from the dugout.

'Yes! But the batsman must hit the ball in the air first,' snapped Neil. 'What's this, a video game?' Neil took Dinesh aside for a chat. 'We have instructions to restrict their total to less than 160,' said Neil, hoping the ten-minute innings break wouldn't give Dinesh enough time to cross-check this statement with Somoresh.

'But why?' asked Dinesh. 'Don't we want to lose the match?'

'Because the bets are shifting away from us,' snapped Neil. 'It's common sense.'

Dinesh snorted, looking suspicious.

'Should I send Somoresh?' asked Neil.

Dinesh looked at his watch and shook his head. 'Okay! Who should I bowl?'

Neil sighed, his heart in his mouth. Offering a meeting with Somoresh had been a big gamble; had Dinesh accepted his offer, the plan to save the final would have collapsed in an instant.

'Bowl Davit and Aarush; they have 2 overs each. And use Antonio to bowl the fifth over. No part-time bowlers please; they will become mincemeat.'

With Dinesh around, Neil didn't get the opportunity to speak with his boys. So he waved towards Davit and Aarush before returning to the dugout, praying they would know what to do.

Over the next 5 overs, Aarush, Divit and Antonio checked the flow of runs, but Rajasthan still managed a final score of 176 in 20 overs. Neeraj and Baldev's poor bowling in the middle overs had caused the real damage.

Antonio's impressive bowling performance baffled Neil; by conceding only 26 runs in 4 overs, he seemed to have gone off script.

Antonio is habitually anti-establishment. Or has the devil suddenly grown a conscience?

During the innings break, Somoresh reviewed the batting plan with Dinesh and Neil.

> » *Batting order:*
>   *Dinesh Singh*
>   *Chander Bajwa*
>   *Divit Varma*
>   *Aarush Barman*
>   *Harish Bhasin*
>   *Antonio Charles*
>   *Ismail Abdullah*
>   *Travis Robins*
>   *Benjamin Roster*
>   *Neeraj Dara*
>   *Baldev Madan*
> » *You and Chander will waste balls and not get out before 8–10 overs, with less than 50 runs on board.*
> » *After you, Divit, Aarush and Harish will waste the next 5–6 overs trying to hit madly, but will not succeed. By that time the match will be beyond repair. Even if the foreign players come in later, they won't be able to do much.*
> » *We have to keep the match competitive till the fifteenth over.*

Somoresh looked away in disgust as Dinesh ditched his underwear and hunted around for a fresh pair. 'The commentators will help us by praising our batting strength,' he said. 'They will also say the pitch is batsman-friendly.'

'You seem to be very confident about the commentators,' smirked Neil. 'Some of them are former cricketers of great repute; won't bend easily.'

Somoresh laughed. 'No one can oppose us. And the former cricketers are the easiest to bend. Just look at what we did to you…'

Controlled Demolition

Dinesh played out the first over without scoring any run. In the second over, Chander Bajwa tried to take quick singles, but Dinesh did not respond, and Chander struggled to save his own wicket every time. Neil had asked Chander to get Dinesh run out by using his compulsive habit of taking risky singles, but Dinesh avoided the trap. It seemed the lure of easy money had helped Dinesh overcome a bad habit he couldn't shake off through his fifteen-year career.

With the score reading 2 runs at the end of 2 overs, Neil was searching for a Plan B, when suddenly Dinesh Singh got out LBW in the third over. The instant replay on the giant screen showed the umpire had made a mistake—the ball would have missed the stumps. Neil used this windfall to send in the Pakistani batsman Ismail Abdullah ahead of Divit Verma.

Somoresh pulled Neil aside. 'Why are you changing the plan?'

'The plan was to maintain a decent run rate till the fifteenth over,' snapped Neil. 'Playing slow doesn't mean he won't score at all. If we send a sixth down batsman in the third over, what will happen to the betting? What will the media say?'

'Okay, you'll explain...not me,' sighed Somoresh.

As Dinesh neared the dugout, he saw Ismail Abdullah stretching near the boundary ropes. He signalled frantically towards the dugout, but Neil ignored him just long enough to allow Ismail to enter the ground. Dinesh flung his bat on the ground and rushed towards the dressing room.

Chander and Ismail stabilized the innings to take the score to 35 for 1 in 7 overs. Dinesh wanted to meet the batsmen during the first strategic timeout, but Neil explained it was not appropriate for the captain to carry drinks. He couldn't allow Dinesh to reduce the scoring rate. A major clash with an unpredictable trajectory was about to happen, and it was important to score rapidly while they still could.

'We must win it in the middle overs—8 to 15—with little left to do in the last 5,' Neil told Chander and Ismail. 'So hit out freely, but save your wickets. I know it is counterintuitive, but we have no other option.'

Somoresh and Dinesh accosted Neil as soon as he returned to the dugout. 'We have instructions to lose 2 more wickets before the end of the tenth over,' said Somoresh. 'Chander and his replacement have to get out ASAP.'

'We can't talk to Chander in front of Ismail,' said Neil.

Dinesh scowled. 'Fuck! Why did you send in Ismail?'

'They're upset about the batting order,' said Somoresh. 'I told them you overruled me.' He shook his head vigorously. 'I can't…I've a family.'

'We can send two guys—one will quickly talk to Chander while the other hands over a bottle to Ismail,' said Dinesh. 'Let me handle this. We will stick to the plan and send Aarush after Chander.'

Chander and Ismail Abdullah scored 9 runs in the eighth over. New Delhi now required 132 runs in 12 overs. Neeraj Dara and Baldev Madan ran in to supply water to the batsmen and whispered into Chander's ear just after Ismail had walked away. Chander looked towards the dugout before walking back to the pitch, and Neil prayed he would remember to ignore instructions delivered by the compromised players.

In the next over, New Delhi scored 12 runs to take the total to 56, and Somoresh lost his cool. 'What's happening? Did you talk to Chander?' he asked Neil.

'Yes, I did,' said Neil. 'Maybe he is trying to get out by hitting the ball. How else will he get out?'

'That's not good enough,' shouted Dinesh. 'Go talk to him now, before the over starts,' he aggressively pushed Neil towards the field. 'If he can't get out, ask him to pretend he has an injury and return to the dugout. We will replace him and quickly lose the 2 wickets. Go! The over is about to start.' Neil closed his eyes and took a deep breath. Then he walked to the dugout.

'Pat, you ready?' he asked.

Pat rose to address the players. 'Boys! This is the last stretch. I need you to fight. We will soon become the first champions of the ICCL. So, get ready to bat at short notice. The batting order will change dynamically according to the situation.'

Somoresh rushed to the dugout. 'Why is Pat...'

Pat's formidable figure towered behind Somoresh like a giant statue. 'Because I am the head coach of this team. I was never officially removed...remember?'

Neil nodded. 'Yes, Pat. Who better than you to guide us in this all-important match?'

'You sit in this dugout and don't try any tricks,' hissed Pat. 'Otherwise I will tell the media you are forcing me to fix the match.'

Pat turned Somoresh around to make him face two cameramen capturing the match live from near the dugouts. 'Hey, Max. You wanted my comments, right?'

Max, the cameraman, shouted over the din of the cheerleaders dancing on the stage behind him. 'Yes please, Pat. Whenever you have time! Give me two minutes' notice so I can call the presenter.'

'Now listen, Mr Somoresh. We will now follow a different script,' said Neil. He signalled to Dinesh, Neeraj and Baldev to come near him. 'The four of you sit in the back seat of the dugout till the match is over. Don't talk to anyone, otherwise we will tell your secrets to the media.' Neil took Somoresh's cell phone and smiled. 'Cell phones not allowed in the dugout. Remember?'

'How many players will you lock down?' said Dinesh. 'Everyone is involved.'

'Not really...it's just the four of you,' said Neil. 'We have the proof to implicate you. So, think if you want to spend your retirement as social outcastes. This country forgives murderers but not match-fixers.'

Ismail Abdullah was dismissed in the eleventh over, and Neil defied the mafia again by sending Travis Robins, the English batsman, to replace Chander. Two overs later, Chander got run out, and Neil sent the West Indian batsman Benjamin Roster with the instructions to hit every ball for a six. Travis and Benjamin hit some big shots to take the score to 127 for 3 in 15 overs. With New Delhi requiring only 50 runs in 5 overs, a win was now possible with two big-hitting all-rounders still available to bat. But Neil knew the mafia wouldn't surrender without a fight. Thus, during the second strategic timeout, he asked the batsmen to try and score rapidly and finish the game by the eighteenth over.

Somoresh approached Neil near the boundary ropes. 'Sir, please have mercy,' he said in a painful voice. 'Mr Akash will hurt my family…'

Neil offered him a carrot. 'I will help you if you help me.'

'Sir…I am only a small servant.'

The stadium was on fire. Travis and Benjamin had hit 19 runs in the sixteenth over. At 146 for 3, they needed only 31 in 4 overs to win.

It's happening. Just ten more minutes.

Neil engaged Somoresh to prevent the mafia from contacting him. 'So you think match-fixing is good?' he asked.

Somoresh lowered his head. 'Very wrong, sir, but what to do? The powerful people always do what they want.'

Benjamin hit the first ball of the seventeenth over for a six, but in the very next ball he was out, caught at long-off, trying to repeat the same stroke. As he walked back to the dugout, suddenly two of the four giant floodlights failed and the stadium plunged into partial darkness. The match stopped, and Neil realized the mafia had struck. By creating an infrastructure problem they had neutralized Pat's threats of a media exposé.

Trump Card

Vikram Singh marshalled Neil and Pat to the basement below the dressing room, where Sanket and Somoresh were waiting for them.

Dressed in an Ivy League-emblemed suit and almost invisible rimless glasses, Sanket Singh resembled a college professor delivering a lecture. His mother had brought him up well; he maintained his trademark politeness even while threatening people. 'Mr Neil, I regret to inform you we have Madame Kanika in our custody. Unfortunately, she will come to a lot of harm if you do not relent.' He handed Neil a large envelope. 'Here is the proof. Don't worry...she is being treated well,' he said with a benevolent smile like a doctor reassuring the family about his patient's health. 'She will be safe, unless...'

Neil tore open the envelope and found photographs of Kanika in captivity—hands and feet tied, mouth sealed with duct tape, hair dishevelled, clothes in disarray, almost revealing her undergarments, and a menacing-looking man standing near her with a bottle with the word 'acid' written on it.

Neil jumped on Sanket and grabbed his collar. 'Bastard! I will kill your family.'

Vikram Singh kicked Neil on the hip and he fell with a loud grunt. He tried to punch Neil, but Pat pinned him with a choke hold.

'Easy...big fella,' hissed Pat. 'Or I'll bust your windpipe.'

'Let's not act like uncivilized buffoons,' said Sanket. He adjusted his tie while Vikram struggled like a chicken caught in a bird trap. 'We can work this out. No one will harm her unless it is absolutely required. After all, we are all reasonable men—businessmen, not murderers.'

Pat released Vikram. 'Switch on the lights immediately...or I will complain...'

'But we won't, unless this is settled,' said Somoresh. He seemed to have regained his aggression. 'And you will complain against us—you wheeler-dealer?'

He pointed towards Neil. 'He, I know, is a disgrace to his family. But you betrayed your employer.'

'Please stick to the point,' snapped Sanket, probably losing his cool for the first time in his life. 'No need for a lecture here. This is not a school.'

Somoresh gulped, looking embarrassed. 'Three things we need. First, Dinesh will control the match; second, Benjamin is already out, so ask Travis to withdraw retired hurt so that we can replace them with Neeraj and Antonio. We will send Baldev next if a wicket falls. Third, if more wickets fall then we have to send in your guys to bat—which can be Harish, Aarush or Divit. So make them fall in line.'

'We can't bend down to these criminals,' said Vikram, massaging his arm.

Somoresh grinned and stroked his face. 'Then acid falls on the pretty face.'

Neil charged towards Somoresh, snorting like a bull, but Pat stopped him. 'Don't! Let's talk outside.'

Sanket nodded, and Pat pulled Neil out of the room. The players had moved to the dressing room, so they sat in the empty dugout.

'See...the rule is...a final match interrupted by anything other than rain will be played the next day. For rain it is Duckworth-Lewis,' said Pat. 'Tomorrow anything can happen, so that's why they are negotiating today. Otherwise they would have first allowed the match to get deferred and then negotiated.'

'So what should we do?' asked Neil.

'Finish the match today,' said Pat. 'Let's pretend we agree; then we'll control the situation once the match starts.'

'How?'

'Very few runs left; we can easily win.'

Neil rolled his eyes. 'But they will send their players.'

Pat smiled. 'Not exactly; I have a surprise for them.'

'What?'

'Antonio! He will help.'

'How?'

Pat's support for a known devil surprised Neil. Was Pat double-crossing him? But it was true Antonio had bowled like a champion. Maybe quite late in life, but he looked like he had become moral.

'I asked him to learn from what happened to Hansie Cronje. Told him South African cricket would disown him if he is caught.'

'That convinced him?' asked Neil.

Pat grinned. 'Yes! But he will only do the minimum without defying them. That's good enough for us. Neeraj and Baldev are poor batsmen, so if 2 wickets fall, they will have to send one of your guys. So it is worth the risk.'

'Hmm!'

'Come on, man! Don't worry.' Pat shook Neil by his shoulders. 'Your conscience is clear, and that's all that matters.' He smiled. 'You still want to win? Or are you scared for Kanika?'

Neil laughed. 'Are you serious, Pat? Can they kidnap the director of operations in front of so many people?'

Pat looked confused. 'So those pictures are false?'

'Man! Those pics are real, but the kidnapping is false. She is working with them.'

'Really? How do you know?'

'Long story, Pat…will tell you later. I got angry to show they can control me using Kanika. Your plan here wouldn't work otherwise. You see…I am learning—I am not as naïve as before.' Neil rose and dusted his pants. 'Come on. Let's do it.'

The Antihero

Thirty Minutes Later

Pat persuaded Travis Robins to fake an injury, and the match resumed with Neeraj Dara and Antonio Charles replacing him and Benjamin Roster. Neeraj played out the seventeenth over without scoring runs. New Delhi then required 25 to win in the next 3 overs.

In the eighteenth over, Neeraj and Antonio swung their bats but scored only 6 runs. New Delhi then required 19 in 2 overs. Neeraj got bowled out in the first ball of the next over, and Dinesh sent Baldev in to bat, who wasted 2 more balls before taking a run to give Antonio the strike. Antonio hit a four to increase the score to 163. In the last ball of the over he attempted a sharp single, but Baldev was slow and got run out. But since they had crossed over, Antonio returned to strike, facing a target of 14 in the last over to win the final.

Harish Bhasin replaced Baldev. Dinesh counselled him while walking to the pitch.

Rajasthan's super-fast bowler Akhil Abbas warmed up to bowl the last over.

Neil hoped Harish wouldn't bend under Dinesh's strong-arm tactics.

He can score 14 if he gets the opportunity. Antonio should give Harish the strike. But will he? Pat trusts him.

Dinesh chatted with Antonio while Harish marched to the non-striker's end.

Antonio is their man so they will trust him to deliver. Maybe that will stop them from switching off the lights again in case this match gets close.

The senior Rajasthan players gathered mid-field for a conference, which went on forever until the umpires intervened to break up the huddle. An eerie silence engulfed the stadium as Akhil Abbas walked to the top of his run-up.

His first ball was outside the off stump, which Antonio's swinging bat did not connect to. New Delhi required 14 to win off 5 balls.

Come on, Antonio, take a single, give Harish the strike.

Dinesh and Somoresh exchanged knowing smiles in the dugout.

In the second ball, Antonio took a single and Harish took strike, with 13 required off 4 balls. Harish hit the next ball for a four, and the stadium erupted in celebration. The Rajasthan players once again held up play with their never-ending conference, and Sanket, Somoresh and Dinesh moved away from the dugout for a discussion.

Fuck! They will again switch off the lights.

The game resumed, and Harish hit the next ball for a big six over mid-wicket, changing the equation to 3 runs in 2 balls.

Sanket hurried away from the dugout and Dinesh again ran in to supply water.

God! They will waste time till Sanket can get the lights switched off.

'Go talk to the match referee—isn't he from South Africa?' Neil urged Pat. 'Tell him the lights have a major problem and can fail again…so we need to hurry.'

Pat's intervention forced Dinesh off the field. In the next ball Harish mistimed a drive over long-off, but Rajasthan's captain Nitin Purohit dropped an easy catch. The batsmen crossed for a run and Antonio returned on strike with 2 runs required in a ball.

Somoresh rushed away from the dugout, possibly to stop Sanket from switching off the lights as the game was again back in their control. Their man, Antonio, was on strike, and he wouldn't hit. Dinesh again met Antonio with a bottle of water, and again the umpires forced him to leave after a few minutes.

'Get ready for the party,' Dinesh told Neil on returning to the dugout. He looked ecstatic. 'Antonio knows what to do. It's all over.'

The fans cheered and Akhil delivered the last ball of the match. Antonio moved towards the offside and swung his bat, connecting a thick outside edge. He ran like a madman as the ball raced to third man. The deep-point fielder returned a wayward throw, giving the batsmen just enough time to take 2 runs and win the match.

Ode to the Master

Arif Aziz, the former cricketer from Pakistan, was the master of ceremonies for the post-match presentation. He invited Neil for a chat.

'Congratulations! How are you feeling?'

Neil smiled. 'Proud of my team for winning after such a tumultuous season.'

'They carried you around the ground.'

'They deserve the credit, not me.'

'Let's talk about your stint as the coach…'

'Can you please call Pat to this podium?' said Neil. 'He is the best person to answer your questions.'

Arif looked puzzled. 'Pat? But, you are the head coach?'

Neil laughed. 'That's not true. Contrary to the news in the media, Pat has been the head coach the entire season. We did not correct the public perception because it allowed Pat to get out of the limelight and focus on training the team. It was a huge honour for me to work under such a great cricketing legend. Pat is a pioneer of match strategy and innovation. I have learnt a lot from him. Pat, can you please come over?'

When Pat reached the podium, Neil gave him the microphone and moved away.

Arif smiled. 'Pat, what actually happened in your team? I mean, the team won, so all is well, but if you can clear the air…'

'Initially we struggled in this new format, and lost six matches in a row,' said Pat in a serious voice. 'There was too much media attention, plus a lot of false stories about conflict in the team. So we gave the impression I am no longer the head coach. It shifted the media's focus from the conflict to the cricket and that really helped us win.'

'So the stories were all false?'

'Yes, totally false. Neil and I have known each other for a long time—much before this tournament. There is a lot of mutual respect. The results show that we collaborated very well. I understand the media has to do its job, but our job was to play cricket.'

'Okay! Fair enough,' said Arif, not sounding convinced. 'Let's now talk about the final. It was a very unconventional batting order towards the end...'

Pat smiled. 'Yes, it was. Both Neeraj and Baldev did a great job with the bat. Since the runs required were less, we asked them to go for it. We knew that if they got out, better batsmen were there to bat. We did not want a situation where better batsmen would get out and then bowlers would bat in the last over. It was a strategy decided by our captain, Dinesh. He has always taken such bold decisions throughout his career. It worked out very well for us.'

Arif shook his head. 'Wow! I have never seen such a strategy in thirty years of following cricket.'

'T20 cricket is all about bold innovation to confuse the opponent,' said Pat.

Flight of the Legends

Neil went to the airport directly from the stadium where a trusted friend handed him a few essentials collected from his hotel and apartment. He was mobbed by fans in the airport but their affection did not touch him. The satisfaction of thwarting a concerted plan to corrupt his soul was more exhilarating than the joy of winning the ICCL.

People use our deepest desires to bend us into submission. They use the emotional bonds that tie us to life to exploit us—our gratitude towards our family, our affection for friends, love for a woman. Our own attitude creates problems for us. My desires had become so big in my head that I saw nothing beyond them. Life is much larger than our goals. Even if none of this nonsense had happened, would I have been happy working under Akash's boots? When people realize we are desperate, they develop ideas to exploit us. Such is human nature. In their minds, uncle, Gagan, Akash and Kanika must have had very valid reasons for justifying their actions to themselves. Instead of appealing to them for help, I should have saved myself by reducing my expectations.

6 a.m., Indian Standard Time

'Congratulations once again; how are you feeling?' Pat asked after their flight to London took off from the Indira Gandhi International Airport.

'Big relief, Pat…more relief than joy, to be honest with you,' said Neil. 'Relief not necessarily because we saved cricket from corruption, but because they were kicking me around and I had the last laugh.'

'Relax dude…it's all over now,' Pat held Neil's hand. 'You are very tense. Go to Bangkok instead of London and let off steam.'

Neil grinned. 'There is no steam backed up. What do you think I was doing in my hotel room?'

'Well done,' Pat winked. 'I would have gladly exchange places with you…if you offered; sharing benefits without blackmail.'

Neil cringed at Pat's snide remark about a woman he had loved, but he let it pass. She wasn't worth it, after all. 'Thanks for helping out, even after my blackmail.'

Pat smiled. 'I helped because I have zero tolerance for any form of match-fixing. South African cricket has still not recovered from the Hansie Cronje issue.'

Neil nodded. 'Thanks, Pat, for showing integrity in situations that matter the most. You are truly a legend of the game.'

'You should move to South Africa,' said Pat, signalling to the airhostess for a refill of his drink. 'There is a big Indian community there. Come, join my coaching business.'

'Thanks, Pat. Maybe I will, one day. But first I want to explore the possibilities in the UK. My friends are hosting me; so…let's see how it goes.'

'I hope you know the danger you are facing,' said Pat, frowning. 'Don't take it lightly. South Africa is a much larger country, and we have the resources to protect you.'

Neil smiled. 'I have nothing to lose, Pat. I can't hide for the rest of my life. So what has to happen will happen.'

'Are you going to get your grandma's money?'

'I have no family, Pat, and thus no share in anybody's money,' said Neil in a low, halting voice. 'It's "over-the-top", but the truth. They exploited me when I was most vulnerable—nothing can compensate for that betrayal.' He smiled. 'I want nothing from them. I am capable; I can survive without their money.'

Pat reclined his seat. 'By the way, your girlfriend was hanging out with the Australian players in the hotel.'

Neil snorted. 'I am sure they had a fascinating discussion. She has the infinite ability to entertain anyone, anywhere, at any time…'

'She met you?'

'No! She is very smart…knows I had understood her game.'

'Don't blame yourself. Few men can resist her charms. And you had history…'

Neil took a large sip of whiskey and swirled it in his mouth. As tears welled up in his eyes, he raised his glass to Pat. 'Fuck 'em!'

Epilogue

No adverse news about the New Delhi Royals appeared in the media in the months following their successful ICCL campaign. Neil's smart move to reinstate Pat as the head coach of the team during the final match presentation ceremony killed the blackmail story. Later, Akash used his political contacts to erase evidence of other blemishes such as Pat's underhand dealings, Neil's minor compromises and the attack on Neil just before the final.

Ramesh and Gagan, backed by Sudha, demanded compensation from Akash for his failure to deliver in the final match. Their conflict festered for a few months till Gagan died in a car accident. Thereafter, Sudha sold all her shares in the Omkar Group to Akash and retired to Rishikesh with Ramesh and Madhu.

Divya learnt about the criminal activities in her team after Neil gave Pat undeserved credit for the team's success and disappeared from India. She wanted to reboot the team with a new captain and coach the next year, but Akash used Gagan's death to convince her that owning the New Delhi Royals would ensure a continuous cycle of bad luck and infamy for the family. Akash sold the cricket team to the Akbar Mohsin family for a hefty profit, and they renamed it as The Dabang Mughals of New Delhi.

Akash became the majority shareholder of the Omkar Group and appointed Divya's cousin as CEO to run the show there. Having eliminated the pesky distractions of the previous year, he focused his creative energies on growing his business empire.

Sudha died in her sleep one night soon after moving to her retirement home in Rishikesh, leaving her sizeable wealth to a variety of charities and educational institutions, and one small but significant portion to Neil. She donated the opulent Upadhyay Palace to the government for setting up a vocational skill training institute for destitute women, ending the tumultuous history of a fortress that witnessed the rise and fall of one of the great business empires of independent India.

After leaving India in the 'darkness' of the most successful night of his professional career, Neil found a new home in Kent, where more than twenty years ago he had spent three summers as a trainee. Supported by the friends he had made there as a teenager, he not only got a job as the assistant coach of Kent's county cricket team, but also a priority consideration for permanent residency in the UK.

Neil ignored requests by Sudha's lawyers to settle his inheritance till a series of incidents forced him to comply. The complications started with a threat letter, followed by a burglary at his home, and finally he was mugged in the streets of London. Neil realized Akash had ordered these attacks to force him to give up his inheritance, because the mafia would have killed him rather than trying to scare him with non-lethal accidents. So he donated Sudha's money to an NGO preferred by Akash, and his life once again returned to the dull normalcy he had enjoyed since moving to the UK.

Nandini continued her job in New York University and strictly avoided contact with her family, including Neil. He respected her wishes and stayed away and focused on the new people and experiences of his adopted country.

Neil never heard from Kanika again, but he read with a lot of interest the report in the British tabloids about her marriage with an ageing German tennis star, and her published interview, where she expressed the desire to give up her 'boring' corporate job to raise kids in the comfort of their villa in Tuscany.

Acknowledgements

This book would not have been possible without the support of my wife, Binda. She inspired and motivated me to write, brainstormed and improved the plot, and patiently provided feedback on my drafts. I am blessed to have such an enthusiastic partner-in-crime who transformed a lonely and personal endeavour such as writing into a joyful team activity between us.

The following people went out of their way to help me during this journey, and I am grateful to them—author Sanchit Gupta for mentoring me in the writing process, advertising gurus Vijay Kuruvilla and Anjali Malthankar for providing marketing and promotions advice, author Koral Dasgupta for introducing me to publishers, and the entire team at Rupa Publications for believing in my work and guiding me through the publication process.

My family members have encouraged me at every step, and I am deeply indebted to them—my late father Salil Dubey, father-in-law Bibhu Dey, brother-in-law Surajit Chattopadhyay and Anirban Dey and sister-in-law Jaita Mullick.

Also, the next generation of my family—Arnab, Gourab and Adriya—deserve recognition for enhancing the hope and joy in my life.

And last but not least, I would like to thank my all-time great friends who included me in their lives and enlightened me with their stories—Ajay Yadavalli, Christos Christopoulos, Deepak Kumar, Jayendran Rajappa, Kanwal Nayan Kapil, Kunal Kapoor, Neeraj Nayan, Nitin Dagar, Omprakash Mishra, Omprakash Singh, Rajiv Kommineni, Rishi Sinha, Saumen Prasad and Soumendu Biswas.

Made in the USA
Monee, IL
03 May 2026